ASTA GEIL

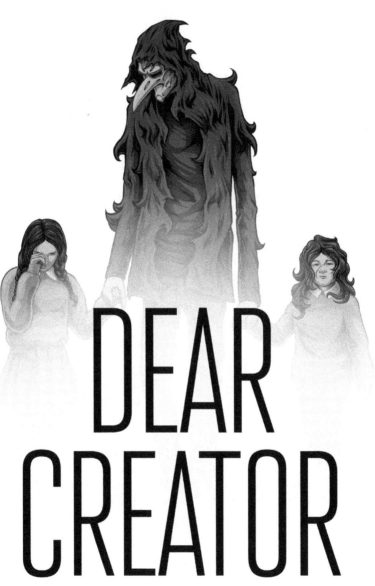

DEAR
CREATOR

DEAR CREATOR
Copyright © 2022 Asta Geil

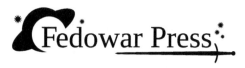

www.FedowarPress.com

ISBN-13 (Digital): 978-1-956492-22-4
ISBN-13 (Paperback): 978-1-956492-23-1
ISBN-13 (Hardcover): 978-1-956492-24-8

Edited by B.K. Bass & Renée Gendron
Cover Design by MiblArt
Interior Design by D.W. Hitz

DEAR CREATOR

ASTA GEIL

JOB 9: 12-15

Behold, he taketh away, who can hinder him? Who will say unto him, What doest thou?

If God will not withdraw his anger, the proud helpers do stoop under him.

How much less shall I answer him, and choose out my words to reason with him?

Whom, I though I were righteous, yet would I not answer, but I would make supplication to my judge.

CHAPTER I

I **HAVE GROWN FOND OF** these children. I live with
them at their military boarding school; in the shadows, in
the closets, underneath the tables, and behind the computers. When I walk the corridors, late at night so the caretakers
will not see me, I can't help but think of the future.

The visions are painfully clear to me. They make me weep.

Blood covers the oval windows. Crimson red mixes with
raven black, and hues of cherry and wine intertwine with
maroon and lava, then clash suddenly with what could be ink,
but most certainly is not. One day, when He returns, mattresses
will cover the floor, strewn with intestines. They will be from
monsters, humans, and what will soon become monsters. They
will lay scattered like playthings in a child's messy room alongside hearts, brains, and dismembered limbs. It will be a massacre, or perhaps a genocide. The walls will echo wails of agony
and distress, the ceilings will hide petitions for help, the doorways will be narrow thresholds, and the corridors will be dirty
crawl spaces.

I can't bear it.

For now, the only thing covering the windows is dust, and the dust allows the white light from the moon to brave through and light up the dark dorm rooms. The homesick children tussle and turn in their beds all night long, blaming both the warmth and the cold on their sheets and protesting their nightmares with muffled mumbles. The young ones heave in mouthfuls of air to fill their tiny lungs, while the older ones unknowingly challenge the pale military clock each night; grunts and heavy snores battling the ticking of time.

The children all know this clock as their not-so-silent protector, as their second or only mother. It lulls them back to sleep each night after they wake to grasp the waters by their bedstands. It lulls them not with bedtime stories or hymns, but with a mechanical tick-tock and a monotone beating, which they are sure holds the power of magical safeguards. After all, who needs an absent Creator or parent when they can hear the seconds ticking by, the world still standing, time still moving?

Their fear is not invalid, but it is misplaced. When they should fear the end of their world, they instead fear a dark presence hunched over their beds. A horror-inducing face hidden beneath a bird mask. Long, bony fingers searching for warm, still-beating hearts.

Watch out, or Birdman will get you, the children tease on the playground, all giggles and smiles. But at night, it is something else.

Don't get up, Elisa.

I have to go to the bathroom.

No, Elisa. Birdman will get you.

Brave pioneers claim to have violated curfew. They claim to have seen this 'Birdman', which they have named me. They claim I am terrifying; a nine-foot-tall monster that has tried to eat them. I've done no such thing. The oldest, the wisest, shake their heads. *He is one of the caretakers,* they say. *Monsters do not exist.* They say I am a fiction to keep them in their beds past bedtime. But everyone, even the oldest and the wisest, tuck in their covers at night and refuse to sip from the water on their bed stands, even when their mouths feel like deserts. Even if they have to urinate, they don't get up. The caretakers heave knowing sighs when they change sheets, like they have unraveled a conspiracy but can get nobody to listen. They don't understand why the children wet their beds, but no one tells them about the monster lurking in the shadows. No one dares to. They are afraid to anger me, they think I'm some sort of malicious god.

But the children who I've grown fond of, Dahlia and Vallesia, are not afraid of me. Not really, no more than an adult who's grown accustomed to the eerie presence of dark corners. I visit them often at night. Today, on Vallesia's ninth birthday, they know I am coming for them. Still, their tiny hearts skip a beat as the hour hand touches midnight and they open their eyes to see a dark presence hunched over their beds. I stare at them, waiting for them, my eyes agonized behind my bird mask.

Long metal wires wrap around my face, soldered to form a bird's beak. My flesh is lost in shadows. It is unnecessarily terrifying, but what lies behind is far worse.

"Come," I whisper to the girls, holding out a hand for each of them. If one believes the stories, I am supposed to have fangs for teeth—sharp as knives and covered in the blood of all the children who 'graduated' or 'left school'. The girls can neither verify nor deny this, even with my face so close to theirs that my rotten breath cloys the air between us. But I'll clarify for you, if anything just to hold back your nightmares: my teeth are no more gruesome than a child wrongly denied braces.

Dahlia kicks her covers aside and lets her bare feet feel the cold marble floor. Vallesia follows suit, gently folding her blanket and reaching for my bony hand, which Dahlia refuses to take. She shakes her head, determined, and whispers, "I'm too old for that," even though she's only eight.

We tiptoe from the dorm room. They hold their breath and move as silently as their shadows. In the doorway, Dahlia glances back and catches a set of fearful eyes lit up by the white light from the moon. They belong to Tomi, quadruple winner of the biannual bed wetter awards in categories including longest streak of bedwetting—735 days in a row and counting, fastest bedwetting—half an hour after bedtime, and provoker of the most defeated caretaker sigh, which was accompanied by tears and, later, a resignation. Rumor has it the caretakers have printed out a picture of his face for their dartboard. I've not seen the dartboards, but I once saw his face in the printer.

Dahlia looks back at me and Vallesia, hands still clasped and waiting patiently, paternally, for her. It must seem absurd to Tomi; the girls willingly following the infamous monster to a buffet where they surely will be the main dish, an unbothered acceptance of a gruesome slaughter, perhaps a suicide. But when Dahlia looks back again, Tomi is pretending to sleep, scared that I will take him, as well. I have a vision of Tomi before we leave, a gruesome one which he does not deserve, but which I won't be able to save him from. Bodies engulf him, a countless throng, and his flesh tears again and again.

"Now," I say once outside the dark, wooden doors, turning my masked face to Vallesia. "How does it feel to be nine?" My voice is deep and coarse. It sounds pained because it is. I've considered tearing out my vocal cords more than once in hope that new, smoother ones will grow in their place, but I've little love of pain. Few people do, if you can call me 'people'.

"I feel older," Vallesia says, her eyes lighting up with excitement and her voice like a sugary princess. She is the opposite of Dahlia, who is boyish and accidentally defiant in everything she does.

"Well, duh," Dahlia grunts and makes a face to let her know how stupid she is being. "A day older than yesterday. Only a few hours older than when you went to bed."

Vallesia buries her nails into her palms and squints at her. "Well," she says, "I am definitely more mature now."

I am quick to act, not wanting this to be the night they become loud enough for us to be caught. "Too mature to get into a fight, I hope." Vallesia straightens her back with pride. "That's right. My sister will have to fight someone else tonight."

I know it is too early to breathe a sigh of relief, but, thankfully, Dahlia only rolls her eyes and ignores what she concludes to be a product of her sister's endless stupidity.

"Where are you taking us tonight?" Vallesia asks, which makes Dahlia look at me with excitement. Vallesia is an expert at diffusing tension, which is fortunate because these spats have sadly become a persistent occurrence on our nightly walks.

I give Vallesia's hand a gentle squeeze and she rubs my fingers, fragile and slim like long bones wrapped in parchment-thin skin, my knuckles like small mountains trying to escape.

It is not very paternal of me to say, but they are not really my children, so Vallesia is my favorite of the two. Easily molded, obedient, and—although I know it's mostly my fault—she reminds me of my mother. This makes it harder for me to look at her sometimes. Knowing her future makes me want to weep, but what will happen must happen. I've always tried to avoid the seemingly unavoidable.

I should say now that I don't know the full tapestry of the future. I only experience glimpses of it; fleeting moments played before me in gruesome images drenched in blood, both red and black. There is roiling fire, crackling electricity, and growling shadows. And there are screams. Terrified, horrified, pained screams. I try to block them out, but they are so loud I cannot sleep at night.

Last night, I had a new vision. In it was a tank, a large gray blob of steel with a rusty barrel pointed at me. The backdrop was dark, almost completely black, with stabs of light flickering by. I felt unsettled, yet safe. There is such a tank at the base where the boarding school is located, where the children live. I have had visions before of things which I try to guide the children away from. I've told them, for example, not to go by the fields behind the halls, where a bonfire one day will come alive and devour everyone in its path. But with this tank, the feeling of safety is so overwhelming that I have decided to show the children the way to it. They need to know where it is and how to get into it, so maybe it can save them later.

I don't know when later is, only that I am running out of time.

"Where am I taking you?" I say, repeating Vallesia's question. "Outside. On an adventure!"

The children squeal with excitement.

The hallway ceiling is so tall that even I, with my long, slim figure, could stand on my own shoulders two, maybe three times. In width, no more than three of me could walk side by side. The automatic lights illuminate the clinical white walls and floor, though the sterility of the walls is broken by fanciful art scrawled by children's hands. I am amused as the girls point at the drawings and commentate on them in carefree tones.

"Joanne drew this," Dahlia says, pointing to a field of flowers. "She peed her bed last night."

"This one is Petro's." Vallesia gestures at a remarkably familiar figure dominating several tiles. "He has a crush on Dahlia."

Dahlia denies this, then confides in both of us that she thinks all boys are disgusting. Other than me, perhaps, but she would never want to marry me. I know all these stories, of course. I sit behind the children when they learn to plot coordinates and I hide behind their ears when they gossip. But I like the stories better coming from them.

We exit through oversized doors and enter the courtyard. The dark sky speckled with stars contrasts the whites of the inside. Buildings surround us. The boarding school is just a small part of the base. Nearby is the academy, the clinic, the pharmacy, and the museum. Beyond this are barracks, offices, armories, and more. Surrounding it all are row upon row of houses that would seem at home in any idyllic community. It is a small city in and of itself.

The tank is near the pharmacy. I walked this way this morning, but the world always seems so different at night, like a mirror image of itself; a strange parallel universe to fall into.

The children debate every detail of their day with glee and I wonder for the hundredth time whether bickering is a sort of love language between humans. I've had no one to bicker with, except perhaps my father and my mother. However, before I attached myself to these children, my parents were the only beings aware of my existence, and it is not lightly you pick a fight with half your entire world.

The children are discussing the correct way to access a short-cut on a computer — I know nothing of computers and have no opinion to contribute — when Dahlia stops dead in her tracks.

In front of us is a marble statue of my parents. My mother, Jarda, is standing proud, one foot in front of another, her gaze straight ahead with squinted eyes and a slight frown. The folds of her dress are so finely carved that the marble looks almost transparent. The pearls of her necklace and bracelets nearly shine in the moonlight and fine holes on her cheeks give the illusion of freckles. In her right hand, she raises a sword. It looks sharp enough for someone to cut themself on. Her other hand holds my father's. He, Gluskab, stands next to her, older but handsome with his iconic full beard and bushy eyebrows. His gaze is not upon the world as hers is, but rather rests on his beautiful wife. A proud smile plays on his lips.

No one knows they are my parents, not even the children. They only know Gluskab as a god, as the only god, the one who created this world with only the sound of his voice. He didn't create your world — truthfully, the jury is still out on *who* created it — but He created the world myself and these children's occupy. Jarda is not a god, or at least she should have never been made into one, Dear Creator rest her soul.

I am the son of a god and no one knows my name, not even I. But this story isn't about me. I have no need for a name. "She's so beautiful," Vallesia says with a sigh, gazing at Jarda. Her eyes are big and her smile even bigger. She has a picture of my mother above her bed in a long, flowing dress with her muscular arms exposed. Feminine, yet the embodiment of strength. She is what Vallesia strives to be, and what she will one day become. Will she be happy then? I try to convince myself she may be.

"She *was* beautiful," Dahlia corrects her sister.

Vallesia's smile freezes and she blinks rapidly. I squeeze her hand and pray to my father that she will contain the anger I know is coming.

Why do I still pray? It's an old habit. I should stop praying.

"Stop it," Vallesia growls at her sister, squeezing my hand back.

"Right," I say, "let's not—"

"But I'm right," Dahlia says.

"You're not right!" Vallesia yells.

I imagine a guard making his routine rounds. He hears the cries of children and sees them with me. He raises his gun at the monster and… "Please, girls, let's—"

"Jarda's gone," Dahlia persists.

"Shut up," Vallesia says.

"Gluskab's gone."

"Stop."

"You're such a baby, you still—"

"Na-na-na-na-na. I-can't-hear-you."

"They're not coming back and—"

"Yes, they are, you're stupid. Just st—"

"Stop!" I snap. The girls both take a step back and look at me with mouths agape. I almost never lose my temper. Like my parents, I am a quiet statue. I walk them places, hold their hands, and try to provide some comfort before what's to come. I never yell at them. Who am I to yell at them?

I could settle their debate by telling them where Jarda

and Gluskab are; that Jarda is six feet underground and that Gluskab is chained up in a shed, and I am the one who chained Him there. I could also tell them that He will come back, but that they won't want Him to, and that when He does, the sky is going to change shades until it falls and then all their bickering will be drowned out by screams.

The screams! Stop screaming!

"Stop!" I yell again, this time not at the girls.

They don't know that. Their eyes grow wide. I can tell they fear me. Vallesia lets go of my hand and bites her cheek, the way she does when she's stressed. Soft nibbles in a circular motion. Both girls have taken a step back. I must regain my composure. I can't stand them looking at me like this.

It strikes me how small Dahlia is compared to her sister. She is one of the smallest girls in their grade. Perhaps even in the entire school. But the many laps she runs, the push-ups, and the crunches—all the military exercises seem to only burn off the healthy meals rather than build new muscle. Vallesia, on the other hand, is proud to show off the subtle bulge of her growing biceps. She draws new lines every month on the wall by her bed to keep track of how much she has grown. Lately, she has been skyrocketing while Dahlia has been at a standstill. You wouldn't think, looking at them now, that Dahlia is only a year younger.

"I'm sorry," I say as I kneel to their level. My long robe sweeps against the ground. "I'm sorry. I don't want you to fight, and there is something I want to show you."

I hold out my hands. This time, both of them accept the offer. Their hands are so tiny in mine. I can't imagine them ever growing bigger than this—becoming adults. I wish they didn't have to.

Now that I see the tank in the darkness, I am uncertain whether this is the same tank. It seems taller, but that might just be an illusion from its placement high on a rocky hill. I think it used to be in active service, but the old model doesn't drive any longer, instead it sits displayed near the museum. When I saw it this morning, orange rust marred part of the exterior. I didn't think much of it, but now I think the shape is all wrong. I wish I could summon my visions, then I could check whether I am on the right track. What if I am, unknowingly, leading the children to a site which will one day become dangerous? I wouldn't be able to forgive myself.

The children run up the hill and both almost trip on loose rocks. Maybe it's just the light. Maybe the stars were just differently aligned on the night of my vision. There were those stabs of light flickering by, like flashlights frantically being waved from all sides.

When I make it to the top, Vallesia has already scaled the tank and is sitting on top of it, while Dahlia is looking at it in hesitation.

"I'll give you a hand," I say and lift her up to the hull, from which she can easily climb to the top of the turret. She lets out small grunts as she does so.

"Daddy has a tank like this in his basement," Vallesia says. She dangles her legs over the edge while humming a sweet melody.

"He does?" I ask.

"Yeah," Dahlia joins. "But it's a *magical* tank."

"Magical?"

Both girls nod and Dahlia sits next to her sister, dangling her legs as well. They have their heads tilted up toward the sky, toward the many stars shining brightly in their intricate patterns. A cold breeze sways their tight braids.

"How is it magical?" I ask.

Dahlia shrugs.

Vallesia turns around with a big smile, one front tooth missing. "Is this tank magical, too?"

I have a vision. A flood of black, tar-like paint falls over the tank, covering it completely. Covering me. It is hot, gooey, and oozes across my skin, burning like acid. Its metallic tang fills my nose as it drips off my mask. The drips fall and hit the metal exterior of the tank with a loud, roaring bang, like the hollow sound of gunshots. Do I hear growls? Howls? The goo sticks to me like syrup. Crimson red. Raven black. It could be ink, but it is not.

Vallesia is still looking at me with that wide smile, clearly expecting me to say yes. I imagine the tank growing wings and flying away, us riding it like a magical carpet with a rainbow shooting out from behind. This tank will be the site of a major atrocity in the future. I can feel death and anxiety and horrible, horrible angst in the air. I take a deep breath in and the metallic tang is still there I realize what I'm smelling is blood.

I look down at my exposed hands, but they are not covered in goo or syrup or ink anymore. Or blood. My skin itches from phantom pains. I am usually in pain.

"Is it a magical tank?" Vallesia asks again. Her smile is more concerned now, and Dahlia has turned around, as well. "Is that why you brought us here?"

Why did I bring them here?

When I put my hands back down, my left falls on the hatch sealing the entrance to the tank. A comfortable feeling rushes over me and carries away all the angst which has burrowed its way deep into my bones. I breathe out, and the tension in my body leaves with the breath. The air tastes sweet again, the breeze caresses me with silky hands.

"Maybe," I say. "Maybe it *is* magical. How about that? I thought we could make this a secret hideout place. If ever you feel unsafe, you could hide here. Inside of the tank. Do you want to try and see if we can figure out how to open it?"

"A hideout!" The girls both squeal.

"Exactly!"

"I always wanted a hideout," Dahlia says.

"Can we bring friends here?" Vallesia asks.

"No," I say in a firm yet gentle tone. "It's a secret hideout. Just for us, okay?"

"Yeah. Of course." Vallesia nods, doing her best to look serious. "Let's just keep it between us."

I nod back with enthusiasm. "It's our safe, secret hideout."

Dahlia peers at the hatch beneath my hand. "I wonder what it looks like inside."

"Maybe we could have snacks," Vallesia says as she edges closer.

"Can we bring blankets?"

This is a good memory. I wish I could catch it in a little jar and place it on my bookcase among my favorite books. Then I could tap the glass and see the dust whirl around and settle, like a snow globe, and I would smile and my heart would grow warm and fuzzy with love, just like now.

This feeling only grows stronger as we work together on the four-digit combination padlock. The children try random combinations, each time announcing that now they've got it, now they're sure.

After a few attempts, Dahlia suggests we work through the combinations in an orderly manner. "There are 9,999 combinations. If we come back every night, or maybe even once a week, and if we try a hundred combinations each time, which would be a good number since we could easily remember where we'd left off, it would take us at most one hundred days, or one hundred weeks, which would be three and one third months, or just under two years. But that would be the max. We'd likely crack it before then. I think, statistically, we'd crack it halfway through, but I'm not sure if that's right."

That becomes our little tradition.

———

Six months later, the day we crack the code, I watch the little children disappear into the dark hull. It is the first time I've felt a sense of safety in years. In that little chamber, the two of them by themselves, no one can hurt them. My father can't hurt them. He won't see them, if only I hide them very, very well.

I should tell you now that I never meant to follow these children out of love. They should have been nothing to me. They are not related to me and I don't know their parents. I wanted to keep these children safe and to prepare them for what is to come only because I have a very special role for one of them, for Vallesia. If I play my cards right, if I do everything exactly as it needs to be done, just maybe, we won't all perish in a screaming abyss of pain and suffering for all eternity.

Those are the screams I hear at night. The souls without bodies. Fragmentations of human consciousness in never-ending spiritual and physical torment. And my soul. I worry if I will join them.

The screams. The screams!

THIRTEEN YEARS LATER

A daisy, a dandelion, the red oak tree, some swallows, and the ants all tell me He's coming back.

CHAPTER 2

THE AIR IS HEAVY WITH anticipation. The dew vibrates and the leaves quiver with excitement. A low chitter runs through the landscape; it sounds like small bells. The trees have grown large and dressed themselves in Gluskab's favorite colors.

When I stop by a daisy this morning to comment on the weather and compliment the blush of his petals, he tells me they are all joyously preparing because Gluskab is soon to make his return. Unnerved, I ask the dandelions and the red oak behind the old dorm, and even a flight of swallows, but none of them can say how they know He's on his way, or when He's supposed to be back. They just tell me that He is coming and they can hardly wait.

Naturally, I go back to the Forest of Magnificent Trees to see if the shed has been opened; the shed where I trapped and hid Gluskab. I thought maybe the door could be unhinged, or that a plank had undone itself, but the shed looks the way it always has and I'm sure He is safely locked inside.

Gluskab must be fuming in there, wriggling around for twenty-two years now, trying to break down the doors. At least that's what I'm imagining. I'm imagining him pulling at the chains, trying to undo the shackles or rip out the hooks from the wall. When I put my ear to the door of the shed, I hear his faint screams and bouts of profanity.

To be sure He isn't shattering any chains, I tell the nearby trees to spread their branches over the shed.

"Like a hug," I say, and hug my own deformed body to show them. I've known these trees for centuries and centuries. Most of them see themselves as my grandfathers and uncles.

"Oh, can't we let him out?" one says, by the side.

"No," I say with a firm tone. "You know the state He's in."

"We hardly recognize you anymore," the biggest one says, the one right behind the shed. "Your face is a new one every time we see you. Please, won't you visit more often?"

I promise to do so and decide against standing guard, mostly because I do not feel like reminiscing with these ancient statues of my childhood. They know too much and, at the same time, they know not enough. It always ends in an argument, and I always feel crazy after having argued with trees. Still, they must be lonely. Nowadays, no one comes to the Forest of Magnificent Trees but me.

The ants are known to get flustered around Gluskab's leaving anniversary, and they gossip. When they decide they know something, their supposed intel spreads across the Gluskabian world in no time at all, yet they are only sometimes right. At best, they are good guessers. When I ask them about the rumors, they deny being the source.

"Can't trust an ant," I mumble to myself as I leave, the sugar cubes in my pocket stolen before I even had a chance to share them.

I know I'm just delaying the inevitable. One day, Gluskab will break free. I've seen it in my visions. I've seen the chaos and agony he will bring. *But not now*, I think. *Vallesia is not ready. Dahlia is not ready.* If I had my way, they would never be ready, and Gluskab, my father, would always be trapped in that shed where he belongs.

Early in the morning, while the sun is still climbing the sky, is my favorite time to walk through the city. Those just awoken or still awake barely look up. They focus on their coffee and on their path and on keeping their eyes open. They walk silently, thinking of the warmth of their beds and why they aren't there just then, and in their groggy haze, they don't notice me as easily. I barely have to hide. During the day is different; I have to slink against walls and make myself small, and it takes so long to walk anywhere when you're only the size of a grape. Sometimes, someone steps on me. It's a dreadful feeling to have my insides squashed like that, and it takes me weeks to recover.

That's not important. What I wanted to show you, to tell you about, is the city square. This is where Gluskab and Jarda used to hold their processions, back when they still ruled this world. Every day at eleven o'clock, everyone living in Capital City, myself included, would huddle around the entrance of the Forest of Magnificent Trees, hoping to catch a glance of our god, Gluskab, with His wife's delicate fingertips resting in His hand. I can feel the excitement still clinging to the air, the anticipation still hiding in the crevices of these buildings.

We slid rugs under them; traditional, beautiful rugs with intricate patterns and vibrant colors, all hand-woven. From the skyscrapers, we would drop a rainfall of richly colored flowers and petals: daffodils scattered among roses, forget-me-nots, sunflowers, and tulips. Every apartment was filled to the brim with plants just for these parades. Shelves upon shelves were laden with them. And we would sing. The entire world turned into one big choir, singing the same blessed song always.

Dear Creator in my street
At my house come meet and greet

Dear Creator in my home
At my table, is a throne
Come, come, oh because I love
You, and I'm so proud thereof

I turn my face up to the apartments, close my eyes, and imagine all the people there. I can almost hear them now. Millions of voices in tune. I hum quietly and sway along to the orchestra in my head before I remember where I am and realize how silly I must look. No one sings that song anymore. I wish they would. I always loved that song.

Behind Gluskab and Jarda, the banshees followed. They walked together hand-in-hand, two and two, like school children going on an excursion. They were quiet, their always-white dresses flowing in the wind. Their pointy, dainty noses and large irises staring straight ahead. No one would meet their eyes, anyway. We were afraid they'd turn to one of us and whisper the name of a dear one soon to die. They never did, not during the processions.

We ignored the somber presences and kept singing as we turned into this street and walked this path. I know you can't see me, but I'm practically skipping along now. A few blocks down from here, there would be a podium on a bedazzled staircase. They would ascend, her hand still in His, she still by His side. He was so infatuated with her, He would look at her more than His people, He would be more impressed by her beauty than their efforts.

How did He not notice? How did I not? We should have noticed.

They took down the podium years ago. Youth kept vandalizing it. Well, they assumed it was youth. Truthfully, it was all kinds of people. In the end, they thought it was better to dismantle it and keep it in the basements of City Hall. That way, it wouldn't be totally destroyed, in case He came back one day. Some people worried He'd come back and be upset about the state of the podium and leave again. It was a cute sentiment. But I do miss the podium, even in its vandalized state. I miss my father and mother even more. I continue down another street, kicking some rocks and whispering hellos to the weeds growing in the cracked sidewalks. When I turn a corner, I hear a familiar voice.

"No, it's fine, fine, fine. I'll just wait. Wait for my ride," it says, slurring. The voice is lively and happy, not how I normally know it.

I push my body against a wall, hoping to camouflage myself and sneak a peek at her. When did I last see Dahlia? It can't have been more than a year. I like to check up on her, even though she was never my favorite. The streetlamps are still on, despite the rising sun, and it is casting a warm light on her. She has changed only superficially since last I saw her. Her big curls are dyed swamp green and she has a nose ring. Behind her, a fluorescent sign announces the name of some shady bar, and I wonder if the sign has been designed to flicker in that seemingly unintentional way. I watch her sway from side to side, clearly intoxicated as she hugs her friend, and I think perhaps she hasn't changed very much in the last year.

"Alright, by'ee," the friend replies, giggling before turning around and swaying down the street. Dahlia waves after her and plops down on the curb, removing her heeled boots before crossing her legs and letting out a deep sigh. A couple walking by glares at her. She glares back.

I look at the time. It's a little past five. I hope Dahlia doesn't have work later.

She yawns and rubs her eyes with the back of her hands, then reaches into her purse and pulls out her phone. She glares at the display for a moment, then tries to tap her code. It takes her three attempts to get in. It's the same background as before; dark with an empowering quote, something about inequality and rebellion. I can smell her breath from where I hide: oddly sweet, like candies and apples, intermixed with something sour, which might very well be vomit.

She's ordering her ride. I can't believe her friend just left her. Granted, these streets are mostly safe, but she's dozing off, resting her face on her arms, which are resting on her knees. She is struggling to keep her eyes opened and catches herself swaying to the side, nearly falling.

How much has she had? I decide to wait with her until her ride comes. I sit on the curb a few feet away from her, but she doesn't seem to notice me. I wonder if she would remember me. I'm not much of a physical presence in the children's lives anymore. I figure they have probably outgrown me, and it is best to let them think I was just some game they played.

I can't help but look at her. She is always off somewhere partying or otherwise making a ruckus. She never seems to stand still or even stop talking. People are always flocking around her and she's always in the center, making everyone laugh or jumping on a table and breaking something. But this morning, she looks so peaceful. I think she's asleep. I listen to her quiet breaths and soft heartbeat as she continues to sway from side to side, almost as if she's lulling herself to sleep. Come to think of it, her arms resting on her knees look almost like she's hugging herself.

I wonder what a real hug feels like.

CHAPTER 3

THE SUN HAS PLACED ITSELF in the sky with confidence and dialed the purple, pink, and orange, back into a pastel blue. After seeing Dahlia, I decide to check on Vallesia as well, so I return to the military base, where she is still living. For Vallesia, today's air is also heavy with anticipation, but for another reason entirely.

I can't believe I almost forgot about today.

Her hands shake more than the leaves as she pours herself a cup of tea. Her fingers are almost too stiff, too jittery, to tie her shoelaces. It takes her longer than normal to get dressed and ready, but setting her alarm early has more than made up for this. When she finally finishes and sits back on her bed to calm her mind, she's left with more than half an hour until breakfast.

Her room is mostly just the bed, which is convenient as she doesn't do much else but sleep in here. The bed is hard and narrow, and the pillow is almost nonexistent, but the ensemble is supposed to maximize her sleep. She doesn't mind; by the time she is dismissed for the night, her body is so broken and tired that she barely registers her face hitting the pillow before she's gone.

The rest of the items in her room could easily fit into one medium-sized moving box. Her uniforms, boots, and workout clothes are neatly stored away in her closet. Coursework books, a calculator, notepads, and pens are lined up on the desk. Towels, toiletries, and a bundle of hair ties to help tame her wild curls into her signature French braids are organized in her desk drawer. The crumbled picture of Jarda from her childhood hangs above her bed, and next to it is a framed inspirational quote, a gift from her husband, Mario.

A calendar filled with crossed-off dates adorns her door. At the end of the long lines of crosses, there's a single word inscribed. The five letters are enough to send a shiver down her spine and make her otherwise-disciplined mind wander.

Final.

She bites her cheek and moves her jaw. In her mind, the letters grow hooks and shape themselves into the word *death.* It's not an unlikely thought at all, considering how out of character the past days were for the administration. The usual afternoon exercises were cancelled, the kitchens cooked a hog roast for the students, then they were allowed an extra hour to sleep. Visitors were even allowed on base for the first time and her and Mario crammed into the small bed until she fell asleep. He kissed her goodnight then snuck out, leaving a heart-shaped candy where her nightstand would have been if she'd had one.

Of course, if passing the Army's Honors Program was easy, more people would sign up for it, or there would at least have been a passing percentage of more than five percent. The last two weeks, as they've been competing in the Honors Program Readiness Evaluation, have involved a constant barrage of physical and academic tests which sharply narrowed the field. They have been ramping up in intensity. They started as simple as timed runs and other physical fitness evaluations, but most recently they had to face off in a close combat tournament where the most consistent losers were eliminated. She was one loss from failing right then and there. There are only twenty students left now, and there's not a single person she could pick out as weak. They are all tough, all of them—is it possible she's the weak link?

That the final test is taking place on a Saturday only furthers her fears. Saturdays are for trust exercises, and not the kind where you let yourself be guided while blindfolded or fall into the arms of a friend. No, Saturday trust exercises take trust falls from falling off a table into the hands of others to breaking both your legs in a thirty-foot drop cushioned only by mud; she has scars where her ankles have been joined together with screws. In her dreams, she relives the weekly tortures. She is dropped several miles from the nearest coast into a roaring ocean where waves swallow her whole; she survives in the cold mountains, wearing only her summer uniform and a ragged poncho she skins a sheep for; she rolls in a pool of sweat and blood on the floor, silently begging for the interrogation simulation to end, but never complaining. Dear Creator, no, never complaining, and never asking the one question that everyone wants answered.

Who are we trusting? How is this a trust exercise?

The sweet summer scent drowns in the overpowering smell of fear. Sweaty soldiers are packed together ten apiece in the beds of two trucks, all shuffling uncomfortably. Dust whirls and rocks rattle around the wheels. It looks strange, clashing with the lush roadside. Here, dew-covered grass grows wild and reaches far up the tree trunks where rosy flowers make up impressive crowns.

They've been traveling for a while and she doesn't know this way. Something that feels malicious is growing in her stomach. She is lightheaded and her legs are numb, but she tells herself, in a firm whisper, that it is all in her head. Fear has no place in her life; it only drags her down. It makes her a worse soldier, unstable, and unable to do what she has to do. It may even decrease her survival odds, or that's what she's been told. Nonetheless, her mind does not care, and the feeling persists, growing until it fills her entire stomach and threatens to push out her breakfast. A silent prayer to her beloved Dear Creator is not much more helpful.

The bumpy, rutted road becomes more uneven when they turn into a field dominated by forget-me-nots. The tiny blue, purple, and pink hands swallow the grass; starving it by denying it any sunlight, but they can do nothing to the white-leaf covered trees enclosing them or the two giant poles towering over the middle of the clearing. The poles are about fifty feet tall. Ladders lead to the top, where two square platforms are connected by a half foot wide, twenty foot long I-beam forming a bridge between them. Underneath the horizontal beam, the flowers are sparser and have an odd color, a more intense pink, almost red. It looks like splatter. Splatter from what?

She gulps.

The beams. The flowers. A shiver moves down her spine and she pushes her neatly cut nails into her palms. After the truck draws to a halt, she jumps from it and lets her newly shined boots sink into the blanket of flowers. The pastel baby hands tug at her shoelaces and she wants to give in. She wants to let herself fall backward, sink into the blanket, and keep sinking until she disappears completely, then remerge after, by some miracle, having passed her final.

Two colonels lead the way for the toughened students.

Among them is Tomi. Tiny Tomi, the bedwetter, who used to jump at his own shadow when they were young and sleeping in the same hall. There's not much of that left—he is taller than Vallesia now, broader, and tougher looking. Maybe, Vallesia thinks, he is not just tougher *looking*, maybe he really is tougher than her. He manages a sly smile and waves at Vallesia as he disembarks from the other truck. Is it possible that he looks a bit excited even, or is he just *that* good at hiding his fear? Maybe they're all tougher than her.

Vallesia waves back at him as they position themselves next to each other in a half circle forming by the poles, in front of the two officers. One of them, Colonel Johns, yells an order. They respond: chin up, chest out, shoulders back, stomach in. At attention.

Colonel Johns's uniform is the same as the student ones, just with silver buttons instead of bronze. The uniforms have mandarin collars on their navy-blue jackets over black buttoned up shirts, complete with matching pants and black boots. Colonel Johns's jacket is the only one which is unbuttoned. It is against protocol, but he doesn't care. He stands with his legs spread far apart and knuckles on his hips, and one can tell by his ear-to-ear grin that he's new and he's enjoying being in a position of power over the students.

"Good morning," he says as he looks at each student in turn to take in their dread.

"Good morning, sir," they echo back in unison, all faking enthusiasm.

The guy at Vallesia's other side reeks of liquor when he opens his mouth. She looks over and curses herself for being happy to see someone who looks even worse off than herself. Tomi also looks at him, but manages to fake a bit more concern.

"Got a good night's rest?" Colonel Johns asks, his smile growing wider by the second.

"Yes, sir," the students reply, the heavy bags apparent below everyone's eyes.

"Nervous?"

"No, sir." Again, they are all lying through their teeth, gasping for air with fists forged from fear buried deep within their chests, but they are too professional to reveal this. Hands fidget behind backs and jaws tighten on pale, expressionless faces. Who are they trying to kid? Now that she is looking at Tomi, *really* looking at him, she wonders if he was usually so pale?

The other colonel, Colonel Lewir, clears his throat and looks with disapproval at Colonel Johns. This is the colonel they are really afraid of, maybe because he is always so quiet, looming in the distance with a threatening aura and glaring at them with either disappointment or no emotion at all.

Colonel Lewir's uniform is deep maroon with golden buttons and the word *Peacer* engraved above his chest pocket. It's a relic from the old world. My mother, Jarda, used to lead The Peacers. That was before everything happened. Since recruitment is by invitation only, The Peacers haven't had new members for twenty-two years and there are only a couple handfuls of them left. Wherever Colonel Lewir goes, people bow their heads and salute him. But he doesn't revel in the attention, like Colonel Johns would if it were him. Like most people would. He stands in silence with that look on his face, like he is upset by being acknowledged.

When she was a child, Vallesia used to write "Peacer" on all her cardigans and shirts, right on the chest. She used to get in so much trouble for that.

"Now listen up," Colonel Johns says as he places a big, blue box at the students' feet. "This one is fairly easy. Or simple. Quickly over with, anyway."

Colonel Johns smiles at Vallesia, then nods at the box. None of the students are strangers to the box, and Vallesia knows her role as self-appointed teacher's pet. She grabs handfuls of the wristbands inside and distributes them. They are made from a shiny metal with no decoration aside from the students' personal numbers engraved in the middle. Vallesia has the number one, as the first one to apply, be accepted, and register for the Honors program. She clicks the band around her wrist and instantly feels her pulse spike. The wristbands are monitoring their pulses to see it they will be able to keep themselves calm. She won't. She already isn't.

When she looks back over at Colonel Lewir, she sees that he is examining a tablet. The device displays the data from the wristbands. She can't read his face.

Her heart beats faster. She can feel it in her throat. More than once has her inability to keep calm brought her grade down to just passing. How is she ever going to keep calm during the exercise if she can't even keep calm now? Maybe she has already failed.

"Like I said," Colonel Johns says, "this is easy. Just walk from one side to the other, but try not to fall." He laughs at this and looks up to the top of the poles, then back down with a quick jerk of his head, as if he is watching a student fall.

Are they going to let them die? I worry. *They're going to die, aren't they, if they fall that far?*

Vallesia looks around, but the other students don't seem too bothered. They've all done their breathing exercises, she realizes. Relaxed themselves to manage their heartrates. Why can't she do the same? Could it be she has already failed? I can hear her blood gushing through her veins. Sweat drips off her nose and her toes cringe in her boots.

"Be brave," I whisper to her.

"Who would like to go first?" Colonel Johns asks. He looks down at the tablet, then momentarily up at Vallesia with a hint of a smile. Is that a challenge?

Her hand is in the air. "I'll go, sir," she says. I think she is more surprised by this than anyone.

Vallesia's foot is on the beam. From up here, it looks like more than a fifty-foot fall if she drops. The flowers are so far away that the ground just looks like it's covered in a pastel blanket. Her friends look tiny, as well, like dolls. She looks straight ahead. Just a few steps to the other side, ten maybe. It's not too far as long as she doesn't look down.

She takes a deep breath.

She can't step onto the beam while shaking or she might as well jump to her death. This, of course, will not matter if she can't figure out how to move. At the moment, her limbs do not feel like her limbs. They are inanimate. Doll's arms and doll's legs glued onto her and fastened in place with nails, but even dolls shake when death is only a misstep away.

"Dear Creator," she prays, her lips trembling, her eyes squeezed shut. She bites her cheek.

A small breeze overcomes her paralysis and pushes her to her knees, but she recovers. Breathe in, breathe out. Is this really worth it? She imagines her husband at home, getting the call that an accident has happened. Then Dahlia, as well, and perhaps even their father. Her neighbors, with their sweet little daughter who sometimes come over for tea and who her husband helps with math. *No*, she reminds herself. She can't be thinking about her family. That is only going to make it worse.

Colonel Johns's mocking smile haunts her, and she steps out from the platform and out onto the beam.

He doesn't think she can do it, but she can do anything she sets her mind to.

She takes a second and third step. Balancing on the beam is no different than walking a curb, the way she did as a child. It's wide. She just has to stay calm so her legs don't shake too much.

She can do this.

She falters on the fourth step. No, she cannot do this. The grass. The grass and the flowers are her friends; she wants to breathe them in, to hug them, to feel them under her skin, to become permanently rooted into the ground with them. The ground. Oh, she misses the dirty ground like no one ever has before.

On the fifth step, she is wobbling and shaking. Her pulse is too high. She can hear it picking up speed, like a tribe pounding their drums faster and faster. Some are out of beat, trying to find out how much her heart can take before it bursts. Oh, Dear Creator! She just wants to lie down, to crawl the rest of the way, puke her guts out, and never look at anything tall ever again. Instead, she continues.

As she takes her sixth step, there are sudden flashes in her mind of a memory that is not hers. A body plummets toward a beach with sharp rocks. She remembers in vivid detail the sound of bones cracking, then pain, then screaming. Her screams.

From atop the beam, Vallesia screams and loses focus and the seventh step.

She trips.

Her life does not flash before her eyes. There is no montage, only one statement repeating like the echo of a coin hitting the floor of a hollow cave: *Try not to fall.* It grows louder and louder, voices intertwining with yells. Her own yell, or someone else's? She does not know, she only knows that despite the warning not to, she is falling. Her arms flail about, hands grabbing, fingers searching.

She grabs the lower flange of the I-beam with her fingertips. They quiver, not strong enough to support her weight, yet she cannot muster the courage to let go with one of her hands and get a better grip.

Gasps echo up to her and she looks down. The ground spins below her. The trees dance, mocking her. The students turn in circles. The air rushes from her lungs. Or is it all in her head? Are the pastel flowers arranged in a never-ending spiral, or is she about to pass out?

She does not want to scream again, but she cannot help but let out a loud sob and imagine herself falling, hitting the cover of flowers, and snapping their necks. She pictures red blood on pastel-colored petals, her skull smashed and limbs bent in impossible angles. Empty eyes stare lifeless at the distant sky. What is left of her is barely recognizable.

Vallesia has a sudden burst of courage, lets go with one hand, and flings herself upward to grab the upper flange. She succeeds and, for a glorious moment, feels optimistic. She pulls herself up, then grabs the upper flange with her other hand. Pain travels through her right arm like thunder as a faint pop echoes from her shoulder. Her optimism is eaten by hopelessness now. She tries to advance toward the goal hand-over-hand, but fails with a cry of agony.

There's that memory again. The one which doesn't belong to her. The one on a beach where sharp rocks look like spears and spikes, and where she is falling willingly rather than slipping as she is now. And maybe she should just accept her fate and fall. Maybe death is inevitable. In that case, the only thing worse than being in pain and dying is being in more pain and dying. So maybe she should just let go.

She can do this.

The wind gushes through the clearing and their collective rustling sound almost encouraging to her. She makes another attempt at survival, flinging herself up to grab onto the beam with her heel, but she misses.

Try not to fall.

She does not want to die, and definitely not like this, so she tries again. This time, she feels her heel kicking against metal, but her excited squeak is cut off when her left hand, slick with sweat, slips. And her right arm, still with thunder-pain rumbling through it, is shaking vigorously.

You must understand that I cannot intervene whenever someone is in danger, even if it is someone I care about. I don't like playing with people's lives like that. I'm not a god in that way, and I try to hold myself from intervening. I really do. There's a natural order to things. People die, and people are reborn. Dying takes such a short time and being dead takes even less. There is nothing cruel or sad about it, and it is the only way the universe stays dynamic. People die, and people are reborn. It is all connected.

And yet, I can't watch Vallesia die. I could lie and say I won't let her die because I have a plan for her, because there is a purpose she must fulfill and I *need* her. The world is going to need her. All that would be true, but more importantly, I just can't watch Vallesia die.

I fold my hands around my mouth and caw like a bird. There is a murder of crows nearby. I saw an eagle, but I don't know if he is too far away. I don't know what else to do. I can't very well climb up there with her and drag her back up. What would people think? How would that look?

"Please save her," I caw out over the landscape. The trees and the air help carry my pleas, and the echo of my caws reverberate all around me. Black dots in the distance grow bigger and bigger until large, black wings, spread wide become apparant.

I can see on Vallesia's face that she is about to give up. Tears make their way down her cheeks.

This is not like me. It's not like me at all. "Please," I caw softly, and even then, I still know that I am doing something wrong. This isn't my place. I am meddling. I promised I wouldn't meddle.

Vallesia looks terrified as the horde of birds swoop in from all sides, circling her. The murder of crows flies straight at her, squawking. She screams and lets go of the beam. As she falls, I almost scream, but then—

An eagle has her arm. Ravens pull at her other arm and jacket. The crows grip her pants with their talons. A blue jay and a robin are each holding a shoelace. There are so many of them, I can barely see her with all those wings flapping about. More and more birds join from every side. They run out of things to clutch at, but the birds keep flying in, creating layers and layers like a cocoon, turning the sky black with wings.

Slowly, she is lowered, floating softly toward the ground like a feather. When her shoes finally rest on the forget-me-nots, squishing their necks, everyone stands around her in a circle. No one says anything. She doesn't say anything.

Her eyes are wide and red and her whole body is shaking. Her hand is bleeding from the eagle's sharp claws and her jacket and pants are torn. She looks down at her torn clothing, grabs a handful of forget-me-nots in her palms, then faints, the world too overwhelming.

I have done something very wrong. I shouldn't have done that. I can feel it; the order of things has been disrupted. The weight of fate is shifting under my feet. What have I done?

CHAPTER
4

VALLESIA RECEIVES THE TEST RESULTS
outside her apartment. The beeping phone nearly
causes her heart to leap from her body.

For a long time, she hovers in front of the door. Too long a
time, weighing the keys in her hand and uncomfortably aware
of the phone in her pocket, which feels at least thrice its weight
now. She finally fishes it out and forces herself to look at the
screen.

Just breathe — In, out, in, out. That's the way. Good girl.

She knows the Honors Program. There are no pity points
for almost making it or passing grades for half completion. Yet,
when she turns on the screen to read the word "unfortunately",
she can't believe it. It doesn't feel real. Nothing feels real.

The screen turns off while she's still staring at it, but she
doesn't turn it back on.

Not only did she fail, but four students died. She was asked
to drive one of the fallen ones to the hospital despite him being
undeniably dead. Tomi helped her carry the student, but when

they lifted him, his snapped neck turned all the way around as if to look at the flowers. She thought it looked as if he were condemning them for not having blanketed his fall, but their necks were also snapped, and their pastel coats were no longer pastel, but deep red. Red splatter, no longer a subtle pink.

When confronted, Colonel Johns merely said that they should not have fallen. It's easy to balance on a beam if you're completely calm. If the students did not fear death and put their trust in the Dear Creator and the knowledge they would be reincarnated and just as happy in another life, they would have passed. The ones who fell did so only because their faith wasn't strong enough. They weren't true Knowers.

That stirred something in Vallesia. Back at base, she scrubbed herself clean for more than an hour until her skin got wrinkled and the water turned cold. Then, somehow, she made it here, to hers and Mario's apartment. She tries to bite her cheek, which is already torn up from the biting, and she shudders in pain.

Now what? The light yellow front door welcomes her with a bold front and silly drawings from the neighbor's girl. *Family Jade!* it says right above a picture of Mario in his smart tux and her in her wedding dress. She feels sick and decides that, once inside, she will go straight for the shower, then sleep forever.

She inserts the key in the keyhole with painstaking hesitation—where it belongs, like her in a uniform. She turns it even slower. Her hand rests on the handle for a long time before she finally pushes it down with another inhale.

How is she going to tell her husband that she failed her final?

Definitely not in front of all their friends, her sister, and her husband's whole family, yelling excitedly as she steps through the door. They have banners and balloons and party poppers that explode with a sound like gunshots in a colorful confetti-hurricane. The kids run up to her and around her with streamers, wrapping her in the thin, intestine-like papers. The silly strings seem especially silly now. Dear Creator, if there is any way to make this matter worse, it is a surprise party celebrating her having passed — when she hasn't.

"Congratulations!" Mario leaps forward with a happy bounce and wraps his arms around her.

She drops her bag and can't help but resent him a little. Maybe because he is the clear organizer of the celebration, but probably because his whole life hasn't just fallen apart. He is even more of a bundle of joy today than any other day, which is saying a lot for him. She cannot recall having ever seen him really down, and it is making her furious as he embraces her.

But he still smells like home. Their rosy laundry detergent, his aftershave, and the cologne she got him for his last birthday. It is a round, pleasant mix of aromas that travels from her nose to her lungs and all the way down into her stomach. But she stills feels as if she is getting strangled with rainbow strings around her neck and dozens of googly eyes sucking the air out of her.

"Thank you," she whispers, her voice broken and shy. Gently, she pushes her husband away, frees herself from his suffocating grip, and turns to smile politely at the crowd.

Can they tell?

It is quiet. She looks around and realizes they have all stopped smiling. Their neighbor grabs her energetic daughter mid-run and holds her close. Mario's mother lets her sign drop and his father swallows hard. Her friends will not meet her eyes. They stare at the ceiling or the floor and act like they are not there. Dahlia bites her lip and touches her cheek, hinting at Vallesia without breaking eye contact.

She raises her sore arm and touches her own cheek. Her fingertips feel numb after the morning's exercise. Even then, she feels the gentle stream of tears. Her smile fools no one.

Snacks are served and recent stories are shared until everyone is updated on everyone's health, living situations, and job offers. The too old and the too young go home, alcohol is served, and the music reverberates throughout the cramped living room. Outside, on the balcony, the bass pulsates through Vallesia's soles like tiny shocks of electricity. The Forest of Magnificent Trees peeks up from behind the skyscrapers surrounding it. That's where Gluskab lived, and where He is now trapped. His mansion is empty, or as good as empty, the walls are deteriorating, the dust gathering.

I remember the day He left.

The sky turned dark gray. If you've ever been to the harbor during a storm, perhaps you can imagine the color: dead and void of life, yet in upheaval. The world halted for a moment as everyone stopped dead in their tracks, overcome with a deep feeling of loss. Not knowing what they were mourning, the whole world wailed, the trees cried, and the rain poured down. It didn't stop raining for weeks on end, except for on the second day, when His banshees ran from the Forest of Magnificent Trees, their angel wings on fire and their screams... oh, their screams. I wish I could forget their screams.

Vallesia wasn't alive back then. Still, she can't seem to look away from the trees towering up just a car ride away. *He lives there,* she thinks. The forest becomes less real the more she looks at it. Her life becomes less real.

Mario is next to her, trying to cheer her up.

"It just means that there are better things out there for you," he says.

"If you don't stop..." she warns.

"We'll figure it out. Maybe we can take some time off. Go traveling?"

"I don't want to travel."

"We can do something else. What do you want to do?"

"To graduate the Honors Army Program, ideally."

"There is something better for you—"

"I'm telling you, there isn't," Vallesia snaps.

Mario sighs.

"Okay" he says. "Then what do you want me to say?"

She shakes her head and turns back to the forest.

Nothing. Don't say anything. Let the disappointment settle and, once it's settled, that's when you speak. For now, let her mourn the life that won't be.

The balcony door slides open and the upbeat pop song grows suddenly loud, filling the space between them, along with clinking glasses, laughter, incoherent yells, cheers. The door closes again and Vallesia breathes out, leaning against the railing. Still looking straight ahead at the forest.

"Hey Valley," Dahlia sings. She makes her way next to Vallesia and hands her a beer. She offers Mario one as well, but he shakes his head and takes a step backward.

"Well, I'll let you two…" he starts and trails off. He looks back at Vallesia, almost as if asking for permission to go.

"Have fun dancing," Vallesia says, sulking. She knows she's not being fair. He's tried to cheer her up all night and she's shut him down, even held back a genuine chuckle when he almost succeeded. She was the one who told him not to send every-one home, and she was, after all, the only reason that she failed her final. There's no one to blame but herself. Is it possible she didn't trust Gluskab enough, is that really the reason she failed? And Mario — the most enthusiastic Knower she has ever known, who loves and trusts Gluskab so whole-heartedly — how could she share that with him?

Dahlia takes a sip from her beer and shoots Mario a disap-proving look as he leaves. She is already a little drunk, or perhaps still drunk. She sways slightly as she leans against the railing beside her sister.

"Doesn't his eternal optimism get frustrating?" Dahlia asks while putting the third drink down. "I mean, what about when you are, like, watching a sad movie? Does he not cry if a dog dies? I mean — Oh, Dear Creator. Valley, don't tell me he *laughs* at dying dogs?"

"First of all, we don't watch sad movies," Vallesia says and catches herself almost smiling. "But also, death isn't sad. Not if you trust our Dear Creator. You are just reborn. That's beautiful."

"You're a freak." Dahlia clinks their bottles and drinks

again, wanting Vallesia to follow her example, but she doesn't. "Is that what they're teaching you? It's a bunch of baloney. They're just brainwashing you to do their bit. You gotta break free, sis."

"I guess I *am* free now, huh?" Vallesia sighs. "But, rebirth? The wonderful miracles of life and death? That's what we were *both* taught at school. Did you forget everything already?"

"I wish I could. It's harder to unlearn things than to learn things. But sometimes I forget for a moment. Such lovely, little moments…"

She nudges Vallesia and lets out a chuckle, and then stops, quieted by her sister's silence. Dahlia twirls a lock of hair between her fingers, calling attention to her free-flowing curls, the swamp green cloud wild and untamed. She cringes at Vallesia's tight braids, straight and practical for military purposes, and wonders whether her sister will let it loose now that she is no longer connected to the army. It is probably still too sensitive a subject to bring up.

"But Mario really isn't bad," Vallesia says. "In fact, I think he's pretty wonderful. I mean, I married him, so I'm sure you're not too surprised. What I mean is, I think you'd like him, too, if you spent a little time with him. We could finally do that double date."

"It'd ruin my image as a brooding rebel."

"I'm not joking. I know we don't see much of each other anymore, but you're my sister and I care about you, and I care about him. A lot. He's just decided to be happy. He's not that bad."

"I don't care that he's a walking children's cartoon—"

"Dahlia—"

"No. I don't, okay? I care that the most important thing in his life is loving Gluskab, and that's not exactly the most important thing in my life. I mean, how am I going to get along with someone like *that*? Right?"

"He's the most important thing in my life. That has to count for something."

There's another silence. It's often like this when they talk.

"I thought Dad would come," Dahlia finally says, reaching

for Mario's beer. "I almost didn't come because of it."

"I'm happy you came. Mario says he invited Dad, but I think it was too many people."

"Or maybe he had the same thought as me and thought I'd show up." She takes another big gulp of the beer. "You know, I thought for sure he wouldn't miss this. His little prized spy finally graduated to top ranks. Have you told him yet that you genuinely love Gluskab, or are you keeping up the spy persona?"

Vallesia winces at Dahlia.

"You know, I find it so funny, I can't help it. Dad sent us both to the military base as spies because he hated Gluskab, right? But he's got two daughters. One loves Gluskab—that's you, and another hates him just as much as he does—that's me. And which of us are disowned? Just because I couldn't stick it out at that awful place. Dad wouldn't have lasted a day there, either."

Vallesia sighs. "Dahlia…"

Dahlia sighs as well. "No, I'm sorry. I really am. I'm happy to see you. I'm happy to be here. I don't know why I'm being mean and making it all about me. I shouldn't. He's just—I mean, I just…" She groans. "I guess I'm just jealous, that's all."

"I just failed my exam, Dahlia. What do you have to be jealous of? I don't have anything."

Dahlia sucks her teeth and looks grim for just a moment, then puts a skinny arm around Vallesia's muscular shoulders. "You have me, don't you? And Mario. You've got such a great life, Vallesia."

Vallesia finally looks away from the forest and right at Dahlia. Her eyes are filled with tears. "I don't know what to do now," she whispers, just loud enough for Dahlia to hear. "This was my whole life."

Dahlia pats her shoulder awkwardly. "It's not the end of the world, you know."

"Not the end of the world, my ass." She laughs dryly. "Dear Creator, it feels like it."

I hope it won't be.

CHAPTER
5

THE TIDE TURNS RED WHEN it sweeps over the sharp rocks and her cracked skull. The new, persistent memory of a death that is not Vallesia's haunts her dreams that night, so much, in fact, that she feels grateful when the doorbell buzzes at five am. Mario growls, still half-asleep as she disentangles herself from their honeymoon grip. She apologizes with a kiss and searches for her panties and a shirt before waddling out into the kitchen, where the doorbell buzzes a second time.

She is off balance from sleep and beers and almost falls over a chair before finding the door. Her body aches from bruising. Her hand is covered in bandages from the eagle talons and she still feels the blood pulsing through it, a slight burn.

"Yeah, yeah," she mumbles groggily and rubs her eye. "On my way…"

She almost doesn't believe it when she opens the door and finds Colonel Lewir on the other side. Colonel Lewir? Outside her apartment at five am? She pulls her shirt down further to cover her panties, then corrects her stance: chin up, chest out, shoulders back, stomach in. At attention.

"Sir," she offers, suddenly awake, or is she? She pinches her arm behind her back and is surprised when Colonel Lewir is still standing in front of her, wearing the uniform belonging to Jarda's special ops. She must still be sleeping. Or she must be seeing things. She focuses her eyes, but reads the same word over and over again, engraved above his chest pocket: *Peacer*. What is a Peacer doing here?

"Vallesia Jade?" he asks. There's something similar to dismay in his tone, but it might just be how he speaks; like a chronically disappointed father.

"Yes, sir," she answers, sure that he knows full well who she is.

"Get dressed and follow me."

She looks for clues hidden beneath his marble mask, but unsurprisingly, she finds none. She discharges herself and retreats to her bedroom, where Mario growls even louder as she turns on the light and looks for her uniform. She kisses him softly and he tries to pull her back into bed, but she is bigger and stronger than him.

"When I get home," she promises. They are good now. Better than good.

A good soldier knows that when no explanation is given, no explanation is needed, so she stays silent as she marches out of the apartment to join the Colonel. Capital City is just waking up, preparing for early commuters, putting drunks to bed, and chasing the distant stars away and shushing the cicadas. It is calm and peaceful. She feels as if she has been let in on a big secret, experiencing this 'before the morning hits' time that few know exists.

However, her heart doesn't bow to tranquility. It is nervous enough to start a riot, so it tries to break through her ribcage. It sets up time bombs and hacks at the grimy prison with hammer and chisel, but she ignores it and gets into the black SUV parked out front. The windows are tinted completely black.

The driver looks at her in the mirror for only a moment, then starts the car. He is wearing the Peacer uniform as well, but she has never seen him before. She has never been fond of Colonel Lewir, nor felt safe alongside him. The army's Honor Students fear him and conspire against him. They argue that he is the one making up the crazy trust exercises, brainstorming with whiskey at ungodly hours at night, and they joke that he is the one to have chased Gluskab away. Tomi says that he is really Birdman, which she knows not to be true. But the other theories about him, she can't disprove.

Vallesia holds her breath as the car pulls up to the Forest of Magnificent Trees and Colonel Lewir steps out. The driver signals for her to stay, so she does, watching as the colonel walks up to the entrance of the forest. The trees tower so high that he looks like an ant in comparison.

Surely this is not where they are going. Even after Gluskab's disappearance, this holy place has stayed protected, its lightning bolts smiting anyone attempting to enter. She has seen it herself, once: a young boy cursing at the wildly growing trees, blaming its dweller on his misery. It was something about a girl, she remembers. He crossed the section between the gray cement and the green grass with a promise of violence and was immediately electrocuted by lightning striking out of the blue sky.

On stay-at-home-weekends, she and Mario liked to bike down here for lunch. They would marvel at the forest and bend their necks back, attempting to see where the tree branches spread to form crowns worthy of their trunks. They would wonder what marvels it might contain. On their first date, while walking by the forest, Mario recited a poem for her:

> *Do the Forest of Ordinary Trees*
> *Feel a jealous twirl or whirl*
> *Breezing through their leaves*
> *When picnickers talk dreamily*
> *Of where pebbles are pearls*

And pearls lay with jewelry?
But I know that the beauty of the forest is not what Vallesia is really interested in. Gluskab and Jarda are supposed to live in there. They did once. Their home, the palace, was a worthy sight to behold, with many windows and spires, and white rock covered in hydrangeas, lilies, and roses. It was nearly as tall as the trees, with a single spire reaching up the farthest. I used to love sitting on the veranda. The light was always just right, no matter what time a day, and it always smelled vaguely like salt water.

Colonel Lewir returns and nods to the driver. "All good," he says.

Are they really going in there? Why? The Peacers are allowed to enter. I've fought my battle, long and hard, to make sure they can so they can guard the shed, but Vallesia isn't a —

Oh, no. I think I am starting to understand. Do they think… She can't go in!

The car starts rolling again. Vallesia holds onto the seat in front of her and protects her face with the other hand. If lightning is intent on smiting them, it will do her no good, but I'm sure it feels better than doing nothing.

I prepare myself. I want to stop them. Perhaps I could make myself big, grab hold of the steering wheel, slam the brake, something, anything. I — I like her. I like her as a person, however much of a person she is. Maybe it is because she reminds me of my mother. But I've already interfered too much. Yesterday, when I felt the weight of fate shift below my feet, I knew I'd done wrong.

But how will I save the world if Vallesia dies? I will think of something. Or I won't. I wasn't supposed to be a god of intervention.

So, I wait.

I wait for the earth-shattering lightning to hit the car and for it to roll around, and if that won't kill everyone inside, the next lightning bolt will. Have you ever seen ten lightning bolts hit one spot? Have you ever seen the culmination of the entire sky's charge?

How about the smell?

Do you know what burned human smells like?

I do.

They reach the edge of the forest, and they enter, and… she survives this act of blasphemy, seemingly with no objections from any gods. Of course, this worries me. I will have to ask *Him* why. The fear almost eats my excitement, but only almost.

Yet, she can't be in the forest. I feel strongly that she shouldn't.

For her, the shock quickly subsides and is replaced by excitement and awe. In the forest, she sees no pearl-like pebbles or jewelry laying free to grab, nor flora shy of textbooks, nor species unheard of, but she does notice that the flowers are more richly colored. The bunnies have cuddlier fur, and the grass—she experiences later when she gets a chance to feel it— is much softer, like well-conditioned hair or silk. The absence of humans has let the soil grow healthy and has fostered life not out of the ordinary, but thriving. And it's magnificent. Ordinarily, magnificently beautiful. My home, my original home.

Oh, I don't like this. Not at all. My bad premonition from earlier is only growing stronger. I wish I could somehow turn the car around and make them bring Vallesia back into the safety of her bed, but I can't. I'm not supposed to interfere.

They reach a clearing and the driver stops the car. Vallesia steps out with Colonel Lewir. The waking sun's light filters through the tree branches and somehow seems to catch every unevenness in the ground, every leaf, and every splinter, even the dew that clings to the grass. It reflects back to her as a million small stars, twinkling and blinking with only the nicest shades a rainbow can have.

"Dear Creator," she catches herself praying. "Let this not be a dream."

In her amazement, she fails to notice that they are not alone. Leaning by a tree trunk a few feet off, a sleepy looking man is watching them, and her in particular. He is wearing the Peacer uniform as well, but he looks much older than Colonel Lewir. Silver hair juts out from his chin in a silent protest against him not having cut it for what looks like years. His skin, with faded, yellow undertones, resembles a crumpled shirt long lost in a teenager's closet, and hangs in veiny strings close to his neck. Despite his fragile body and the way his chest expands too widely with each troubled breath, she feels no fear of him collapsing and is sure no one else would. Maybe it is because of the stance he so easily slips into as soon as his droopy eyes meet Colonel Lewir's.

"Is this the girl?" he asks and looks back at Vallesia, squinting and blinking swiftly. The squinting might be less to do with him judging her and more to do with him not being able to open his eyes fully, but she still feels him examining her. His eyes jot all over the place from behind the thin slits, running over her skin, stopping to examine her bruises and scars.

"Yes," Colonel Lewir says.

"Are you sure?" the old man asks, failing to hide his skepticism, or not even trying.

"Yes."

Although she doesn't know what is going on, Vallesia feels strangely thankful to Colonel Lewir for what seems like defending her.

"Has she even graduated yet?"

Vallesia cringes.

Colonel Lewir hesitates. "No."

She blushes.

He adds, "I told you what happened. I trust that you will be good to her."

The man turns to examine her again. "It's been eons since I've last had to fill a recruit in."

Recruit. Recruit, recruit, recruit, recruit... The word bounces back and forth in her mind until it doesn't sound like a real word anymore. Until it is merely a sound, undeciphered vibrations with lost meanings.

"Mister Crado," Colonel Lewir says, sternly. "Be good to

her. Hopefully it won't be the last."

"The last?"

"Recruit."

"Hopefully."

"I'll leave you to it, then." Colonel Lewir turns around and heads back toward the car. When Vallesia realizes he is going to leave, she finds herself wishing he wouldn't. I find myself wishing that she would get back into the car with him. "May the Dear Creator bless you."

"And may he bless your ride back."

They watch Colonel Lewir take off. She can do nothing but stand there, completely baffled. And then they are alone. Vallesia, somewhere where she should not be, with a stranger she knows nothing about. I curse her for being so excited that she is practically vibrating.

"I've always wanted to ask Colonel Lewir to bend over and cough," Mister Crado says in a loud, confident voice.

Vallesia is so surprised that she forgets how to breathe mid-breath and ends up in a coughing fit. Mister Crado just looks at her with a suppressed smile.

"What?" she asks in between coughs now forming into hiccups.

But he waits until she's done, so she can fully appreciate his joke. "So I can get the stick out his butt," he says. And then he shows off his gray teeth in a warm smile.

Vallesia is almost too baffled to laugh, but she does manage a chuckle.

"But he's a good one," Mister Crado says. "Devoted like no one else. I'd trust him with my life."

She nods, but she is not sure she agrees. All she'd ever trust him with would be the development of torture devices. Instead, she looks around, taking in the scenery. Trees and flowers and indescribable beauty and then a contrast, something dramatically lackluster in the midsts of all the beauty: a shed.

I admit, it is no impressive piece of craftsmanship, at least from the outside. Rain and the changing seasons have taken their toll. The door is rotten and the walls look ready to collapse in on themselves. The only thing keeping the structure together is the tree which it is leaning against, reaching out its branches to smother it. Have you ever gone camping and had to use one of those primitive toilets, the ones where you sit on a bench and relieve yourself into a hole? Vallesia knows them too well from army retreats, and, she thinks to herself, loud and clear so I can hear, *this one isn't even a nice one.* Ouch. I crafted this shed with my own hands and—curse my humanity—I can't help but feel a little insulted. It's not as easy as it seems, to slam together a shed in that amount of time. Time was a factor. You try it yourself.

I get closer to the shed. Does it look more fragile than when I went to check on it yesterday? Is the door holding up? Are the nails still in? The trees have indulged me; they are hugging it tightly. Yet, I cannot help but be concerned by what the daisy told me.

The shed is buzzing. Energy. She can feel it too. She is being drawn toward it.

"Are you really not going to ask?" Mister Crado finally breaks the silence, but she doesn't hear. She is still watching the shed. Above it is an inscribed plaque: *If you open me, the sky will fall, the blood will turn to ink, the shadows will eat flesh, and no one may save you then.*

I'm not the poet. Don't look at me.

"They really make them dull these days," he continues. "No mind of their own. They just want a gray blur that will obey orders, no questions asked. It wasn't like that back in my days."

Vallesia looks back at him.

"You can ask me," he says. "Anything. You must have so many questions."

She does. Where to begin?

"What does this mean?" She points to the plaque, then corrects herself. "Sir."

"Huh, the plaque? That's what you're interested in? Okay. No need to call me sir, by the way. But the plaque, huh? I guess you could call it a prophesy. A warning. That's how we're interpreting it, anyway. We're here to make sure it doesn't come true." He sighs. "It's a bit of a boring job, but it's important. I keep myself busy when I'm out here. I like knitting and I can juggle. I've been dabbling with the mouth organ lately. Maybe you want a show?"

She squints at him.

"Whittling too," he continues, presenting a bad attempt at a man. The torso and arms are much too long, and the head is too small. Mister Crado smiles with pride.

Open me...

She is distracted. For some bizarre reason, she wants to open the shed very much. It is like it is calling her name, like gravity is centered around it, pulling her in.

That's it. I can't let this go on. I have to stop it. She will open that shed, I can feel it, and Gluskab? I can feel the energy. He must have squirmed out of one of His locks. He's calling her, and she isn't ready yet. I try to make myself bigger, but something stops me. *Someone.* An evil laugh echoes somewhere. Only I can hear it.

"You must have more questions," Mister Crado says. "Unless you want that concert now?"

She snaps back. That's a good girl.

"Why me?" she asks. "Why could I cross the border? Why am I here?"

"Right, finally. That's what you should have been asking from the start. I mean, I was almost starting to doubt my sanity here. This is a bit weird, isn't it? All this secrecy? And then here you are, asking me about a shed. I'd be much more interested in what in the Dear Creator's name is going on, if I were you."

He looks at her, but she's not sure what he wants her to say. She can't help but feel that she's out of line even asking him. "Right," she finally offers.

"Right. So, what *is* going on? What do you think? Why *are* you here?"

Vallesia had a whole car ride to think about this, but she's still not sure. An hour ago, she was still in bed. Some hours before that, she was watching the forest she's now in from afar, thinking about how her life had fallen apart. "You're both Peacers, Colonel Lewir and you. I suppose the Peacers can get into the forest. The driver was a Peacer, too. But I'm not. I'm not even an Honors student. Yesterday, I failed, I—"

The exam. She's been so caught up in the failing and in the deaths, the one student whose neck snapped all the way around, that she hasn't even had time to process what happened. The birds. She'd been saved. *By birds.*

"Yesterday, I was going to fall and die," she says, suddenly realizing. "I was sure to die. But then birds flew in from everywhere and grabbed me. They saved me. Was that... did Jarda do that? Does that mean... was I recruited?"

Mister Crado nods.

They are wrong. That is not what happened. I messed with something I shouldn't have.

"Does that mean..." she continues, her mouth feeling dry. She swallows hard. "Does that mean... is she back? Jarda?"

No, it doesn't. What have I done?

"Maybe," he says. "To tell you the truth, I have the same question. We *all* have the same question. But no matter the answer, what happened yesterday was a miracle. It means something. It means we're not alone in this world. It means you're special. There's no other explanation for it."

I have an explanation—I messed it up. I messed it all up.

The air is buzzing. All the flowers and trees have turned their necks toward the shed, but neither of them have noticed.

"Actually, it's good that you're here," Mister Crado says suddenly, full of excitement. "I've been waiting to go number two for a while now and we're not allowed to take our eyes off of the shed, not even for a minute. Well, with me, it's a bit more than a minute. And I feel so awkward maintaining eye contact with a shed while taking a dump. You wouldn't mind, would you?"

I scream at the top of my lungs, "No!" But they can't hear

me. My father continues to laugh at me. He is so loud now that I can barely hear them speaking.

Mister Crado looks around as if deciding on the best bush to go behind.

"Hey, Mister Crado?" Vallesia asks, that smile still on her face, and only growing bigger.

"Yes?"

"I think they're back."

He nods. "I hope so," he says, then he finally settles on a bush further away. "No touchey-touchey." He points to the shed as he skips away. "And don't let the bunnies in, 'aight?"

It's not about what comes in. It's about what, *who*, comes out.

She laughs. "I won't."

The sound of rustling, of sticks being stepped on and branches being pushed aside, subsides, and then he is gone. And with him, his words are instantly forgotten, as well.

What is this shed? She thinks. *A toilet? Why has Mister Crado not gone there instead?*

She looks around for him and is about to shout his name when the shed catches her attention again. Demands her attention, rather.

What is it?

She walks over to it.

A whisper. Deep and raspy. *Open me.*

Her fingers are hovering in front of the door.

Open me.

I am telling her — screaming at her — not to do it, but she cannot hear me.

The wind has betrayed me. My old friend, the wind, is now pulling her toward the shed, and the tree, who has been like an uncle for me, is loosening its grip. Traitors. They will regret this.

But there is no distinction between man and beast. There is only her primal instinct to obey this simple command. Everything in her body is screaming at her to do so. Everything in the universe is screaming at her to do so. I am the only one telling her not to, and my screams are not being heard.

Open me.

She wants to open it.

Open me.

She wants to know what is inside, or maybe she just wants to obey. I realize why it must be her, why she must be here, and why she must be the one to open it. She cannot disobey a command. It is my fault; I am the one who made her this way.

Open me!

I cannot stop her.

She gives in. The door moans as it opens. She feels an almost orgasmic relief, like a lost man in the desert gulping water, or a starved girl in the mountains shoving berries into her mouth. It tickles her cheeks, her arms, and her hands. She looks down at her body with a giggle. Her freckles are making their way from every part of her body, moving toward the shed.

I cannot stop this.

Mister Crado returns from behind the woods. "False alarm," he says while tightening his belt, but he stops wide-eyed when he sees the scene.

He cannot stop this.

The ground is rumbling. Sparks fly into the air, wrapping themselves around Vallesia and the shed, catching them in a cocoon-like tornado. The wind picks up. Her hair lifts into the air and her clothes hit her skin in powerful slaps.

"Let go!" Mister Crado's roar is almost as loud as the sky and the lightning which strikes from it. Gravel spews up to either side like stray bullets as a powerful sword of pure energy stabs and rips up the dirt in front of him, leaving a crater by the end of his foot.

It is too late.

It has started now.

"I can't!" Her breaking voice does not reach him from within the storm. She cries, but her tears never reach her cheeks and are instead ripped away from her, merging with the tornado.

"No!"

It feels as if her fingers are glued to the door. Pulling with her whole body makes no difference.

"Let go! *Now!*"

There is a loud crackling behind her.

"I can't! *I can't!*" she screams with all the air that the wind is crunching out of her.

The wind picks up speed. Her hair is a mess, her eyes have no business staying open, and when another lightning bolt hits behind her, her feet leave the ground.

The sky will fall.

The whispering voice is no longer whispering, but yelling. Loudly, while everything else mutes around her. It seems to come from the sun above her, the ground below her, and from the violent wind.

The blood will turn to ink.

The plaque releases from the shed and flies into the air with her. It whirls around, bruising her body with every strike, but her choked cry is lost in the cacophony.

The shadows will eat flesh.

She falls. Her knees hit the ravaged ground with a loud thump that she barely hears over a high-pitched tinnitus. The ringing crescendos until it peaks briefly and washes out into total silence. She opens her eyes to see that the bruises covering her whole body, and the agony as she wiggles around is only a taste of the hell that she has broken loose.

The presence in front of her makes her crawl back, squirming on the ground. It is a large, dense cloud; wicked black, hovering without dissipating. She feels as if it is watching her, as if it is somehow a conscious being—alive and organic, its breath mixing with hers. It whirls around, shifting matter and pushing dust clouds aside to reveal a set of glowing red eyes. They look human and tortured and so angry that it makes her own blood boil with rage. She gasps for air.

And no one can save you then.

The cloud takes off and soars right through her. It is hot and bitter inside; she feels claustrophobic, as if her skin fits too tightly around her bones. It passes her. She turns and watches it approach Mister Crado lying paralyzed on the ground. Five craters surround him from where the lightning has struck, but he has gone unharmed. Now, the cloud swallows him and holds onto him for much longer than Vallesia.

He screams as Vallesia pushes herself up to attempt to chase the cursed being away, but before she reaches it, he stops. Then, the cloud finally dissipates, but not into the air. It surges into him. It stretches itself into thin funnels and enters his ears, eyes, nose, and mouth. He sits up, suddenly and awkward, as if possessed. When he opens his eyes to reveal a set of glowing red ones, tortured and angry, she realizes that this is exactly what he is. Possessed.

She blinks and he disappears. In his place, there is only wicked black smoke. And then there is nothing, and she is all alone. The trees have fallen in a wide circle around her, their roots reaching for the gray clouds. In front of her, a gaping hole seems deeper than to the core of the ground and the wood from the shed lies scattered by her feet where it has been ripped apart.

She picks up the plaque, then falls into the traumatized grass and bites her cheek.

It is my fault. I am so sorry.

We look up at the clouds to watch the sky fall.

DAY I

If the sky cannot have eyes, then neither can you.

CHAPTER 6

WATCHING THE WORLD IS LIKE watching a bubble grow larger and larger, not knowing when it's going to burst. Yet, there is nothing I can do but watch. In the last pre-apocalyptic hours of the Gluskabian world, I find Dahlia marching down the streets of Capital City.

This must be the biggest protest that she has ever been a part of. It starts off peacefully. At noon, she joins twenty-five thousand others, racing down the main roads, screaming at the top of their lungs for change. The chants fill the air, creating a static atmosphere which pushes the blood through her veins, fast and hot, making her fingertips tickle. She is at once smiling, proud, and enjoying the feeling of being alive, but she is also, of course, angry like the others.

"Run! Run! Run!" Dahlia screams at the top of her lungs. She is louder than everyone else and she holds her sign higher and higher until her arm hurts. The years she has spent at the military boarding school before escaping have given her an unreal relationship to pain, so her arm will not go down before its message is revealed to all, it is cut down, or the world has ended. She feels her voice breaking with each command to flee. "Run! Run! Run!"

Mothers try to contain their curious children who, now that they are not allowed to join the parade, peek their heads out from their windows, ice cream in hand and all smiles. They watch from their towers, skyscrapers towering far into the air. Fresh green vines and blooming flowers are attached to cold steel and rustic brick walls, alongside soothing pastel colors in blocks like big, intricate quilts. The protesters rage through the streets past murals on houses; portraits of dear ones, beautiful landscapes, children's drawings, abstract compositions, and the most popular ones: drawings of space. Stars impossibly close and the moon shining as bright as the sun.

The protesters wear their shirts like quilts as well: knitted patches randomly sewn on buttoned up shirts with no sleeves ever matching. Comfy trousers and loose shirts coated in green, yellow, and pink. To tell you the truth, I've never seen much gray until I traveled outside of my world. A man to Dahlia's right is wearing a neon green dress shirt, and another is wearing a long skirt with flowers embroidered by the seams. Dahlia is wearing a euphoric smile despite a brutal hangover which she has softened with more than one beer.

People open their windows and chant with them. Kids fold magazines into cones and use them as megaphones to amplify their voices. Parents let banners drop from their windows, the words waving in the air. *Run! Run! Run!*

This protest must be for the banshees. Before Gluskab made humans, he made banshees. They were innocent beings, youngsters running around The Forest of Magnificent Trees. They didn't have any language, in fact, they still don't, but they were happy by nature just to be around Gluskab and Jarda. When Jarda insisted on the creation of humans, banshees became their protectors of hurt, letting them know whenever a loved one was soon to pass. The banshees ventured out of the forest only when a name tugged at their hearts. They would find the person whose parent or child or love was soon to pass and discreetly whisper their name, allowing for a chance to say goodbye. To my knowledge, they haven't whispered a name since Gluskab disappeared.

When He left, the banshees were forcibly removed from the forest. There are things you can't forgive, and His treatment of the banshees is one of those things that sour my heart so much that I struggle to think of Him in any way kindly. I am not talking of how He threw them out, although imagine that—to be thousands of years old, and to have lived in the same place for all those years, and then suddenly be thrown out. What I am talking about is the fire.

I remember seeing hundreds of pillars of smoke reaching toward the sky. And then the screams. Almost too high pitched for me to hear. They came running out of the forest then, with the pillars of smoke following them. Their wings were on fire. It would have been beautiful, had it not been so horrifying. The fire seared off their wings, and then their backs, and threatened to envelop their whole bodies. When we finally extinguished the fires, the skin of some was completely black and peeled off by the faintest touch. They were angels—innocent, then condemned as witches on stakes.

After that, they became homeless, without identities, without purposes. But they weren't met with much sympathy when they tried to join society. At first, everyone thought that the thousands of banshees must mean that an impending catastrophe was on its way. Then, they were blamed for their own banishment, some even believing that they were the ones who drove the Dear Creator away. When they walked the streets, mothers would hold tightly onto their children, as though the banshees were not just messengers of death, but bringers of death. Naturally, people were just scared, but I really don't think that's any excuse. After everything they'd been through…

At least Dahlia, and everyone here today, is trying to make amends for that. This new generation seems, in so many ways, so much more sympathetic than the last. I have long theorized that people can become spoiled from too much divine protection.

A small boy bumps into Dahlia. He is wearing an 'I love banshees' shirt and a big smile. He looks faintly like a banshee himself, with unsettling big irises and high cheekbones. I think he is half. He looks up at Dahlia and smiles as if he doesn't have a worry in the world. She smiles back at him and spots his mother in the crowd. The banshee smiles at her as well, then she grabs his hand and disappears with him. Dahlia's heart is beating fast and she raises her sign even higher.

She feels so *alive*. I can feel it and I almost, just almost, allow myself to forget that the world is literally going to end anytime now.

Yells suddenly fill the scene. They aren't the passionate yells of protesters. It must be a little further down, but close enough that Dahlia can easily hear them. Someone must be having a problem. The shouting gets louder, more immediate. She moves quickly, pushing herself through the masses, heart beating fast. She is certain that something is wrong. The closer she gets, the louder the people scream. There is a ruckus, dissatisfaction not caused by what the protest is meant for. Hooligans, that's what it is.

She is right. When she reaches the corner of twenty-fourth and twenty-fifth streets, the crowd becomes too dense. She can hardly move, hardly breathe. And there is a car, oh, Dear Creator, a car on fire. In the middle of everything. And the protesters—she looks around to see one with a gas can. And another has a torch. This was not the intention. This is all wrong.

The military fills the role as police and stands ready at every corner to ensure that nothing turns violent. Now that it has, they don't know what to do. Dahlia is hoping to find Vallesia among them, but she is off starting an apocalypse.

"Run! Run! Run!" The protesters' commands sound more and more threatening with every chant and the military rushing in only heightens the confusion and the violence with their rubber bullets, mace, and batons. Enemy and friend become blurred. Official military jackets are mistaken for fashionable military jackets. The young and old are shoved to the side. Mothers close their windows. The fire spreads. Somewhere, a woman's scream tops every other noise before ending abruptly.

Dahlia looks for the source. It sounded inhuman, like— she knows what it sounded like. But there are so many people around them and the scream was too quick, not long enough for Dahlia to have been able to determine even the general direction. She jumps on a nearby car. Two young girls like her idea and join her, but instead of searching for a distressed banshee, they start to yell at the military.

"Where is your god now? Where is your god now?" they yell it over and over, one of them giggling. Two soldiers rush toward them.

"Get down from there!" one of them demands. The giggling girl laughs, but the other one can barely contain her anger.

"Stop trying to silence our voices! You're what's wrong with this world!"

Dahlia is trying her best to tune the arguing girls out. She is still searching. Searching, searching, searching.

There!

There she is.

But before Dahlia can get down, the soldier has climbed the car. The girls have dissipated, so he grabs hold of Dahlia in their place. His sudden grip around her elbow startles her and she turns to him, ready to explain, but he doesn't wait for an explanation. Instead, he takes wriggling as resistance and hits her side with his baton. She cries out in pain, the world momentarily blurred.

"Get down from there," he grumbles.

She would if he'd let her. She hears the scream again. But there are too many people—she has lost track of the banshee.

"Please let me—" she starts, but is silenced with another blow, this time to the knee. She falls.

Never mind, then. If he's not going to be nice, she'll show

him that she is not nice either. She's not her sister. He tries to pull her back up, but she kicks him, bringing him to his knees. She is freed and on top of him, and she returns his violence with a solid fist squarely to his face. The soldier let's out a cry, but she's far gone by then.

The banshee.

Where has the banshee gone?

There! Where she saw her before!

The banshee has pushed herself against a wall and is completely frozen. Her dark eyes are fixated on a wrecked car that protesters have turned over in a frenzy. And this is the source of her screams: A hand of heat enveloping the car in its palm, sweat sprouting from it like acidic rain. There are monsters dancing in the clear of her eyes, horrid creatures of the past.

It started off as a peaceful protest. It is no longer.

If only Dahlia had been as big and strong as her sister, it would have been no trouble for her to push past the people. She tries but is immediately punched in the face and stepped on. Instead, she uses her size to cram herself into the small spaces between people, bending down and to the side like a human Tetris block and finally, she is beside the creature. She looks so frail, like a baby bird.

"Are you okay?" Dahlia yells at her, but realizes it's a stupid question. The banshee looks at her, or maybe through her, her eyes glassy. She is clearly not okay. "Let's go somewhere, okay? I know somewhere close."

The banshee doesn't answer, but she also doesn't fight Dahlia when she grabs her wrist and drags her along. Someone elbows her in the side and they stumble into each other. Dahlia drops her sign and gets a tight hold around both the banshee's arms. The banshee barely seems to notice. She is too far away.

They stay close to the wall but they are still getting pushed. The road seems so narrow, the surging mass of protesters seems less impressive and more terrifying now, angry and, for some reason, armed with torches. A classic mob, minus the pitchforks. The skyscrapers are fireproof, praise the Dear Creator, but there are plenty of things that can burn. Other cars. Trees. Clothes. Herself. The banshee.

Dahlia is filled with a new purpose: to get this angel with her flickering eyes and wobbling legs to safety. She looks lost, wide eyed and her body tense while skirting all over the place. She must be seeing attackers coming from all sides with the way she twists her head in a frantic attempt to cover all angles. Dahlia fills with rage toward the protesters—can't they see that the last thing the banshees need is yet another fire threatening to destroy them? Who was mindless enough to bring torches, anyway?

"Run! Run! Run!" The protesters do not give up their chants, but instead directs them at the military. They are retreating as well. Cowards, Dahlia thinks. Spoiled children that do not know how to stand on their own legs without their parent, their Creator, to support them. I can't say I disagree.

The banshee is breathing heavily now. Hyperventilating. On the verge of tears, Dahlia sees. She guides her into a side street, away from the turmoil. Solitarius Café is not far.

CHAPTER
7

SOLITARIUS CAFÉ HAS A HISTORY, ONE that makes me feel like a traitor following them inside. Let's not sugar-coat it—it's a café for the resistance. Even before Gluskab's disappearance, it was a place where disgruntled men came to complain about their own failures in life and sought some greater being than themselves to blame. Why does Gluskab have a palace, and I don't? Why won't he cure my wife's headaches? Why can't we all be immortal, anyway, and why does he even get to decide? How about a democratically elected god! After today, their complaints will be completely validated, I'm afraid. The conspiracies will gain a new degree of credibility.

Dahlia comes here often, to complain about life to a stranger over beers or just because she likes the cubicles. That's something else that sets this café apart from others. You get your own cubicle, completely soundproof, with as much privacy as you want. There is service, but only when you press a button. Or you can order through the computer from the comfort of your chair. There are huge windows covering the entire wall out to the streets, but you can only see out, not in, and if you tap the glass twice, the outside blurs out. The cubicles are designed to keep Gluskab out, or at least that's how they were marketed back in the day. I think it was just to attract more disgruntled men. I don't think it actually works like that.

Gluskab's disappearance has been good for the café's business, and it's busy enough that it has had to expand several times. Often, it's hard to get a cubicle, but Dahlia is a prime member and they get theirs immediately. They sit down at a table with a wooden surface, rough around the edges but with delicate engravings containing snippets from speeches made by people Dahlia sees as brave rebels.

The banshee doesn't reply when asked what she'd like, so Dahlia orders a small assortment: water, tea, coffee, cupcakes, and cookies. What she really wants is a beer or a nice glass or two of wine, but even she can tell that now is not the time. The protest continues outside the window, but it has quieted down. The fires have been extinguished and the culprits seem mostly to have been hauled off. Dahlia breathes a sigh of relief.

"We can fog it up if it bothers you," Dahlia says, pointing to the window behind them. "If you feel a bit... Well, I don't know. You know. I promise you, it wasn't planned on our side. The fire, that is. It was supposed to be completely peaceful. Anyway, I'm sorry."

The banshee looks up at her, the first sign of her listening. Dahlia was wondering whether she might be deaf. She has stopped shaking as much, as well. Her eyes look questioning, interested perhaps.

"Oh, yeah," Dahlia, who doesn't mind leading a conversation, continues. "I'm one of the lead organizers. Me and a couple of people from work. We planned some of the protest here, actually, in this cubicle. It's our favorite café. We come here after we get off and have a few beers. To relax, you know."

The banshee tilts her head and squints at her. Maybe she is mute? Many of the banshees do not have a language, Dahlia reminds herself, only the ones who have permanently left the forests and moved to the cities have one—but this one is a city banshee, isn't she? She's in the city, yet she doesn't quite appear to fit in.

"I work down at Reynard's, the TV station, as a reporter. Do you know it?"

The banshee shakes her head with infinite slowness. She has completely stopped shaking now.

"Oh. Okay. Maybe you don't watch a lot of TV?"

No response.

"Okay, that's completely fine. My channel, where I work, it's very famous for being, well... Anti-Gluskab. I hope that doesn't offend you. In my experience, most of the banshees are not too positive toward Him either."

She doesn't reply, but her eyes turn glassy again. She leans back into her chair and makes herself even smaller than she is. Her thick, light gray hair falls down to cover most of her face. Dahlia has a thought which surprises us both—she thinks the banshee is cute. A bit like someone you want to protect and keep safe at all costs.

They hear a knock on the door before a waitress enters with a filled tray. She looks from Dahlia to the banshee as she places the order in the middle. Banshees are not uncommon here, so the waitress doesn't seem surprised by her presence.

"Would that be all?" she asks with her usual flirty smile.

"Yes, thank you, Ariel." Dahlia returns the expression. Last time she was here, she promised herself that she'd ask Ariel out the next time she saw her, but she will have to wait for another chance.

"Enjoy," Ariel chirps back. "Just buzz if there's anything missing."

"Ariel..." the banshee whispers after she has gone.

Dahlia is surprised, but pleased. The banshee's voice is small and light, like a little girl's, with the typical, exotic banshee pronunciation.

"Yes! That's her name. Mine is Dahlia." She laughs and

smiles wide. "Did I really forget to introduce myself? I'm sorry about that. What's your name?"

"Sera-phina."

"Seraphina." Dahlia repeats it as if tasting the name. Then she smiles again. "I like it. A lot." She puts her hand forward and nods toward it. Seraphina shakes it reluctantly, her long sleeves covering most of her fingers. Dahlia catches herself thinking that she likes the way Seraphina's skin feels. "Do you mind me asking, where do you live? With someone?"

"Angel. Forest," Seraphina says with her brow furrowed, as if she is trying to solve a hard math problem.

"Oh." Dahlia leans in closer. Intrigued. "That's outside of town, isn't it? It's the reservation. I've been there. They've got that big sign out in front, the one that says 'Welcome Home'. It's very beautiful."

The banshee nods slowly, still with an intense concentration. "Beauti-ful," she repeats. Every word she speaks sounds pained, as if it physically hurts her throat to form the unusual words. "Not magnifi-cent."

Dahlia furrows her brows, processing the words individually and together. Finally, she nods back. "Yeah, it's no Forest of Magnificent Trees, I bet. Still, it's a good reservation. I'm sure you know, but that's in part what we're working on, with the protests and so on. Getting more reservations, that is. I know some banshees have been forced to move to the city in these... *blocks* are really the best way to describe them. It'd make anyone depressed, no less someone so connected to nature."

Is that a smile on Seraphina's lips? "Thanks," she says.

"No problem." Dahlia smiles back. "I can relate, at least somewhat. I was thrown out of my home too, when I was sixteen. Or, I ran away from the boarding school where I lived when I was sixteen, then my dad threw me out of his house before I even stepped inside. It's a long story. My point is just that I think I understand somewhat what you guys have been through. There's nothing worse than feeling unwanted. Well, constantly having to worry about where to sleep and how to get food is not too great either."

Seraphina's eyes fog up with tears. She wipes them with her sleeve and reaches for the tea, folding her hands around the warm cup and placing it in front of her. She looks down at it, a little unsure.

Dahlia smiles at her again, and Seraphina answers with a careful smile. Then Dahlia lifts a cup of coffee and takes a big, confident gulp. Seraphina responds with a careful sip, then puts the cup back down with a grimace that shuffles between emotions of surprise and shock.

Dahlia laughs. "Have you not had tea before?"

Seraphina shakes her head no.

Dahlia laughs again, then narrows her eyes. "Is this your first time here, then? In the city, I mean. Or, I assume, before… you must have been to the city before? Before… everything happened."

Seraphina nods.

"But not after… not for the last twenty-odd years?"

She nods again.

Dahlia is surprised and doesn't try to hide it. It is inconceivable to her that Seraphina stayed within the reservation for so many years. The place is nice, she supposes, at least from the perspective of a banshee. There is nature aplenty — flowers, trees, and bushes all things a banshee might like — although it is not cared for very well. The huts are primitive, the place is bizarrely quiet, and though Dahlia does not like to admit it, it has an apparent lack of culture. The only things of value there are what volunteers have built, like the sign in front, the big fireplace, and some nicer huts. The banshees there seem content with their pointless, static existences, and any of the volunteers' attempts to stimulate them have been unsuccessful so far. Seraphina does not appear comfortable in the city and with human culture, but she also doesn't seem like she'd never been to the city. Somewhere in between, maybe.

"I am sorry to be asking so many questions," Dahlia says. "You don't mind, do you?"

Seraphina shakes her head no again.

"Why did you come here? To the protest, I mean. You came alone, right? Did you know there was a protest today?"

Seraphina turns in her chair, looking out the window. Contemplating her answer, it seems, as though it's the first time it occurred to her that she needed a reason to come to the city or the protest.

She wets her lips before responding with in a measured, solemn tone. "People act. I want be people."

Dahlia leans back in her chair, musing over the response with an intense gaze on the banshee. What does that mean, she wants to be a person? Isn't she already a person? But before Dahlia gets to ask more questions, the heavens interrupt them, illuminating the room with a bright light.

Oh, Dear Creator. It is time.

CHAPTER 8

LIGHTNING RIPS THROUGH THE CLOUDS with a rumble like a deep drumroll. Dahlia and Seraphina can't hear it, but they see the world light up from their cubicle. The clear sky turns gray, like the clouds are made of ashes. Grimy dark spots like sinister slugs loom above them, awaiting the perfect time to unleash another volley of lightning, which stabs the ground with a mighty roar. Its sheer power tears open the streets, tossing bricks aside and burning a crater that crackles with electricity for several long seconds. It flickers like pulsing veins, like alien snouts suckling on the breasts of the ground. Then, anvil crawlers appear. The lightning strokes stretch over the sky like the fingers of a starving man grasping, begging for food. All of this occurs as Dahlia turns around and Seraphina stands up, blood like ice, her whole being numb. When she opens her mouth, only a raspy sound escapes her.

It is like watching television. It seems so unreal, so overly dramatic.

Only a few meters from the window, right in front of them,

a girl turns on the sidewalk, looking for somebody. She searches with frantic eyes, her orange, red, and yellow hair rising and falling as her head spins around, like sunsets and sunrises, wild and untamed, answering to no one. She seems full of life, fifteen years old, maybe.

At least she was before the lightning.

It shoots from the clouds, angry, cold blooded, purposeful, and obstinate. It wraps itself around her and she spasms as the electricity courses through her body. Her eyes empty before she falls, her body lifeless on the ground. People jump back, covering their ears, stomachs turning in the deep roar-like laughter of the lightning.

If panic reigned before, chaos has now declared itself the absolute ruler, turning whimpers into full-blown wails and heating fires under everyone's feet. Dahlia's first thought is of anthills and boots, confused and terrified swarms scattering and running, stumbling into each other, eyes wide open, hysterical. Searching for someone they know — distraught, hopeless, and lost. They scream. Seraphina and Dahlia cannot hear inside the cubicle, but they can see their mouths stretching wide.

The next victim is a man. Seconds later, barely giving them time to process the first. He is standing right beside her fallen body. Tilting his head up toward the gray skies, the treacherous vault of heaven, the cruel slugs — he is searching for an answer, or perhaps expecting one. He condemns the heavens, denouncing them. And they answer. Oh yes, the clouds, they answer. The lightning splits before finding his head, piercing both his eyes and sending shock waves through his body. He spasms before he drops and joins the girl.

A mother grabs her children and jumps the bodies. Bigger people plow through the crowd, forgetting social niceties as they throw smaller, fragile innocents to the ground. They trample them, breaking ankles and backs, smashing faces into the pavement. Bodies are pushed up against walls. Grown men cry and weep, pray and shake. The blood is not from the lightning, the first or second, third, fifth or tenth — twelve deadly lightning bolts have left bodies in their wake — the blood is from boots.

Seraphina turns away from the window with a terrified squeak. Tears fill her eyes. "What happening?"

Dahlia looks away as well, and back at the banshee. "I don't know," she says, although she does. She knows what is happening, and she is, in theory, prepared for it. She just doesn't want it to be happening, but that doesn't change that it is.

Seraphina is panting. Dahlia is better at suppressing the fact that she is completely and utterly freaking out. She looks out the window again, processing what she knows this must be. It is the only thing it can be. While she looks out, Seraphina makes her way over to her and wraps her arms around her waist. The banshee is shorter than her by a head, so small and fragile, and her sobs sound like a mouse. Slowly, Dahlia puts her arm around the stranger.

"Listen, Seraphina," she says, her voice shaky. "This is a safe place. The walls are cement. Nothing is going to happen to you in here. They are prepared for this kind of thing, so you just stay here. Okay?"

"This… thing?" Seraphina repeats.

This kind of thing. What kind of thing? Dahlia can't bring herself to say or even think the word. She has said and heard it so many times during her life, more than most, and now… Maybe she never actually believed this day would come. Maybe it was just an idea to believe in, something to make sense of everything, not something that would actually happen.

"You are going to stay here," Dahlia says, ignoring the question.

"Me?" Seraphina asks and takes a step backward. She looks up at Dahlia, her eyes wide. "You?"

"I'm going to go to work," Dahlia says. "I need to know what's going on. It's a news station. If anyone knows, it'll be them."

That's the first step of the apocalypse prepper's plan. Gather information. Then, resources. A safe space. Weapons. Retaliation. She glances at the lightning outside again. *Retaliation against what?* She wonders.

"Outside!" Seraphina squeaks.

"Yes, I'll have to go outside. I know, but I need to find out what's happening."

Seraphina looks genuinely distressed, her eyes darting around, her hands clutching her chest. "Call?"

"That's not good enough. Plus, my car is parked there and I need my bug out bags."

"Bug... out." Seraphina tries to repeat, but loses it halfway through. Her brows furrow again. She's thinking harder than she is made to think.

"Bug out bags. Look, it doesn't matter. You just stay here."

Seraphina shakes her head. Her whole body is shaking. "No," she says.

What is with her? Is she afraid of being left behind?

"Yes," Dahlia insists.

"No!"

Dahlia sighs and glances out. The scene has calmed down. People have rushed into the nearest apartments or sit huddled together, stacked in hallways. The streets are clear; all that remains are turned over bricks, trampled signs, lost shoes, and, of course, the bodies. She could count them if she wanted.

I count them. There are twenty-four.

Twenty-four fellow beings lying dead or dying on the ground, limbs bent and eyes wide open in a last moment of horror. Some of them are breathing faintly, but no one dares to enter the streets to help them, even if the sky above is baby blue. They don't trust the above anymore. I wouldn't either, if I were them.

I am trembling with anger. I knew my father would do this.

"Look," Dahlia finally says. "I really think you should stay here. It's safer."

Seraphina is small and weak, physically and mentally. She'd be a liability. *You can't afford too many charities at times like these.* The phrase is imprinted within her and this, today, is the day where she will finally be able to follow it in its true meaning. She thought the day would never come when the phrase would apply, and yet, today, she doesn't want to apply it.

"No."

Dahlia walks over to the window to feel the cold surface with her fingertips. She knows the lightning bolts targeted the people. *It's almost as though... as though...* Dahlia takes a deep breath before finishing the thought, letting the truth be clearly pronounced in her mind.

It is almost as though it was the act of a Creator.

And she is right. Except for the almost part.

"Then let's go," Dahlia says.

CHAPTER 9

I **KEEP AN EYE OUT** for Mario as well. He doesn't wake up until the afternoon is well on its way, to an empty bed and with only a faint memory of his wife leaving in the middle of the night. He reflects on this while he makes himself a cup of tea. *Why did she leave? Did she give him any explanation?* She took her uniform, kissed him on the cheek, and told him she'd be back. *Don't go,* Mario said, but she left nevertheless. She was shaking. *Was she scared? Nervous? Excited?* He wasn't sure, and still isn't sure. Her scent lingers on the pillow, on the covers, on his skin.

He tries to locate his phone, thinking maybe there's a text from her, or maybe a voicemail to let him know what's up. But there are no messages, only an apartment wrecked from the night before, a party gone awry in more ways than just the usual drunkenness. At first, he thought Vallesia's tears were of happiness and he was the last one to hear the pin drop, preserving his naïve enthusiasm even after Vallesia ran off to the balcony and Dahlia turned to him and prompted him to follow.

Gluskab works in mysterious ways. That's what he thought to himself before sharing this with Vallesia, who didn't seem much comforted by it.

He can think of many positives to his wife's predicament while his tea is steeping. The pay in the army isn't great. She might have been deployed and they would have to move. Whenever she came home, she was always too sore, too tired, and too busy with diets and training. It isn't a job ideal for an expanding family, which he very much hopes for. It is a dangerous job as well, and it gets even more dangerous every year Gluskab is absent. People are losing faith that he will be back again. They are becoming braver in their crimes, and beginning to think there might not be consequences to their actions. The military isn't nearly large enough to handle these new cases; they were never meant to handle this. Yes, Mario is convinced that their life will be much better now. Calmer. Easier.

His thoughts are sweet, but there is no possible outcome in what's to come where Mario wins. His misery has always been in the cards since he met Vallesia and married someone who was never meant to be his.

I'm sorry, I'm getting ahead of myself. It's all very upsetting to me, but I will try to stay calm for you.

Mario looks around the apartment to assess the damage. The floor is messy. Streamers float around. There are pools of something sticky, hopefully just alcohol. The furniture is displaced; the couch is a few inches too far to the left or right—he can't decide which, but it's unsettling. He finds a lamp in the bathtub. There is cereal in the hallway. Carrots lie under the living room table. Empty and half full bottles of alcohol are stacked on every surface that, from a drunk person's perspective, looks capable of carrying the weight. He is going to have to clean today. If he were rich, he thinks, he could call someone instead.

Today was supposed to be a day off from work. Well, it was supposed to be a day off so he could spend the day massaging Vallesia's feet and really spoiling her the way she deserves.

But she isn't here, so he decides to get to work, anyway. He steps outside on the balcony with his overly sweetened tea, a dry piece of toast, an apple, his work PC, and letters. The sky is light blue like the sea in paradise, the birds are singing, and the summer air is warm but not humid.

He weighs the heavy envelopes in his hands.

To
Mario Jade
Identity Detective, Inc.
Mirror Street 1667, apt 73
Capital City

He loves his job and he is proud to say that he is one of the absolute best at it, although, of course, the competition is very slim and the job is anything but prestigious. The most common reaction to him telling anyone his profession is laughter followed by *'Oh. You're serious!'* But Mario doesn't see why it is funny. Jarda herself taught the world about reincarnation, explaining how any dead organism is reborn in a new body. A fly might become a bird, or a horse a puppy. Sometimes, a human becoming a human, and that's what Mario studies, human-to-human reincarnations. There is nothing like the feeling of a solved case with family members and loved ones reunited once again.

How does he do it? Babies are, of course, ensouled the moment the water breaks. Doctors have gotten impressively accurate at determining the exact time of ensoulment, and his database is growing more and more intricate with more hospitals reporting this to him. His PC is so filled with numbers, it's about to burst. Once he's found all the possible contestants, that is, everyone whose ensoulment date matches the dead's death date, he can rate them based on likelihood. Those ensouled closest to the place of death rates higher, as a soul will simply slip into the nearest vessel.

Then, he looks for connections between the likely. Tragic deaths will result in nightmares and sudden flashbacks. Those are more or less considered proofs, but they might not start until late into the reincarnation's life, often after or during traumatic or stressful events. A math professor's reincarnation loves numbers, a zookeeper's reincarnation loves playing with the neighborhood dog. A strong enough trait will always persevere. Lastly, Mario will let the client meet with a few preselected candidates. They will usually be able to recognize a tick, a smile, or a way of sitting or walking. Sometimes, there is just a feeling that can't be quantified.

Some people call this a pseudoscience, but, impressively, he is right. This *is* exactly how it works. There is only one type of assignment he consistently refuses — the constant stream of people claiming that they are the reincarnation of Gluskab or Jarda. The requests have exploded these past years. Anyone born around the time of his disappearance suddenly thinks they are a god. He finds it to be grossly blasphemous. Just thinking about it now, he feels a lump of annoyance, like others would when confronted with a noisy fly. Watching him for many years now, I can tell you that's as upset as he ever gets.

A few hours into his work, a bright flash disturbs Mario. The thunder follows less than a second later, bellowing just as he raises his head to shoot a confused look at the city. The balcony windows shudder and the birds stop their chattering to yell at the heavens.

Gray clouds storm in from every side, swallowing everything from tenth to thirtieth street, creating a dome of horror. He can hear the screams all the way up here. Flashes appear from inside the horror dome at regular intervals, each time unleashing more terrified yells. The thunder is so loud his cup clinks against his plate and his whole body trembles with fear.

He rushes back inside and busies himself by moving the couch back into place, first left, then right, then finally he realizes it has only been moved a little forward. He continues on to a new task. The TV runs in the background, zapping between channels: a reality cook who probably feeds her children nuggets, a sitcom opting for a laugh track every few seconds, a documentary conspiring against Gluskab, two beauty queens fighting over a bedazzled crown, then suddenly broken up by a breaking news segment.

He locks the channel to watch in breathless suspense, plastic sack in hand, streamers at its mouth along with an empty bottle halfway into it. A reporter stands in front of an empty street holding an oversized microphone. She speaks slowly, her voice shaking as she stumbles over the words. There is almost nothing to add about the thunderstorm. It started at 14:00 and ended at 14:30, lasting for thirty minutes. The estimated death toll is fifty-six. The reporter calls it a catastrophe the likes of which has never before been seen. Scientists offer no explanation, and neither does the military. The Peacers are silent shadows, disappeared, it seems, the same way the gods did.

"A catastrophe? Or perhaps... a massacre?" the reporter closes. Mario flips the channel and grimaces at the screen.

"A massacre?" he repeats at the TV, as if it is personally responsible for the blasphemy. "A brutal slaughter led by *whom*? Gluskab? That's just ridiculous. That reporter should be fired."

I wish he, and not the reporter, were right.

Another channel is showing footage from the storm. A scientist is analyzing atmospheric readings, the shape of the clouds, even the color of the sky — gray like ashes and black like iron chains — doesn't escape his attentive eyes. He explains how there couldn't have been a thunderstorm, rather than how there was.

"There were no cumulonimbus clouds"," he whines, his voice high pitched and distraught, as if everyone should focus on the cumulonimbus clouds or the lack thereof.

They show a young woman with bright orange hair being hit by lightning in slow motion again and again. The scientist pushes up his glasses and comments on the shape of the lightning. By the third replay, Mario turns off the TV. He makes himself a new cup of tea, abandoning the empty bottles and plastic sack.

Mario tries to list the positives to the situation, as he has a habit of doing. It is his opinion that there is nothing sad about death when every soul is recycled. Every ended life means the beginning of a new, and Gluskab takes lives for a reason. He picks souls out of bodies before the bodies atrophy and he saves beings from suffering before they even know they are suffering. Death, Mario thinks, should be met with a smile and a thank you to the Dear Creator, who might work in mysterious ways, but always knows what is best.

Certainly, there was a point in history where Mario would have been right. But that point in history is as far from now as it could be.

Anyway, it is not the dying I am worried about.

CHAPTER 10

THE WEATHER HAS GONE MAD.
In Antonia, a girl hides under a table, hands around her head as if they can save her from the diamond shower. Deadly spikes plummet from the sky like daggers as she listens to the sound of murder. The sky tears everything down with it. If it cannot have eyes, then neither can we, and so it stabs with diamonds, aiming perfectly from years of practicing with raindrops while it silently plotted. Diamonds like daggers, butcher's knives, and saws tear into the population.

If it cannot have legs, then neither can we. The diamond rains cuts and slices legs away.

The blood only angers it — how dare you complain about bleeding, moaning, and screaming when the sky cannot bleed? So, it keeps on aiming and shooting, loading its cloud-cannons with beautiful gems to cut through the skin.

In Larba's inner city, the same sky is crying the dead a river. Then two rivers, and three rivers — the whole town is flooded by ten meters of water, which then rises until the tallest skyscraper becomes an outlook post for this new ocean, this Ocean of Despair. It is a monument for the dead which only grabs hold of more dead, hugging them until they choke. Swallowing rivers, puking up rivers.

The ground, too, is throwing a tantrum. In Hopefield, it knocks everyone off their feet. It makes the gravel dance and the trees moan, then it opens up and swallows a playground whole; swing set and slide, children and all. It swallows the corner store too, a library, and three schools. It moves on to the outskirts, to fields with tractors and lakes with ducks. It laughs and demands yet more sacrifices, not satisfied until it has devoured everything.

CHAPTER

II

MARIO LOOKS OUT HIS KITCHEN window and notices that it is snowing. Really, properly snowing. For the first time ever in Capital City, white flakes flutter down, soon covering the streets in a white blanket. He watches, bewitched, as snowflakes form patterns on the window, stretching their baby arms and legs. It seems like they are waking up, yawning with happy contentment.

The murderous thunder and many dead are soon forgotten, the cold successfully distracting Mario, who was looking to forget about the whole thing, anyway.

He opens the window and cold air rushes in to greet his cheeks with chill kisses. When he breathes in, it tickles his lungs. He runs to the balcony and leaps into the white. His feet freeze in moments, and the wind almost knocks him over. It bites at his skin like a million scissors gnawing into his bare arms or a bag of ice slapping his cheeks.

Inside again, he is shaking hard. His blonde curls are stiff with frost. He turns with a slowness like a robot that hasn't been oiled properly and looks at the round clock above the dining room table. 15:05, it reads. An hour ago, he was sitting outside on his balcony, enjoying a beautiful day with the sun's rays shining down on him and warming his bare shoulders. He scratches his neck with baby blue nails and he doesn't even know what frostnips are.

He wraps the biggest and comfiest blanket he can find around himself and struggles to put on socks, then decides on slippers instead. When will Vallesia be home? He doesn't want to venture outside again without her. He wants to share this historical moment with her. To dive into the cold, make a snow angel, build a fort, a snowman, whatever. Do whatever. The possibilities are endless.

I don't trust this snow. I don't think he should go outside, but I fear nothing will stop him.

He dials her number with numb fingers, but it goes straight to voicemail.

"This is Vallesia Jade." It isn't her voice, it is Mario speaking in falsetto. In the background, she is squealing, protesting the mutiny, so instead he continues in the lowest, manliest baritone note, he can muster: *"I'm busy lifting weights and drinking protein shakes, but – "* His voice is broken off suddenly by loud laughter and, he remembers, Vallesia tackling him. It beeps.

He stares at the phone for a while, then decides to call Tomi. He picks up after the third beep and Mario tells him about last night.

"She left when?" Tomi asks in disbelief. "In the middle of the night? Why?"

Mario balances his phone between his shoulder and ear while rubbing his still-frozen hands together. "I was hoping you'd know."

"Oh," Tomi says. "I mean, no. No. I haven't got a clue."

"Ah."

"I'm sorry."

"No, I'm sure she's fine. It's just because it's snowing. Where are you? It's snowing where you are too, right?"

"No."

"Oh?" Mario tries to blow on his fingers, which are slowly warming.

"Yeah. Look, I've got to go. The military has been called in, lots of crazy stuff right now, so..."

"Oh, yeah. Sure. Take care, right?"

"You, too." Tomi pauses. "And call back when you hear from Valley, yeah? I'll call too."

"Of course. Will do."

"And Mario? The snow, right?"

"Yes?"

"I'm not sure you should go out. It could be dangerous." Tomi sounds grim. He is a smart guy and Mario should listen to him, but he won't.

"Alright, thank you."

They hang up. Mario puts on all his sweaters, layers on layers, then his thickest jacket and tracksuit bottoms over jeans, plus Vallesia's oversized scarf and gloves found under the sink. He also puts hairbands around his ears, and as many socks as his rain boots will allow. How could snow ever be dangerous? He skips out the door and jumps down the many stairs, too excited to wait for his wife.

He struggles to get the front door open and has to push his entire body against it, so he is sure his shoulder is going to bruise. When he finally gets it open, he takes a step forward, where steps should be, and slides into knee-high snow. It makes it into his boots, freezing through the layers of socks. The wind cuts right through the glove fabric, so he pulls down his sleeves and cups his hands into fists. It doesn't take long before he is diminished to a human popsicle; blue lipped, bones rattling against each other, and legs shaking like leaves in the wind. He ventures out into the sea-like landscape with icy tongues licking far up streetlamps and buildings. Piles of cold imprison cars tightly in their palms.

He is far from alone. A group of boys in spring jackets run away from their concerned mothers, throwing snowballs at their friends and shoving ice down each other's shirts. A dog leaps from a door and disappears for a moment before its tail shoots straight up out of the snow. A little girl eyes the snow with care, like she fears it is going to attack her, then marches outside, almost disappearing into the white seas with a tiny squeak. She looks like a hacky sack with entirely too many layers of sweaters and jackets.

A man curses in anger as he tries to free his car with a spatula and a broom, and he accidentally hits an old lady behind him. She screams, then reaches for her chest as her son grabs her arm and maneuvers her back indoors with words of caution. When the man turns back to his car, which is further buried under the ever-falling snow, a teenage boy has climbed on top of it. He poses for his friend, who is taking photos and shouting like an erotica photographer for him to show him more butt and unbutton his shirt a little. The boy obliges, stripping and posing sensually. The angry man only yells at first, but when the teenager does not respond to his threats, he swings his broom, knocking him down. He looks surprised when the boy lands on his behind, then falls face first into the snow. The surprise turns into a paternal concern, then back into anger when the boy pops his head up and it is clear that he is unharmed.

Mario laughs.

Next to him, a couple walks by hand in hand. The girl is shivering and the guy, trying to warm her up, stops and hugs her. Mario imagines the couple as him and his wife: his skinny, pale arms around her muscular body and his blonde locks contrasting her black curls. When Vallesia gets home, he thinks they'll be just like that—happily walking hand in hand, laughing about the beauty of nature, and thanking their Dear Creator. For now, he greets the couple with a wide smile. He is considering venturing further out into the scene when something grabs hold of his ankle.

He leaps back, his heart in his throat and his whole body alert when he sees a white, boney hand reaching out from a pile of snow, clutched around his ankle. After taking a deep breath,

Mario bends down and scoops the snow aside to uncover an old, frozen man, buried whole and barely alive, it seems.

The man is moving his lips, which are light blue, but no words escape them. His silver beard and long, unkempt hair have ice clinging to them and frostbite is claiming his shaking hands and deathly pale face. Whatever he is wearing, it is covered in a thick layer of ice and snow, so the man almost looks more like a snowman than a real human being.

Oh no, I've just realized who this is. What in His own name is He doing here?

"Sir!" Mario exclaims, helping Him to his feet. "Sir! Can you stand?"

He neither responds, nor moves. His bodyweight fall on Mario. His nails are buried deep into Mario's jacket. The god's eyes are wide open, white and stiff. If it weren't for the shaking, Mario could have been fooled into thinking that He was already dead — dear, I might have been fooled into thinking He is actually struggling.

"Okay, let's get you inside," Mario says as he turns the body around and steers the god back into the building. He worries that a wrong move might cause a leg or arm to fall off, that's how thoroughly frozen He is, and how little Mario knows about being frozen.

"S—so... C—cold," the god stutters once inside. "C—cold."

Mario nods. It is not until he starts brushing the snow off the god that he realizes what He is wearing. A uniform. A military uniform, and not just any military uniform. Deep maroon. Golden buttons. 'Peacer' embroidered above His chest. He stops and looks at the soldier with the old, wrinkled skin and hunched back. His eyes are soft and helpless in this stolen flesh suit.

"I'm C—Cr—Crado," Gluskab whispers. "Mister... C—Crado."

Gluskab disappears into thin air in front of Mario's door. Just like that, Mario turns and the god he doesn't know is a god is gone.

"Sir?" Mario asks, but there is no response. There is only an empty, silent hallway.

Puzzled, he glances back into the apartment and jumps when he sees a silhouette lounging on his couch. The god has made himself comfortable with a freshly brewed cup of tea in one hand and the TV remote in the other. There is no sign of frostbite or any sort of freezing. He pauses His zapping and turns His head, as if He has been waiting for Mario.

"Hello," Gluskab says with a sly smile.

Mario is too shocked to respond.

"I'm sorry," He continues. "I didn't want you out there in that dreadful weather. Now that you're here, you can help me."

Gluskab flashes a warm smile while Mario stands still and attempts to make sense of the situation. He considers, shortly, if the being before him may be Gluskab. But, he determines, the being looks nothing like Him. The air around Him, the way He sits, and the way He gazes at Mario with a somewhat pleasant smile but also eyes a shade darker than black — it is unsettling. It is nothing like Gluskab's smile, which is said to calm better than a cat's purr.

Gluskab is not the god Mario knew as a child.

"Who are you?" Mario asks. He is still in the doorway, ready to run.

Gluskab smiles wider, then leans forward and holds up the teapot, wiggling it around in His old, veiny hands. "I made tea," He says, but it is Mario's teapot and tea.

Mario steps into his apartment with care, as if the wooden floor below him might hide spring traps. The closer he gets, the more unsettling the god's smile gets: it looks painted on and His eyes are like the eyes of a wolf — angry and hungry. His face is like one stolen from a princess it has devoured whole, skin, bones, and all.

Gluskab pours a cup of tea and lets the aromatic steam

fill His nostrils before passing it on to Mario. "Lavender," He exhales. "So calming."

"I'm sorry," Mario says with caution, but I'd like to know how you got in here."

"Why, I walked."

"You walked?"

"You opened the door for me yourself."

Mario stops in front of the couch. There is a clear flaw in the god's logic, but he cannot pinpoint it. After all, he *did* open the door and the god must have walked in here — how else would He have gotten here? Mario wants to say something, but what?

"Well," Gluskab chuckles. "You *definitely* look like someone who could use some lavender tea. Come here, will ya'?"

Mario unwraps his makeshift winter clothes, then sits down on the couch arm with the warm cup between his hands. "Are you not cold anymore?" he asks.

"Cold? No." Gluskab shakes His head, then leans in closer to Mario. This close, Mario only feels a stronger urge to run. "I need you to find my wife."

I believe I've solved the mystery.

"Your wife?"

The god nods.

Mario does not think the lavender tea is relaxing in any way at all. In fact, he feels more confused by the second. He would like to find his own wife, as well. *Maybe it is the day of the missing wives,* he thinks.

"Did you lose her outside?" he asks. "It's snowing quite a lot. I could see how she could have gotten lost, but I am sure you guys will find each other once it passes. She's probably searching for you, too."

Gluskab looks up at Mario with His hungry, wolfen eyes. Mario is afraid of being swallowed whole and instinctively leans back.

"She is not outside," Gluskab says, His voice cold and dead.

"Oh." Mario is sweating now. A less polite person would have asked the god to leave. "I'm not sure I'm the right person to help you."

"Mario Jade," the god says, taking the cup from Mario's hands, sipping from it, then placing it on a coaster. A sudden, violent gust of wind shakes the apartment, threatening the thin windows. His voice is shaking when He continues. "You're a famous identity detective. You specialize in finding reincarnations of those who have passed, and you are the very best there is. Am I wrong?"

"Your wife is dead?" Mario asks. Years of experience have taught him that there is no sensitive way of posing this question.

Gluskab pushes himself up from the couch and looks toward the window, a low hissing emerging from Him and smoke escaping from His flaring nostrils. Something which sounds like small bullets, but is probably hail, slams against the windows at an alarming rate. They are too fragile for this kind of weather.

"She is," Gluskab says through clenched teeth. "She should never have died, but she did."

"We all die one day," Mario says. "You will, and so will I. But Gluskab made it so it's not sad, praise to Him. I do specialize in finding reincarnations, you're right, and I could help you one of these days. I just have a lot of work right—"

A cloud of smoke emerges from the god as the sky outside darkens. Something rumbles. Perhaps it is a new thunderstorm gathering, but it seems to be coming from Him. It seems He Himself is a storm building up and ready to be set loose.

"You will help me now," Gluskab growls.

Mario sinks further into the couch. "I can run it in the system real fast, shouldn't take too long," he says. "That'll give you some initial candidates, but there's a lot more work than that, of course."

"You put in the information and search for the potential candidates?" Gluskab now appears calm. Mario would somehow prefer Him not to. It unsettles him. The old man's smile is phony.

"Y—yes," Mario hesitates. "I'd just need some information, of course"

"I know all there is to know. She died twenty-two years ago. She plummeted to her death. I know where. I know the hour."

Mario disappears into his home office, then returns with his tablet. "If you'd like me to take you on as a client, I—"

A glare from Gluskab silences him.

Stumbling for words, Mario attempts to continue. "I have... an opening. We could maybe discuss..."

The god wets His lips. Something icy drops down Mario's back.

"Prices?" Mario finishes.

Gluskab holds out His hand, wiggling His fingertips. It does not take long before Mario has handed Him the tablet, defeated, sure that his life's work is less valuable than his life.

The storm outside calms as Mario stands there, waiting amid an awkward silence, for the god in front of him to finish. Does this count as robbery? Sure, the god is not threatening him at gunpoint, but what would the legal implications be, if any, of intimidating someone into, well... Mario is, arguably, not doing his job. Someone has borrowed his work gear; is that a crime? Mario is just letting a god help Himself, a god who is clearly distraught and in need of help. He would not have dreamed of charging Him for letting him inside the building, either.

"This is too complicated," Gluskab says after a while and plops back down into the couch, still clutching the tablet. Every time He growls, a branch outside smacks against the window. "Who designed this?"

"I did," Mario admits as he retreats to the kitchen to make himself a proper cup of tea, one with heaps of sugar. This will take a while, anyway.

Mario gazes from the window at the winter-in-summer land-scape. The snow is still falling and the people are still enjoying it, jumping around in the white masses, frolicking in a cold beauty which most, if not all, have never experienced.

He wonders if his Vallesia is enjoying this, as well. If she is out there, he may spot her if he stares long enough. He imagines her muscular body coming around the corner, her strict, marching gait, and her persistence and strength vibrating in the air around her. He wishes she was there. Certainly, she wouldn't be bullied into whatever he has been bullied into, although he is not quite sure what it is yet.

He pours too much milk into his tea. It will not only need sugar, but honey as well, and will have to be accompanied by two large chocolate cookies.

Ah. That's it. Mario feels calmer, the warm brew filling his mouth, making its way down his throat. For only a moment, while staring out the window, nipping at his cookie and sipping his overly sweetened tea, he forgets about the mysterious, inappropriate man in his living room.

Then Gluskab is suddenly in the doorway, and Mario's heart sinks with a silent sigh.

"It says Mario and Vallesia Jade on your door," Gluskab says, His dark eyes almost inhuman now, more like a demon's than a wolf's.

"Yes. That's me and my wife," Mario explains.

"And where is she now?"

If Mario knew where Vallesia was, he is not sure that he should tell Him, but almost sure that he could be bullied into it. Thankfully, he does not know where she is, and tells him so.

"You don't know?" Gluskab does very little, if anything at all, to hide the annoyance in His voice. He looks at Mario through squinted eyes and flashes His grinding teeth at him. The matter is settled. Even if Mario wanted to lie, he would not dare to.

"She left last night," Mario takes a step backward. "She took her uniform, but she didn't say where she was going."

"When?"

"I'm not sure..."

The windows clatter again as the storm outside rages. A large, vein throbs on Gluskab's forehead.

"I was barely awake..."

There are screams outside. They are so loud that they travel up the colorful skyscraper to reach the fifth floor, where they struggle through the cracks in Mario's closed windows. He jumps in surprise and runs to open the window, listening in horror to the agonized cries. What he sees, he cannot believe.

He tears up and does not even dare to gasp. Every muscle in his body tenses, then he feels like jelly, then as if he does not even belong in his body anymore. Hopelessness embraces him and pulls him down. He hopes his eyes and ears are betraying him, but they are not.

"When did she leave?" Gluskab asks again, but Mario barely hears Him. He is agape, staring at the scene. His eyes tear up and as he moves his hand up to cover his mouth as the reality of the unimaginable situation hits him.

Fire.

The snow has burst into flames. Everyone is screaming as they burn alive. Thousands of people, one moment enjoying the icy weather, then the next... *No, no, no...* his mind rails. Tiny flames and sparks fall from the sky when they should be floating upward. I It is the Gluskabian world's largest wildfire ever, as wide as the streets and reaching as far as he can see.

The screams. Oh, Dear Creator, the screams. They might be faint, but Mario hears them louder than anything he has ever heard before, and he is sure that he will hear them for a long time after they end. I'm sure I will, as well.

"She might have left around six," Mario whispers, his voice quivering. "Or seven. I heard some birds, but it wasn't light outside yet."

Mario wonders how he can help, but knows that he cannot. *What is happening?* he wonders. *Gluskab, oh Gluskab, why have You allowed this to happen? Where are You*, Mario wonders foolishly. *Why are You not stopping this horrible, horrible...*

And the little girl? I wonder about the girl who braved out

earlier, looking like a hacky sack. Is she…

When Mario turns back with the absurd thought of demanding an explanation, the god is gone. Mario searches the apartment. The windows are all shut, not that he'd expect the god to jump from the fifth floor into a maelstrom of flames. He checks his office, his bedroom, the bathroom, and in the cabinets. He even checks under the bed, sprawled out on all fours with a flashlight in hand. The places which Mario looks become more and more improbable: under the rug, in the fridge, in his wife's jewelry box.

He turns to storm out the apartment and comes face to face with Gluskab. He is so close, Mario can smell his breath. It stinks of rot and death, as if something is decaying inside of Him. Mario lets out a surprised squeak, but is silenced, agape once again when he notices Gluskab's eyes.

They are glowing red in a way he has only seen fire burn. Not the controlled fire from a match or a torch. No, not even the passionate, hungry flames of a bonfire or a fireplace, where dry leaves and sticks are devoured whole and the flames lick the ground in hopes of finding something more to destroy. No, it's more like the sheer destructiveness of a single flame consuming a house, feeding on everything and anything it can get its lips on, growing like a demon, savoring objects with the most sentimental value—family photos, inherited jewelry, and children's drawing going up in flames, the memories lost to an evil force that only grows stronger and stronger until everything is gone.

Mario moves his lips to say something, but cannot. Gluskab cups his hands around his face and bends down to get even closer, then He breathes out, his mouth wide open. Mario can see His sharp fangs. He feels himself slipping, his mind emptying, and his legs weakening. He pushes out a silent protest before collapsing on the floor.

Mario doesn't deserve this.

CHAPTER
12

CATASTROPHES ARE A complicated matter for those working in the news. While they are horrible by nature, they also bring in good viewers and, by extension, good money. Dahlia's boss is grumbling over this exact conundrum as she leaves Seraphina sitting outside his office and enters with a polite knock and a careful smile.

"Hey Chief, just checking in," Dahlia says, relieved to see him alive and well at his desk. He has clearly not been outside yet. The station is untouched so far, at least by the angry weather, although masses have gathered in front of the gates, demanding answers that the building is more than happy to provide them with, had it any.

She is not surprised, of course, to see him doing well. He, like her, is an apocalypse prepper. She thinks he'd outlive them all, should it come to that.

When he sees her, he flashes one of his warm, pleasant smiles reserved for her, his favorite prodigy. The huge, bear-like man escapes his chair with some difficulty as the sides attempt to hold him down, then moves toward her, arms outstretched. The bottom of his belly is exposed underneath a treacherous shirt and his well-tailored suit, which he has already grown too big for. He hugs her, and she gets a whiff of his strong odor. It is not of cigars and whiskey as one might expect, but of condensed lemon tea droplets and hot cocoa. His hugs are legendary, as he has just the right height, level of fluff, and tightness of grip. She relaxes in his comforting embrace.

She remembers the first time she met The Chief. She was sixteen then, homeless and lost, but had somehow ended up at the same party as him. He'd been dancing on tables, the host begging him to stop, until a leg gave up and folded under him, sending him to the floor with a loud crash. He continued to laugh as he got up. "I'm bubble wrapped!" he'd yelled before climbing up to dance on a sofa, blood spreading from a gash on his leg and staining the cushions.

At the height of the commotion, as the host was trying to salvage her table, some guests yelled at The Chief to get down from the couch while others laughed. Dahlia had slipped out into the kitchen. Her face was buried in a stranger's fridge when a guy rushed The Chief in there, then left to find bandages.

"Hey, kid," The Chief said while tying a tea towel around his leg.

Dahlia jumped.

"You hungry?"

She immediately slammed the fridge and felt her face heat up. "Just munchies," she lied.

He must have seen it on her emaciated face, sharp cheekbones, and jutting collarbones, or the way she hunched over like she couldn't stand properly and had to lean against the counters. Possibly, it was the way she wouldn't meet his eyes.

"Tell you what..." he said, suddenly serious and sober. "Let's go get a bite to eat, huh?"

The Chief wouldn't have been my first choice for a surrogate father, but I was relieved when he took her under his wing, made sure she was fed and had a place to live, and even gave her a job at the station. I often wonder where she would have been without him. She certainly wouldn't have been here.

"I'm so happy you are alright, kid!" he beams. "I've been trying to call you, but the signal has been terrible. My provider must be overworked. But here—I've got just the solution!" He lets go of her and turns around to a cabinet, from which he pulls out a two-way radio and hands it to her. "It's state of the art. I just bought it. A thirty-mile radius and a twenty-four-hour battery life. I'll give you some batteries, too."

"That's awesome, thanks," she says, accepting his present, her body already less adrenalin-filled. He's like a sponge, soaking up all her anxieties. "How are things here?"

"Well, busy."

"I've noticed. It's like sardines in a can out there. Both at the station and out on the streets, that is. I mean, have you been outside? There's a mob. I was almost afraid of getting trampled. I had to go through all sorts of side streets. I really regretted never learning parkour."

I have always wondered what it is about chaos that seems to lure everyone out on the streets. Maybe safety in numbers? Maybe no one wants to die alone?

The Chief nods and slumps back into his chair, which screeches in protest and threatens to give up. He reclines, to its further dismay.

"I think you better be careful," he says, then and leans forward, suddenly serious. He speaks in a hushed voice, as though letting her in on a big secret. "There's a lot going on out there, I'm telling you. Ice and fire and floods and earthquakes—it's horrible. Gruesome. The pictures our reporters are getting... and we can't broadcast fast enough. Some of it, I don't think we should be broadcasting at all. It's the first time I've even considered that. We're making one breaking news segment after another, each an even more horrible thing, and we can't keep up, and... Well, just try and stay safe, yeah? And keep me updated for as long as you can."

She swallows hard, biting her lip. "So, you think... You

think this is... it's it? What we've been expecting? You're sure it's not just coincidences or... well, I don't know."

His face hardens. "I think you better be careful, that's what I think. The footage we've received... it's vengeful, I'd say. Like someone has a vendetta, and I think we both know who."

She nods and thinks about what she'd heard the reporter call the events on the way here. *A massacre.* It had sent a chill through her spine.

"Are you going to head to your dad's?" The Chief asks.

She lets out a small groan. He's right—her dad's would be the best, the safest place for her to be now. His compound is built to withstand Gluskab's wrath. The only problem is that she hasn't spoken to him for years, and last time she did, it was with rifles pointed at her and a strongly worded warning never to return. "Yeah, that's the plan. I need to get my sister first. He loves Valley. He wouldn't turn *her* away."

"Good, good. If he gives you any trouble, you know... I know you can throw a good punch."

Dahlia raises her fists in front of her face and play punches the air. "Hey, if Gluskab is behind this, I'll punch Him too."

The Chief nods, smiling. "You don't think... Well, I hear things, sometimes, from people who've talked to your dad. They say he might have a way into the Forest of Magnificent Trees. That would be crazy though, wouldn't it?"

Her fists drop to the side as she takes a deep breath in. "It would be. No one can enter there. I mean, they're probably just rumors, although I'll ask him when I find Valley." She shakes her head, as if to dismiss the thought. "But what about you? You've got your bug out bags ready, don't you?"

He shrugs, his gaze drifting out the window. Outside, the crowd of protesters is growing. In the distance, the sky looks gray and heavy. "I don't know," he says. "I might just stay here. Keep the masses updated for as long as we've got a signal. Someone ought to do it, right? And besides, I'm too old to be running around like that."

Dahlia's heart sinks. "You're not too old," she says.

"I've made up my mind. I'm staying put. I'm too old and too tired. Got a station to run."

"Chief..."

"No. Don't argue with me. I've thought about this for a long time, and I really think it's important that I stay."

She opens her mouth to object further, but he interrupts her.

"I've got an interesting angle," he says, breaking into a big bear smile. "How about genocide? We'd be buried in complaint letters, of course, if this blows over, but then who cares? We shouldn't hide who's at fault here. Who knows why he's doing this, but either way, we aren't his puppets to play with. I'm going to let Gluskab know how upset we are. It's not right."

It feels like she's got something stuck in her throat. There's nothing more to say; she won't be able to convince him. "Well, then," she says as she stands up. Her voice is croaky as she continues. "You've got that covered, then. I've got someone waiting for me."

The Chief nods. She wants to say something, something terribly sentimental and short that she's never said to anyone or had anyone say to her. Three words should be easy enough, but she can't form them in her mouth and her throat constricts and her eyes are itchy. He wants to say it back, but she wouldn't know that. Instead, she waves the two-way radio at him.

"I'll be in touch," she says before leaving the room, breathing a little heavier than she intended.

Seraphina is gone. She is not waiting outside the office on the soft, red couches, like Dahlia asked her to. When she grabs hold of an intern rushing by and asks her if she's seen a banshee, she is met with a blank expression. Dahlia almost worries that she's made the banshee up.

In all honesty, I didn't even pay attention to where she slipped off to, either.

It won't be long until Capital City will be completely wiped out, and Dahlia would prefer being on the road by then—hopefully with Vallesia by her side. Of course, the streets are already backed up, so driving is not an option. She should already be putting on her hiking boots, but what about the angel? *It's Seraphina's fault for disappearing,* she tells herself, but isn't convinced.

The secretary who checked them in returns to his desk, sitting down with a cheery sigh, as if the world isn't ending.

Dahlia leaps at him. "Where's the banshee I came with?"

"Hmm?" he asks, smiling at her and blinking slowly.

"The banshee. She was sitting on the couch. You said you'd look after her. She's gone now."

The secretary follows her line of sight to the couches, which are completely empty. Journalists, interns, and workers walk by, an endless line of people rushing through. *I don't understand why they aren't home with their loved ones Why would all these people be at work at a time like this?*

"The banshee," Dahlia says again, more firmly. She places both hands on his desk, looms over him, and tries to look threatening. She's never liked this secretary; she's asked The Chief to change him many times, and she can't for the life of her comprehend why he hasn't. He's not normally shy about firing workers.

"Look, honey," the secretary says, taking a long, slurping sip of his drink. "I don't know. I was in the bathroom."

"But you *said* you'd look after her," Dahlia growls.

The secretary shrugs, and Dahlia realizes there's no point. She turns around and scans the room one more time to the clicking sound of the secretary typing. There is no banshee anywhere—no bird like nose or soft hair or scarred back, no adorably small voice or big, child-like eyes. So, what now? Make a run for it? Out of the building, or to look for Seraphina?

You can't afford too many charities at times like these.

Seraphina would have been a liability anyway, wouldn't she? Maybe stopping at the station was already a waste of time. She should have been on the road by now.

"Oh, hey," the secretary says behind her. "Isn't that her?" He points up.

Dahlia follows his gesture to a big flat-screened TV on the side of the wall. She clutches her chest, eyes wide open, when she sees that Seraphina is in the studio.

It is a live news segment. The reporter is saying nothing, merely staring in confusion at Seraphina, who seems to have just entered the studio. The subtitles reveal that he is supposed to be talking about acid showers—about a whole city being destroyed, the houses melted, the people nothing but bones, and the whole place left an empty, sizzling pool.

Seraphina pushes the reporter aside, placing herself in front of the camera instead. She stops and looks straight into it. She opens her mouth but says nothing, then closes it again. She pulls her hand up to her throat and claws at it. You can feel the tension. The whole studio holds their breath, knowing, somehow, what is about to happen. Her eyes are wild and distraught, reminding Dahlia of earlier today. She is quivering, her whole body shaking, her face porcelain white, then she speaks.

"Janeh Stills, Tayah Stills, Don Stills. Tara Bay, Smith Bay, Karen Bay, Marah Bay…"

The secretary and Dahlia both look at the screen in stunned silence as the listing continues, now faster and more confidently, bursting out of her like a waterfall. All the while, her face turns paler and paler, now almost supernaturally pale. It sounds as if she can't breathe.

"Jennyfer Hefney, Courtney Hefney, Braff Hefney, Mertha Hefney…"

"What is she doing?" the secretary asks. His once so cheery voice quivers.

Dahlia takes a deep breath, sucking at the air between her teeth. "Well, she's a banshee, isn't she? And banshees—they warn."

"Brand John, Day John. Jown Anders, Jack Anders…"

"Dear Creator," the secretary says, gasping. He holds his

hands to his mouth. "Those people... They are all going to die, aren't they?"

Banshees soon storm the station. Employees have to set up a barricade. Outside, there is a sea of name murmuring, bird-like statues who have not been entrusted with a job for twenty-two years. Now, it seems that every person has to die, all at once.

There are too many loved ones to warn. There isn't enough time.

On the streets, people are stopped and a name is whispered to them. Radios broadcast nothing but long strings of names. At the train stations, the announcements are of deaths, the megaphones screeching and high pitched. The library does not warn of an impending closing time, but of an impending doom of everyone and everyone's loved ones.

There are too many loved ones to warn. There isn't enough time.

CHAPTER 13

MARIO WAKES IN HIS BED feeling sick and after what he believes to be a very odd nightmare — something about snow, and fire, and a man with rotten breath like death. He sighs at the empty side of his bed, disappointed that his wife leaving in the night was not a dream. Stifling a cough, he gets up to make himself a cup of tea. After all, he thinks, everything is better after a nice cup of tea.

He takes notice of the twilight outside, but mistakes it for a dawn. Maybe, he thinks, he will go on a morning run before getting on to his work. As his tea steeps, he tries to remember the last time he'd had a nightmare, but he can't. Usually, his dreams are all edible clouds and puppies.

He coughs again. He doesn't feel well, but is sure it's nothing that a good, strong herbal tea won't be able to mend. Maybe it's just a minor cold, a dry throat, or the effects of last night's alcohol.

I wish it were. Right now, his arteries are filling with black goo, and soon all of his insides will be slimy, hot, and oozing.

Then, it will spread to his lungs, filling them like a pitcher of tar. After that, he won't have long. Not long at all.

The kitchen is straight ahead. He walks past the empty bottles of alcohol that someone has already started throwing into a big, black plastic bag and steps in something sticky, which he hopes is just alcohol. He thinks it odd someone would start cleaning and not finish, even leaving the half-full bag on the floor in the middle of the room and all the cleaning articles out. While he fills the kettle, the doorbell buzzes and he remembers what woke him in the first place.

He also finds it odd for anyone to be at his door this early in the morning. Perhaps it's a friend out jogging? A very important letter? His wife? Yes, Vallesia! He wonders if she lost her key. He loves it when the doorbell buzzes. Worst case scenario, it is a salesperson; even then, he can still enjoy a nice conversation. Everyone has stories to tell, and everyone has mysteries which Mario loves to ponder about late at night. Once or twice, he has even picked up a client this way—not the ones who pay the most, but a mystery is a mystery.

The presence at his door is not at all who he would have expected. He is more than surprised to see Dahlia standing there. She only just set foot in the apartment for the second time yesterday. She's rarely ever around, and he can count their interactions on one hand. He just can't crack her, or why she'd live such a second-rate life devoid of meaning, filled with benders and sleeping around and friends who only enable her. Mario imagines his life in shambles and himself at a café, writing out a list on how to solve it. Dahlia, he knows, does not like lists.

He's also never seen her with a banshee. Seraphina hides behind Dahlia, her sleeves pulled over her hands, her eyes big and wary. Vallesia always tells him about her sister's many conquests, but a banshee? That's not natural, and she doesn't have to come here and rub it in his face.

It occurs to him that Dahlia must have forgotten something from the night before.

"Hey," Dahlia says. "Is my sis here?"

The memories return to him with such haste that he feels lightheaded. The snow, then the fire—not a nightmare. Lightning and mayhem. And the god. The god he didn't know was a god, the one who had been looking for his wife, or Vallesia, and whose presence made Mario's stomach turn. Even now, remembering his unsettling eyes, Mario feels unsafe in his own home. He checks the time for the first time. The clock reads 18:53. Evening, not morning.

"Was there a fire?" Mario asks, searching for anything to confirm his distant memories. His teacup from earlier today sits half drunk on the table. His improvised winter outfit is slung over one of the chairs.

Dahlia squints back at him, nodding. "And snow, and lightning, and a million other things. Earthquakes, diamond spears, tsunamis, you name it. Are you alright? Were you sleeping?"

"I guess so," he answers, touching his hair in an absentminded stupor. "I just don't remember going to bed. The last thing I remember…" He cannot recall it, so he stands like that for a long time, thinking, before Dahlia grows restless.

"Look, Mario. Is my sis here?"

"No…"

"No?"

"No."

"Well, where did she go?" Dahlia asks. She is fidgeting with one of the two bug out bags she has slung over her shoulders. Seraphina behind her has a third one.

Mario coughs again, harder this time. "I don't know where she is," he says and leans against the doorway. He explains, as well as he can, that Vallesia left last night with her uniform and still has not returned. Someone came and got her, he thinks. He does not know much, does not know anything at all, really. There was a peculiar… someone came and asked for her. Or did he? He might have dreamed that part. No, he does not feel well at all. He coughs again, harder and longer. When Dahlia asks what's wrong with him, he waves away her concern.

"She took her uniform?" Dahlia asks. "So she must be with

the military, right?"

Mario shrugs. "I called Tomi earlier. He says she isn't with him."

A window clatters somewhere down the stairwell. Dahlia jumps and looks for it, tensing her hold of the straps, then she turns back to Mario. "Look, it's really important that we find her. Now."

Mario feels something icy in his stomach, like a big clump of... of what? Worries? When is the last time he's been worried?

"She'll turn up soon, I'm sure," he says, attempting to calm either Dahlia or himself, though he's not sure which. "You know how the military is. Not too reliable. Maybe it's part of her examination yesterday. Maybe they changed their minds."

"No, you don't understand. You don't know what's happening. What's *going to* happen. I need to find Valley."

"What *is* happening?" he asks, but regrets it right away. No, he does not want this. Horrible things do not happen, not in this world with his Dear Creator looking over them from his place of hiding. Mario feels himself regaining even just a hint of energy: the Dear Creator is good. Whatever lies Dahlia is going to try to fill him with, he will not listen.

"You saw the fire," Dahlia says, her voice low and shaky. "That's just the beginning."

"Look, I'll go call Tomi again, alright?" Mario tries a smile. "If she took her uniform... it only makes sense. I'll call real quick. You guys come on in. I'll make you some tea."

Dahlia insists on being the one to call Tomi and leaves Mario with Seraphina, whom she quickly introduces. Mario admits that he is already biased against her. The banshees still in hiding at the reservations are generally thought to be good Knowers loyal to Gluskab, but the ones in the city, not so much. Personally, he thinks they are acting like disgruntled teenagers, belittling the Dear Creator whenever they have a chance, shamelessly abandoning thousands of years of paradise because of a few rough years. He thinks that he would never act like that. However, he is nothing if not a good host. He reminds himself it is not his place to judge, so he flashes her a warm smile and attempts to perk up a little.

"Would you like some tea?" he asks.

She does not answer, and she does not have to because Mario has already decided on being a good host, which he is certain must include tea. She sits by the kitchen table, watching him as he prepares the warm drink then makes his way through the mess on the floor and hands her a cup the size of her face. He also serves sugar, honey, milk, and the chocolate cookies he didn't get to finish earlier. Seraphina nips at one, not wanting to be rude but also not feeling any urge for sweets at a time like this.

There is too much to process. The weather going crazy, everyone is dying, and all the people who are going to die... the names still tuck at her vocal cords. And this odd man seems unbothered. He has dismissed everything Dahlia has said, sighing and mumbling some praise to the Dear Creator instead.

"Do you live on a reservation, or in the city?" Mario asks as he sits down next to her.

"Angel Forest," she whispers.

"Ah," he says, nodding. "That's good."

She doesn't know what to respond to that. She matches his nodding and stares into her tea. The quiet continues.

"You know, you shouldn't believe everything Dahlia says," Mario warns her. He leans forward and stares at her, as if measuring her reaction.

She wants to tell him about the names pressing their way to the top of her throat. It feels like a boiling kettle and soon, if she is not careful, the names will sputter everywhere, just like at the station. The lid must stay on. Sweat gathers on her forehead.

His name is one of them. *Mario.* It rages at the top of her throat, threatening to claw its way out, but she chokes it back.

Seraphina looks around the room to distract herself and notices the TV. The volunteers at the reservation have a TV in their building; she's walked by the window and seen the vivid images dancing over it. More than once has she snuck in while everyone was asleep and tried to make sense of it, studying the language, the strange sounds that she'd always heard on her missions but never understood. She'd always been so in awe at the idea of a language and the complex meanings it can convey, at how it seemed to tie everyone together like an invisible thread. Now, she wishes that she'd studied harder.

She gets up and walks toward the TV, grabbing the remote from the table. If she were to move to the city, would she be able to have her own TV? She'd love nothing more than to sit by it all day. That would be her dream. She remembers that the TV has the news — she knows what that is. Maybe that will tell them more of what is happening. But before she hits the button, Mario is beside her, pulling the remote from her hand.

"No!" he says, a little too loud, his face panicked. "No," he says again, calmer. "I've seen the news. I know what's on there."

Seraphina watches him in silence, covering her mouth behind the rolled down sleeve.

"It's all blasphemy, all of it," he says. "I can imagine what Dahlia has told you. What, is it the end of the world suddenly? Because of a little harsh weather? Did she tell you that Gluskab, somehow, is causing all of this? Why would He? It's insane. And you're a banshee — you should know better. You really should trust Him more."

Seraphina freezes. She agrees. Why would Gluskab do this? That isn't the god she knows, the god she has known for thousands and thousands of years. But then, the god she knew wouldn't have left like this, and who else could cause this?

"I'll tell you something," Mario continues, confident now. "It's just a story, but it might make you see and then you can stop this nonsense and relax. It's from a fantasy book with all kinds of short stories that Jarda brought back from one of her travels. I think it was from a universe with a planet called 'Earth'."

Oh! That must have been your world! This is your story too, isn't it?

"One of the stories involves a guy named Job. Job is one of their god's most favorite followers, good, kind, and trusting in Him above all else. But the god, for nonsensical reasons, allows this angel, Satan, to take everything away from him—his health, his farm, even his family, who are all killed in gruesome ways. Absolutely gruesome. They burn alive. And there are no banshees to warn him, either. The reason why He lets Satan do this is to prove to him how good a man Job is and how much faith he has in Him. Imagine what Job says. I've memorized: 'He destroys both the blameless and the wicked. When a plague sweeps through, he laughs at the death of the innocent.' And, I mean, his *whole family* dies. And servants and all the animals. In the end, yeah, this 'god' gives him back twice as much as he had, but it is real lives we are talking about, not jewelry or money. Never mind Job, what about the family? Did they not want to live? And here's the kicker, no reincarnation!"

Seraphina tilts her head, listening intently.

"Our Dear Creator is not like this false god," Mario says. "He is good. He is benevolent. He doesn't destroy the 'blameless' or the 'wicked'. When has he ever done anything like that? So, I know that whatever Dahlia thinks is going on is not."

Seraphina can think of one time when the Creator destroyed the blameless—she has scars to remind her of it. Now it seems he is doing the same thing to His humans, as well. She can't wrap her head around it. Is He testing them, like in Mario's story? What happens, then, if they fail?

Dahlia reenters the room at a jog. "There's a storm coming up," she says, a wild look in her eyes, then holds up her hand.

They stop and listen. The wind is screeching. On the skyscraper opposite them, the vines are holding onto the steel frames with their frail fingers, then give up and wave them like white flags. Today, the sky has gone from bright yellow and sunny to dark and roaring with thunder. It sent white freckles of snow which turned to murderous red flames. Now, the sky is gray. Threatening gray, it seems, as the clouds gather like gang members preparing for a fight.

"That looks pretty bad. We should probably stay inside," Mario says, then pours Dahlia a cup of tea. He pushes the cookies toward her with a much-too-forced smile. Dahlia eyes the cookies, confused.

"Are you kidding me?" she erupts. "We can't stay here."

"Of course we can."

"No, of course we *cannot.* The whole building is going to give."

"You are both so tiny," Mario says and waves a dismissive hand. "If you go outside, the wind will pick you up and you'll fly away. We should stay here. We will be just fine."

"We are *not* going to be fine. Look across from us. That building is swaying."

"What? Nonsense. I've seen it do that many times before."

Dahlia sends a hopeful look to Seraphina, pleading for help, but the banshee only offers a shy, worried look.

The windows clatter. The walls creak and groan, growing louder.

"Do you remember that children's story?" Mario asks Dahlia. "You must have heard it; Valley knows it. It's about the witch. She flies on her broom through the city, leaving a whirlwind behind her. The more excited she is, the faster she flies, and the worse the storm becomes. You can tell how excited she is by her scream— the higher the pitch, the more she is enjoying herself." He feigns a high-pitched scream. "What blasphemy. Don't you agree?"

Dahlia is practically pulling out her hair by now. "You're an idiot," she says. Mario glares, then pretends to ignore her and takes a bite of a cookie.

"What did Tomi say?" he asks.

Dahlia looks confused, then remembers why she went to the balcony in the first place. She takes a deep breath. "He said she might be at base."

That's a lie. I overheard the whole thing. She couldn't even reach Tomi, or anyone else.

"He doesn't know for sure, but she could be there," Dahlia

continues. "I think we should get going now. You want to see Vallesia, right? Let's go."

"Let's tell him to text us when he sees her. If she's at base, she's fine, anyway. There's no rush." Mario coughs. His eyes have specks of black in them now.

Another violent gust of wind hits the building. A lamp falls over and they all jump.

"Mario, seriously, we have to go," she tries again. "At least, let's go to the basement, or whatever. It's seriously not safe."

A cabinet opens and plates tumble out to break on the floor, the pieces spread all over.

Mario mumbles, "No." He gets up and closes the cabinet. It slides open again, along with a mug cabinet, and he decides to leave them. He disappears, then returns with a broom and dustpan.

Dahlia's face turns red. She looks over at Seraphina, then shoots to her feet.

You can't afford too many charities at times like these.

"Let's leave, now," Dahlia says one last time.

Mario is sweeping a floor that will soon be no more. "We will be fine."

They will not be fine. The room tilts. Seraphina tumbles from her chair. Dahlia falls over the table. Mario stumbles and crashes to the floor.

There is a thunderous crash outside. From the kitchen window, they watch the skyscrapers across from them smash into each other, taking down the long line of buildings like dominos. Screaming fills the air as ashes and blood cover the streets.

People storm from the ground floors while others leap in desperation from on high. Some who make it to the street are missing limbs. They crawl, screaming and bleeding as they claw at the ground to escape their inevitable deaths. The streets become a sea of gray and red, like something from a dystopian film or comic, or an unfinished art piece. Buckets of blood spray up in the air. Then the debris and smoke cover everything and the streets become a ghostly sea of dust and ash.

"Out. Now." Dahlia grabs hold of Seraphina's arm, pulling her out of her shocked trance.

They move toward the door, but Mario does not follow. He sits on the floor, staring into the wallpaper. Then he gets up, serene in his movements, and finds a plastic bag above the sink. Dahlia and Seraphina stare at him in disbelief as he opens the fridge and ponders for several moments before placing an assortment of food into the bag. Meanwhile, the building they are in cries in agony. He stumbles as the room tilts from side to side, shuddering.

"Leave," Seraphina begs.

Mario does not listen. He fills a water bottle while humming an old psalm to drown out the sounds of terror. The apartment quakes again, knocking him off his feet and sending the water spraying everywhere. There's a loud crash from upstairs, then the ceiling lamp smashes into the living room table, sending shards of glass flying through the room.

"No way," Dahlia mumbles, pulling Seraphina with her out the door.

Seraphina pants as they sprint down the stairs. It feels as if there is a fire in her lungs, or behind her, above her, and around her. She cannot see; dots of red and orange flutter in her eyes. Perhaps there is a fire, or perhaps it just feels the same as that day long ago when everything was burning.

Run, run, run!

Dahlia guides her. They hold hands — sweaty, disgusting hands. There is only one way to run for your life down stairs, and it involves not thinking too much about it. But Seraphina's feet refuse to obey and her legs feel weak, like soft clay. The staircase grows steeper and steeper in her mind.

She trips and rolls down the stairs, falling to the next landing on her hands and knees, which instantly feel warm. There will be bruises later, if there is a later. She gets up, runs a few steps, then falls again. Her face strikes the wall, sending pain shooting through her head and warm, sticky blood dripping from her nose.

Dahlia stops, scoops her up, and throws her on her back.

The flickering lights in the stairwell go all the way out. The walls cry. Seraphina cries. Her knee cries, dripping wet, warm, crimson blood. She goes limp. As Dahlia runs down the stairs with her, it feels as if time is infinite. The staircase reaches from the clouds to the core of the world, but once they make it to the lobby, their entire flight is forgotten.

The building moans, telling them it is ready to give up. They beg for it to hang in there, then Dahlia lets Seraphina down and they both feel a sense of accomplishment as they push through the door. They are free. They made it. They survived. They run out into safety.

As soon as they hit the street, they are knocked over by the same powerful wind that is sending buildings tumbling to the ground around them. If the wind is strong enough to knock over tall buildings, do you think that they are any safer?

They go flying, like dandelion seeds blown from the flower. They grip each other's hands as the air around them roars like the inside of a jet engine or underside of a train. Seraphina's ears pop and she worries the terrifying roar will be the last thing she will ever hear, even if she makes it out alive.

The wind pulls at her in every direction. She is weightless, but much less graceful than a feather.

They crash into something. Seraphina still cannot see. Even if not for the red and orange dots, the swirling dust and ash occlude her vision. Her back is numbed by the impact.

Numbed by pain, blinded, and deafened by the roaring maelstrom, she wonders if she is dead.

She touches her face with numb fingers. It doesn't feel real.

Dahlia speaks. She sounds as if she is far, far away, but she cannot be; they are still holding hands.

The last of the skyscrapers implode under the onslaught, their corpses oozing with death.

Did Mario make it out? I didn't see him. I can't find him

Seraphina prays to her Creator.

DAY 2

Arteries filled to the bursting point with tar-like black blood.

CHAPTER 14

I **SPEND MOST OF THE** night and morning trying to squirm out from a piece of skyscraper that impaled me. It pierced my stomach, ripped out most of my intestines, and left me in an uncomfortable half standing and half sitting position. The blood flows from me undisturbed and I repeatedly pass out and wake hours later when my body has regenerated enough blood. It gets harder and harder to free myself as my skin grows over the hole around the metal rod, making for tedious work. On my third attempt, I worry that I might be permanently stuck, that this is my life now — trying to free myself from a metal pole over and over again, dying a million times. Then, on my fifth attempt, I hear a swooping sound as I am finally freed from the metal pole. I fall to the ground, face first.

There is nothing I could compare this pain to that you would understand, because your kind could not possibly survive this. I'm unfortunate enough to have died and lived a thousand times before.

When I wake, the sun has risen and revealed a world of after-chaos. The streets are cracked and overturned and I cannot walk some stretches, only climb and jump around. Guilt wrenches my stomach. I watch the collapsed buildings and nod to the few miserable beings still alive. They sit on top of the ruins with blank eyes and inexpressive faces. They look like dolls. Grown men seem like children, helpless, so over-come with shock that they might sit by the streets until they die from hunger—if only nothing else kills them first. While most walk around with no clear destination or sit by idly, one man attempts to lift a heavy beam, but his heart is far from in it.

Two kids, siblings, are digging through bricks, murmuring a call for their mother. They have been at it for hours. Perhaps they think someone will come to help. If so, they will certain-ly be disappointed. This is why I have always disagreed with Gluskab's major interventions—they have made the people of this world weak and helpless. When fear comes knocking, they curl into a ball and start crying, pleading for a savior.

What else can they do? Punch weather in the face?

A little girl sitting on top of a staircase leading nowhere coughs blood, black like ink. I stop as my heart skips a beat.

Already? Is it really already at this stage? He certainly isn't wasting any time.

The girl's cough persists. When she stops to look down, black tar covers her hands and arms. It seems she understands its evil nature as she, unsuccessfully, attempts to wipe it off in her trousers. She gives up, as these humans always do, and resumes her empty stare into nothingness. Does she know that she is dying? Does she care?

I can save her, of course. I can spend all day here, putting my scarred hands over the people's lungs and save them one by one. I can move on to the next city and undo the apocalypse slowly, then gather the people in a shed and protect them until Gluskab rips the shed apart. There would be no use in me doing that.

I find Mario first.

He wakes in a crater, coughing and surprised to find himself alive. He must have been lying there all night, pressed against the ground underneath the scattered bricks. He hugs a dead girl with wild, untamed hair in two braids, fried and orange. The sunrise is now a sunset.

At first, he remembers nothing. Why is he in a crater in the middle of the streets instead of his bed? Why is he hugging a dead girl? Why does his whole body hurt like he is one big bruise? The memories slowly return. But how did he make it out of the skyscraper? He remembers running, the walls literally crumbling behind him and the stairs disappearing as soon as his feet leave them. Then, a beam falls in front of the front entrance. Did he somehow crawl over it, or under it? He screams out in pain when he tries to move his ankle. Maybe the beam fell on top of him?

All he knows is that once he made it out, the storm witch picked him up on her broom and flew him several streets down, where he managed to grab onto something and crawl into this crater. That's where he is still lying, and maybe, he thinks, should continue to lie. He has never felt unsafe anywhere, not late at night or in dark alleys. In fact, he does not remember ever feeling afraid in his life, but now he wants nothing more than to curl up and keep lying in his crater until the world decides to fix itself, until Gluskab comes back. Gluskab? He had been surer of a godly salvation yesterday.

Mario pushes himself up and coughs again. This time, he coughs up blood. At least it tastes like blood, but it is black, almost like ink. He thinks he might be bleeding internally. If only it were just that.

When he looks around at the dystopian setting, he notices that almost no building nearby is standing. He must look far out to the horizon to see any remaining upright. The Forest of Magnificent Trees still towers tall and proud, which he takes as a sign of Gluskab's incredible and amazing powers. As for the streets, they are littered with furniture and clothes blown out from the buildings, as well as debris and ashes. Cars are overturned and thrown around as if a child had been playing with them and gotten bored. There are many more craters than the one he is lying in, all stacked with two or more bodies in various stages of dead and dying.

The air is still heavy with dust, which makes it hard to breathe or even see clearly ahead.

So many people—*and a demi-god*—have been impaled by beams and metal sticks, car antennas, and the hoods from streetlights. All are dead or will be very soon. Dear Creator, there is so much blood. Mario has never seen so much blood. I have never seen so much blood. With the way the light is hitting it, it looks like paint. A new initiative by the mayor to liven up the streets, perhaps.

Mario staggers out from the hole, not really sure with what purpose. It all feels so surreal. There is a persistent ringing in his ears, and it sounds as if he is under water.

He checks for other survivors, limping around with a maybe-broken ankle, checking for pulses but finds none. Some are too obviously dead—one is just a torso and a head, another is everything but a head. Mario's snot, dripping down his chin, is also black. He is white as a sheet.

Finally, he finds a man who still has a pulse. He is covered in glass, the shards buried deep into his stomach. He looks up at Mario with pleading eyes, irises jumping around frantically. When he tries to talk, he gurgles instead and his mouth is filled with fresh blood. *Please kill me.* That is what he is trying to say. Mario does not need him to say it because he can see that he is in great pain and, deep down, they both know that no one will come to save them. But Mario cannot kill the man. He is too much of a coward. So, he gets up instead, swaying, and staggers away. The man reaches out his hands and gurgles something, yet Mario continues.

He is not sure where he is. The city looks completely different. The skyscrapers that had once been so familiar to him now look like they have been plowed by a giant wrecking ball. The streets are littered in stone, rubble, bricks, glass, and a thick blanket of bodies. It takes him a lot of confused stumbling around before he finds the remains of a wall with a graffiti motive he recognizes:

On the first day of Creation, Gluskab caught a sense of responsibility. He lost it, I guess.

The wall makes a mockery of the Tale of Creation. It should have said, *On the first day of Creation, Gluskab caught a speck of dust between His fingers.* What then? *Gluskab held up the dust, looked at it in the sunlight that His father had created, and decided to create His own sunlight for His own world.*

And what now? Now He's just changed His mind?

Mario has considered scrubbing the wall clean many times. Vallesia has more than once been there as the sound of reason, reminding him that whoever wrote it was just angry and shouldn't be blamed for this. With a gentle hand on his, Vallesia reminded him that not everyone was as fortunate as them to be able to see Gluskab's greatness. He misses her. Oh, Dear Creator, how he misses her. She would bite her cheek the way she always does and know exactly what to do, and then she would extinguish the small ball of doubt in his stomach that he will not admit to having.

He never understood the people's anger before now. His first memory is from when he was four years old and Gluskab had just left. It was when the banshees crawled out from the Forest of the Magnificent Trees and through the cities with their angel wings still in flames. They cried as the entire city went silent. He watched from the window, his tiny nose pressed against the cold glass and his eyes wide in amazement. He remembers the small, wailing figures, their red hands reaching toward the sky, and the pillars of smoke chasing them. He remembers the faint smell of ashes.

"It's Gluskab!" his mother yelled, outraged. "He has shut the banshees out. He has left. There was a shooting in Antonia last night, and he wasn't there. And now, this! How dare he?"

Several days after that, the people took to the streets. They walked all the way to the Forest of the Magnificent Trees and surrounded it with posters and megaphones. Mario had been holding on to his mother's legs.

"Where are you? Where are you?" They yelled at the forest, but no one answered. Some tried to enter but, despite Gluskab's apparent disappearance, the forest was still protected by lightning, which slaughtered them. Mario watched through his mother's legs as someone was electrocuted in front of them. He can recall the smell of burned flesh even now.

After that, poems and books were written and, for a while, the topic of Gluskab was unavoidable in every art piece. Everyone had an opinion. At first, most people were still loyal to Gluskab, sure that He was good and kind, and they did not turn their backs to Him just because He appeared to have let them down this one time. There were thousands and thousands of years of greatness to remember. These few years were only a blip in comparison.

Mario never strayed. To the depths of his stomach, there was never any doubt. His love of Gluskab was a physical, tangible thing, he was sure. You could touch, if you opened him up. The whole world was a testament to his glory. However, by the time Mario made it to high school, a teacher scoffed at him for exclaiming 'Dear Creator', an expression now seen more as a prayer and which was slowly being erased from everyday language.

I am sometimes confronted with how much the world has changed since He left. I both feel the old world was just yesterday, and that it was so long ago I can barely remember it. Now, the new world will be the old world again, and I might be nostalgic for yesterday.

Mario picks up a sign from *Solitarius Café*. Normally, he would have spat on it, knowing that this was one of the cafés that branded themselves as rebel strongholds against the fickleness of Gluskab, but today he feels an emptiness where the love of his Creator used to be. Instead, he lets go of the sign with a deep-felt sigh.

He still loves his Dear Creator. He tells himself this and then he says it out loud, to no one at all. He says, "I love you, my Dear Creator."

Then he turns around and yells at the Forest of the Magnificent Trees. "I love you, my Dear Creator!" When he is about to yell it a second time, he starts coughing. The black, gooey blood is everywhere. Everything in him hurts.

He resumes his limping. Of course, he knows his apartment block has suffered the same fate as all the buildings here, but where else is he to go? What else should he do?

On his way, he meets five others, excluding the many, many bodies. As if the rules of traffic are still viable, they limp alone along the sidewalks, crawl on top of the scattered pieces of road, and jump with a great effort. As they pass one another, they exchange tired grunts.

It makes Mario think of zombies. He thinks that if a zombie apocalypse ever happened, the day after, everyone will get up and walk along the sidewalks and grunt at each other, displeased. They will also limp, and their eyes will be dead like the people he has met and like his own eyes must be. They will be as pale as him, as tired as him, and as pained as him. In fact, Mario both feels and looks like a zombie, so he thinks maybe he is one. His head hurts too much for him to ponder it further. Whenever he manages a clear thought, the dreadful cough returns. His hands and arms are covered in black goo.

He has no idea what to do when he finally turns onto the street where he lived just hours ago. It is already midday, and he thinks Dahlia and the banshee must be long gone. He is not sure what he was thinking. Maybe that he would walk here and they would just be sitting around, kicking rocks and waiting for him. After how idiotic he acted last night, almost getting all of them killed?

Perhaps they are dead. He definitely should be.

He searches the ruins with little effort and no hope, kicking bricks, sighing, and whimpering. Half an hour later, he walks out in the middle of the road to lie down on top of a car. With a dramatic sigh and more coughing, he goes to sleep and hopes that he won't wake up again.

CHAPTER
15

I **FIND DAHLIA AND SERAPHINA** just as they are
waking up. Sometime last night, they must have crawled
into one of the ruins, because that's where I find them—
close but not too close. Seraphina is lying on top of a pad with a
sleeping bag wrapped around her while Dahlia is off in a corner,
resting against a pole with her head near her chest. Only one of
Dahlia's bug out bags has survived. It is safe by her side, and
it must be where Seraphina got the sleeping pad and bag from.

Dahlia hasn't slept much in the awkward position and is the
first one to wake up, groggy and with a vague feeling that her
dream is one she ought to remember. She sits and waits for it to
return to her. They are not in a hurry anyway. She glances over
at Seraphina's sleeping form, her chest expanding and deflating
slowly, light pink lips gently apart. She wouldn't dare to wake
her up.

When the dream does return to Dahlia, suddenly and all at
once, she wonders if she might have been happier without it.
It is more of a memory than a dream, a scene in a sort of haze,

the details slightly altered and the emotions heightened. She must have been around seven, at home during one of the holidays. Why was she down in the basement? Had she stumbled across it, or gone there intentionally, or had her father shown her there? She is not sure, but she was there.

From the wooden, creaky staircase, she watches the gigantic white sheet in the middle of the room hiding an unknown monstrosity, big and square and with something long and round poking out. Had she walked down the stairs? Yes, she remembers the creaking sound, each step like an exasperated sigh. But the sheet... had she taken it off, or had her father? He is beside her suddenly, looking at her with an expression she cannot read—in her dream, his face is wiped clean, polished, and completely bare.

Under the sheet is a military tank, big and shiny, the tracks taller than her. She stares at it in amazement. She is small, even for a seven-year-old, and it looks enormous before her. Then it grows and grows to the size of a small house.

"What is that?" she asks, her voice full of frightened wonder.

The tank keeps on growing, as tall as a three-story house. The room grows around it.

"My great secret," her father answers. "It is *our* great secret now."

It grows, or maybe she is getting smaller. It is a full palace now. She is like an ant before it.

"A tank..." she whispers.

"A magic tank," he corrects her. The word 'magic' does not fit in his mouth; it is cornered and prickly and he does not like it. She can feel the discomfort oozing off him. "A very special tank indeed. It will be important. Later."

The tank grows to the size of a planet and engulfs them both. Then the dream ends and so does her memory of the scene. She neither remembers what came before nor after. It is a snapshot which does not fit into the narrative of her life. Yet, it feels too real. No. She shakes her head, attempting to rid herself of the memory. It is no use to her, especially not now.

She inspects the only surviving bag instead, busying herself. It contains a gallon of water, a weeks' worth of food supplies if rationed, a first aid kit, a torch, and the two-way radio. A flask has also been stashed, containing vodka. Thankfully, it is bug out bag number one, and thus the most important one with the most basic supplies. It worries Dahlia that the bag is meant for only one and she quickly calculates that the supplies will last them only a few days at best, but she has a plan where they won't need the supplies, anyway.

Next step, or next distraction, is scouting out the terrain. She doesn't remember how they got in between the ruins in the first place, but she thinks it looks safe. There's shelter and a few holes where the sunlight braves in. It's dusty and dirty, the floor is not really a floor, and they can't stand up properly because the place is too cramped, but that's no issue. They won't stay for long, anyway. Slithering out is hard. Dahlia locates a hole big enough for her to slide through. When she makes it halfway out of the hole, she decides against her original plan to have breakfast outside.

Now that all the skyscrapers are toppled over, she can finally, for maybe the first time ever, clearly see the sun rising. It is bright and halfway up the sky, which is a gradient of blue, purple, and pink. There isn't a cloud to see.

The streets are littered with corpses and it smells of blood and burned flesh. The ash covers her view, whirling in the soft breeze, and distorting the scene in a gray filter. A streetlight stands at forty-five degrees and there is a long crack down the middle of the road. In front of her, a severed hand juts out of the rubble, the fingers pointing straight up, like a zombie in a movie. It is wearing a ring. She can see the veins. It rests in a puddle of blood. Her stomach turns, and she throws up immediately. Everything is quiet except for her retching and birds chirping.

Inside is much nicer.

She slithers back and takes a chug of water before noticing that Seraphina has awoken. The banshee looks around, confused and with groggy eyes, and a bad case of bed-hair, or perhaps tornado-hair.

"Morning there," Dahlia says with half a smile as she crawls back toward the bag. "Are you okay? All in one piece?"

Seraphina pulls her hands out from inside the sleeping bag and inspects them, turning them around. She winces when she moves her elbow, but she can move all her limbs. Nothing broken. There's dried blood down her chin from her nose and her arms are covered in bruises. Dahlia doesn't look much better herself. Her left eye is red, puffy, and swollen.

"Great," Dahlia says. While Seraphina comes to, Dahlia lays out the food supplies in front of her—calorie blocks, energy bars, and some odd-looking, smaller bags. "What would you like for breakfast?"

Seraphina tilts her head and points at the bags. "What that?" she asks.

"Rations," Dahlia explains. "They are made for the military or loonies like me. It's just proper, hot meals, really. Would you like a hot meal? I have two bags of porridge here. There is apple and cinnamon or apple and cranberries. I hope you like apples?"

Seraphina stares, confused. First toward Dahlia, and then around. She rubs her eyes and picks up a brick, weighs it in her hand, then puts it down again. With her brows still furrowed, she returns her stare to Dahlia and tilts her head to the side.

"I think we're in like a basement or something, or under a building," Dahlia says. "We must have crawled in here. I don't really remember. Do you?"

Seraphina shakes her head.

"Right. I must have completely blacked out," Dahlia continues. "But I'm thinking we were lucky. Really lucky. Do you—I think it would be really good to get something to eat. Why don't I show you how this works?" She lifts a bag and shakes it a little. "We don't need heaters. I've got some flameless ration heaters. I'll show you, okay?"

Seraphina nods, curious.

"Okay, right," Dahlia says and opens the bag again to find two other bags and their water. One is bigger and, it turns out, empty. The other is smaller with a little pouch. Both are in the style of the ration packs—gray and plastic. Dahlia explains as she sets them up. "It's really quite simple. You open the smaller bag here, that's the heater. Just take off the top and put in your ration next to it, like that. There's a little line here at the bottom, can you see? Yeah, so you pour the water in right to the line. It starts to activate pretty quickly, so you put it back in the bigger bag, which is more heat resistant. Close it up like this, and then you wait."

The big bag quickly expands like a balloon while Dahlia holds onto the ends tightly, preventing the air from escaping. "Excuse me if I don't know the exact science of this, but the heater contains, I think, magnesium. It reacts to the water, then heats up the food. It takes a little while. Here, can you hold it while I make the other bag?"

Seraphina accepts it with some apprehension and Dahlia repeats the steps with another bag.

"My old man taught me," Dahlia continues. "He's a bit of a looney, even more than me. He built this big prepper's compound believing that when Gluskab came back, it wouldn't be pretty. People used to call him a conspiracy theorist, but I don't know… it always made sense to me and back then, I wanted to impress him. Not that I possibly could, but that's another story. We'll go to his compound. As soon as we've found Valley, that is. I doubt he'll let us in without her, especially not if I bring a banshee with me. No offense."

Seraphina shoots her another of her confused but genuinely interested glances, where she purses her lips and furrows her brows. She looks like a little child when she does it, her cheeks big and puffy.

"In his eyes, I'm not his daughter," Dahlia explains. "It's a long story, okay? Maybe it's not the kind of story for breakfast, hm?"

Seraphina nods as if she understands, although she does

not, and their meals are soon ready. Dahlia is too used to talking and too used to being surrounded by extroverts and know-it-alls to enjoy her meal in silence.

"You know," she says between mouthfuls, "I'd like to get to know you a little better. I mean, we don't know what will happen today. It'll be good to know each other, right? And I just keep monologuing. My friends all tell me I need to remember to breathe when I talk."

Seraphina reacts with a shy smile and takes a tiny bite of her porridge.

"You understand what I'm saying, don't you? So, your language must be pretty good. Really. I'm sure you just need to try and say some stuff, and I'll try to listen. It's not my best suit, but I'll try. We'll both practice, right? Why don't you tell me about your home? About the reservation."

The conversation is long and strained, and I won't relay it to you in its entirety. Dahlia doesn't always understand Seraphina, but when she doesn't, she asks more questions and fills in the blanks with what she already knows.

Seraphina explains that the banshees are not created for feelings and love, or maybe they just forgot it along the way. She seems to remember a feeling of happiness once, in the very beginning, and remembers laughing, just faintly. The banshees at the reservation keep as quiet as possible, and do not speak. She never knows if they can't or won't. Sometimes she thinks it's just because they have nothing to talk about. The weather is of no interest to them, the scenery is nothing but ugly compared to their distant home, and they don't do much but sit around all day. Seraphina explains that they are all waiting for their Dear Creator to return and take them back home, to restore their lives and purpose. There is, to them, no point in establishing a life when Gluskab will soon come and bring them home, anyway. When Dahlia wrings her face, she reminds her that banshees are almost as old as the Gluskabian world and that the last twenty-two years is, for them, the equivalent of about a day in Dahlia's life.

Seraphina grows more confident as she speaks, even managing a four-word sentence toward the end, but then she runs out of things to say, or words to describe them, and Dahlia can see the exhaustion on her face.

"I'm sorry I can't offer you any coffee or tea," Dahlia says. "That's all in another bug out bag. This one is just the essentials. I know I could use a bit of caffeine now."

"Thanks," Seraphina says with a polite smile. She then puts the porridge down next to her, crawls over, and begins stuffing the sleeping bag into the compression sack next to her.

"Oh, thanks," Dahlia says. "I guess we should actually start to get going, shouldn't we?"

"No," Seraphina stops her stuffing and points at herself. "Me."

"Wait, what? You're joking, aren't you?" Dahlia examines her face and finds that she is not joking. She does not seem like the joking type, either. "You're going to leave on your own? Why? Where are you planning on going?"

"Angel Forest."

"Your reservation? Seraphina, that's... I mean, that's likely been destroyed. When I talked to The Chief yesterday, he said things weren't just going on here. It was all over. And I mean, how would you get there?"

Seraphina presses the half stuffed sleeping back to her body and buries her face in it.

"I'm really sorry," Dahlia offers.

Seraphina looks up from the sleeping bag, still squeezing it.

"You think..." Seraphina starts, brows furrowed, pressing her lips tightly together so it's nothing but a thin line. "Gluskab?" She gestures out at the broken world.

"Do I think Gluskab's doing this?"

Seraphina nods.

"Of course, I do. Who else would it be? Who else *could* it be? I mean, *someone* has caused this, and it can only be Gluskab. You saw the lightning yesterday. That's, like, his signature killing-people move."

"But... why?"

Dahlia bites her lip. She asked her father about that once, too. She was five, and he was dropping her and Vallesia off at the boarding school at the military base for the very first time. He parked well off base, refusing to walk them inside like all the other parents. Dahlia remembers him scowling at the large gates.

"That place there," he said, pointing indignantly. "That place is home to the world's biggest idiots. Everyone in there are mindless followers. You're going to have to assimilate. Act. Pretend you're one of them. But I'm not worried. You're both smart enough to not listen to anything they have to say. You're my children, after all."

Dahlia and Vallesia packed everything in one suitcase. Uniforms, towels, and a picture of their parents taken before their mother died. That was all. They hadn't been allowed to bring any of their toys from home. Their father helped them unload the small case and offered it to Vallesia, who was already half a head taller than Dahlia and much stronger.

"Learn everything you can," Father said. "But without giving yourself away. What are you, again? What are we always playing at home?"

"Spies," Vallesia said with a big smile.

"Spies, yes. It will be just like playing. Now, off you go. I'll come get you when the year is over. Okay? Dahlia?"

Dahlia looked uncertain. She glanced back at the car, where her monkey toy was still fastened in a seatbelt, looking stiffly ahead with its perpetual, forced smile. They fought all morning about whether she should be allowed to bring him with her. Her father wasn't going to give him the cuddles he needed. She knew that. Her monkey would be starved of love and missing her. How could she just leave him?

"Dahlia, forget your stupid monkey," Father said. "This is life and death we're talking about. Gluskab is coming back. And what will happen when He does?"

"The apocalypse," Dahlia mumbled.

"Exactly. We need to know everything about our enemy before that happens. So, stop acting like a baby. Make me proud instead."

"But what if He comes back and it's not the apocalypse?" Dahlia asked without even thinking. Vallesia gasped. Her father's smile stiffened, the disappointment painted all over his face.

"Of course it will be," he said.

"But why kill us?" Dahlia shouldn't have asked that. Her father was visibly vibrating with anger as he grabbed onto her arm, hard, and yanked her toward him.

"Maybe He's tired of you," he said, spitting as he pushed the words out of his reddening face. "Maybe He's tired of all your endless questions and stupid actions. Maybe He doesn't want to deal with you anymore after thousands of years of babysitting. Did you think about that? Maybe He didn't want you in the first place. Maybe He just doesn't love you anymore."

Sitting in the ruins after the apocalypse her father predicted, Dahlia looks at Seraphina with a sigh. "Maybe Gluskab is disappointed in us."

The two-way radio emits static, which makes both of them jump and turn toward it.

"Dahlia?" The Chief's baritone voice resonates in their small crawlspace. "Dahlia, let me know if you hear this. Over." There's a squelching sound, then the radio goes quiet.

Dahlia leaps to it and inspects the radio before finding the right button to push.

"This is Dahlia. Where are you? How are you?" She stops, listening for an answer. "Oh, right. Over." She lets go of the button and looks back at Seraphina, who edges forward to better hear. There is no need. His voice fills their little pocket of shelter.

"Oh, dear, I'm so happy to hear from you," he says. "You were supposed to keep me updated. I'm fine. I took a helicopter from the station before things got bad. I'm parked out in the middle of... I don't even know... nowhere. How about you?

Where are you? Over."

"I'm fine. I'm with a—a friend. We got caught up in the storm last night, but we managed to ride it out in a shelter. My legs and arms have felt *and* looked better, but we made it. I don't even remember how we got here. I think I basically blacked out. It's brutal outside. I went to check this morning and…" Dahlia stops to look at Seraphina, who seems unsettled, and realizes that she has still not seen the slaughter outside. "Anyway. We're safe for now. Over."

The response is instant. "Good, I'm happy to hear that. What's the plan now? Are you on your way to your dad's? What about your sister? Over."

"I haven't found Vallesia yet. We think she might be at the military base, so we're planning on heading there next. Can't go to my dad's without her. Over."

"Ah."

The radio goes quiet.

Did he say that he has a helicopter?

"It's a pretty long way to base," The Chief says. "Over."

"It is. Probably dangerous, too. Over."

There is another long, anxious silence, then just what Dahlia needs to hear: "Where are you?"

As they pack up, Dahlia slips the flask from the bag into her pocket. She climbs out the opening first, then gives Seraphina a hand. The small banshee chokes a squeak when she sees the carnage, then puts her hand around her throat. There are less names tugging at it today, but there are still so many.

They decide not to spend energy looking for Mario, since Dahlia believes there is no way he has survived. When they crawl out from their shelter, it takes a moment for them to realize that it is him dying on top of a car in front of them. The sight is merely an artist's detail on this painting of despair. It is Seraphina who points to him with enthusiasm and yells his name. He doesn't wake immediately, but as they move closer to him, he spasms.

He looks awful. His whole body is one big bruise, more blue, purple, and yellow than white. The black and gooey substance covers his arms and hands and hangs in thick strings from his mouth. He mumbles something impossible to understand, but it proves to them that he is alive. It takes them a while to get him up and even longer to make him drink. Once they do, he coughs and the water spills out along with more of the black, gooey substance.

When his glassy eyes fall on Seraphina, she can't help but whisper his name, quiet enough that no one hears her. His wife is the one who needs to hear her say it, but Seraphina still feels like screaming it to the world.

CHAPTER 16

IT IS TIME FOR ME to update you on my dear Vallesia. Something horrible and most worrisome happened during my detour, and now I fear the consequences.

Vallesia was picked up by the Peacers yesterday and has been locked in a cell in their headquarters since then. I thought she'd be safe there. If there were any group I could trust, it would be them. Her cell isn't particularly unpleasant; there's a bed, a desk, a chair, and even a few books—all of them pro-Gluskabian, of course. Her cell is more comfortable than her dorm room.

Colonel Lewir broke the news to her last night, after the lightning, acid showers, and earthquakes; but before the floods, the flaming snow, the tornadoes, and everything else.

I did not watch everything. Who could have watched everything and still been a whole person after? I admit to closing my eyes at one point.

Vallesia sat on the edge of the bed, back straight, as Colonel Lewir entered her cell.

"Look," he led as he sat on the chair across from her. "I

know we've been asking you a lot of questions since you were brought in—about the shed, about how you opened it, about what happened when you did. We really need to get some answers. Soon. Like what happened to Mister Crado, and where he is."

"Sir," she said, trying to hold it together, "I'm not hiding anything. I've told you. I touched the shed and then... something came out. It was like a cloud. I've explained it. When it left, Mister Crado was gone. I'm really sorry I touched the shed. I don't know what happened. I don't know why I touched it, I—"

Colonel Lewir held up his hand and she fell silent, biting her cheek. "That's enough," he said, then pulled a phone out of his pocket. "This isn't a game. If you're holding something back, you need to tell us. I'm going to show you why."

Colonel Lewir handed Vallesia the phone as a video started to play. Screams and explosions, crashes and crying, and the thunderous roars of lightning emitted from the device. Vallesia's eyes grew large and filled with tears as she covered her mouth. The color drained from her face and her body shook.

"What is this?" she whispered.

"It's what's happening—right now—because the shed was opened."

None of this is her fault. It is mine. I should have let her fall. I really messed up. I messed it all up. And now she thinks she's done all this.

There is no knock on the door this time, only keys clattering as it unlocks. Vallesia jumps from her bed, exhausted from a long night of interrogations.

She barely slept at all. Even when they left her alone, she laid in her bed and stared at the ceiling, the horrible videos continuously playing in her mind. The bags under her eyes are heavy and dark. No one has answered her questions about

Mario or Dahlia, and they haven't let her contact them, even when she begged.

Peacers enter her cell in silence, then motion for her to follow them. Most of the interviews were in other rooms, so this should not alarm her, but it does. She has not seen these men before. They look younger, their faces are rough, and their eyes are filled with loathing. She considers not following them, but their arms are bigger than her legs and her legs are not small.

The hallways are empty despite it being midday. She slows the pace to look through open doors and finds only empty rooms. Two other Peacers pass by them as they turn a corner, and she is at first relieved to see them, but their faces are as rough as the Peacers who came to get her. They glare at her with disgust. Her heart skips a beat when she sees what they are dragging after them: A body bag. She tries to calm herself, reminding herself that Peacers are good people, they wouldn't hurt her, and everything is going to be okay.

The men grab her arm and shove her into a room with such a force that she trips and falls to the floor. One locks the door with deliberation while the other forces her up and pushes her into a chair. She feels sick, her breathing quick now.

"Can I have a glass of—"

"Shut up!" The man slaps her, then turns his frown into a smirk when she cries out in pain.

Vallesia realizes what is about to happen. She is no stranger to torture, at least in theory. She has gone through her fair share of simulations, but she never thought she might be interrogated like that. The practices felt like farfetched imaginations, like something they were playing. She has nothing to hide, but these men won't stop until they have the answers they need. She doesn't even understand the questions well enough to make up answers.

Fight or flight, then? It is too late for flight. In a sudden rush of bravery, she decides to give fighting a chance. She jumps from the chair just as the shorter one, who is still inhumanly tall, turns to her with a bundle of rope. She tries to headbutt him, but they are both at least a head taller than her, so her head slams into his chest. Then she tries to kick the taller one's leg, but he locks his ankle around hers and brings her to the cold floor. He lowers himself atop her and uses his weight to pin her down, his hands wrapped tightly around her wrists. She raises a knee and tries to push over on the ball of her foot, but he is in complete control and does not budge. She tries pushing up from her hip to make him fall forward, but again, he does not move. He is too large and experienced.

As Vallesia falls limp in defeat, the man lifts her from the floor and sits her down in the chair. The shorter one ties her hands behind her back and fastens them to the chair, then ties her feet together. It is too tight and she whimpers. Tears spring to her eyes. They work in silence with quick, coordinated effort, then stand aside to conspire in low voices.

She is helpless. All she can do is pray for it to be over quickly. How will they make her suffer? No, she doesn't want to go through with that thought. She needs to calm her breathing. Distract herself. She decides to get a good look at them to try to remember their faces for later, if ever there will be a later.

The fear and pain make her sight blurry, but she is able to discern some key features to remember; an unusual nose, some hollow eyes, and the shape of their jaws. If I were a vengeful god, I would remember their faces as well and smite them later, but I am not and so I make no effort to remember their faces.

The tallest seems to be in charge. He ends their hushed discussion and turns back to Vallesia, grabbing a chair from beside the door and pulling it out in front of her. He turns it around and sits down, puffing up his chest and tilting his head while squinting. He intimidates her despite her knowing that this is the intended effect.

"Well, there's no reason to keep this hidden from you, is there?" the taller one asks. His voice is incredibly deep. Perhaps he is making it deeper on purpose. Something about the two men makes them appear boyish and unprofessional. She would have preferred a professional. "A few of us think the others have been treating you too kindly. After all, you are the lowest level of scum I've ever had the displeasure of coming across. So, we decided that we'd do this our way."

Her heart skips a beat. The man smiles. It is not a polite smile.

"Are you scared?" he asks, tilting his head and leaning forward. "It's alright if you are," he whispers. "You're not a real Peacer, anyway."

She attempts to toughen up, feeling the burn of the insult, but she does not dare to answer. Her throat feels dry.

"The fact that some of them actually believed that she was a Peacer…" the shorter one mumbles.

"It must have been a joke," the taller one says.

"Yeah, oh well. They're all gone now."

Vallesia flinches. *Gone?* She remembers the body bag being dragged across the floor and feels as if she is about to throw up. The whole room is spinning with green and pink spots dancing before her eyes.

"What?" she asks. It sounds more like a croak, but they understand, grinning faces and all.

"Oh, yes," the tallest says and leans forward. He speaks slowly, as if she's a child, with that devilish smile played across his face. "They are all gone now. No one left to protect you. Especially that Colonel Lewir. We took *really* good care of him. Some of them, you know, just didn't have what it took. They just sat around and waited for orders, and they made us sick. But don't you worry." He leans in even closer, his lips hovering right above her neck. "We are going to have so… much… fun…"'

I was so foolish, trusting these people. A mutiny… And now she, despite her innocence, will suffer the consequences.

I, too, feel like throwing up.

The shorter one leaves the room without another word, locking the door behind him as he does. The click makes Vallesia flinch. It sounds like the click of a gun.

"I've already told the Peacers everything I know," Vallesia

says.

"You have told us nothing." He leans back in the chair, inspecting his fingernails.

Several minutes pass. He looks back at the door behind him, impatient, but the shorter one is taking his time. Then he turns his callous gaze back at her. "Now that Jarda and Gluskab are dead, no one is going to punish us," he says in an even tone. "You know that, right? All actions are unpunishable now. No one is watching us. Isn't that exciting?" He stops and awaits an answer. When he doesn't get one, he scoffs. "This isn't looking very promising."

The shorter one reenters with one of the men who was dragging the body bag. Now he is carrying a heavy bucket in both his arms. Water splashes over the sides when he puts it down, a cloth and a sponge sloshing around inside. She looks up at them with wide eyes, her heart beating fast.

They enjoy her suffering. They look at her and see she knows what is about to happen, and they *enjoy* it. She is disgusted by their sadism. *How can Jarda ever have appointed them?* she wonders

I wonder the same thing. Maybe Jarda did so because, after all, she was merely human.

"Now," the taller one says. "Are you ready to give us some real answers?"

"I don't have any answers. I've told you—"

The short one kicks her chair. She falls to the floor, then the taller one pours water into a pitcher, ever so slowly. She struggles with the ropes and tries to free her hands, but it is pointless. She accepts her fate and closes her eyes.

"I'm not scared of you," she says. Somehow, she manages to make it sound somewhat convincing. She knows if they want to torture her and kill her, they will. She cannot stop them. The only thing that she can do is to ruin their fantasy by not playing along.

"You should be," the taller one says, putting down the pitcher beside her and submerging the sponge.

She bites her cheek.

The taller one stuffs the sponge in her mouth and covers her face with the cloth, then grabs the pitcher. She tells herself that she will not resist, that she will not give them that, but when he starts pouring the water, the drowning sensation makes her forget every noble cause. She coughs and gasps for air, a big mistake as the water moves up through her nose, then down in her lungs, where it burns. The nightmare. The memory that is not hers, the beach and the rocks, and her drowning and bleeding to death at the same time. She feels now as if the shards are piercing through her skin, as if she is being impaled. The darkness turns red, blood getting washed out into the sea on pink foam. A thousand different shades of red and screams. Her screams? Is she screaming? Is she drowning, really drowning?

Her body screams, her lungs especially, and she thinks she is just about dead before, suddenly, they have run out of water and she can breathe again. She coughs up the sponge and keeps coughing, coughing, and coughing, then she throws up through her mouth and nose. The whole contents of her stomach spread all over the cold floor and down her chin and lips, smeared all over her cheeks. Her nose burns, but it is nothing like the forest fire in her lungs.

Oh, I really cannot watch... Have they finished now?

"She doesn't look ready to me," the taller one says. She has still not gotten her breath back, and she is still coughing up an entire week's food when they shove the sponge back into her mouth and cover her face.

No, I really cannot watch this. Don't make me watch this. I have to go—

CHAPTER
17

THE WEATHER REALLY IS LOVELY today. The sun is high in the sky, with not a single cloud to be seen. It extends its golden arms in search of skin to touch and comfort with warm hugs. The air is clear and fresh and attempts to mend tender lungs and sore throats. The birds chirp cheerily.

It is hard to enjoy the weather in this ravaged and traumatized scenery, but I make a determined try. It is important to appreciate when the world is being good to you, especially when a hundred not-so-natural catastrophes have just more than halved the entire world's population, you have spent your night and morning speared by a beam, and you have just witnessed the person you love most being tortured. In such cases, it is good to stop and close your eyes, shut out the death and destruction around you, and let rays of sun stroke your crippled body.

Dahlia and her group arrive shortly, disturbing my deep meditation and attempts to convince myself that all will be okay.

The helicopter is loud and I cannot hear the birds while The Chief lands it on the empty field. It is impossible to make out which crop might have grown here. Wheat, perhaps? It wasn't empty yesterday. Even the grass and the weeds are gone. As the helicopter lands, clouds of ash whirl into a maelstrom. Fields of dark gray greet them when they jump out. They shudder. A breeze hits them with the nauseating smell of charred livestock. The ash swirls in the air, sending them into coughing fits.

None of them notice the lovely weather.

They try their best to cover their mouths. Mario does not follow suit, nor does he need to. He has been coughing since yesterday anyway, so the ash won't make a difference. His eyes are glazed and he walks as if in a trance. Have you ever hurt yourself so much you don't even scream or cry or *do* anything, you just try to move as little and as mechanically as possible and detach yourself from your body? Mario is doing no better than his wife, but I can tolerate observing his downfall. Even when they are apart, they are in sync. It is like that for married people, I suppose. Not that I would know.

The group unloads The Chief's three bug out bags and Dahlia's one. While they do, The Chief eyes Mario, as if he is not quite sure if he should or could convince the others to leave him behind. If he had known that Mario was this sick when he went to pick them up, he would probably have made a fuss about it earlier, but the man was half asleep and The Chief thought his poor state was merely a result of his disturbing amount of bruises. It wasn't until he threw up all over the helicopter, which had been The Chief's pricey birthday present to himself, that he realized his error, and now they have landed with this half-man, half-zombie. The Chief looks to Dahlia, who is keeping a safe distance from her sick brother-in-law, and he knows she is thinking the same as him — that it might be contagious and they would not like to catch whatever he has.

You can't afford too many charities at times like these.

Maybe Mario can just limp behind them until they arrive at base, where they can pass him on to a soldier and run away like a game of ding dong ditch. As long as Mario does not make trouble, The Chief will agree to this plan. However, when Dahlia points them toward the base and they start to walk, Mario does not move. They look back and see him still standing by the heli-copter, motionless, staring off into the distance.

That's it. The Chief looks back at Dahlia. Their eyes lock as she gives him a miniscule nod, and he is just about to open his mouth to suggest something controversial when Seraphina surprises them both. She walks back to Mario and lays a gentle hand on his arm. He retreats with a whimper, almost like a frightened puppy, as if her touch burns him.

This takes a bit of processing, the gears in Seraphina's brain visibly turning.

"Okay?" she asks. He doesn't respond, so she looks back at Dahlia and The Chief, pleading for help. Dahlia looks down into the charred field and The Chief looks up into the clear, blue sky. They are like children in class, scared to be called on.

Seraphina grows unsure of herself. Everything she has learned from watching humans through the centuries is telling her the right thing to do is to not leave Mario behind, but why are they not helping? Do they want to leave him behind? She is confused and feels suddenly more out of place than usual.

There is a long, uncomfortable silence while The Chief chooses his words. He finally suggests, "Maybe Mario will do better waiting in the helicopter?"

Dahlia nods with enthusiasm.

He continues with renewed confidence. "He can lie down and get a bit of rest. Look at him, he's in pain. It's a bit of a walk, right, Dahlia? We'll be back to check on him once we find Vallesia. It should just be a short stop, anyway, right?"

Seraphina feels as if something is amiss, but she is about to agree with him regardless, if only because she finds no cause for her to trust her instinct over his reasoning when it comes to human behavior.

"Vallesia?" Mario mumbles as he looks up in a sudden fit of clarity. Black drool drips down his chin. "V — Valley?"

There is another long, uncomfortable silence.

Dahlia sighs, then reminds herself this man is family, after all. "Right," she says. "Come along, then. This way."

They are not the first to stop by the military base. When they reach the gates, they are shocked to find a long line of people waiting, and even more shocked to see that Mario's condition is not just a poorly timed, enormously aggressive flu, which it in retrospect definitely was not anyway. Wherever Dahlia looks, there are people showing the same symptoms as Mario, but at different stages: Some are just coughing, some look a bit pale, and some are throwing up the black tar. One guy in front of them falls to the ground with a huge thump and does not appear to have any plans of getting up. When no one steps forward to help him up, a soldier comes over, lifts him over his shoulder, then carries him away, the man still completely unresponsive.

Mario has moved on to a new phase in his illness, in which he has gone absolutely, feverishly crazy. The entire way there, Seraphina attempted to talk to him, but his half-conscious answers have been those of a madman.

She asked him how he is feeling.

"No," he said.

She asked him if he was feeling bad, to which he replied by commenting on the dark green color of the leaves which the trees no longer possess. He stopped at one point to mumble about how nice the grass felt against his toes, except he was wearing shoes and there was no grass. Most of the time, he addressed an invisible Vallesia, pretending to pick her flowers and showering her with absurd compliments.

Dahlia feels a clump forming in her throat. It occurs to her that she has not been the most sympathetic to Mario. Although she dislikes him on a fundamental level, he is the man that her sister chose to love. He is possibly dying, and he *is* a person. Still, she feels the same repellent force as The Chief and the same desire to change her plans and run away as fast as possible from all these sick people gathered before the gates. Yet she realizes the soldiers are not wearing masks, walking amongst the people, and letting them in through the gates. Surely, she reasons, they wouldn't be doing so if they thought whatever they have is contagious.

But if it's not contagious, she thinks, *what is it?*

It becomes their turn to pass through the gate into the base. The Chief stands aside as Seraphina ridiculously attempts to support Mario's body, which is twice as big as hers. Dahlia makes sure that no one touches her and approaches a soldier by the entrance to the gate. He looks frantic and overwhelmed by the surge of people, his eyes darting all around, his breath sharp and constant.

"We're looking for my sister," Dahlia tells him. She fails to lock her eyes on his since they are all over the place.

"Go to the sleeping halls," he says like a robot, as if he's repeated the same sentence a thousand times today already, which might actually not be an exaggeration. He glances at Mario but does not seem phased in the least. "F and G should still have some room."

"Her name is Vallesia Jade. She took her Honors examination this weekend. She might be with the military," Dahlia attempts.

"She's probably in the sleeping halls with the rest," he says and waves them through, not seeming to have time for her.

There is no point arguing. As they enter the base, Dahlia has to remind herself not to be surprised to find the usually tranquil setting anything but that. The base is overcrowded because people trust the military in times of trouble.

"Are you sure we need your sister?" The Chief asks. He looks overwhelmed, both by the amount of people and by the sheer size of the place.

Dahlia does not blame him for being overwhelmed because she would have been overwhelmed even if the place hadn't been filled with wounded and coughing souls. She has not been back on base since she left late at night so many years ago, at sixteen and with nothing but a small backpack of essentials on her back. She remembers the statue peering at her with displeasure as she did, the same statue they are standing in front of now: Gluskab gazing lovingly at Jarda, her with a sword in her hand and a determined look demanding peace and justice. I always thought it was telling that Gluskab was looking at her, but she was looking at the world. This representation of priorities was unintentionally true. The statue fills Dahlia with a sense of dread and shame, although she cannot pinpoint why. By reflex, she reaches her hand behind her back to make out the outline of her flask. She feels about sixteen again.

Pre-death clings to the air, a sort of gloomy atmosphere graying the view, but she can smell something else, as well—the specific smell of a specific place, the kind of smell that you cannot describe or even remember before you recognize it, and then you can't believe you could have ever forgotten about it. It makes her stomach turn.

"Dahlia," The Chief presses, breaking her from her thoughts. "Are you sure we need to find Vallesia?"

"Yeah, I'm sure," she answers, her face caught in a grimace. "We need her. My father won't let us in without her."

"Are you sure about that?" The Chief asks. "You could call and ask..."

"I don't have his number, and my phone isn't working, anyway. Come on, let's go."

She stomps away, toward the sleeping halls F and G. Where else should they go? Her entourage follows behind, surprised by her sudden fit of anger. With each step, she imagines fire spewing from her feet and hopefully burning down this entire wretched place. She will be damned if this is where she goes to die.

Dahlia must fight a fit of nostalgia as they reach sleeping

halls F and G. This was where she and Vallesia slept when they were young. She remembers listening to the mechanical clock ticking by, holding hands during thunderstorms, and grinning at the other children when they told ghost stories about me. She takes a deep breath.

It helps that the sleeping halls are completely unrecognizable, having been converted into sick wards. There are people everywhere. Mostly the ill, lying spread out side by side on a floor completely covered in mattresses. The room is in constant movement, the half-dead twisting and turning. They cough and throw up everywhere—on themselves, the mattresses, the floor, and even on each other—but they are all too weak to care. There is only pain and death to care about. The room reverberates with groans and crying and screams from sudden jabs of cramps. There is a constant cough which sounds almost rhythmic, like a deep drumroll building up. In between the brooding zombies, soldiers pass through, zigzagging on small paths with desperate, quick movements. Their faces are as pale as the sick ones and they, too, often must stop to release the contents of their stomachs. The soldiers carry in cloths and sheets, blankets and water. They carry out dead bodies, heaps of them, three to a stretcher. The room reeks.

The four new arrivals stand in the doorway, mouths agape, and even Mario is quiet. A soldier passes behind them, his arms full of sleeping pads, but rather than bring them into the crowded room, he dumps them by the wall in the hallway. He drops them with little care, kicking them against the wall before nodding to himself. As he turns to leave, Dahlia and the others catch his eye.

"The halls are full," he says, unprompted. His face is paler than porcelain and he looks young with not-quite-stubble not-quite-growing above his lips. Dahlia realizes with horror that maybe he is not even a soldier; maybe he is just a boarding school student.

"We can see that," she says.

"He can lay down here," the soldier nods at Mario. "Fresh

pads. No… goo on them."

Mario grunts dissatisfied. Seraphina does not look thrilled either.

A soldier pushes them out of the way and a stretcher emerges from the room. A hand has fallen over the edge and drags over the floor as the stretcher bounces from side to side, leaving behind a trail of black.

"It's quieter in the hallway," the soldier continues. His voice is shaking. Why is he trying to sell them on the idea of a hallway sleeping pad, as if they are young adults shopping for a new car?

"No," Seraphina says, determined, and grabs onto Mario.

"There are more and more people coming, but we have room for them, because even more are leaving," the soldier says. "They don't leave because they get better. They don't. None of them do. They just don't."

Something happens inside of Dahlia, something which makes a faint click, only audible to her. She raises her chin at the soldier and looks him right in the eyes. Her palms hurt from where her nails are buried in the tender flesh. "We're not leaving him here." She is surprised to hear the words pronounced from her own mouth. "He's my brother-in-law. I'm not going to have him rolling around here. It's inhumane."

The soldier does not protest, instead nodding with understanding, then turns and walks away. He probably does not know where he is off to—just somewhere better than here.

The group copies him, allowing themselves one last glance at the horrific scene before leaving. Dahlia and Seraphina support Mario as he staggers along. On the way out, they all silently decide to purge the whole of the experience from their minds. They do not even stop to ask anyone about Vallesia. They just keep walking in silence, as if they are afraid that something will emerge from behind them and tug at their shirts and pull them back in.

Not yet.

Once outside, Dahlia and Seraphina agree that there are two

priorities: getting Mario somewhere quiet and finding Vallesia. "Let's get Mario somewhere first, then we can look for Vallesia afterwards, okay?" Dahlia asks.

Seraphina nods with enthusiasm. The Chief would rather run out the damned gates, get into the damned helicopter, and fly as far away as humanly possible. Mario does not weigh in, but not even The Chief can think of any reasons why he should not agree with the girls. He is outvoted.

"Let's see," Dahlia says while looking around, "somewhere where we can make camp, maybe even stay for the night, if it comes to that. We should be able to barricade it, but also get out quick. There might be more… things happening. And it needs to be somewhere close."

"How about a nice spa, too? And a fridge and a double bed." The Chief pouts and crosses his arms like a petulant child.

Dahlia shoots him a stern look. How easily the roles switch; it requires nothing but an apocalypse to put Dahlia in charge of her boss, her second father.

"Vallesia…" Mario mumbles, his eyes drifting. He looks like a tree swaying in the wind, threatening to topple over at any point.

"First you," Seraphina says and struggles to stay upright as he falls into her.

"No, Vallesia…" Mario insists while looking around. He appears a little better as he pushes himself away from Seraphina's caring grip to take a careful step of his own. He keeps his arms out for balance but doesn't fall over. "Vallesia…"

Seraphina looks, pleading, at Dahlia, who tries to step in, but Mario ducks her arm and takes a step away from them.

They look in disbelief as he staggers off, then Dahlia shrugs and they set off after him. Occasionally, Mario looks around at the buildings to orientate himself, and then sets off again. He mumbles incoherently, but Dahlia makes out enough to understand that he is having some sort of conversation with an imaginary Vallesia. It sounds mundane.

"What do you want for dinner?" He asks. "I went shopping… Are you coming to bed? … Are you coming home soon? I made dinner."

Mario possibly knows the current layout of the base better than Dahlia, and it is not unlikely that he has understood some of their discussion. He did not grow up here, but he has been with Vallesia for long enough that the base must be a sort of home to him as well. He has been a good husband, visiting her whenever allowed, staying over, and putting up with her ridiculous routines. The army's Honor Students only get a single day off once a week, and they are usually in so much physical pain, they barely leave their beds except to go eat. How anyone would ever be able to maintain a relationship, much less a marriage, in that environment is beyond Dahlia. Perhaps, she thinks, she has not given Mario enough credit. Her longest proper relationship lasted for less than a week, if that can even be considered a 'proper' relationship.

Mario finally stops in front of a door. Next to it, there is a pad, which he opens and enters a code into. The doors swing open with a high-pitched beep and they enter the building, which appears deserted.

"Where are you?" Mario mumbles at the white walls and makes a sharp turn down a hallway.

Even The Chief is glad to follow him because the building, which they soon find to be a dorm, is quiet and clean. All the soldiers who live there are off dealing with the end of the world. It feels like a vacuum. A safe vacuum.

After some time, Mario stops in front of another door, fiddles with the frame, and watches a key fall out and land on the floor with a hollow clink. He picks it up, his hands only shaking slightly, and unlocks the door with it. He turns back to them and mumbles, "Vallesia's room."

Then, as if his body decides that he has performed well enough, he collapses on the floor. They carry him inside with much effort, which would be reduced if The Chief were not too frightened of his condition to help, and put him on the single bed. The room is beyond minimalistic. Besides the bed, everything else would easily fit into a medium sized box: slippers, toiletries, hair ties, a calendar. Just the essentials. The only thing that throws Dahlia off is the inspirational quote above Vallesia's bed, but it must have been a gift from Mario.

Seraphina converts an empty trash bin into a puke bin, which Mario breaks in as soon as it is placed next to him. He then curls back into a ball and passes out again. For a long time, he doesn't make any sound and they have to check to make sure that he is still breathing. For now, he is.

"Well, that's one part down," The Chief says.

They sit on the floor, worried, while Seraphina strokes Mario's sweaty head. Dahlia passes around some protein bars from her bug out bag. Along with The Chief's three bug out bags, they should have enough food and drinks for at least a couple of weeks, if it comes to that. They are not too hungry, though.

None of this feels real. Dahlia pinches herself and only realizes afterwards that she genuinely expected to wake up. Yes, she has been planning for this apocalypse since birth, but she liked to believe that her father and The Chief were crazy. She had done all her preparations like a good kid does, but she had not actually expected to need them. Now, her preparations seem painfully inadequate as she struggles to think of what should happen next.

Dahlia feels her own body, touches her throat, and swallows. Does she feel sick? Is her throat a little sore? Is she a little dizzy? A small headache is setting in, then her toe feels funny. Before long, everything feels wrong and she is not certain if she is sick or if it is just the placebo setting in. The longer she sits idly by, the more the unease spreads.

Time to find Vallesia, she decides.

"There is a registry office," Dahlia says, amazed that she hasn't thought of this sooner. "We can go there and ask for Vallesia. If anyone knows, it'd be them. Right?"

The Chief and Seraphina both nod. No objections.

"Great," Dahlia concludes. "So, who's going to go?"

They look around at each other. Seraphina halts her stroking. The Chief clears his throat.

"I'll stay here," he says. "To look after Mario, that is. In case anything happens."

"What a hero," Dahlia mumbles. "Seraphina, is that fine with you? We can go together."

Seraphina looks back at Mario, biting her lip and furrowing her brows. With a last stroke of his greasy locks, which are now completely wet from sweat, she nods and tears herself away.

In the doorway, The Chief holds Dahlia's arm. He pulls her away from Seraphina and leans in close to whisper in her ear. "Maybe get some stronger drugs." He steps back and looks at her.

Stronger drugs. There are painkillers in both their bug out bags, but perhaps he is right. Perhaps painkillers will not be enough for Mario. She looks back at him as he mumbles and turns in the bed as if possessed. It is soaked with his sweat and puke. He will not make it through the night, doubtfully even the evening. Perhaps the right thing, the most humane thing, would just be to put him out of his misery. Dahlia does not like it. She has never killed anyone, and never thought she would kill her brother-in-law, no matter how much he annoys her at times.

CHAPTER
18

MAYBE THERE IS STILL TIME. Maybe I can stop it. Yesterday's episode pulled too hard on my heartstrings; I don't know if I can go through it again.

I pluck a bouquet of flowers — lilies and daisies and sunflowers — whatever I can find on my way. Whatever wasn't scorched or blown off or otherwise horribly mangled yesterday. My selection is limited.

I take them to my father. He, or this version of Him at least, is still on the tattered, old couch where I left Him twenty-two years ago, staring straight ahead, His mouth slightly open. His palace reeks even more than I remembered. The walls are hairy from mold and there is a constant buzz of flies and spiders at war. He is covered in a light layer of dust and seems unbothered by the cockroach exploring His ear.

You'd think He was dead. I almost do. He wheezes, annoyed, when I poke His side.

There is something I've forgotten to tell you about in this

whole chaos. Or maybe I just didn't know how to explain it to you. There is a version of my father, of Gluskab, who came to see Mario in his apartment, and there is another version of Him now in front of me. In some ways, They are not the same. In other ways, They are.

It happened that day. He was sitting on the porch, smiling, waiting for Jarda to come back home after our walk. The weather was beautiful. There was not a single cloud in the sky and all the flowers were in bloom. A rainbow sea of forget-me-nots surrounded His rocking chair.

I was carrying Jarda's lifeless body in my arms.

His smile stiffened. His mouth twitched along with His eyes. He clutched the arms of the chair so tight the wood splintered and blood poured. I didn't know what to say. We were silent for a long time.

Then, the clouds opened up and rain poured on us so violently my shoulders ached. The rain intermixed with hail, then the wind picked up and I had to reposition myself not to blow away. The trees were nearly horizontal and the flowers' heads blew off. In the distance, I heard the rumbling of thunder, narrowing in on us, and the grass beneath us withered and became a slump of brown-gray mush.

My father's face kept twitching, and I knew — I understood in the way I so weirdly understand these human emotions — that He was sad and He was angry. In fact, He was so sad and so angry that He couldn't contain both emotions. He wasn't made for this. My father switched between blue and red shades, His hair set on fire and His body grayed, and He grew and shrank and then... Then, suddenly, there were two of them.

I don't know how to explain this.

I think the Gluskab before me is the part still in mourning. The Gluskab who threatened me with violent prophecies and the painful end of all mankind, who is out there *right now* causing all the misery, He is the part who wants revenge. Revenge because His wife is dead and someone must be blamed, and the only ones He can blame is the collective called humanity. That is my theory, anyway. I don't pretend to understand the workings of gods. I'm only half.

I carry my father outside in a firefighter hold. He weighs nothing and I can make out every single bone as if He is only a skeleton wrapped in skin. The porch, which was once white and radiating, is now gray and looks ready to collapse. The rocking chair, which He used to sit in while smiling at His creation, has equally given up and is now a pile of rotten wood.

I look around, weighing my options, and finally prop His body against a tree on the outskirts of the clearing.

"Isn't this nice? It'll be good for you to get some fresh air," I say and fill my lungs with the fresh, cold air. I want the air I breathed in inside the palace, out of my lungs. I feel it is tainted, containing every illness in the world. It tasted heavy and sticky and made my mouth taste bitter.

Gluskab lazily rolls His eyes and closes them, then collapses His body against the tree so He is almost lying down. I wince.

"You're not feeling too good, are you?" I ask. "When did you last eat?"

"Gods don't have to eat," He replies, barely moving His lips as He speaks. He is so pale, and His hair is thinning so that there is barely any left. His eyes rest in big craters and His lips are so dry that when He moves them, they crack and the blood tickles down His chin.

"Apparently they do need lip balm," I mumble.

Gluskab looks up at me with a frown and a raised eyebrow, then His lips heal in a second and He closes his eyes again. It occurs to me, as I am watching His troubled breathing and pointed collarbones, that He is choosing to look like this. He is so melodramatic. I sigh.

"Maybe you'd be less depressed if your palace didn't look like the inside of a molded gingerbread house," I offer.

"Will that bring her back?"

I bite my lip. *Her*. Jarda. My mother and his wife. The one whose absence has caused all this. "She *is* back. You know she's back," I say as I crouch down in front of Him, trying to catch

His eyes. This is why I've come: not to visit my sickly father, whose depression has swallowed Him whole and left Him a shell of Himself, but to convince Him that what I'm saying is true. "Jarda is back. She's reincarnated. I can lead you to her." He sighs and rolls around, facing the tree instead of me. "*He* came by and told me. The other one. He said He'd gone by an identity detective and found her."

A scene with Mario on the bed, black puke everywhere, crying for my father to save him, plays before me.

"If... He visited you and told you that, then you know I'm right," I say. "Jarda is out there. She's a real human who's suffering right now. We can save her. We can end this, together."

He sighs, His shoulders rising far above His ears before falling back down.

"You can have her back," I continue trying. "You can have her back. You can."

"Even if it *is* her, it won't be the same. She won't be the same."

"Her soul is the same."

He waves as if swatting a fly. "What is a soul? People are so much more than that. They are memories, too. There are so many things that make us into what we are."

I bite my lip. He's right. After all, I have made Vallesia into someone she is not. Look how easy that was for me.

"Do it for the people, then," I say. "They are the same. They haven't changed. You love your people. And they need you. Let's go save them. Please."

He shakes his head.

"You made them, Dad. You need to save them. You owe them that. They are *your* creations. You can't just make someone and then leave them."

Gluskab is silent for a long time. Then He rolls back around to face me. His face is grave as He musters an answer. "You know," He says. "It's weird. Being sad, for me at least, feels like being empty. It feels like I am completely and utterly empty on the inside. Like if you cut me right up, there would be just nothing—no organs, no heart, no nothing at all. But being angry... I remember it. I felt so full, I felt as if there wasn't enough space inside of me. I felt as if I was going to burst right open."

I listen. I'm not sure what to do with that.

"If you pour a full glass into an empty glass, you know it's just going to be full," He finishes. I don't know what that means. He closes his eyes and moments later, He begins to snore softly.

I take a step back and look at what is left of my father. He has crawled into a fetal position. His hands are covering His face, His knees up to His chest. His clothes are tattered. What is left of His hair hangs in greasy strips. Every time He heaves in for a breath, His body quivers. I think He is crying, like a dog losing a fight in their sleep.

This visit was pointless. I carry my feeble father back inside and place Him gently on the couch. I find a vase for my flowers and place it on a nearby desk. Maybe they will cheer Him up. Probably they won't.

This Gluskab won't save the world. He can't.

Only I can. Me and Vallesia together. When the time is right.

CHAPTER 19

DAHLIA DOES NOT REMEMBER WHICH way the registry office is, but she is intent on hiding that. She walks through the streets with feigned confidence, glancing at signs in passing and trying to not get overwhelmed by the memories. There is the bar, the one that she was too young to go to, but into which she snuck in the morning, after it had closed, to steal bottles. There, on that bench, she had her first kiss on a warm spring evening with cherry blossom petals falling around them like snow. And there, the library, where she went on the last night and crammed as many of her favorite books into her bag as possible. She'd sworn to never step foot on base again. Younger Dahlia would be so disappointed to see her here now.

Seraphina is silent but keeps close, either not noticing or not commenting on their circular paths. Dahlia keeps glancing over at her, at her soft profile, small nose, fine, frizzy hair, and blank stare. She can't help but wonder what Seraphina's thinking about, if she's even thinking about anything at all. Dahlia has always thought she is good at reading people, and has always bragged about her ability to box strangers into neat categories within the first five minutes of meeting. Yet, she can't seem to read even the first thing about Seraphina.

"You don't have any family," Dahlia says out of the blue. "Do you have any friends? Anyone close to you at all?"

Seraphina misses a step, surprised to be addressed. She hadn't seemed to mind the silence. "No," she says.

Dahlia waits for her to expand on this, but she does not.

"You must know someone. I mean, you've lived for thousands of years, haven't you? You can't just go through life without anyone. Have you lost someone, maybe? Don't answer if you mind, of course. I'm just curious. I've been told I'm bad at small talk."

"Gluskab," she says.

Touché.

This time, she surprises Dahlia by expanding on her answer. It takes her time and effort to say what she wants to say, but it is clearly important because she pushes through the challenge. "Easy hate, when not know."

"Huh? Hate who, Gluskab?"

Seraphina nods.

"And I don't know him, so it's easy for me to hate him. But you know him."

"Know…" Seraphina smacks her lips as if tasting the word. She's pondering the tense.

Dahlia ponders the claim instead. Her generation, and therefore most the people she knows, has never met Gluskab or were too young to remember. But Seraphina, of course, has been there since the beginning. The banshees lived in His backyard almost from the beginning.

"Have you ever met Him? Personally?" she asks.

Seraphina nods. It takes her time to find the words again. "Took time. Met us. Name us. Know names."

It is Dahlia's turn to nod. She struggles to imagine Gluskab coming out from His grand palace to sit around bonfires with the banshees, ask them about their day, make jokes with them, and play catch. Then again, she can't imagine Gluskab doing any kind of normal activities: going on dates with His wife, strolling the parks, or solving a puzzle. That doesn't mean He didn't do those things. If ever I told Dahlia that Gluskab had even taken the time to raise a child, to raise me, I am sure she wouldn't believe me. No one would, probably. But my secretive childhood is another story entirely.

"Being god stress," Seraphina continues. "Not human. Empty."

"What?" Dahlia scoffs. "Was it too tough being the big puppeteer? I suppose you're going to tell me He has some deep, dark backstory. That He was a complex person with complex emotions, and that He was actually just really sad."

"Yes," Seraphina says without hesitation. "But... not always."

Dahlia grimaces at Seraphina sympathizing with Gluskab. Especially now, when it is clear He does not care about *them*, she sees no reason to care about *Him*.

"I can't believe you're actually excusing Him right now," she says. "After all of this. After everything you've seen. After what He's done—what he's done to Mario."

Seraphina stands still. Her round eyes fill with tears as she pushes up her shoulders and looks down at her fingers fiddling. "Don't know..." she whispers.

Dahlia doesn't hear her whisper and continues walking, picking up her pace. "What's wrong with you, anyway?" she asks as she strides away, Seraphina following moments after with careful steps. "Did you fall into a big pot of emotions or something? You're a banshee. I thought you were supposed to be unemotional, or logical, or whatever. Didn't you tell me that?"

Seraphina doesn't respond. Instead, she bites her lip while she looks at the ground and hurries to keep up with Dahlia.

Their existential crises are put to an end when they arrive at the registry office. Here, they realize there is a gaping flaw in their brilliant plan: They are not the only ones to think that going to the registry office is a brilliant plan. The unmoving queue extends outside the building and writhes, snake-like, around it.

Dahlia sighs. Another letdown. They will still be standing here by sundown, and Dahlia knows better than allowing that. A non-contagious plague is too easy. Something else must be brewing.

Seraphina doesn't seem to mind, happily getting into line and planting her feet on the ground. She is doing what is most natural to her: waiting. She will stand here the entire night if she must.

"This won't work," Dahlia says. "We've got to find a way to skip to the front."

Seraphina looks at her, confused, but Dahlia does not have time for the banshee's moral quandaries. She looks around for some sort of plan until, with a defeated sigh, she realizes she cannot come up with one. Instead, she leaves Seraphina and goes to the front of the line, where she turns to a man and asks him how long he has been waiting.

"Some hours," he says, yawning. "Maybe longer. What time is it?"

"Seventeen forty-five," she says.

"Oh yeah," he nods. "More than a few hours, then. I think I got here around oh two hundred."

"Thank you," Dahlia says, turning away.

Who would wait in line for that long? Not her. Her feet are already itching to get a move on. She is about to give up and go back to find Seraphina when she notices a familiar face.

"Tomi!" she yells and jogs toward her childhood friend.

She nearly hadn't recognized him. He has grown much taller and is not wearing glasses anymore, nor is he skinny. Of course, Dahlia knew that him being in the same class as Vallesia would naturally imply that he must have become a larger and stronger than last she saw him, but she had not expected this beast of a man to appear. He used to be her partner in suffering, after all. They would get the same meals as kids, the ones for the smaller ones, with more calories and in larger portions. They were next to inedible and the only way they got through them was by making a game of it. She wonders if she would have been as big and strong as Tomi if she had continued eating those meals, but she doubts it. The man is a blatant display of pure dedication.

"Dahlia!" he exclaims, his somber face lighting up as he sees her. He is eyeing her as well. Physically, she is sure, she cannot have changed much. She is still a miniature, scaled-down version of a normal person. Instead of her physique, he observes her general appearance: The wild, swamp green cloud of curls is a contrast to the once tight braids. Her yellow spotted teeth and slightly reddened nose, which are evidence of another lifestyle than his. He smirks at the loose but dirtied tee-shirt with pro-banshee messages. The septum piercing completes the general air of rebellion around her.

"I didn't expect to see you here," he says. His smile is stiff and his forehead is damp with perspiration.

"No," she says. "This is probably not where I had expected to see myself, either. I guess it shouldn't surprise me to see you here, though. Valley has been keeping me updated."

He nods. "Yeah, I'm working. But hey, it must be weird being back. Have you been here since…"

He trails off. Her not-so-dramatic exit was carried out during the night to give her a head start and, clearly, it was well timed because no one ever caught up with her. Vallesia told her little about the morning reactions, only that the caretakers eventually announced she had gone home to her dad, which she obviously hadn't. Did Tomi know why she left? Was he sad? Did anyone go looking for her? The last question has been on her mind lately. Could it really be that a puny sixteen-year-old was able to out-walk the military? It seems unlikely.

"No, I haven't," she says. "I'm only here because I'm looking for Valley. You wouldn't have heard anything, would you?"

Tomi's hardened face gives Dahlia little hope. "About that," he says, looking anywhere but at her and scratching his head. "I'm sorry. I was just at the registry office to ask about her. She's not been called in for some reason. I assumed she would have been, even if she... Well, you know what happened Saturday. There are all kinds here. Retired soldiers, dropouts, discharges. Everyone who made it past year seven at the boarding school, really. But I asked the lady about her and her face kind of went... it was all wrong."

Dahlia imagines the look.

"She's a chirpy one," he continues. "Always smiles. Her name is Bertha. Her son is going to medical school. We talk about him a lot. So, what I'm saying is that I know her fairly well and I'm not sure what that look was or what it meant... Anyway, Val hasn't been called in and she's definitely not here. Bertha seemed certain of that, and she also told me, in strictest confidentiality, that it would be no use at all to go looking for her. I'm sorry about that. Everything's a bit of a mess right now."

"Right," Dahlia says.

"She's not dead, though," Tomi adds with haste. "At least, I don't think so. I don't think that was what it was about. She's just somewhere and it's not here, and it might be hard to get to. Again, I'm sorry."

Dahlia has no reason to doubt him, so she doesn't.

"Right," she says again. What else is there to say? "Thank you for your help."

Her voice is monotone, mechanical. Even she hears it. She tries a smile, but it is unsuccessful. It is a smile with no emotion, the sort a robot might try.

"Right." He shuffles his feet and pretends to look at a wristwatch he does not have. "Anyway, I should get going now. Get back to work. We're very busy at the moment, clearly."

Dahlia doesn't object, which he takes as her answer. Then, he disappears with another muttered apology. She doesn't mind his hasty disappearance—he has given her all the answers he has, anyway. No use standing around, loitering, talking about old times. There's no time for that. Although, what is there time for? She feels weird, disoriented. Her plan for the apocalypse has always been getting a hold of Vallesia and going to their father's place. Now, that seems impossible. She was expecting the unexpected, except that Vallesia wouldn't be there with her; that was never an option. She feels hollow, and it takes her more than some moments to shake the feeling.

Get yourself together, she commands herself. *Stop moaning. Find another plan.*

Vallesia is lost, and that is it. Dahlia feels the cogs in her brain spinning, working up a solution, but nothing comes to mind. Finally, she gives in, deciding she will just have to buy more time. She needs to set up camp, get the last of the things, and go barricade the room. A long night is awaiting, and there's no time to waste standing by, thinking. Tonight or tomorrow will be a time for thinking, if she makes it so far.

∞∞∞∞◆∞∞∞∞

Seraphina frowns when Dahlia comes to disturb her natural position of waiting. She is reluctant to leave the queue, but Dahlia does not seem open to feedback with her long strides and the look of determination in her narrowed eyes.

"I just need to get something," Dahlia says, "then we'll head back."

"Okay."

They walk in silence. Dahlia grumbles, scanning the base, hoping with clenched fists and no sense of optimism at all that her sister will have snuck into camp anyway and might be just around the corner. She is too preoccupied to notice Seraphina's endearing eyes with their large irises staring at her.

Seraphina clears her throat. "You," she says, catching Dahlia by surprise as she is pulled out of her deep, mostly unconstructive thoughts. "You have family," she asks, forgetting the proper intonation for a question and noting this for herself.

Dahlia slows her pace and looks with surprise to Seraphina. "Yes," she replies, uncertain. "A sister and a father. I guess I've told you about my father already. You know what... the deal is."

Seraphina nods thoughtfully, then forms her next question with care. "Any close?" she asks, this time remembering the intonation but executing it poorly.

Dahlia narrows her eyes. It is the same line of questions she asked Seraphina earlier, and now she realizes how unfair she was. But, Dahlia realizes with regret, Seraphina answered truthfully, and so now must she.

"Do I have anyone close?" she repeats. "Some people, I guess. There's Vallesia, but we've been a little distant the last years. I don't know. There's The Chief. He's always been there for me. He's like a father, I suppose, although I wouldn't know. And I have friends, I'd say. Most people would even say I have a lot of friends, and my weekends are always booked, you know, so that fills... something. But close... I'm not quite sure what close is, to tell you the truth. I haven't given a single thought to my friends since yesterday, really. Not since any of this happened. So that would suggest maybe I don't actually care that much for them."

Again, Seraphina nods thoughtfully, although Dahlia is not convinced she's absorbing the information. She's got the face of someone who is trying hard to solve a mathematical problem and failing.

"Lonely?" Seraphina asks, her brows furrowed and her teeth clenched from effort.

"No," Dahlia snaps, trying for a chuckle and a shrug, but failing all attempts at nonchalance. Seraphina's stare makes her feel uncovered, caught in a lie. She bites her lip. "I'm not lonely, no. As I said, I have tons of friends."

"Okay," Seraphina says.

"Of course..." Dahlia continues, hesitating. "This—you know, everything that is happening—I'd call that an apocalypse. My whole childhood, my whole life, I was told it was coming and I'm prepared for it, but… hmm… it's… I guess it's… no, it sounds stupid, anyway."

Seraphina looks at Dahlia with interest, willing her to go on.

Dahlia sighs, shrugs, and looks away, fighting with the words she doesn't want to say, but relents under the banshee's scrutiny and obliges her. "I guess what I mean is that I'm not lonely, but I also don't have a person. You know what I mean by, a person?"

Seraphina keeps staring, her expression unchanged.

"I don't have anyone I'd like to go through the apocalypse with."

At this, the banshee's eyes grew larger and rounder.

"No, not like… not like you, that's not what I mean. I'm sorry I didn't put that better. I guess what I mean is I would have liked to have someone who, immediately when this started happening, I would want to be with them. Someone to fight with but also for. My person."

"Sister," Seraphina offers.

"Yes," Dahlia says, blowing air out her nose. "You're right, this whole thing was meant to be with Vallesia. But she isn't *my* person. She's Mario's person, and my dad's person, and probably other people's person, too. We barely talk anymore."

"Not too late."

"Isn't it? I think it probably is."

They arrive at a pharmacy, one from an ordinary chain in an ordinary building which is untouched by the previous day's trials. Dahlia steps up to the door and pushes it open. The bell chimes with a cheery tone as they step inside. The store isn't very busy, but there is no cashier or anyone who looks to be working, so buyers are walking down the aisles, inspecting the remedies, picking up a variety without anyone to ask for help, and leaving with their find. Whoever used to run the place must have realized that money is now pointless and that running a business is no way to spend the rest of your limited days. Or maybe they're sick, as well. Some of the shoppers look ill, though not severely. One woman stands out though with glassy eyes, slow and pained movements, and gritted teeth. She brings her hand to her head, wincing.

"Why?" Seraphina asks.

"Why what?"

"Not talk anymore."

"Why me and my sister don't talk much anymore?" she asks.

Seraphina nods.

"Because we disagree."

Dahlia divides her attention as she slips behind the counter and examines the cabinets, pulling out bottles, reading their labels, wincing, then carefully putting them back.

"About?" the banshee asks.

"Gluskab. She adores him, and I don't."

Seraphina makes a face which almost amuses Dahlia.

"Silly," she says.

"Is it silly?" Dahlia asks, then pouts. "Maybe it is silly. But it was a big deal to us. *Is* a big deal."

Seraphina shakes her head, seeming to be in disbelief. "Silly," she repeats.

A hand reaches out and clutches Seraphina's wrist. She leaps back and looks up to find the glassy-eyed woman latched onto her. She lets go of Seraphina as a violent cough bends her forward, and holds her stomach with one hand while covering her mouth with another. What comes out coats her hand in a thick layer of the same tar-like substance that Mario was coughing up. Seraphina takes a step back and continues eyeing the woman, not sure how or whether to interfere.

"Dahlia…"

"No, I guess you're right. Maybe it didn't matter," Dahlia says, head still buried in the bottles. "It's just difficult to fix the past, you know? To mend bruises like that. They don't just go away. There's just a lot of hurt, I guess, on both sides."

"No. Dahlia."

"No?" Dahlia looks up, not expecting what she sees. She drops the bottles and moves toward Seraphina and the woman.

"Don't get any closer to her," she warns.

But Seraphina doesn't listen. She is overcome with empathy, and takes a hesitant step forward. The woman holds up her hand, pleading for the banshee to not get any closer, but Seraphina misunderstands it as a plea for help and presses on. The tar drips from the woman's hand to the white floor.

"Seraphina, I'm serious. Step away from her."

The woman's cough ceases and she falls to the floor with a hollow thud. She isn't moving. Her eyes and mouth are agape, and her face pales.

It's begun.

CHAPTER
20

THE SOLDIERS HAVE ABANDONED THE idea of a civilized graveyard and are throwing bodies into piles on the fields behind the dorms. The heaps look like bonfires, but with arms and legs jutting out instead of sticks. A thick coat of the suspicious tar-like vomit saturates the whole thing and covers the lawn like mud. The soldier's boots sink into the sticky ground as they pass through.

Priests stand by the heaps and pray that the people's reincarnated bodies will decay in a less painful manner. The soldiers shove them out of the way, asking them to help instead.

Vultures circle the piles then fly away, disgusted by the smell.

At 1800 on the dot, every single sick person in the Gluskabian world dies. The ones who are mumbling like madmen, the ones who are rolling around in the contents of their stomachs, the ones who cannot walk, and even the ones with only a minor cough. Their eyes roll back and their bodies go numb, then that's it. Their hearts are still. Death does not discriminate.

At the sleeping halls, a distinct sound like a gust of wind moves through the halls as they all take a collective, final breath. Then, everything is completely quiet. The halls, once buzzing with pain, return to static. Peaceful static. The soldiers stop what they are doing, discouraged and relieved at the same time. They plop to the floor and cry. Their hearts dropping is the second collective sound, a sort of thump.

You must be worried about Mario. I'm afraid there is nothing positive for me to report on that front. I can only say that I wish his death would have been more dignified.

The Chief stays with Mario after the others leave. They are two strangers who know nothing about each other except what Dahlia has told The Chief about her religious sister and brother-in-law. If they had known each other, they would probably have concluded that they had very little in common except for a previously unbothered life with an unbalanced amount of positivity. However, it is a task too grand for either of them to think of any positives in the current situation. For Mario, it is a task too grand to think of anything at the moment, positive or negative, as he is consumed by intense pain.

He is not dying peacefully. He twists and turns in the bed, screaming between mumbles. He alternates between insulting Gluskab and pleading for forgiveness. At one point, The Chief thinks he is suffocating in his own puke, but Mario is not so lucky.

The Chief, despite his disgust, takes pity on his patient. In Vallesia's closet, he finds a bundle of undershirts which he soaks in water from the bathroom down the hall and presses against Mario's forehead. The cold calms him down for only a moment before the undershirts become steaming hot and The Chief has to go soak them again. Acknowledging the losing battle, he instead tries to feed Mario painkillers, shoving them into his mouth, but he quickly throws them back up.

There is not a lot more The Chief can do except sit beside Mario, talk, and try to calm him down.

"I'm not sure what to tell you," he says, then he stops for a long time because he really does not know what to tell him. He considers for a moment singing to him, but his voice has never heard much but insults, so he decides to spare his patient further anguish. *How about a story?* He is the chief in command of a successful radio and TV station, and yet he cannot, for the life of him, think up any stories that might be worth telling this man. He is in the business of fearmongering, mostly.

"I'm sorry that you have to die alone," The Chief finally says. There is not much else after that except his own realization that he will likely die alone as well, and soon. He swallows a few painkillers himself to celebrate the occasion. At least, he thinks, Mario has a wife who will mourn him. Who will mourn The Chief when he dies?

He looks down at his stubby fingers and sigh at their nakedness.

"You know," he starts, hesitating. He takes a deep, ragged breath. "I was never married. There was a girl once. It was not too long ago, actually. A couple of years. She wanted to marry me."

Silence.

"We'd been dating for, dear, I don't know. Four years? We were both getting older, and she wanted kids, a family, and the big wedding—a big dress, hundreds of guests, the whole shebang. I don't know why I didn't want that. Actually, I don't think it was that I *didn't* want it. I guess I didn't want it enough, and I was busy. I've always been so busy."

The Chief glances over at Mario, who says nothing, yet has quieted down. Is he listening?

"You strike me as the kind of guy to take the time to smell the flowers. I looked down on guys like you, you know. I mean, I heard what you do for a living, and—" He stops himself, realizing that fighting a half-unconscious man about his occupation on his deathbed perhaps isn't appropriate. "Anyway. I thought I was right. I thought I didn't have time to settle down. I thought my broadcasting company would be my legacy, that I was giving some big gift to humanity and that it was worth so much more than kids. Than family. I thought that was enough. And then, suddenly, yesterday, it was gone. My company was gone. Just like that."

The Chief sighs and looks up at the ceiling, closes his eyes, and bangs the back of his head softly against the wall.

"The worst part about all this is I feel like nothing matters anymore. Like nothing I've done, ever has mattered. I wonder if I would have felt different if I'd married her. Maybe I wouldn't have. Most likely, nothing matters either way."

He wonders where she is now and tries to remember every detail about her. What did she smell like? What did her laugh sound like? Did she have freckles? What was the color of her eyes? He fails to remember anything of significance about her at all. He tries to imagine her now, in the apocalypse, perhaps overpowered by the weather yesterday—drowned or blown away by a tornado. Or today, sick like Mario, lying on a bed in a strange room next to a strange man. Alone, in pain, and begging for death and vengeance and forgiveness. Knowing that when she dies, so will the memory of her. There will not be enough people left in this world to remember everyone who dies. There may be no one left at all.

Will he remember her? Will she remember him if he dies first?

He wishes he would be terribly sad thinking about her death. He wishes that, when this started, his first thought had been to get in the helicopter and spend the rest of his short life hunting her down. He wishes that they would have found each other and loved each other very much and that they would have died heroically, together—perhaps kissing and holding each other. He wishes he loved her. He wishes he loved anyone like Mario loves his wife.

Mario mumbles Vallesia's name. What name will The Chief mumble?

"What's the point of this?" The Chief asks. "What's the point of any of this?"

Mario heaves and wakes to throw up all over the bed, splattering his caregiver with black tar. The Chief withdraws in disgust. He doesn't even want to touch the gooey-ness to wipe it off. Instead he grumbles, grabs the undershirts, and makes another trip to the bathroom. He grabs paper and tries to rub away the stain with no luck, then dabs his forehead with cold water.

"Did I focus on the wrong things in life?" he asks his reflection with a sigh. "I wonder if everyone regrets how they lived their life when they realize it is almost over. If anyone is ever really satisfied in the end."

But this is his life now, he realizes on the walk back to the room. It is now a dirty apocalypse, a rapidly ticking clock counting down the seconds to an early end. And what does he want? He's always had a goal, to work hard and make enough money to give himself whatever he wanted. That goal is meaningless now.

You can have four goals in an apocalypse: Try to survive as long as possible, for no reason but basic animalistic instinct. Try to die peacefully. Try to stop it. Or live for something bigger.

The last one always intrigued The Chief. It's certainly not what he's been doing with his life so far, but how can he live for something bigger? What's bigger now? In the context of an apocalypse, The Chief decides, that would mean saving others. He can do that, he thinks. Yes, he could be very good at that. New goal sorted, then. Once again, he has a purpose for his existence and it feels good, existentially reassuring.

The Chief drapes the cold undershirts over Mario's face, and wonders how to show him some final kindness.

There was a guest on his show once, an 'expert', whom he invited to discuss his thoughts on death. It had been a mock segment, of course. The man was a supporter of Gluskab, after all. *What did he say?* The Chief rummages around in his brain, remembering snippets of dialogue:

Death isn't an ending, it's a beginning.
The beautiful cycle of existence will keep the life count stable.
Crying over a death is the same as crying when a caterpillar begins its metamorphosis.

Something like that. *What a load of garbage*, he thinks, but that's what Mario must believe. That he will soon become someone or something else. A worm, a daffodil, or a cat. Perhaps an infant which will never have a chance in this new world anyway.

The Chief sits down next to Mario on the bed, carefully avoiding the black puddles. "Which is your favorite animal?" he asks, not expecting a reply, and not getting one. "That's what you will be. If Gluskab loves anyone, He loves you. You will be the most majestic, happiest animal in the whole world."

The pale old military clock, still with its mechanical, monotone ticking slaving away in the old dorm, tics just one time too many. At 1800 on the dot, death embraces every last suffering soul. But Mario is already dead. I was so focused on The Chief, I didn't even notice. The Chief didn't either. Mario passed away quietly, with absolutely no one in the entire world noticing.

The sky does not turn a depressing color and time does not halt for even a second. No one cries or wails or challenges the Dear Creator. The Chief does not shake Mario or call his name or break into tears. Mario's death is met by the universe with not as much as a shrug. It is not Mario's fault; he is loved by many and many would cry at his death, but they are not here. They do not know. Vallesia's heart does not suddenly hurt and beat out of sync, nor does she have sudden images of her husband popping into mind. His family is dead and dying and his friends are too busy.

If anyone were to mourn his passing, they would not have long because Death is not done yet. Death rubs his hands together and smiles a wicked, villainous smile. This is just the appetizer — now for the main course.

CHAPTER
21

THE PHARMACY SCAVENGERS STOP TO look at the collapsed woman, the shop momentarily quiet. Dahlia's eyes fall on another woman, who looks at the scene wide-eyed and shaking then grabs a handful of bottles next to her and bolts out. Within moments, the shop is empty. Seraphina moves closer to the ill woman, inspecting her.

"Don't touch her," Dahlia warns as she reaches out to hold her back.

Seraphina's eyes narrow and her lips tighten as she ignores Dahlia's warning and moves closer to the woman, bending down and feeling for her pulse. There is none.

"I'm serious!" Dahlia says, then leaps forward to grab Seraphina's hand.

"Why?" she asks.

"Why? What do you mean, *why*? Because we don't know what she has, what everyone else has. How do you think it spreads, huh? It's got to spread somehow. Get away from her, now. She's dead. Gone. Let it go."

"Soldiers touch."

"Yes." Dahlia groans, stomping. She feels as if she's arguing with a child. "At the sleeping halls, they touched. I know. But it has to be spreading somehow. People don't just get sick like that. That's not how illnesses work. They don't just appear."

"Maybe."

"Maybe what?"

"Maybe sick appear."

"What, out of nowhere? Just randomly?"

"Yes."

Dahlia groans again. Then it occurs to her that the banshee might be right. If the plague is Gluskab's work, and it clearly is, then why would it need to follow the patterns of normal illnesses? Why couldn't some people just get sick, completely at random, and die, completely at random? If Gluskab wanted to, He could snap his fingers and have everyone fall over dead. Or He could just say a word or think a thought or vibrate at a certain frequency or nothing at all. So why only kill some?

"Listen," she says, shaking her head as if trying to shake off the thought. "Let's just finish up here and go. It's late and the sun will be down in an hour or so."

Seraphina shrugs. She sits next to the woman with her long dress tucked underneath her feet and her tiny, pointed chin resting on her bruised knees. She tilts her head and watches the woman, accepting that there is nothing she can do. A steady stream of black tar drips from the woman's nose into her half-opened mouth, then from there, down her chin. A small pool grows beneath her and soils the clean, white floor. It spreads, threatening Seraphina's now spotted and dirtied dress. She draws back, continuing to watch the woman, deep in thought.

Is this empathy? Seraphina thinks. She sits completely still and quiet, as if meditating, trying to hold on to the feeling, pinpoint it, understand it, and examine it from every angle. Then, hopefully, she can save it within herself on a little shelf so she can bring it out later when she needs it. This empathy, she will treasure deeply. Empathy — what a lovely human capacity.

Five minutes later, at 1805 on the dot, all the dead come back to life.

No, that's not quite right. They're not alive. They don't breathe, they don't think, and they have nothing in common with the people they once were except for their appearance.

No, they are possessed by an evil force which compels them to leave their humanity behind and fills them with a thirst for yet more death.

Their fingers, their toes, and their eyelids twitch as if spasming. They move in sync, as if to the beat of a song, but I doubt my father has that much humor or attention to detail. The twitching intensifies until they are flailing around like fish.

A positive person might be compelled to believe that the corpse in front of them is not a corpse at all, and never was. They might even, if they are the religious or spiritual kind, be inclined to believe this is a miracle. Outside on the fields, with towering mounds of bodies, the soldiers do not witness a miracle. They feel neither excitement nor awe nor a religious awakening. No. They feel only terror.

The hills become buzzing beehives. A low baritone groan is caught by the wind and travels across base like ghost whispers. Tomi has just thrown a girl into one of the piles; she was clutching her teddy bear with stiff fingers, and her icy eyes follow him around like your renaissance paintings.

The soldiers do not run. Why do they not run? They stand still like trees, their feet planted on the ground. I want to grab them by their shoulders and shake them. Especially Tomi, whom I have always had a soft spot for. *Wake up! Run!* They do not run; the conglomeration of feelings is too overwhelming.

The flailing intensifies until the undead gain mobility one by one. They struggle to untangle themselves, then fall or jump or roll down from the hills until they become an army, tripping like babies learning to walk, bumping, and falling over each other like deer on ice.

"Dear Creator," Tomi whispers, but the Creator is not dear. He should know that by now.

The soldiers finally start to run and scream to alert the others, but there are screams at every corner of the base now, a chorus, a consistent underlying track. It is too late. The army of undead outnumbers them by far too many. They leap and jump using all their limbs like animals. They grab hold of the soldiers, hunting them down one by one. Gunfire rings out, teeth are barred, blood sprays from open wounds, and flesh is ripped apart.

Tomi runs from a mound, which rolls and changes shape, charging at him with arms outstretched, grasping for him. They catch his shoes and his pant legs and squeeze his ankles as if they are trying to squish him. They pull at him and the mound becomes a tidal wave of undead, swallowing him whole.

The undead feast, look up at the sky, and howl in victory.

The woman twitches. First her fingertips, then her hands, then her arms. She looks like a robot with misaligned gears— moving a few inches, getting stuck, then moving again. Seraphina notices it first and leaps back, gasping as she lands on her back, scraping her already-abraded elbows against the floor.

"Dahlia," she tries, but her voice is low and soft and not immediate enough for Dahlia to pay her any attention. Her eyes are wide, impossibly wide, almost bulging out.

The woman moves again, this time in spasm. Her arm flails and slaps against the floor. She opens her eyes and looks toward Seraphina with an unseeing gaze.

"Dahlia," Seraphina tries again, this time louder and more immediate. Her voice is shaking. Her eyes are begging her to look away from the monster, but she cannot. Dahlia turns around and sees the woman, as well. She freezes.

The undead woman's arm bends at impossible angles,

which her skin cannot follow. It tears like fabric, opening a wound that ruptures arteries filled to the bursting point with tar-like black blood. It spills all over the floor, then pours from every opening she has; from her ears and nose, from eyes down her cheeks and from her mouth, drooling in a pained expression. The pool underneath her expands to reach Seraphina's feet, and the liquid feels horribly warm between her toes.

"Get up," Dahlia says, her voice cool. "Slowly..."

Seraphina does as she is told, pushing her body up from the floor with meticulous care until she is upright, her eyes still locked on the creature.

"Don't move closer," Dahlia says. "Just stay completely still. And don't ever turn your back to it."

That's something Dahlia learned at boarding school: never, ever turn your back to something you thought was dead. And the woman, she *had* been dead. She definitely had been.

"Okay," Seraphina says as the creature reaches forward, toward her. She doesn't dare to breathe, worried that the vibrations in the air might unsettle the beast and provoke a reaction.

The creature motions become more fluid, more and more confident in its new body. It blinks and focuses on Seraphina. The creature rolls onto its stomach and pushes itself up to all fours, then bares its teeth and moans in pain as they extend into sharp fangs. Bones crackle and tendons tear as its fingers extend and its nails grow to sharp claws. It tilts its head, its eyes almost questioning

What am I doing here? Seraphina imagines it thinking.

It blocks the way to the exit, with Dahlia and Seraphina on either side of it. The air is filled with tension. One wrong move and the creature will leap at either of them. The way it moves is not human. It is hungry, like an animal hunting for prey. But they cannot stand still like this forever. It will leap at them, eventually.

A distraction. That's what they need. Perspiration beads on Dahlia's forehead. Can she throw something? What? She is holding a container of pills in her hand. That might work. Or does that only work in movies? She glances over at Seraphina, who is still holding her breath, her face approaching a light blue undertone.

The creature growls. It starts off low, a sort of purr, but soon it is loud, angry.

Someone enters the pharmacy, a man in mid-run, fleeing from another creature.

The bells chimes with a cheerful tone.

The creature leaps. The man does not have enough time to react. The undead woman is on him in the blink of an eye and tackles him, burying its fangs into his neck with a loud roar.

Blood spills everywhere, spraying from his neck in a way none of them thought blood could spray. It coats the shelves, windows, door, and across the white floor. It sprays across Seraphina as Dahlia pulls her away. The man screams behind them, a deep and horrid sound which rattles even their bones.

Seraphina, surprised to be suddenly jerked, loses her footing and slips in the puddle of fluid below her. As she lets out a faint whimper, the creature turns its head toward her.

It is not hungry for brains or meat, Dahlia realizes. *It is hungry for death.*

It lets go of the man, who squirms by the door in a puddle of his own gore, still screaming in pain. The creature's attention is now on Seraphina as she struggles to stand back up, her bruised legs flailing about. It hisses and repositions itself, half sitting with its palms pressed against the cold floor like a cat or a lioness. It leaps toward her and she is up, running toward Dahlia. Adrenalin pumps as her heart beats so fast she might throw up. Colors dance before her eyes.

A window crashes behind them.

Another creature flings itself into the pharmacy, sending shards of glass everywhere. The sound is deafening. The beast crashes into a shelf, sending it toppling. It rises on uncertain limbs, disoriented, then throws itself at the screaming, dying man by the door.

The first creature grabs hold of Seraphina's dress, pulling

at it, its strength overwhelming the brittle banshee. She tries to pull away, fingers tight around the counter. Dahlia waits in an open doorway leading to a small storage room. The dress tears and Seraphina falls forward. Dahlia catches her and pulls, but the creature curls its claws around the banshee's ankles, dragging her back to the floor. Dahlia presses a foot against the doorway from outside and pulls harder. Seraphina screams as they stretch her. Hot tears stream down her cheeks.

You can't afford too many charities at times like these. Let her go.

Dahlia is not certain she even has a choice to make. Her hands feel slippery. She wishes she would have gone to the gym at any point these last nine years. Outside, a loud siren wails across base, warning everyone that they are under attack, as if they didn't know already.

Seraphina cries out. Blood trickles down her leg under the undead claws, red and black mixing.

A weapon. Dahlia looks around. What kind of weapon is there in a pharmacy?

The second creature stirs. The man has stopped screaming, and it has gotten bored. It leaps toward Seraphina, knocking over shelves on the way, grunting and huffing as its body slams against the floor. Its beats and pounds on the floor as it draws nearer.

There! On the wall! Dahlia finds her weapon. *A fire extinguisher!*

She will have to let go of Seraphina to grab it. She can't do that. They will be all over her in seconds. Yet, they can't stay like this. The second creature is edging closer, and another is coming, knocking over more shelves on the way, sending the displays clattering.

It's the only way.

Dahlia lets go and leaps back inside, her awkward position stealing valuable time. The fire extinguisher is leaning against a wall, not locked away, and that might make all the difference. She grabs it and spins around. Seraphina is fighting, kicking the creature, screaming at it, and not giving up. Dahlia's heart is pounding so hard it might explode. Her hands are shaking. This is no time to drop the fire extinguisher, but it is heavy. Why is she so weak? Panicked screams fill the air. Seraphina tries to scurry away, avoiding fangs and claws, kicking and punching. The second creature is almost upon her.

You can't afford too many charities at times like these. No. Screw that. Dahlia wields the fire extinguisher like a hammer, bashing in the creature's head. It whimpers and retreats. She raises the fire extinguisher again, now painted black with the tainted ichor of the foe. The other creature stops, seems to think, then leaps at her. She holds the fire extinguisher out to block the attack. The creature buries its claws into it, ripping it from her grasp and flinging it away to clatter against the counters.

Dahlia is exposed with no weapon. She raises her hands to her face and waits for her inevitable dismemberment.

The creature leaps at her. Dahlia prepares for death, closing her eyes and holding her breath... Then, against all odds, the creature falls with its head bashed in. Seraphina stands above it, holding the fire extinguisher above her in both hands. Black blood spatter covers her face, arms, and clothing. A wild look covers her face, her eyes almost crazed. She huffs and puffs, standing there, staring down at the beast she just killed.

Dahlia grabs her arm, drags her through the door into the storage room, and closes it behind them. They lean on it, putting their full weight against it, not sure if they're holding it closed or if it is holding them upright. Tears stream down their faces and they breathe quickly, panicked, as if there isn't enough air around them. They grasp for each other's clammy, bloodied hands while the monsters throw themselves at the door, each impacts sending shockwaves through their spines. Finally, the creatures stop and move on, looking for other lives to take.

All is quiet for a moment, then a low groan sends their hearts racing once more.

CHAPTER 22

WHEN MARIO'S FINGERTIPS start twitching, The Chief does not jump to his feet to thank the Dear Creator for bringing him back to life. No, you can say much about The Chief, but he is not stupid. He knows very well that dead people do not come back to life, and he knows very well that the Creator is not one to perform miracles. Not anymore, anyway.

Mario lets out something like a quiet wheeze. He spasms with quick, jerky motions, then falls still.

The Chief moves closer to the door, slowly, wary. "Mario?" he asks. It is worth a try, but the corpse only replies with more wheezing, then a growl. The Chief fumbles with the doorknob.

What used to be Mario opens its eyes. Completely black orbs scan the room as if it is the first they've seen it. As the creature struggles to rise, it reminds The Chief of someone waking up, disoriented, after sleeping off a heavy night of drinking, but it is evil. He can feel the evil oozing from it, tainting the air around them.

"Mario? Look. I need you to say something, or I'm out of here."

It growls.

"That's not—"

It pushes itself upright, tilts its head, and looks at him. Black ichor drips from its mouth as it pants. The blood drains from The Chief's face and a shiver runs down his spine as if someone dropped a bucket of ice down his back.

He fumbles behind him, opens the door, walks outside, and closes it behind him His eyes are wide open and his breathing rapid as he tries to make sense of what just happened. The first thing to do, he reminds himself, is not panic.

He closes his eyes and breathes deep, struggling to remain calm. Something screams within his mind, urging him to flee down the hall, but he stands there, breathing deeply, slowing his panicking heart.

The door shudders against his back as something bangs on it from the other side.

He presses against it with his entire bodyweight, which is thankfully a lot, and realizes he should have been locking the door rather than wasting time breathing.

A woman walks down the hallway toward him. She is the first other person he has stumbled across in the dorm. She is unnervingly attractive, her hips swaying in a way only famous people's hips sway, and her hair cascades down her back. The Chief almost forgets the dead person banging on the door behind him.

Yes, he thinks. *That's the kind of woman I could live to protect.*

The woman comes closer. He smiles at her. She seems wary, but stops in front of him. In her perfect arms, she is carrying strawberries, grapes, and banana slices on a plate. She must be on a break.

What was Mario bangs on the door once again.

"What's that?" she asks in a sugary, cautious voice.

"Oh," he says, trying to sound casual. "That's just my friend. He's alright."

She squints at him.

Mario bangs again, louder.

"Doesn't sound like it," she says.

"No? Well, that's Mario for you. Playing a joke, really."

Somehow, she squints even more.

"Open the door," she says.

"Oh. No, thank you."

She tilts her head. He tries to smile back. She is muscular, her military trousers tight around her legs and her broad shoulders peeking out from a white tank top with no bra underneath. She could easily beat him up or remove him from the door, no doubt about it.

"I'm *telling* you to open the door," she says. Her voice is no longer sugary or cautious, but instead filled with authority.

"I really don't think that'd be a good idea."

More banging.

"Why not?"

"Well..." He is sweating. The door, he feels, is giving up, and so is he. He wants to tell her the truth, but... "Mario wasn't feeling well, then he died. And now I think he's not quite dead anymore."

She rolls her eyes, then takes a step forward and pushes him aside. Despite the rough handling, The Chief is relieved to be unburdened from the responsibility of holding the door closed. She opens it just as a well-timed siren wails across base. Her plate falls to the floor and breaks into a dozen pieces.

The Chief refrains from saying 'I told you so'.

The beast that emerges is not Mario. It is a monster, animal-like, covered in the black tar with wild eyes, claws, and fangs. Mario's usually crazy curls seem even wilder. It slumps down, touching the floor with one of its hands, then lifts its head and howls at the ceiling.

The Chief wastes no time being stunned. He grabs the woman's hand without thinking and runs down the hallway as fast as he can. She soon takes the lead, sprinting much faster than him. Adrenalin rushes through his body, his heart galloping even faster than his feet, which barely meet the floor between paces.

Mario's body is as fast as it is strong. The Chief had pegged him for the type of guy to stay indoors all day, but whatever inhabits his body appears to be a world-class athlete. As they turn a corner, he can hear it scrambling along the walls, digging those wicked claws into them. The Chief glances over his shoulder. The thing is running on all fours, its gait clumsy like it is not used to the body, like it thinks that it is some sort of animal. It forgets that its legs are longer than its arms and trips, falling face first and rolling along the hall before springing back upright with a howl.

With each step they take, it takes two. It trips, falls, and bashes into walls as they turn corners, but it picks itself up and keeps going like it feels no pain. It barely is slowed down, and The Chief and the woman's head start is dwindling.

All around him, he hears flesh tearing, sprays of blood, and screams.

The Chief's heart rises to his throat.

He has not run since he was a little boy, chasing butterflies. The woman, in contrast, is fit and agile — they turn another corner and she leads him up a staircase. She jumps two steps at a time, and his lungs burn and his breath is strained as he struggles to keep up.

They will not make it.

Rather, they will not *both* make it.

The monster reaches out and claws at The Chief's vest.

His hand is slippery in the woman's. Sweat cascades off him, ruining his shirt and pouring down his forehead. It stings his eyes. His legs burn and feel heavy as they cramp up. He cannot run much longer.

Mario's nails slide around his calf. When the woman pulls at him, something in him decides to pull back.

And he pulls back hard.

The woman tumbles back.

He lets go of her hand and keeps running, something exciting bouncing within him. Ecstasy. He will survive. Her screams echo throughout the hallways, reverberating off the walls and creeping underneath his skin. When he reaches the top of the staircase, he looks back toward her. It is a mistake that he instantly regrets.

So much for living for something bigger.

CHAPTER
23

DAHLIA AND SERAPHINA'S pounding hearts remind them they're still alive as they lean against the door leading from the small storage room to the pharmacy. There's another groan, louder this time, seeming much closer, from somewhere within the storage room.

"Is that..." Seraphina whispers and scoots even closer to Dahlia. The black stains on her face make her look like a vicious warrior, but when she lowers her head, slides down to a squat, and pulls her knees up, her wide, round eyes and trembling lip make her look like a child.

"I think so," Dahlia answers, whispering as well.

Perhaps it hasn't heard them. Perhaps if they just sit very, very still, it won't hear them.

They can hear it banging against something now, a shelf. Some pills fall to the floor in the distance, clattering.

Footsteps.

Louder.

A deep groan.

"Dahlia…" Seraphina whispers, her tiny, bird-like voice soaked with fear.

Another plan, then. Dahlia didn't get away from the other creatures just to fall to another one.

She needs a weapon. Seraphina dropped the fire extinguisher on the other side of the door. It is not worth the possibility, however small, of releasing two additional creatures to get to it. She cannot see any other blunt objects in the back room, just shelves upon shelves of medicine.

An escape, then. It does not take her long to locate the exit with a large red sign glowing with the word 'exit' in bold above it. But what is on the other side? Even more danger? She would rather they locked themselves in the back room for the night and gear up later. Or will it be easier to get to the dorm room tonight in the midst of all the confusion, rather than tomorrow, when there's less prey to distract the monsters?

Footsteps.

Louder.

A deep groan.

"Dahlia," Seraphina says, still in a whisper, but a more commanding one.

There are loud sniffing sounds, like a pig on the hunt for truffles. A bony hand emerges, curling its deathly white fingers around a shelf. A head peeks out and they realize it belongs to the pharmacist who had so conveniently gone missing before. He has thinning gray hair, glasses, and patchy stubble. He presents a bony figure, almost like a skeleton, wearing a sleek, white buttoned-up shirt with dark stains all over and sporting a name tag that reads 'Stan'. He must have died in the storage room soundlessly and bothering no one.

Dahlia shoots up, her heart still beating fast, and Seraphina follows. This only alerts the monster, and what was once called Stan sees them and charges at them. The fragile thing before them does not look threatening, but when it leaps and almost flies toward them, they jump back. It sinks to the floor and hunches over, slouching its arms close to the floor and spreading its legs like a gorilla.

They do not notice this; they are too busy running. Dahlia tries to knock over a shelf, but it is bolted to the concrete floor. The monster hurtles toward them, throwing its body forward, then turns and crashes into a shelf. All the pills come rushing down, clattering against each other, scattering all over the floor.

When it stands up, Seraphina and Dahlia almost by the exit. Its arms and legs are bent, a bone is sticking out, and the tar is rushing out from several openings. It pants and huffs, then it jumps again. It smashes against the exit door, slamming it shut as they reach for the handle.

It bares its teeth at them and grunts again. Its breath smells rotten.

Without hesitating, Seraphina punches the monster square in the face. Its nose crumples with a loud crack and black ooze sprays across its face. The monster lets go of the door and stumbles in confusion, not because of pain but because of surprise. The little banshee, looking innocent in a white, ripped, and stained dress with big, bright eyes didn't seem like a threat. Even Dahlia stops for a second to register what happened. Then, Seraphina pulls her through the exit with her.

They emerge into an alleyway. From here, they watch the scene playing out in front of them in absolute horror. Packs of corpses dart down the streets, hunting for flesh and sparing no one. They are hungry—screaming, grunting, and roaring like a parade of savage animals gone awry, leaving behind a trail of destruction.

They overturn trucks, rip mailboxes from the ground and throw them like spears, and mount trees to rip off branches. They break into houses and apartments, smashing windows and dragging residents out for a feast. They spread the insides of their victims across the pavement, painting the roads red.

Gunshots echo in the distance. The military moves shoulder to shoulder, maintaining safety in numbers. Yet, the parade of undead continues undisturbed.

They press their bodies against the door and Seraphina

silently prays for them both. It is half-dark in the alley and they make a point of not moving, not even an inch. Maybe they can just hide here?

"What now?" Seraphina whispers, her lips barely moving as she speaks.

It is only a matter of time before they are noticed, so where should they go? Climb to the roof? But if they can, so can the undead. They might be noticed, and then what? Maybe they should hide inside the trash bins. But if they loot them next, what chances do they have? What if they can smell them? There is only one place on the entire base Dahlia can think would be safe enough, and it is just across the street. But the street is a battlefield, that they cannot possibly cross. The only way across is directly through.

"I don't know," Dahlia whispers back, her lips moving even less.

They hear gunfire again, this time much closer. The wall of soldiers, fully armed in their uniforms and with rifles, push in unison, attempting to overwhelm the swarm. They try to be as merciless as the creatures, firing round after round without even aiming. The bullets open up the creatures like leaking water balloons with tar-like black blood gushing from every hole, but this only slows them down. The creatures jump the soldiers in response, bury their sharp teeth in their necks, and rip out their vocal cords. They look like bloody fountains or bloody sprinklers.

This is their only chance. Now or never. They can sneak behind the soldiers while the creatures are distracted. Dahlia grabs Seraphina's hand and drags her forward. The banshee does not protest, though perhaps she should.

It's a sea of hostility. The soldiers think Dahlia and Seraphina are monsters attacking from the side. One turns and is about to fire at them, but a monster leaps at him. His rifle points upwards, the shot aimed at the sky, and blood sprays everywhere. The monsters know they are not monsters; everyone is their enemy.

The stream moves upward while the two try to move straight, but they are being pushed from all sides as the monsters and the soldiers press into each other in a bloody melee. They experience life in flashes, a sort of unconnected chaos — crouching down, pushing through, fitting in. They dodge and swerve, then drop with their palms on the rough asphalt, small stones cutting into them.

A soldier is impaled, his blood sputtering on them. The dark red face of an undead, jaw unhinged, lunges at them, misses, and continues on its rampage. Crazy eyes glare from every angle, and something grabs Dahlia's shoe. She kicks it off, just as a sudden white flash blinds her. Heavy panting fills her ears. Someone's shoulder dislocates near them with a loud pop.

A bullet swishes by. Seraphina touches her cheek, feeling for blood. It felt as if the bullet went right through her brain, but it only clipped her hair.

Ringing. The world is ringing — a constant tone. Everything around them is black, red, and grimy, like a noir film.

Dahlia stumbles over a pan, picks it up, and slams it into a nearby face. Her target stares back at her with wild curls framing wild eyes. It tilts its head and screams until the veins on its forehead pop. It's face turns bright red.

Mario?

It's gone.

The cacophony returns. Dahlia wishes it hadn't. Howls, roars, screams, and crying fill her ears., A little girl with long braids emerges from the press of bodies for a moment, then is consumed by it. The undead dance around the bodies of the recently dead which litter the streets. The smell of fire, suddenly strong, fills the air. Ashes sting in their eyes.

Somewhere far off is a light, perhaps an exit from the mass of flailing bodies. They crawl toward it, dirt under their fingers, scratches covering their arms and legs, and the rocks piercing their soft palms. Keep climbing, keep struggling, keep getting back up. .

Grass is between their fingers. They are mostly sure they

are not dead.

Ahead of them is a memorial. On top of a rocky hill, a huge tank is on display. Our tank. The one I showed the girls when they were young. My visions connect. This is exactly what I saw then. Death and destruction. A wave of tar-like black blood.

Dahlia hopes she can still remember the combination. It's been so many years.

No time to waste—they scale the rocky hill, almost stumbling on the loose rocks, then scramble on all fours like the beasts beneath them: animalistic and fighting on pure instinct.

Dahlia climbs atop the tank and locates the padlock.

She doesn't remember the combination! Sweat beads on her forehead and tears gather in her eyes. To get so close, only to fall short on memory.

She struggles to think in the cacophony. They used to get drunk down here, her and her friends, with their stolen booze. That was so long ago. She tried so hard to forget everything from that life.

"Hurry!" Seraphina yells, panic filling her voice. She is in front of the tank, pan in hand, ready to fight whoever or whatever comes near. It doesn't take long before she spots an incoming monster, creeping up, clawing at the base of the hill. Its head tilts from side to side bearing a murderous grin. It wheezes.

Dahlia finally tries a combination, but the padlock doesn't unlock. She screams in frustration, then tries to kick it with her remaining shoe, but only hurts herself.

I don't think I remember the combination either.

Sweat dripping from her brow, Dahlia's damp hands struggle to spin the small numbers. She muffles a scream.

Seraphina swings the pan at the creature. It slams into the things face, jerking it back with a spray of black blood, but it turns its wicked grin back to her as if it felt nothing. She swings again, screaming and baring her teeth, mustering all her strength. She strikes its leg with a loud crunch of shattering bone and it falls, tumbling down the hill. It lie still for a moment, then with jerking, spasmodic movements, gets up again. It resumes its climb up the hill unfazed.

Concentrate, Dahlia. Don't look back, I urge her.

She looks back and her breathing quickens.

Concentrate! Concentrate, Dahlia! I want to scream at her, but I can't interfere, not even now.

She kneels lower and closes her eyes, then takes one deep breath. She pretends nothing else is happening—forgets about the fight, forgets about the monsters, forgets that she might die at any moment, and that Seraphina might die. That her sister might be dead. And The Chief. That Mario is definitely already dead.

Concentrate.

She takes another deep breath.

It took us five months to crack it the combination lock, trying one hundred combinations a week.

Oh, I know! I know the combination. Interference be damned. I yell the combination to her, but she doesn't hear me.

The sounds of battle intensify behind her. The pan whistles through the air and bones break, hopefully the monster's. Seraphina yells, but Dahlia does not look.

"Don't look," I yell, not sure if she can hear me. "Concentrate. Good. Listen to me."

She will save the banshee by cracking the tank open, and herself. The pan goes flying down the hill, then it is hard to decipher who is winning.

I yell the number again.

She jumps as if electrocuted, then looks around. I think she's looking for me. Then she turns back to the padlock and resumes spinning the little numbers.

The top swings open and she wants to cry with happiness. Behind her, Seraphina kicks and punches and the monster falls down the hill again. There are more coming. They have taken notice. The soldiers have fallen back, and less and less khaki is visible in the stream.

Dahlia and Seraphina are next. They are interesting and full of life. Tasty. Drool falls from the monsters lips as they smack them and imagine the taste of young life being drained, their stomachs never full.

"Get in!" Dahlia screams at the top of her lungs. Her voice is hoarse and tired.

She does not have to tell Seraphina twice, who leaps for the tank, the swarm running behind her. She approaches with them on her heels, climbs with them just behind her, then plunges into the engulfing darkness.

Dahlia pulls the hatch closed above them and latches it. Inside the tank, they are finally safe. But they do not feel peaceful. The sounds of the monsters scratching at the metal echo through the old vehicle. Adrenaline, excitement, and shock keep them rattled. Both their bodies are vibrating with a chaotic flurry of emotions. Their breathing is heavy and labored. Dahlia feels claustrophobic in her own body and wants to claw off her own skin, and then she leans forward and finds Seraphina's face in the deep darkness.

Seraphina kisses her.

People act. She wants to be people, so she acts, and now she is people.

Their kisses are hard and aggressive. Passion drives their lips into one another. The closer they get, the hotter that passion burns. Their hands wander, caressing and holding at first, then grabbing, their fingers buried deep into one another's flesh. The dark interior of the tank seems to light up with every kiss, like flint sparking a fire alight.

On the roof, The Chief is throwing up, it seems, everything he has eaten for at least the last decade. It pours out of him like a stream and does not stop. He falls on his knees and lets his expensive cashmere trousers get soaked, then continues to let his puke mix with his tears.

The creature bangs on the door, which The Chief has safely sealed behind him. It makes a horrible sound, a hollow clang of metal as a skull cracks against it. But the door holds. The door holds.

So much for living for something bigger.

What a failure he is.

Still shaking and wailing like a child, but now unable to throw anything but air up, he staggers toward the edge of the roof.

It is the day where words have finally become meaningless. After this, humans will stop talking. They will revert to grunting, because they will realize that when words are really needed, they will always fall short.

There is nothing to say.

CHAPTER 24

THE **TORTURERS FINALLY LEAVE** Vallesia alone to bleed to death in the bare room, and hours pass. She does not know how long she has been lying on the floor, still tied to the chair, whimpering and shivering. It may have been minutes, hours, or even days. It feels like days to her. She also does not know if they will return. Or, rather, if they will return before or after she dies. She decides the latter would be preferable, although she feels she has endured such pain that she may be numb to whatever torture they have planned next, however creative they get.

Maybe I can take away a little of her pain? Would that be okay? Would anyone notice?

I approach her.

Could it be, she thinks, that she really deserves this? She shuffles around on the floor, grunting, trying to pull her hands from the ropes gnawing into her wrists, but knows it's impossible. This knot, no one can break out of. They have the same training as her.

I lay a hand on her, trying to ease the pain, but there is too much. I don't think I even make a difference. She squirms. Soon, she will bleed out. I'm not qualified to help.

She wants to be with Mario. She wants to be at home, under the covers, in their bed. She wants him to hold her tight, the way he always does, as if he is afraid of her leaving. She wants to hear his voice, his stupid voice and his stupid laugh—his stupid him, that she loves wholly. She wants to watch cartoons with the duvet on the sofa and drink too sweet tea, then complain about who has to do the dishes. She just wants to be anywhere but here.

She cannot bear being alone with her thoughts on this cold, dirty floor and then her prayers are heard.

Oh dear. Oh no.

The door unlocks with a hollow click and opens with a loud creak. A ray of light enters the room from the hallway outside and her blood turns to ice. *Them again,* she thinks. But no, it is not them again. This is something else. Someone else. She lays still, like an animal pretending to be dead, and awaits the cruel footsteps she is sure will soon approach her. However, no one enters.

She counts her breaths, listens for just the smallest sound: shoes on the floor, exhaled breath, fabric brushing against skin. But there are no sounds. They have not snuck in. They are not here. She fears that when she moves, they will appear above her and drag her out of the cell. That they will pour water over her again, or draw more blood with their wicked blades. She thinks they are soundless demons, so she lies frozen in terror.

Time moves. She counts her breaths and the seconds. Then, something brushes against her hands and her feet. It is them, surely, but no, the motions are gentle and loving. The rope falls off, untied in a single second. Yet, there are no sounds, no sign of anyone else in the room with her.

She looks around but sees nothing. Finally, she turns around and pushes herself up with her palms pressed into a pool of mixed bodily fluids. She watches the door and waits. Nothing?

Who unlocked the door? Who untied her?

You're free! Oh no, just kidding. She can hear their laughs so clearly that she briefly believes they are real.

Her muscles cry when she moves. The joke has gone on for too long. She will show them. She will get up, right now, and they will see. She'll kick them and punch them and they will be in pain and then, then they can do whatever they want with her again. As long as they suffer as well.

No, little dear one, I urge. *Stay there. Don't get up.*

But she doesn't listen.

She gets up with pained, slow effort. Her legs wobble and she falls, then hauls herself back up. She stumbles toward the chair, picks it up, and hurls it to the floor. It clatters and she groans. She picks it back up and hurls it again. This time, it falls apart. She picks up one of the legs and hefts it like a club. They will hear her now, surely, and they will come charging in.

No one comes charging in.

No one hears her.

She stumbles toward the door, chair leg raised high like a bat, ready to bash whoever she imagines is hiding behind the door, but there is no one. She opens the door all the way and jumps out, only to find the hallway abandoned.

Her bare feet leave a trail of blood behind her as she continues down the hallway, suspicious and careful, her weapon still raised high. Her breathing is troubled, her lungs aflame with every breath. The hallway curves. It appears endless. She is not sure this is real. It feels like one of those dreams where you keep walking but make no progress. Is she dreaming? Is she even alive?

She picks up the pace. There is no one here. She turns a corner to the left, then down the hall and turns right, then left. She slips into a trance, a military march, but from time to time, she falls down on the floor or into the walls. Everything looks as if in a deep fog, her vision blurry. She drags her weapon behind her, almost letting it go a few times. Her eyelids feel heavy. Her legs feel heavy. Her whole body feels heavy.

She turns another corner, gasps, and almost walks back from where she came. In front of her is a body. There is no blood, just a contorted body with its arms and legs bent in impossible angles and its neck snapped. Is it one of her torturers? She squints and tries to look at his face. Maybe. It does not seem real to her. She needs to keep moving.

The hallways are filled with bodies, all contorted and with snapped necks. There is still no blood. One of them she recognizes as the shorter torturer. Who has done this? She bends down to feel for a pulse, and finds none. He's still warm. Her breath grows more troubled, then she tries to run, bumping into every wall as she does so.

She is amazed to make it to the front entrance without running into whoever has slaughtered an entire wing of professional Peacers. The door is open and outside the moon bathes her in its white light. A breeze envelops her and she falls to her knees. The trees rattle in the wind, seeming to laugh with their branches. *What now?* They ask her. She does not know. There is a dusty road leading into the forest surrounding the Peacer headquarters, but where should she go? She is sure she would die from blood loss before getting very far. *What now? What now?*

I would take her, but He is watching. I need to stay hidden and wait for a better time. I am no match against Him.

Here He is.

A hand rests on her shoulder. She flinches, then gives in. It is her own fault, she thinks. She should have kept running when she had the chance, and now the crazy neck snapping maniac will kill her as well.

"Dear Creator," she prays into the cold night, folding her hands. "Don't let what they told me be true. Let everyone be okay. Let Dahlia be okay. And please, I beg you, let Mario be okay. Thank you."

When she is done, she breathes out and tells herself that she is prepared. But her neck is not snapped. A familiar voice fills her ears.

"Vallesia?"

Her eyes flood with tears as she turns around to see who she thinks is Mister Crado with his silver-gray hair and crumbled skin. Overjoyed, she leaps into His arms.

"I thought you died," she says. "They all said — what happened to you?"

Before He has time to answer, her eyelids grow heavy, and then her body is drained of energy. Her mind wills her to fight, but she has no fight left. She falls asleep in the god's arms.

DAY 3

The shadows stretch themselves long and wave their thin arms.

CHAPTER 25

IT IS ANOTHER DAY IN the Gluskabian world. The sun rises at dawn like it always has and the light uncovers the many dead bodies draped across the landscape. Trees try to rattle their leaves for morning stretches, but vandals have chewed their arms off in the night. Houses want to greet their owners with creaks, but their mothers lie cuddled up next to their intestines on the road outside and do not hear them. Mailboxes await the daily mail. The cars have checked that their gas tanks are full and have prepared an upbeat playlist for the daily commute.

It is silent yet again. Last night, at midnight precisely, all the risen dead once again died and collapsed to the ground. The military was defeated by then, and the monsters were free to roam the streets, screaming, jumping off benches, and bumping into each other. They growled at each gust of wind, sniffed for humans, and howled at the moon. They ran and climbed and scurried along walls. Then, suddenly, mid-action, they stopped as if caught in a spell and fell to the ground where they stood.

Only a few dozen survivors were around to witness this. A well-dressed man covered in his own puke could not sleep for the noise and saw everything from a rooftop. A banshee and a young woman only notice it the morning when they dare to sneak a peek from within a tank.

Dahlia jumps out first, landing in a pool of sticky tar where green grass should have been. It is humid, moist, and the warmth only worsens the smell of decomposing bodies. The smell is so foul that she must cover her mouth with her sleeve. The picture in front of her is also foul, and she wants to cover her eyes, but cannot make herself do it.

The bodies lay scattered on the streets, piled on top of each other, and only a few are still intact. Mostly, it's just limbs. A head here. A leg there. An arm with no home. The entire scene is a myriad of red and dark hues, deep maroon and inky black.

As though the world does not know that it has broken, birds are chirping.

Dahlia limps down the hill, partly because her knee was bruised in last night's fight and partly because she's lost one shoe. The lost shoe should be in the streets somewhere. Her socks are soaked through with the tar, which has somehow not solidified yet.

At the edge of the hill, she pauses and takes a deep breath. She can barely see the streets for all the bodies. Few made it up the hill. The real battle was fought here. She has to commend the soldiers; her only priority was to run and hide and survive. They stood their ground and fought the monsters, who so easily got up after eating their bullets. She's sure, if she had been in their shoes, that she would have taken one look and run the other way.

Dahlia steps onto the street, tiptoeing between bodies and pools of tar, forcing herself to look down. She covers her mouth and nose with her hand to lessen the smell, but she's unsuccessful and retches more than once. It is so quiet. She worries.

Finally, she locates her shoe. The tip peeks out from under a uniformed soldier, lying on his chest with brown, greasy hair covering his face. Her heart skips a beat as she kneels, holding her breath.

"Tomi?" she whispers, her lips barely moving.

No one answers.

She takes a deep breath, forgetting about the horrible smell, and retches again. Then she reaches down to move the soldier's hair aside. It's not him. She sighs with relief.

She wouldn't even recognize Tomi if she found him. I saw what happened to him. His face is completely gone. His own mother wouldn't recognize him.

Dahlia wiggles her lost shoe out from under the soldier and is relieved to see it is almost clean, protected by his body. She carries it back toward the hill, where she climbs the tank and sits down to put it back on.

Seraphina climbs out and sits next to Dahlia, looking down at her hands rather than out at the scene. Dahlia finishes tying her shoelaces and sighs again, looking up at the sky.

"Enough," Seraphina declares, her little voice filled to the brim with determination.

"What's enough?" Dahlia asks in a monotone voice.

"Everything."

Dahlia nods. She understands. I understand, too.

"I'm going to punch Him in the face," Dahlia says, equally determined and confident. She jumps down from the tank and looks back to Seraphina, then extends a hand to her.

"Him?"

"*Him.*"

"You can't. He god."

"Watch me."

Seraphina looks with uncertainty at Dahlia's hand and bites her lip.

"Don't you want to punch him in the face as well?" Dahlia asks.

Dahlia expects her to agree—who wouldn't? Who could have seen this level of genocide and not condemn the perpetrator? At the very least, if Seraphina still is not convinced that

He is behind it, He still allowed it to happen. But Seraphina looks down at her own hands, inspecting them, clenching and unclenching them. She imagines punching her Dear Creator in the face.

"Want answers," Seraphina decides with a deep inhale.

Dahlia cannot believe what she's hearing. "You want answers?" She retracts her hand and narrows her eyes, her voice suddenly not as monotone anymore. "What could He possibly answer that would make any of this remotely okay?"

She shrugs. "Don't know Him."

"Yeah. I don't think you do."

Seraphina glares back. That's not what she meant. But Dahlia might be right. Seraphina never imagined Him leaving, and He did. She never imagined being forced out of her home, and she was. She certainly never imagined Him allowing anything like this, yet here she sits on the side of a tank amidst a sea of blood.

Seraphina jumps down, her head held high, and swaggers down the hill.

"Where are you going?" Dahlia demands, catching up to her.

"Answers."

"You are going to get answers?"

"Yes."

Dahlia shakes her head in disbelief.

Seraphina stops and looks back at her with a tender look, the sun highlighting her face. The light glows on her soft curves, silky skin, and pale pink lips.

Dahlia's eyes grow wide. *Last night... What happened last night?* Adrenaline and fear overwhelmed her in the darkness of the tank, and relief, and it had been just that — surely — and yet...

Seraphina reaches out and takes Dahlia's hand, cupping it in her own. Dahlia's heart flutters. She doesn't remember feeling this way before: weak, cheeks burning. Yet, she thinks Seraphina is ridiculous. She supports a god who does not deserve anyone's support. She infuriates Dahlia, and yet, her hand feels safe in the banshee's palm. Last night must have been a dream, but why would she dream of such things? And why can't her heart seem to settle?

There was another dream. Another dream with another tank. A magical tank which grew and grew to the size of a house, and someone else holding her hand, but surely — surely that one must have been only a dream. Had her father ever held her hand?

Seraphina gives her hand a squeeze and Dahlia is brought back. She puts her brave face on and they swagger down the road, zigzagging to avoid stepping on bodies.

They devise a plan. There will be a large element of luck involved and, as such, it is not a good plan — but it is the only plan they have.

First on the agenda is to gather troops. Every military needs an army, but the real army has perished in their brave yet senseless efforts, so they must improvise. The helicopter is a must, and someone who can fly it. They have no hopes of Mario being alive and few for The Chief. They *know* this, yet… have you ever explained something terribly important to a child? That you are going to move, for example. That their worst fear, which they don't yet know is their worst fear, is soon to be realized? It is not that they don't believe you. They simply don't have the frame of reference to process it.

This is how Dahlia and Seraphina feel.

Their friends could be alive, so which other way is there to go but toward the dormitories, toward Vallesia's old room? They feel stuck in a game where the walls are narrowing in on them, pushing them in one direction, and not allowing them any side quests or opening up for any other options. There is one plan which makes sense and there is one way to carry out this plan. If Gluskab somehow has meant for them to follow this road for some cruel, sadistic reason, then so be it. What else are they to do?

The roads are exactly as you imagine them: filled with

corpses and puddles of blood wherever they go. Even the quiet alleyways are scarred. I am in no mood to describe it — I am sure, with what terrible wars your world has hosted, you must understand. Those war pictures I've seen... The bombings. I assume it would be fine if you imagined something like that.

On their way, they bump into only a handful of other survivors. They stop each of them and ask if they would like to join in their efforts, to probe the Creator for answers or, possibly, punch Him. It's not important which, what's important is that it's a plan of action. Some follow: a teenaged girl filled to the brim with defiance the way only a teenage girl can be filled, a young priest in his robe, a mother who tells them, again and again as if it is a mantra, that she watched her four-year-old eat his father's face last night. Her hair is wild and so are her eyes.

They do not ask hard questions. How did everyone survive? What must they have done to do so? Did the mother sacrifice her husband? Did she not protest when he offered to sacrifice himself? Did the priest hide somewhere instead of trying to save his flock? Does he still pray? Does he want part in Seraphina or Dahlia's plan? How about the teenage girl—the exaggerated defiance, crossed arms, jutting chin, and squinting eyes; all daring someone to challenge her. What is there to be challenged? Wasn't it just luck that Dahlia did not sacrifice Seraphina? Didn't Seraphina, for only a split second, think the same?

None of these people came to the base alone.

They say little to each other. They are ashamed. Pointing out someone else's flaws will only reveal their own. They haven't even told each other their names. There's safety in anonymity.

"You cannot fight the Creator," a voice of reason tells them. It is an old man who has survived against all odds. His presence is a mystery. Left are only the strong, the young, and the selfish. Those who put their own needs above others. If humanity outlives the apocalypse, what will we be left with?

"To Him, you are ants," the old man continues, his voice raspy. His eyes are made of steel. "You cannot overthrow a god more than an ant can trip you over."

"But a horde of ants might do some harm," Dahlia counters, refusing reason as it stands on her threshold.

He shakes his head and sighs. "You are not a horde," he says, then turns around. He continues down the road, his old hips swaying as he supports his body with a stick. I wonder where he is off to. How will an old, lonely man spend his last few hours? And in a massacred ruin, nonetheless.

They are not disheartened. Their parade continues, but they find no other survivors. They soon reach the dormitory and try to open the door, but it is locked and Dahlia did not check the code Mario put in yesterday. Instead, they move around the building, toward Vallesia's room. It is easy to tell which one it is through the windows. The minimalist one. White, clean, and stocked only with essential items.

Except that today, the room looks different. The bed is covered in the black, tar-like matter and the sheets are all tussled up. A trash bin near the bed has goo coming down the sides. The calendar has been ripped down, as well as the cliché inspirational quote. The door is scratched, black and red, and hanging off its hinges. Most notably, the room is empty.

No Mario. No Chief.

The thumping sound is not the sound of their hearts dropping. This is not something they have not seen coming. They accepted the facts of this new, terrifying world. Instead, the thumping sound is coming from above. The roof, maybe.

"Chief?" Dahlia yells out, surprised by the sound of her own voice. Everything is so quiet here, like early in the morning, before everyone wakes up.

They crane their necks to look up at the roof.

Yes! A shy head pops out from above. The Chief. But not like she has ever seen him before. It is a cliché, but it is the truth; he looks aged. Is it possible to grow wrinkles overnight?

Dahlia, especially, can barely contain her excitement. She even dares a small smile. It is not until now that she realizes how much she has wanted him to be alive, and not only for him to fly the helicopter. She allows herself a brief moment of positivity, then packs it away in the back of her mind. This is no time for hope. She will only be disappointed.

The Chief does not smile, nor does he make a sound. After a while, his head disappears. This is followed by a clanging sound, a door opening, and retching. Then sobbing, the door closing. After a very long time, so long, in fact, that the group has started questioning whether he is coming down at all, he emerges with infinite slowness, like a turtle. His eyes are puffed up as if he's been stung by bees, and he doesn't look at anyone's faces. His soul quivers. He gulps. He pushes rocks aside with his bloodied shoes and awaits orders.

The shame pours out from him. It becomes a physical, tangible thing, like a big, round ball creeping up behind him, threatening to roll over him. It reminds the group of their own shame, and suddenly they are surrounded by big, round balls creeping up behind them.

Dahlia is happy that she packed away the positivity before it could be ripped away from her. Better to be realistic, then. This way, there is still hope that she might find the box later and unpack it when the time is right.

"What's this," The Chief asks with no intonation. He's barely got a voice at all and he's still looking down at the ground. "You picked up the kids on the way."

Dahlia looks perplexed. She's taken to looking down at the ground as well. "We've found an angry mob."

"Where are the pitchforks."

"We don't have any. Torches, either. Or gasoline, or banners."

"What a shitty mob."

"Yeah."

"But angry."

"Very."

They are not soldiers. They have no kick or bravery or fighting spirit, and yet they are the ones who have survived — the cleverest, the fastest, and the strongest? No, they are simply the lucky ones, or maybe the unlucky ones, depending how you view it. Chance is the only thing humanity has left now.

CHAPTER 26

THE SUN MOVING ACROSS THE sky is like a ticking time bomb. When it reaches a point, and who knows what point that will be, time will be up and— well, I don't know what my father has planned for today, but I can only assume total annihilation.

I remember the plaque, the one I wrote and hung above the shed because my father kept screaming the words from his cell. It said that today, the shadows will grow fangs. I don't know what that means. As I stand in the sun, in the middle of the charred field by the helicopter, I look down at my shadow.

Is it going to attack me? Is it going to leap at me? How am I going to run away from that?

When Dahlia's group enters the field, they are relieved to see the helicopter unscathed.

"Thank the—" the priest starts but does not finish. He bites his tongue, as if punishing it.

The group gathers by the helicopter to plan their next move, eating dried nuts and protein bars, a light breakfast from one of

The Chief's bug out bags. They are completely different people now. The ravaged fields which shocked them yesterday look like child's play after what they've witnessed since. When did they weep about burned crops? How silly that was. How pure and naïve they were.

I stare at their shadows, squinting, waiting to see them move of their own accord. Perhaps a jerk of an arm, or a shift of a leg.

Could the shadows be sentient already? When are they going to strike?

I must sound like a crazy person.

"So, where are we going?" the teenager asks, finally defying the awkward, shameful silence. "To the Forest of Magnificent Trees, I guess?"

"No," the priest says, raising his brows and taking a step back. "Of course not. We'd get slaughtered. You can't enter the forest."

"Right, but we were going to go find Gluskab, right? He's in the forest."

The priest is about to protest again when Dahlia cuts them both off.

"We're not going to the forest," she says. "You're right. We'd be slaughtered."

"Where *are* we going?" the mother asks.

Dahlia takes a deep breath and clenches her fists. "To my father's."

"Wait, what?" the teenager asks. "You said we were going to go punch Gluskab, not go on some family reunion tour. I wanna punch Gluskab."

"I'd like to check on my niece," the priest says. "Could we check on my niece after?"

Dahlia sighs and rolls her eyes. "Look, I don't *want* to go see my father. I'm telling you, I really, really don't. In fact, I'd almost rather take my chances getting fried by lightning in the forest than go see him. I'm not even sure if I'm more upset at my dad or Gluskab at this point, to be honest. I don't know how to convey to you guys how much I absolutely don't want to go, but my dad's an apocalypse prepper, and a pretty hardcore one at that. If anyone has found a way into the forest, it's him. He's our best bet."

Dahlia feels Seraphina's worried eyes on her. Her palms sting from the nails digging into them.

"I think that sounds like a really great idea," The Chief finally says as he places a hand on her shoulder. Her fists loosen. "But we still didn't find Vallesia. Do you reckon he'd be okay with us showing up without her?"

Dahlia has thought of that. There's a very good chance he won't let them in without Vallesia. He's not below leaving his daughter outside and vulnerable to attacks. After all, he left her outside that one night when she was just sixteen, hungry and shivering in the rain.

If only Vallesia were here, she could vouch for them. He would never deny her anything—not that I can blame him—his sweet little princess who he still, to this day, believes is a dedicated spy for the 'anti-Gluskabian organization'. How many times has Dahlia dreamed of exposing her, to let him know that Vallesia isn't playing the military, she's playing *him*? Maybe then she could finally convince her father that *she* is the one who hates Gluskab, that *she* is the one who is making real change and stirring up a real resistance at her anti-Gluskabian network? But Dahlia has never convinced him of anything, and this is unlikely to be the first time.

"We should probably try to sneak in," she says.

"Wait," the teenager says. "He might not even let us in? What?"

"We should find somewhere safe instead," the mother says. "If he might not even let us in, then... could we go somewhere else? What if... What if there's... more..."

"We have to take that risk," Dahlia says. "Look, you don't have to come with. I get it. But we can't just hide somewhere safe for the rest of our lives. Gluskab is going to find us. You can't hide from Him. My dad's really our only hope. I would take any other way if there was one. Do you have an idea?"

After a short silence, the mother shakes her head. But she's right. If Dahlia's father won't let them in, where will they go? Will there be any time left to go somewhere else?

"Is he — is he really that bad?" the priest asks.

Dahlia nods and sucks air in between gritted teeth. "I wish there were another way."

The Chief slides into the cockpit, leaving little room for Dahlia with her instructions. The others follow in the back. The door slides shut, and The Chief begins turning on switches and pressing buttons. One hand on the cyclic and another on the collective. The helicopter makes a sound, then the rotor blades start spinning, the monstrosity lifts from the ground, and they are off.

The helicopter gracefully floats across the landscape, the propellers deafeningly loud. They put on their headsets, though none of them talk to each other. Instead, they look down at the landscape below, completely changed and foreign to them.

They fly across small towns with red brick houses and cute little button chimneys blown away by the Big Bad Wolf. Past market squares filled with red pools. Across open fields, burned down or filled with craters. Livestock litters this part of the landscape, still and abandoned to their own horrors. They fly by a sea where they have never seen a sea, debris floating quietly in the current, chimneys peaking up. Then a city which looks unharmed by the weather, yet a wide rift splits it in the middle, the wound so deep it is completely dark.

They cannot see the bodies from this far up, but Dahlia wonders whether the rest of the world looks like the base. Perhaps wondering the same as Dahlia, The Chief lowers the helicopter and flies closer to the rift, which is still pitch black. He turns to a side street, and they can see the bodies. There are not as many as there were at the base, but it is a horrible scene, nonetheless. There's a woman spread out on the streets with half a baby next to her. A head stares up from the middle of the road. A leg is draped across a bench as if its owner got up and forgot to bring it with them. A monster has collapsed with someone's hand in their mouth. Without the military uniforms, it's nearly impossible to discern who were the chasers and who were the chased. They see multiple people wandering the streets as if in a trance, and a child running down the sidewalk yelling for their mother.

The Chief raises the helicopter back up. He hovers from a safe distance, but his passengers have stopped looking out the window. Instead, they fixate on the roof, on the floor, or on bloodied shoes and sweaty hands. Dahlia struggles to make out where they are. None of the landmarks fit the map. It's as if they have entered a parallel universe.

She offers her best guess for directions, and about an hour in, they reach a massive forest which stretches out as far as they can see. Dahlia recognizes it immediately and is amazed to see it untouched. They spot a clearing, in the middle of which is her father's compound, what should have been her childhood home. The structure is made up of four steely rectangles organized in a square, with a garden protected in the middle. A moat stretches all the way around. A ball in her stomach grows bigger and bigger until she feels sick, and her throat turns dry and prickly.

"Don't land too close," she croaks, the headset repeating back the words to her in a voice as foreign as the world.

He obliges, landing on a much smaller clearing further away. They jump out of the helicopter and are met with fresh grass. Death has passed by this forest, it seems, and everything appears normal. The trees are so tight they can barely see ahead except for the flowers in red, blue, yellow, and pink. A butterfly flutters along the flowers and the sound of birds fills the air. A bunny peers at them from within a bush.

Destruction, it seems, comes in stages.

They gather themselves quickly, stretching like cats, breathing in the fresh air, and grabbing their assigned supplies. Perhaps it is the unnerving illusion of normality, but the group speaks freely as they walk. It is as if they are pretending that death isn't right around the corner. They point to the pretty colors, touch the bark of the trees, and exchange parts, only small parts, of their past lives. Still, their names are hidden.

With only a compass to navigate and no trail, nature is hesitant to provide access. Hills, thorn bushes, and trees stand guard, but the travelers do not mind. They are way tougher than nature. They go through and around, but they never stop. They roll up their sleeves and continue through the thorns, cutting deep like knives, yet they do not complain.

I'm still watching their shadows. I think the shadows know that I'm watching them, but are trying to act normal, like shadows. What can I do if they slip up?

The Chief and Dahlia walk in front with their compass and map, leading the way. They bury their faces in their navigation tools, frowning, until they stumble into a small clearing of grass covered entirely in forget-me-nots in pastel shades of blue, purple, and pink; tiny hands almost too pure to step on. They stop and look at the scene lit by bright light filtering through the leaves.

"I remember your dad," The Chief says out of the blue.

Dahlia glances up at him. "I forgot you two met."

"Yeah, I'm sorry about all of that. You were such a little brat. I didn't believe you when you told me about how terrible the guy was. I thought you were just a runway teenager. You know, all teenagers fight with their parents, and most kids run away at some point. I thought he was probably worried about you, too, and I was doing both of you a favor, returning you to him."

"I remember that. You told me you were taking me out to eat, but then we just kept driving for ages, and I guess I fell asleep. When I woke up, we were pulling into my dad's. How did you know where he lived, anyway?"

"You'd told me the week before when you were drunk."

Dahlia scoffs. "Sounds about right."

The Chief smiles. The rest of the group look impatient, and they begin walking again.

"I thought you were still just being a brat when you wouldn't come with me to the door. You were sitting in the car with crossed arms and fuming like a toddler, pouty lips and everything. I was going to joke about that with your dad. I thought we would get a good laugh out of it."

"Did he even open the door for you? I don't remember."

"No, he just spoke to me through the intercom." The Chief shakes his head. "He asked what I wanted, and I said I was returning his daughter, then he asked which one. 'Which one?' I asked. I didn't know about your sister. When I said it was you, he just told me to go away. I thought he was joking, but when I rang the doorbell again, he didn't answer. I had to take you back home with me after that."

"I remember that now. I think we waited for a really long time, didn't we? You kept ringing the doorbell. I mean, you just wouldn't let it go."

"But it was ridiculous!"

"You were so stubborn," Dahlia says, smiling carefully. "You just kept ringing the doorbell and banging the door. Honestly, I'm surprised he didn't shoot you."

"Really? You think he'd do that?"

Dahlia shrugs. "I don't know. He threatened to shoot the mailman once. I never knew how serious he was."

"Wow. I'm happy I made it out, then."

"Me too," Dahlia says and reaches over to touch The Chief's arm. She gives it a squeeze. "I don't think I ever thanked you for all that."

"For me wasting your whole day? I don't think that's anything to thank me for, kid."

"No, not that. For caring about me. You took the day off from work to drive me out there. You didn't have to do all that, and I was so embarrassed when I found out where we were. And then my dad reacted like that and afterwards, you know, you took care of me when we got back home. I'm just grateful, and I don't know if I ever told you that before."

The Chief looks back at Dahlia, nodding. He blinks to wipe

away the tears and crosses his arms. "Of course, I took care of you. Of course, I did."

Dahlia shakes her head. "It's not 'of course'." She takes a deep breath. She doesn't remember them ever talking so frankly. Maybe it's the imminent death pulling at her heartstrings, finally allowing her to open up. "You didn't have to do all that. You're a good man, you really are. You saved me. I don't know where I'd be without you. I know that's cliché, and I'm sorry about that, but it's true."

The Chief's lip is quivering. He's stopped walking. She squeezes his arm again, surprised by this reaction. She's never seen him cry before.

"Don't say that," he whispers.

"Hm?"

"Don't say I'm a good man. Not after—"

The Chief is barely holding it together. A single poke and he'll fall right over. She doesn't know what to say. The ball in her own stomach is growing and her throat is constricting.

"Not after I—" The Chief starts but does not finish. He wants to unburden himself about last night. Maybe, he thinks, if he tells Dahlia what he's done, and she tells him it's okay, he will feel better. Maybe he can live with himself. But what if she doesn't tell him it's okay? What if she's disgusted? What if she leaves him here, shunning him? What if she'll never be able to look at him again? No, he decides, he will say nothing. He will carry his secret to his grave, however close that might be.

"Look," she says, "we've all done things. If you're talking about… recent things, we've all done things. But we're going to be okay. This isn't our fault. You've got to remember that. It isn't our fault."

"What if it is?" They both jump at the sound of the priest's voice.

"It isn't," the mother says before Dahlia can insist on the same.

"How can you be so sure?" the priest asks.

"What do you mean, how? Gluskab called Himself our father. Don't you see that? We call Him the Creator, but we also call Him our father. That's how He wants us to see Him."

"So?"

"So? I don't care what we've done. If we're His children, it doesn't matter. There's literally nothing we could have even thought of doing which would warrant anything like this."

"People punish kids," the teenager chimes in.

"Not by torturing and killing them," the mother hisses. "You take their phones away or put them under house arrest. What's the worst thing you've done? Actually, it doesn't matter. It literally doesn't matter. We're being collectively punished for something we have no idea we've done, and it's not fair. Not if He's our father, not if He's anyone. *She's* right, none of this is our fault."

As they near the compound, Dahlia ponders fathers and responsibilities, punishments and fairness, but her thoughts are silenced when she feels something warm, tiny and delicate, brushing against her fingers.

Seraphina has caught up with her and, now side by side, their sweaty palms are pressed against each other. Dahlia's face flushes and she is too scared to turn and look at the banshee — what if she is looking at her as well? What if they make eye contact? It is hard to breathe. Her lips are quivering, remembering last night.

Her heavy breathing seems deafening to her, and she is certain everyone else must hear it. She bites her lip. If this is no time for charities, it is certainly no time for distractions, either. Dear, she feels just like a silly schoolgirl, and she cannot help it.

She wants to say something, but she is not sure what. *Do you like me?* No. How silly. They are about to be slaughtered. The world has turned into a slaughterhouse and they are its defenseless cattle, and she wants to know if the banshee by her side *likes her.* What if she does? What is she supposed to do with that? And besides, banshees are not made for love. It is not in their DNA. If it were, how would they be able to perform their grim reaper jobs? An image of the banshee at the protest — smiling, child in hand, with make-up and dyed hair — pops into her mind.

"My father doesn't like banshees," Dahlia says, maybe just to say something.

Seraphina looks up at her with furrowed brows.

"It's, ah... he thinks you're spies," Dahlia continues. "So, if he's... well, he's not going to be nice to any of us. If he says something to you, just ignore him. He will think you're still working for Gluskab, that it's some big ruse or a conspiracy. He's like that. Don't worry."

"You worry," Seraphina says. It catches Dahlia off guard.

"Sorry?" Her mouth feels dry. "I worry?"

They share a look. Dahlia is confused.

"Worry," Seraphina repeats, then looks down at their sweaty hands, clasped together, as if to suggest evidence. "Fear. Your dad?"

"Am *I* worried about my dad?"

Seraphina nods.

Dahlia is about to argue because her father isn't the reason for her sweaty palm, but she decides not to. How else can she explain this bout of unwanted emotions? And really, truly, it isn't a lie. She *is* worried about seeing her dad. It's been so long since they last talked, and back then...

The last time she talked to her dad was also through that stupid intercom. It was days after she'd run away from the boarding school. She had been traveling for days, sleeping on park benches and with nothing to eat. Her feet were full of blisters and she'd racked up a handful of fines from sneaking on busses. And finally, she'd made it. Here, to her father's compound, where she'd been met with rifles pointing at her. He saw her coming, evidenced by the way the rifles stretched their necks to look directly at her.

But the front door did not open.

"Dad!" she yelled. "Please!"

It was raining. Pouring down, in fact. She was drenched, every part of her, even her socks. Her clothes were heavy. She could barely move and held herself in her arms, shivering in the cold, the tears carried away with the heavy droplets.

He didn't respond.

She took a deep breath and yelled with everything she had. It was a loud, high-pitched scream, which prompted the birds to lift off and fly away. In response, a red dot appeared and perused her heart. She jumped away, but the dot followed her.

"Go away," the intercom screeched at her.

She looked right at the little camera, imagining her father on the other side of the device, probably not even looking at her. She shook her head no, her blue lips quivering, the tears falling even heavier. Her head throbbed. He'd always said he would do this if she ran away. He said he'd disown her. She hadn't actually thought he would.

I hadn't thought he would, either. Who would disown their own child like that? Who would watch them suffer like that and do nothing? How cruel would you have to be to do something like that?

"You're embarrassing me," the doorbell said. It was calm. Collected. Then the father sighed on the other side. "You're no use to me here."

"Please let me in."

He didn't respond after that. She screamed and lunged forward, kicking the door, but the speaker remained quiet. When she lunged forward again, the rifle fired. I'm not sure, to this day, if it was a warning shot. I think it would have hit if she hadn't jumped at the right time. In fact, the more I think about it, the more certain I become that it wasn't a warning shot at all.

Seraphina gives Dahlia's hand a squeeze. The sweating has stopped, but Dahlia preferred her ridiculous crush over the anger now filling her.

"I just don't want to see him," she says.

He has denied her two times already; I'm certain that he will deny her a third.

CHAPTER 27

GLUSKAB NUDGES AT THE SLEEPING
Vallesia, waking her up. Her eyelashes flutter. She is in
a jeep with Gluskab at the wheel in His stolen Mister
Crado skin suit. He has taken her to the only place He could
have thought of: His own backyard, the Forest of Magnificent
Trees.

Her fingertips are tucked underneath her cheek and against
the window. The corners of her mouth twitch, then she cracks
opens her eyes, her innocence disturbed. She looks confused
before recognizing the god by her side. Or she thinks she does,
anyway.

She looks out the window to place herself. They are parked
by a clear, blue lake with swans blissfully floating across it, the
water glistening in the sunlight, which hits it just right. The
trees behind tower far up, covered with lush green shades. It's
a forest, and a big one at that. She feels she has been here before,
but she can't place it. Maybe not here, right at this lake, right at
this spot, but in this forest, surely. *It's so beautiful,* she thinks. *It*

must be famous. I must have seen pictures.

"Good morning," the stolen voice says.

She flinches, surprised. The setting has drawn her in and she almost forgot about Him. He stands next to her, His lower half hidden behind the car, His hand resting nonchalantly on the open door. He tries to sound casual, stretching His body as if He has just woken up as well. He has been staring at her for hours, sniffing her hair, even. He has taken in every detail of her face and mapped every freckle. Right now, He is trying to decide on the exact shade of her golden brown eyes. His stolen face smiles.

I can't decide how I feel about this situation. It could be the answer to everything. It could end this thing right here, right now, or it could make everything worse—ruin everything, even. Ruin it forever. The dust buzzes in rhythm to my heart, my poor anxious heart, which has regenerated a little too big for my ribcage.

I can do nothing. I can only watch. The moment I stir, He will notice me. He will know I'm here. I don't want Him to. I can't face Him yet.

"Good morning," she says with her sugar-coated voice and a genuine smile. She feels oddly drugged, the contentment too complete. Dream-like. It doesn't bother her.

"Well, are you going to stay in that sweaty car all morning, or come out and play with me?" He jokes.

My stomach turns.

She giggles and steps out of the car. Once outside, she removes her shoes and feels the soft, dewy grass beneath her toes. Behind her, the branches of the impressive trees wave good morning. The setting buzzes with life. The gentle breeze spreads its fingers through the plethora of flowers. The frogs croak, the birds chirp, and a bunny jumps out in front of her, then scurries away.

She nears the side of the lake and dips her toes into the just-right water.

"It's beautiful, isn't it?" He asks.

She nods, but a tiny frown and a concerned crease on her brow appear. The splashing ceases as she looks down at her arms, studying them, turning them to search every inch of them. Then she rolls up her trousers and inspects her legs, as well.

"What's wrong?" He asks.

"I had a horrible nightmare. It must have been a nightmare, anyway. I just remembered it. Someone cut... and I was... but I'm fine. I feel completely fine."

"Oh, dear," He says. He sits down next to her, taking her arms and inspecting them with a gentle touch. What a good excuse to feel her. "Sometimes, nightmares seem almost more real than reality. It's a shame. I'm sorry you didn't sleep well."

She doesn't feel as if she didn't sleep well. She feels well-rested, and in no way tired at all. She even feels energized and ready to seize the day. Something prods inside her, a feeling which doesn't belong.

"Where are we?" she asks.

"A secret place only I know about. Now, are you sure you're okay?"

She nods, finding her smile again. "I'm really good. I feel... just really good."

"Me too," he says as he moves closer to her — uncomfortably close.

Why... why didn't he find a younger, better-looking body if this was what he was planning?

The feeling inside of her, of something being just a little off, only grows stronger. And now she can identify it — how did she get here? In Mister Crado's car, but from where? She searches her mind, but all her memories seem covered in a deep fog, especially the ones from the last few days. She feels as if this is a dream. The beautiful setting in front of her, the sun on her, the feeling of euphoria, the bliss. It's not right. She can't remember anything.

"What happened last night?" she asks, only turning her face to glance at him, her smile more strained.

She couldn't have seen through Him already, could she?

He frowns, scrunching His eyebrows together, the plethora of wrinkles revealing worry and deep contemplation, then He breaks into a huge smile. "Don't you remember?" He asks. "We were working all night, with the Peacers. We've just gotten back from headquarters."

She remembers, or thinks she does. Flashes of memories, rose-tinted, of her at the Peacers' headquarters, joking and laughing with the others and finally being one of them, which is what she has always wanted. They played cards and had competitions. She did more push-ups than all of them and earned their respect. Colonel Lewir patted her shoulder, and she felt a surge of paternal pride oozing from him. She is startled that she could have forgotten, but then...

"I'm sorry," she says. "I must be forgetting. I don't remember what we did. Our work, that is. It's odd..."

He feigns confusion. "You don't remember? We've just been traveling around, helping out wherever we were needed."

Again, the memories manifest as soon as He explains. They drive around in their trucks in Peacer uniforms. She is proud, standing tall as she hands out water to excited children, all laughing and giggling. The cities have suffered minor damage. Heavy winds have knocked down parts of buildings, and some of the canals have risen. A few basements have been destroyed, and there have even been fires claiming a handful of cars. Then, yesterday, some people got sick, and she was handing out medicine. The pictures are so clear. Almost too clear.

"And why are we here now?" she asks, then blushes as she realizes the rudeness. "I mean, I should be getting back to my husband. How long have we been gone?"

He attempts to laugh it off, but His laugh comes out nervous, awkward.

"I think you hit your head," He says while taking off his shoes to reveal a set of veiny toes, which He dips into the water. "It must have happened last night." He reaches out to touch her head, slowly, intimately, tugging some of her curls behind her ears. He smiles. "What a pretty little head. We will have to get that looked at."

I can sense her discomfort at His touch. He is looking at her in a way she does not understand, His eyes filled to the brim with love.

"Should we be getting back?" she asks, uncertain.

"We're in no rush. Let's just enjoy the morning for now. It's beautiful, isn't it?"

"It is. I feel like I recognize this place. Are you sure it's not somewhere famous?"

"My, oh my. You do realize that everything you've said to me since you've woken up has been a question, do you not?"

"I'm sorry."

"Don't apologize. Never apologize. It's not your fault."

"What's not my fault?"

He's said too much. His worry-lines manifest unnaturally and His hair grays rapidly. Then, in an attempt to pivot, He lights up as if He has just had a splendid idea. He jumps to His feet, walks toward the car, and retrieves a picnic basket from within it. His movements are quick, youthful, and not at all the movements of an old man. "You must be starving."

A picnic basket? What an odd thing to just have in your car. Is He even trying? He's overeager. He's been chained up too long. He's forgotten how to interact with humans. She realizes the absurdity as well, furrowing her brow and tilting her head.

"What's wrong?" He asks.

The problem is right at the tip of her tongue, but it refuses to manifest.

"I've got your favorites: cream cheese and salmon bagels. Come on, you must be hungry!"

Oh, father. How would you know her favorite lunch item?

She squints at Him. What's the answer, here? She understands something is amiss, but what would this be, if not what He says it is? Where would they be, who would He be? Why would He lie? No, she must just be paranoid. It is because of her nightmare, she decides. Because she hit her head.

Rather than listening to her instincts, she accepts the bagel.

He pulls out a blanket from the car and lays it out on the grass with two pillows. In the middle, He places the picnic basket, then lies down, spreading Himself on the blanket and propping Himself up with His arm. She follows, placing herself on the other side of the basket, eyeing Him. By the looks of His relaxed, eager demeanor, He is blissfully unaware of her suspicions.

Is He attempting to seduce her? In Mister Crado's old wriggly skin-suit? He has realized that she is married. Does He feel that He has picked a worthy look to compete with Mario, dead or not?

"You could get closer, if you want," He says.

I shudder.

She shudders as well and inches further away from Him.

Now he realizes His mistake, yet not the gravity of it. He is too smitten, and He has lost control of Himself and of the situation. He laughs, and all the wrinkles on His face fold on top of each other. "I'm sorry," He says. "I'm just so excited. I can't believe I finally found you."

"You found me?" she asks, her back arched, her mind alert, and her hands around her knees. It is a position from which she could spring away, should she need to, and I'm sure it is intentional. "What do you mean, you found me? Was I gone?"

"Well, I, w — well…" He stutters.

I can hear her heart pounding. Her blood rushes through her body, and her thoughts rush through her mind. In which direction will she run? Could she outrun Him? Track exercises against a god? Of course not.

"Mister Crado, I think I'd like to get back now."

She fiddles with some grass and looks away.

His face is falling apart. It twitches, His eyes blinking, His mouth raising, then lowering. Then He emits odd sounds — a grunt, a cluck, a bark. She moves away from Him, scooting backward, afraid that His meltdown will climax in an explosion and then — remembering.

The cell, the torture, the dead soldiers. Mister Crado's mysterious reappearance. She feels like throwing up and clutches her throat, covering her mouth. The drowning. Her lungs burning, the gasping for air. She can barely breathe as she wraps her arms around her, then pulls them out to inspect them. They were bloody. The wounds were so deep she'd been bleeding to death. That had all happened. She is sure of it. But she can still not make sense of any of it.

He stops twitching, regaining His motor skills all at once. His murky green eyes rest on her. They are dark, pulling her into a swamp, further and further until she feels her whole body immobilized by the mud. Above them, the clouds darken and the birds stop chirping. The waves in the lake surge and swallow the swans whole.

"You are tired," He says. His voice is again calm, but cold and steely. It almost hurts her when He speaks. "Why don't you take a nap?"

She does not want to take a nap. She wants to run away, but her body is becoming heavy. Her arms, her shoulders, her eyelids… It is no use attempting to stay awake when your Creator is telling you to sleep. She feels herself going in and out of consciousness, her eyelids fluttering, then closing completely.

She's gone.

CHAPTER 28

DAHLIA'S GROUP WATCHES A SPOT of darkness gather and spread on the horizon. It is eerie, empty, and not quite like a cloud; yet it moves across the sky as one. They can't decide why it is not quite like a cloud, but they all have the profound knowledge that it cannot be. It reminds them of a big thundercloud, electrically charged and getting ready to spear them. Its darkness is so intense, so completely black, that they feel drawn into it as the temperature drops.

It is too late, they think.

Should they run? Should they drop down and give into their fate?

Their shadows stir. The group is too preoccupied to notice their shadows moving of their own accord, but I notice. A chill moves down my spine. The shadows stretch long and extend their thin arms. Their fingers grow nails and their mouths gape open. The shadows of the trees, as well, close in on the clearing like an enormous mouth chomping down. In a moment, we are all going to be devoured.

And then they stop.

The darkness above never reaches them. It stops suddenly and lingers. The group watches in breathless suspense, then it retreats, swallowing itself, folding until it is gone and the sky is clear blue again. The birds sing once more, seeming to confer among themselves.

The shadows pretend to be just shadows.

It isn't time yet.

When they finally close in on Dahlia's father's compound, more time has passed than they would have liked. A couple of hours, perhaps. Dahlia holds up a hand to bring the expedition to a halt. They are hidden behind some trees, but from here, they can clearly see the huge structure, the tall, metal walls rising to the sky. They are made of pure titanium, a bullet-proof vest wrapping the compound's never-harmed body. Cameras adorn the sides along with the rifles which she remembers well. They are not pointed at them at the moment, luckily, but it does more than unsettle the group.

As they creep up on the structure, Dahlia warns them in hushed tones, "Careful. There are motion sensors." She leads them down a specific route through the trees.

"No sensors here, just cameras," Dahlia whispers, then adds, mostly to calm herself, "If we move quickly, he probably won't see. I'm sure he's busy."

They circle in on the compound and stop in front of a moat sheltered from view by an enormous weeping willow. She takes a deep breath. The congregation looks puzzled, then anxious that she will attempt to make the leap toward the other side. Surely, they think collectively, the moat, though narrow, is not narrow enough. Yet, she jumps, not far enough, but her foot lands on what must be a stone hidden beneath surface. Agile, she jumps the last of the way across, reaching out for the wall and pressing herself against it.

The stone is hidden, but if you squint, as the following does now, you can just about make out the outline of it. They are afraid to follow. The teenager goes first, then Seraphina, the mother, and then the priest. The Chief is the least elegant of the bunch, but they all make it across.

"A little more," Dahlia whispers.

They make their way on the narrow path between the wall and the moat, their bodies pressed against the cold surface. They feel like spies. Secret soldiers. Finally, a door manifests as they turn a corner. It is another thing which you'd only see if you knew it was there. Underneath some ivy, curiously growing up the metal frame of the building, a smaller panel is hidden. Dahlia wipes the leaves aside to reveal it, smiling. The lid slides off to reveal a screen.

This was a fantasy of hers many years ago: To gather a group of unlikely peers and lead them around the house, let them in through the back entrance, and plunder her father's most prized possessions. Back then, she just wanted to punish him, to get back on him for leaving her, metaphorically and nearly literally, in a ditch to starve. The objective may now be altered, but the thrill is the same.

This is the epic moment in the fantasy where she presses her thumb on the screen and the computer grants her entry, but her fantasy is —as fantasies often are —just that. She presses her thumb against the screen, looking back at them with her eyebrows raised, and then the screen flickers red. There is a loud, unfriendly beep. Her heart drops. She tries again, but with the same result.

"I don't understand," she mumbles, ears burning. Has her father reprogrammed the computer and made sure his own daughter cannot enter? Of course, he has, after their fight. Or fights. Why, she thinks, did she believe he wouldn't? Has years of neglect and disappointment taught her nothing? Her stomach churns and sputters in some emotional distress, but it will not tell her which.

She does not get to confront her stomach before the door opens and she almost leaps back in surprise. What? *DENIED ENTRANCE* had flickered across the screen in bold, red letters, hadn't it? And now the door sliding open in a smooth motion with the sound of metal clanking. They collectively hold their breaths.

And before them appears a man.

Who is he? Dahlia wonders.

He is large and muscular with a neck tattoo and a clean-shaven head. He easily towers two heads taller than Dahlia and he fills the entrance with his massive frame, much like a bouncer. In fact, he may just be that, clutching a gun and muscles tensing beneath his wife beater, as he squints at the group. If he intends to inflict fear, he has succeeded.

"Who are you?" Dahlia asks, knees weak.

The bouncer looks equally puzzled and, for a moment, less menacing before he regathers himself, pushing his chest forward and tightening his grip around his gun. "No," he says, revealing a deep baritone voice to match his appearance. "Who are *you?*"

Dahlia hesitates. Is there a guest list? A password? Is her father watching, right now, on a screen? Who is this man, and what is he doing in her recluse father's house? How has he possibly gained entrance? It occurs to Dahlia that the man may not have anything to do with her father, except that he may have overtaken his house. It's an unlikely thought that anyone would have overtaken the impenetrable compound, yet it seems more likely than her father in any sort of alliance.

"We're just passing by," Dahlia tries, uncertain, attempting to gather herself. She instantly regrets her answer.

"Just passing by?" the bouncer says, a faint smile playing on his lips. "You were out here, in the middle of nowhere, and happened to fall over this... here, and thought you might attempt to sneak in through the backdoor, which you... just happened to spot? And you avoided all the sensors, *accidentally?*"

They all shuffle their feet. Dahlia feels the group's discomfort, their distrust in her. They want to run away. Does Seraphina want to run away too? But running is not an option and she needs to find out whether this man is anything to her father, and if so, what.

"Something like that," she says, trying to keep her cool. Her face feels red and flushed. Her palms are sweaty. "Do you mind telling my friends and me where we are? What, exactly, is *here*?"

The bouncer seems to be enjoying himself, perhaps because he is proud to have seen through Dahlia's obvious lie, or perhaps because he has not gotten many visitors. At any rate, his enjoyment is to their advantage. He won't get rid of them just yet. He may just humor her.

"What do you think *here* is?" he asks.

She pretends to ponder. "I wouldn't know," she says, pouting, pressing a finger to her lips. She looks up with big doe eyes. She is an attractive young lady, after all. Better to use her gifts. It is a gift she has used often enough to become infamous. It feels wrong to use it now, though, with Seraphina right behind her.

"Somewhere safe, perhaps?" she continues. "Are you here all by yourself?"

He smiles, smitten. Easy. What a shame for him that Dahlia plays the other team.

"I'm not," he says. "I'm just the muscle."

"Oh," she says, flashing a playful smile. "I can see that."

He grins. "I'm sorry, but you're going to have to come up with a better explanation than just passing by," he says, adjusting his grip on the gun. "Or else... well..."

"I know the owner of the place," she says, surprising herself as she says it.

"Oh?"

She takes a deep breath in through her nostrils, fills up her lungs, and breathes out. She attempts to look as confident as possible. "My name is Vallesia. Vallesia Jade. I believe you should know who I am."

The bouncer's expression freezes. That's a good reaction, she thinks. He knows about her sister and therefore her father, as well. His body relaxes, the grip around the gun easing up.

"Oh." He breathes out.

She smiles, impressed that it worked. The man believes her, although he glances at her noodle-like arms and legs with slight confusion. He has seen a picture of Vallesia, then, but they are sisters, after all. Their faces are similar despite their bodies and styling being polar opposites, Vallesia's muscular army body, feminine dresses, and pink workout clothes to Dahlia's stick figure, tight trousers, and oversized lazy shirts. They are like the same person torn in different directions. Vallesia could have gone through a phase, starved herself, released her curls, and dyed them grunge green.

"Oh," she mimics, gloating.

"I'm sorry," he says.

"Me too. I had to make sure, you understand, if you were my father's friend or not. He has many enemies."

Does he? She doubts it. He does not socialize enough to make enemies. But it sounds good, and the muscle seems to accept it, nodding with what he must feel is profound understanding.

"Of course," he says. Then he looks behind her as if he's seeing her group for the first time just now. "And these?" he asks.

"Back-up," she explains, shrugging.

He accepts this as well, nodding again.

"Now then…" she says, tilting her head toward the inside and taking a small step forward.

"Yes, of course. You'll want to see your father. He will be overjoyed to know that you are well. He's called many times, you know. You should pick up your phone, call your old dad back. Let me walk you there, now."

Perhaps needless to say, he has not tried to call Dahlia. She wonders how the situation may have unfolded had she revealed her true identity — would the bouncer have kicked her out instead? Would he have yelled at her and called her a traitor or a disappointment, mirroring her father's words? Or would he not even have known who she is? Likely it would be the last scenario.

"Oh, that's not necessary. I know my way. In the lounge, is he?"

"Don't be silly. I'll walk you there."

"Aren't you busy keeping guard?"

"It should be fine. You're the firsts to pass by, anyway."

The bouncer wants recognition. A clap on the back. She does not have any counters to that, so she lets him walk them there. At least he will be disappointed; no glory will await him once her father finds out what the cat's dragged in.

"Thank you, that is very kind of you," she says, nodding at her entourage to follow.

The temperature drops notably as they move through the hallway. Despite the warmth outside, the inside is freezing. The cold from the steely floor permeates their feet, cooling their insides. They all have goosebumps — I have goosebumps. Something is off inside the compound. It feels strangely uninhabited.

The décor, or rather the lack of décor, adds to the eerie feeling. The walls are covered in strips of steel rather than windows, completely cutting off the outside world. The only furniture is utilitarian and functional; there are no paintings or artworks, no vases or rugs, only simple lights along the walls. Most of the rooms they walk by are bare, huge areas containing nothing but air and dust. A tarp lays over a chair in one, the armrest exposed with the fabric covered in a thin layer of dust. None of the rooms have any doors. Doors are unnecessary.

There must be ventilation somewhere, but the air feels heavy, as if it has been breathed in and out too many times. It makes them feel drowsy, drugged. There are no sounds except the clattering of their shoes against the floor and their heavy, rapid breathing. Something, somewhere, pounds against metal.

The teenager clears her throat and glances to a paling Dahlia, who's moved closer to Seraphina in hopes of protection or protecting.

"How long have you been working with my father?" Dahlia asks the guard. She's still trying to understand the development of her father letting anybody into the compound or in any way interacting with humanity. It is, of course, still possible this man does not work for her father and that he is luring them into a trap. But that wouldn't make any sense. That doesn't make any sense at all.

"We've been working together for years. Online, of course. I arrived here yesterday. Most of us did. A few arrived here the day before that."

Most of us? Dahlia now has to process that the bouncer is not the only one here. There are more, and they have been working together for *years*.

"I don't know my father as the big socialite," Dahlia says.

"No," he says, chuckling. He looks at her in a way which reveals that he is still smitten, but he is making an effort to hide it. Perhaps he is afraid of her father. "He is not. But there's a common cause, you understand."

"Of course," Dahlia says.

"If you called you father more often, I'm sure he would have explained everything."

Dahlia smiles at him. Her nails are cutting into her palms and she can feel the blood pulsating.

They reach a door at the end of a long hallway leading to the lounge, the only room with a door so far. It is heavy titanium, just like the exterior door. Instead of a door handle, it has a keypad similar to the one outside. A light illuminates it from above, like the object of a quest. Again, Dahlia ponders whether it is not all predestined, whether she is not just following the intended and ultimately disastrous path laid before her. What if she ran out, right now, and did something that wasn't expected—or would that be what Gluskab expects of her? You can't fight fate.

The bouncer inputs the code, taking little care for the posse to not see it. Dahlia holds her breath. She and Vallesia were never allowed in the lounge.

"I'm building something," their father would say. They were toddlers and preschoolers, too young for the boarding school. They would play with their dolls and toys right outside the big, heavy door towering above them like a solid pillar, trying to be as close to their father as possible. Sometimes, they would imagine the inside: A treehouse, new bunk beds, a pink room with butterflies and unicorns, puppies and kittens and toys. Lots and lots of toys.

The bouncer leans on the door, pushing it open with an agonizing slowness.. It is nothing like either of the sisters could have ever imagined.

The room is not a lounge, and Dahlia wonders why it was called a lounge. There is no furniture, no couch or coffee table, plants or paintings. It is packed with a dozen strangers standing around tables with computers which beep and ping. Flashy screens cover the walls, showcasing maps, and featuring a number which increases with a slow, steady pace. Below the number is the label, *Death Count*.

Dear... that is large. Is that in the billions? Not even I would have imagined that. That cannot be true. Is that right? Are there so few left, then?

The wall adjacent is covered in a huge, printed map with red push pins and adhesive notes with eerie titles: *Acid showers. Electric water. Unbearable heat.* A man is trying to connect them, pulling his beard, stretching his chin. In the middle, a crowd of people crouch on the cold floor, working on some sort of device with red and blue lights flashing on it and tubes to connect the different parts. They are looking at books and pointing to different parts of it, discussing loudly, yelling in an agitated manner, each intent on being heard.

And there. Quietly observing the strangers, unnerving them, shaking his head to let them know when they are wrong, is Dahlia's father.

CHAPTER 29

THE BOUNCER CLEARS HIS THROAT and Dahlia's father slowly raises his head to look up at the group. His mouth is a thin line and his small irises peek out from underneath heavy, almost closed eyelids. His narrow glasses rest on a pointy nose, as do his elbows on his skinny legs in pressed suit pants. Despite being seated, it somehow feels as if he is looking down on them.

Dahlia is visibly sweating when they lock eyes. I can tell she wants to look confident and nonchalant, but she is failing. She hides her hands behind her back, fiddling with them, and bites her lip.

Her father's only reaction is a long, deep exhale, almost like a sigh. Then he pushes himself up from his chair and proceeds toward the mob. The working mass, beyond busy just moments before, has stopped its work and watches him instead.

Surprised by the reaction, the bouncer takes a timid step back. His cocky smile is gone. His eyes are filled with fear. The father doesn't even deign him a single look.

"Dahlia," the father says.

She nods in response, the word 'father' choked in her throat. It constricts. She feels the tenseness. Equipment beeps somewhere seemingly far, far in the distance.

"Dahlia?" the bouncer begins, visibly sweating. "She said — I thought — Vallesia!"

The father shuts him up with a glare. The bouncer takes yet another, bigger step backward and mumbles an apology, which the father does not seem to care for, completely disregarding him and turning his whole body toward Dahlia.

"Where is your sister?" he asks. The words sound off in his narrow mouth, as if he is not used to speaking. Perhaps he merely looks at people with disapproval, telepathically guiding them to do his bidding.

The question was bound to come. She shouldn't have been surprised, and she tries to convince herself that she is not. There is a small ball growing in her stomach.

"I've been looking for her," Dahlia says, and dislikes how apologetic she sounds. She has nothing to apologize for, nothing at all.

The father scoffs. "You have, have you?"

"I have."

They stare at each other long enough for everyone else to shuffle their feet awkwardly. Dahlia grows more confident and pushes out her chest, holding her ground. The father does not stir at all. She is not the first to succumb to his steely glare.

"We went to her apartment, and she wasn't there," she says. "We were at the base yesterday and she wasn't there, either. Mar —" She stops herself. He doesn't know who Mario is, doesn't even know that Vallesia is married — or widowed now, technically. She deemed it too difficult to hide her husband's overwhelmingly religious views, so she never told him the happy news. There was no danger of him finding out, having never visited either of them. "Her friends didn't know where she was, either."

"I've been calling her," he says.

"We've been, too."

The father exhales again.

"You'll have to make do with me instead, I guess," Dahlia jokes.

He emits a sound like a hiss. She is not acceptable seconds, that's what that means. She is not surprised.

A man approaches them. He is round with friendly brown eyes and disheveled long hair. His beard reaches his chest, where his greasy plaid shirt has several pens in the pocket. His jeans are patched. He looks to be in his early fifties. As he makes his way toward them, he places his hand on the father's shoulder. It is like petting an angry tiger, yet the man seems at ease with the action.

"You'll have to excuse him," he says. "We don't let him out much."

The father hisses again. This time, it's definitely a hiss, like that of a feral animal.

The man extends his free hand toward Dahlia with a polite smile. "I'm Brand," he says, even though Dahlia does not accept his hand. She stares at it with suspicion. "And you must be the previously secret daughter."

He nods at the gathering behind Dahlia. "And you," he says. "Friends?"

"*Mob*," Seraphina corrects him.

Dahlia fails to hide a smile.

"It doesn't matter who they are," the father snaps, "because they are not staying. I don't want you here. I have no idea why you came. You are of no use to me, and I want you to leave."

Dahlia breathes in sharply, feeling blood rushing through her. She stops fiddling with her hands and forms them into fists instead.

"Let's just calm down for a second," Brand says. He might not have the body of a yoga instructor, but he has the presence.

"I'm calm," the father says. He does appear calm. "And I'd like them to leave." He gestures at the bouncer, who has retreated further and further into a corner. "Escort them out, please."

"You can't just throw us out!" Dahlia protests.

"I cannot?"

"I'm your daughter!"

"By blood, maybe."

Dahlia barks a sharp laugh in disbelief and shakes her head. I, like her, would really like to slap him.

"What's wrong with you?" The Chief asks, stepping forward, in front of Dahlia. "Are you actually serious right now?"

The father doesn't care to answer him, but stares at him too with an inexpressive, dead face.

"Answer!" The Chief demands. "What in the world is wrong with you that you'd treat someone—your own daughter—like that? This is crazy!"

"Please," the father says, motioning from the bouncer to Dahlia and her group.

The Chief steps forward again, now right in front of the father. His face turns completely red and his teeth are bared. The father blinks slowly. When The Chief raises his fist, Brand steps in and grabs his wrist.

"How about we discuss this calmly," Brand says.

The Chief lowers his arm but doesn't break eye contact with the father.

Brand turns to Dahlia. "Dahlia, was it?"

She does not respond. There are so many things she would like to say, but can't, and not because the sentences won't form or the words won't leave her mouth. Rather, she is stumped by the profound knowledge that nothing she could ever say would make her father realize the injustice of the hurt and pain he has inflicted on her. Yet, they can't leave the compound. It's not an option.

I inspect the shadows again. They do not stir, but it must be nearly time.

I hear the beating of drums. The heavy footsteps of death.

CHAPTER
30

VALLESIA AWAKENS AND IS SURPRISED anew by the beautiful setting around her. Swans, bunnies, and birds chirping above her. *Such happy chirps for such a happy day*, she thinks, still groggy as she stretches her arms. The sun warms her with its gentle yet powerful hands. She leans back with a happy sigh, smiling at the sky and making herself big, pretending to photosynthesize, then reaches out to touch the grass, which makes her think of newly conditioned hair. It is smooth like butter and smells newly cut.

"Ah, you're awake," Gluskab says, still in Mister Crado's skinsuit and smiling at her from the lake. He holds a fishing rod and has folded up His trousers to not get them wet.

She smiles back at Him. *Ah, Mister Crado*, she thinks. *Such a nice man*. All their funny, wacky adventures these past few days rushes over her: The way they joked, the way they laughed, the way He suggested they go fishing to celebrate her official initiation into the Peacers. Yes—she is a Peacer now! They have really gotten close. She feels as if she has known Him her entire life. His eyes, she thinks, are so gentle and calm. It is like being hugged from afar.

I wonder if my father is planning on brainwashing Vallesia for the rest of her life. Could He be that naïve?

"Did you sleep well?" He asks.

His voice is pleasant, as well, she thinks. *Calm and soothing.*

"Yes," she says. "I don't remember what I dreamed, but I remember it was nice. I feel so well-rested. It was a good idea for you to propose we take a nap."

"I'm full of good ideas. Would you like to fish with me?"

She is all smiles. "Yes! I love fishing. Do we need to get back at any time?"

"We're not in a hurry. Everything is well and fine. The world is at peace."

She accepts this easily and joins Him, picking up a rod from beside her, which she prepares with surprising ease. When did she learn how to fish? She is uncertain she has ever fished, yet she hooks the bait with little effort before casting it. He really has made the scenery even lovelier; the lake seems almost blush pink and the clouds above are whiter than snow. The grass is almost aggressively lush. Each animal is coupled with a partner, snuggling up close to each other, the swans on the lake, bunnies sleeping under a tree, and doves in the sky.

"Oh, look at that!" He says, pointing at a cluster of heart-shaped clouds as if surprised by His own creation. She looks up and laughs, impressed.

"And look at that!" she says and points at a disturbingly realistic dog cloud.

"Wow, yeah!"

They go on like that, the clouds surpassing each other, spelling out words and sceneries, then portraits to flatter her. The clouds seem to shine, glitter even. She is not suspicious—not yet.

Before long, something pulls at her rod and she squeals excitedly.

"I think I've got something!" she exclaims.

He is by her fast, smiling.

"Bring it in!"

"I'm trying!"

She giggles while reeling, pulling the rod, lowering it, and reeling again. How did she learn how to fish? She doesn't question it, she merely continues the fight with skill until the fish shoots from the water and toward her, flapping its tail, its body squirming against the grass filling the air with a soft rhythm. Its scales glisten in the sunlight, pink and green against purple, orange, blue, and yellow. It genuinely looks as if it is smiling.

Are you creeped out? I am. She's not. Not yet.

"Wow!" they both exclaim, hovering above it, taking it in. Gluskab measures it against His forearm—just about the same size. He pulls out an instant camera seemingly from nowhere.

"Let's get this on film," He says.

The fish stops moving the moment she picks it up. It is warm and soft, not at all slimy or slippery. It looks as if it poses with her, its smile uncannily human. They wait for the photo to develop in suspense, wondering if the quality will capture the bliss. It does. The quality of the picture would put professional photographers to shame.

"Wow," she exclaims again.

He is about to say something inappropriate. It is written all over His face. I am already cringing.

Before He gets the chance, she sighs as if the whole of it is just too perfect and says, "It is so beautiful here. It would be so lovely to bring my husband one day."

He pales. She doesn't notice at first, too engaged in her senses, but His silence becomes too palpable.

"Oh, are you feeling alright?" she asks, her brows furrowed. But her worry isn't complete; it is too minute compared to the rest of her feelings.

"Your husband," Gluskab says with a disapproving scowl.

And so, it begins. Again.

He seems to have more wrinkles than before, and His skin has a grayish tone to it, but then, the whole scene seems suddenly gray-toned. His grip around the rod is tight.

"My husband," she repeats, clueless. "Mario. I don't think you've met, but you two would get along very well, I think. He is the most dedicated Knower I've ever met. Sometimes he hosts church meetings at our apartment."

Gluskab stares straight ahead, His jaw clenched. The wind plays too violently in the water and it churns with waves.

"What is it?" she asks, concerned.

"You don't love him," he says, his mouth barely moving.

Oh no, this again.

She laughs, but it is brought on by discomfort rather than mirth. Perhaps she is hoping that He is joking.

"Of course I do," she says. "I love him with all my heart. He is the most amazing man I have ever met, so kind and thoughtful, and always with a smile on his face. I'm telling you, you would love him. Everyone does. He is much too good for me, really."

It is as if the air is pressed backward, creating a vacuum in which she finds it hard to breathe. A cloud moves across the sky, hiding the sun, and the temperature drops. She shudders, looking around for a shirt or jacket, for something to cover her bare arms.

"It's so cold, suddenly," she says between nervous chuckles. "Do you mind lending me a jacket?"

"You do not love him," He repeats. His eyes do not feel like hugs from afar anymore.

Something breaks inside her and memories disappear like pages being ripped out of a photo book, dropped into acid, and then replaced. The air is sucked out of her and when she finally remembers how to breathe again, her lungs feel different. The air feels foreign. The setting is like a black-and-white picture, the sky now completely void of color, and the grass now grainy.

She is quiet, much too scared to talk.

"You do not love him," He says again, softer, putting His arm around her. "It's okay. Sometimes you just stop loving people."

She wipes a tear away and collects her arms around her ankles, burying her face into her knees.

"Do you remember when he hit you?" He asks. "He was always so angry. Always angry, and never happy. Do you remember that?"

She remembers. No, no. Yes! No... She does not want these memories. They are fuzzy and odd, like a single tile slightly discolored against an otherwise pristine wall. They do not fit in, but she has them. They are her memories. They must be. She remembers the hand against her cheek, the smack, and the pain, but the pain does not matter. It is the surprise, the confusion, and the betrayal that hurts the most. How could Mario have done that to her? He did not, did he?

He would never.

"It's alright," Gluskab says again, caressing her arm.

I shiver with a chill not brought on by the clouds. This is a low point, even for him. How am I going to fix this? He wants her all for Himself, but this is not the way.

She looks up and catches Him staring at her, His eyes are intense and thrilled, but His hug is not quite friendly. It is too close. The colors return to the scene, fading in like a sunrise. His wrinkles fade out, the creases around His eyes are gone. His dusty skin becomes lively, even vibrant. His hair changes from gray to a dirty blond. She notices. She is aware.

"You don't love him," Gluskab repeats with an assertive tone.

It is warmer now, almost too warm, and the colors are aggressively vibrant. The flowers are too red and the birds are so noisy she almost does not hear Him speak.

Gluskab leans in close. "You only love me. Oh, my darling, darling, Jarda."

I cannot watch this. It will never work. He is millions of years old and socially inept. He's made these humans, He's fathered them Himself, and yet He does not understand the first thing about them.

I intervene. My intervention brought all this on, and it will end it. I whisper in her ear, it is not important what, but when I do, she pushes herself up.

"What?" she asks, squinting.

Don't wait for the reply.

She does not. Good girl! She understands that if she lets Him say it again, she will believe Him. Her memories will disappear and new ones will manifest at His urging. Everything will be distorted, and the air will taste like metal scraps. Who will she be then?

"Who are you? *What* are you?" she asks, taking a step backward.

Don't wait for that reply, either. You know. Get out of here. Fast.

"You—"

I whisper again, *Run!*

"No!" she yells, covering her ears. Tears stream down her face. She is confused. Mario? Did He plant memories? Did He erase memories? Who is He? Does she love Him, really? Him? Whom does she—

Run! Run!

She runs away from the god. He reaches out His hand for her, jumps up after her, and follows her into the woods. The sky turns dark again. The trees get closer until she has to force herself between them, pushing her body through them, her arms and legs ripped wide open by the thorns. All the while, she feels His fingers—her god's fingers—grazing her back, reaching for her.

I appear in front of her in my horror-inducing mask, my long, dark coat, and my lithe, slender body. I catch her. My arms encase her like the branches of a tree, and then I carry her away. I have stolen her from my father.

"You're okay now, child. You're okay," I tell her. "No harm will come to you now. As long as you do what I tell you to. No harm will come to anyone."

CHAPTER
31

A **GUST OF AIR TRAVELS** from the Forest of Magnificent Trees over the ravaged lands and reaches the compound. It presses itself through locked doors and windows and makes its way down the corridor. Dahlia, in the doorway to the lounge, is nearly knocked over by the force of it. Apparatus clatter and swivel chairs slide. When the gust of air leaves them, moving on to warn every corner of the world the atmosphere has changed. The air becomes heavy and hard to breathe, and everyone feels momentarily lightheaded.

A shriek is the next thing they hear.

"Sir!" a man in front of a computer yells. When everyone turns to look at him, including the father, he points to the massive screen displaying the casualty numbers and a satellite feed of the world. A completely black blob, seemingly originating from The Forest of Magnificent Trees, is spreading across the landscape. Blinking lights are all that is visible beneath it. The source of the blob is unclear.

"What is that?" Brand asks, walking further into the room.

He watches the screen, attempting to make sense of it. But the danger is not on the screen; it is outside, and it is rapidly approaching.

The man at the computer shakes his head and his glasses almost fall off. "I have no idea..."

It is *that*. Death. It has begun. I look down on my shadow, which is growing, stretching itself, readying. It won't just be the people's shadows attacking, though, I realize. Soon, the world will be covered in a single shadow completely cutting off the sun. Then, where will they run? There is nowhere to run.

This is it.

The rest of the team gathers around the screen, observing the blob with terror. The shocked man swirls back around in his chair to type on his computer with what appears to be limited results.

"It is darkness," he says. "The area is turning completely dark, like nightfall."

"That wouldn't spread like that," another replies. "Darkness doesn't *spread*."

"I'm telling you what I see."

"Where is the sun?"

The man hesitates. "In—uh, I think behind."

"Behind clouds?"

"No, it's not... It's not clouds. It's just darkness."

"That doesn't make any sense."

"I know. I'm just telling you what I see."

"But darkness doesn't spread like that!"

Dahlia and her group are uncertain what to do with themselves. They shuffle their feet and share concerned glances. Of course, Dahlia knew something was coming, but confronting her father felt like enough challenge for one day. Are they safe in here?

The father turns to Dahlia and spits through gritted teeth, "What a coincidence this happened when you arrived."

She is caught off guard but quickly recovers, narrowing her eyes, puffing herself up. "What are you saying?"

"It certainly is a coincidence." His eyes glide past her and behind her, resting on Seraphina. He takes a step forward. "You've brought a spy," he says. His voice is cold, emotionless.

Behind them, his team is still bickering, the volume increasing. Dahlia almost believes that she has misheard him in the noise. Almost.

"She's not a spy," she snaps.

"So?" he says. "Are you perhaps the spy, then?"

"None of us are spies."

"The banshees," he continues, pointing to Seraphina. "They work for Gluskab. You know that. You brought one into my house, and now... now this!" He gestures back to the screen.

Is he afraid?

Dahlia feels an unnatural rage rise within her. She cannot control it. It fills her. Her petite body cannot contain the anger and she is about to overflow, the lid popping off, her knuckles growing hard, her muscles preparing...

"Sir!" another tech yells behind them, trying to get the father's attention. Brand rushes forward and places his hand on the father's arm, not gently this time, but pulling.

"Come on!" Brand yells. "It's narrowing in. It's going to be here soon. And we need to get the bomb finished."

Bomb?

The father stands firm like a pillar.

"We need to bring it down to the tank," Brand begs. "Come. Please. It's coming."

The father turns with hesitation to oversee the team already gathered around the device from before, which is apparently a bomb. Their work is now hurried, frantic, and intense. Wires of different colors are exchanged and everyone's hands are shaking and sweat drips from them. They are bound, one may think, to make mistakes. They shouldn't be handling a bomb like that.

"We're safe in here, though, right?" the priest asks Dahlia. "Right?"

She does not know how to respond. She wants to calm

them down but cannot find the words. How would she know if they're safe? Something else is on her mind, something which demands her attention, but she is not sure what it is. Something she is remembering...

The tank? Had Brand mentioned a tank?

"Of course, you're not safe," the father hisses at the group.

"But the walls..."

"The walls? The walls are *walls*," the father says, now clearly distracted from his work. "You think a *god* can't tear them down?"

The priest presses on. "The other days —"

"Were not like today." The father cuts him off, wetting his lips in a quick, reptile motion. "All the best things come in threes. Today, we perish."

Darkness engulfs the world. It is a darkness which is unpleasant only because it is worrisome. It brings with it a sense of dread. The air quivers in trepidation as the few survivors collectively hold their breaths. It is a promise they have not been forgotten, though they may wish they were. The people sharpen their spears and ready their fists and wait. They squint to see better and position their feet squarely on the ground as they wait. From somewhere, very soon, danger will leap at them when they least expect it.

Isn't waiting worse? What quality does your life hold in those few moments before you die, when you know that you will die? When you are alone and afraid, when they truly have nothing else to do but to wait? Best to get it over with. To be free from the pain and terror. In my nightmares, when death comes for me, I beg for immediate release. I never put up a fight. I lay down and roll up into a ball and I beg, not to be saved, but to be free. Grant us thy peace, according to thy word. It's not that I don't want to live, it's only that dying is so infinitely worse than being dead.

They wait. No one comes to relieve them, so they wait.

Soon, very soon, it comes.

Oh my. There it is.

Darkness engulfs the compound as well. The event passes unnoticed. There are no windows, so they would not know it is happening if not for the man at the computer announcing their doom.

"It's fine," Brand says with a smooth, comforting voice. He turns to the man, but speaks loudly, hoping that everyone will hear him. "The compound will hold. A little darkness won't hurt. We just have to finish the bomb."

I wonder about the bomb. Dahlia does too, and so does the rest of the mob. No one seems willing to tell them, or me, about it. Dahlia turns toward the bouncer, but he meets her with a cold shoulder and announces that he wants nothing to do with her.

She bites her lip. It seems whatever comes next is dependent on the bomb. She wonders what sort of bomb it is, what it's for, and how they will bring it where it needs to be set off. Will they blow up the entire world? She is sure her father wouldn't mind exterminating humanity as long as he takes down the Creator with him. However, a bomb such as that doesn't exist. It couldn't, surely?

She takes a step toward the bomb. Maybe if she can get a closer look. The answer is right on the tip of her tongue.

"Don't get any closer," her father warns with a pointed finger. "You're lucky I haven't thrown you out yet."

"You *did* try," she mumbles and huffs. She stands there for a little while longer, much to her father's visible dismay. He is seething, not paying attention to the task in front of him. She is getting nothing out of being closer to the bomb, yet remains out of stubbornness. She looks back at her group. Where has she brought them? To what purpose?

The answer is on the tip of her tongue. Right there.

What is it she's remembering?

The lights go out suddenly, then flicker back on. The

computers are rebooting. Someone lets out a soft whimper. The lights all continue to flicker.

"What was that?" the father snaps.

"I don't know!" the man who first announced the darkness says, clearly frustrated with the quantity of unfair questions being directed at him, or perhaps at his own ineptness. "A power shortage, maybe... Hold on."

"The batteries are draining," another chimes in, her forehead glistening with sweat.

A bomb. Dahlia tastes the word. What else did Brand say? Something about... a tank. That's it. She's getting warmer, she is certain of it. The bomb and the tank...

The tank! The tank. How could she have forgotten about the tank?

"How's the bomb coming along?" Brand asks.

"Almost there," someone answers.

Dahlia catches her father's eyes just as her lips part in a wide smile. The tank the sisters told me about that night on base when Vallesia had just turned nine. The tank that has been haunting her dreams since everything started. She didn't make it up. She didn't imagine it. She relives a memory. Home for the holidays. Down in the basement. The basement they were never supposed to go into. The big, white sheet, covering...

"It's a magical tank," Dahlia says, remembering his words. Her father's eyes grow wide in surprise for the first time. "A very special tank. Just our secret."

He doesn't respond.

"I bet I can guess how it's special," she says, her eyebrows arched and wearing a sassy grin.

His mouth is a thin line.

"It can get into The Forest of Magnificent Trees. You're going to drive the bomb there and blow Him up."

Really? Is that what he's planning?

The father neither agrees nor disagrees. He merely looks back down at the bomb, suddenly disinterested in her. In what's before him. In his supposed plan.

There is a click as something is pushed into place. A woman looks up with a wild smile across her face. Her fingers hover over the bomb, quivering. Her eyes are beaming and big, like a child's.

"It's done," she announces.

A flurry of motion, the scrawnier of the workers push themselves away from the bomb, the father included. Two bigger, younger men move toward it. The change happens quickly and smoothly, as if practiced. They reach under the bomb and lift it. Clearly it is a heavy bomb, judging by the sweat on their brows. A heavy bomb designed with enough destructive power to kill a god. I can't help but feel a tug at my heart, imagining my father blown up. I think of the palace I grew up in with my mother, and the gardens, and all the pleasant and unpleasant memories, gone. I feel my insides turn a melancholic gray by the very thought.

Dahlia is about to follow them, but the female engineer pushes her back. When she frees herself, an announcement distracts her. They may or may not be, but most likely are, under attack. No one seems to be able to answer by whom, or really in what way, despite several desperate enquiries.

"I don't know," says the man who has announced the bad news, in the way someone would announce a diagnosis of stage four cancer: helpless, pitiful, somehow distanced from the situation and in denial that their own mortality may be challenged as well. "The sensors have detected heat signals outside, but none of the cameras show anything. Not even the infrared night vision cameras, which doesn't make sense at all. I just don't know."

"Maybe the sensors are broken," someone suggests.

Cute.

"It doesn't matter," Brand assures them, his loud, authoritative voice booming once again. "The compound will hold. It will protect us. Whatever is outside will never make it in. This is, right now, the safest place you could be in the entire world. Believe me."

As he says this, there is loud banging at the walls. Each outburst crashes against the outer wall with the force of several cars. The compound shakes and grown men lose their balance and fall over. The sound of equipment breaking is barely audible between explosions.

Brand's face looks as if he is trying hard, but failing, to hide his doubts and fears.

Dahlia motions for Seraphina and The Chief to follow her to the door, but the gesture is lost to darkness as the lights cut off again. When a single light flickers on in the corner, shadows play on the wall and on the floor—threatening like hungry monsters, their large, abyssal fangs reaching out for solid matter to consume.

The compound groans.

Someone yells from down the hallway, perhaps the bouncer. Then everything drowns in deafening sounds: A large explosion, the banging growing louder, the screams, the compound itself howling. Dahlia is knocked over and falls, busting her lip against the cold floor.

When the explosion is over, hearing gradually returns to Dahlia as a high-pitched tinnitus growing in intensity. The return of sight is even more damning: the scene is nothing short of chaotic. The lights are flickering intensely, and bodies are scattered all over the floor, unconscious or groaning in pain. Blood pours out of them from what looks like huge bite marks, large enough to be caused by bears. The screens have fallen to the floor and smashed into dagger-like shards of glass which has impaled several. The mother has a huge shard going through her stomach.

Dahlia catches sight of her father recovering and staggering onto his feet. He looks at her for only a fleeting moment before grunting and pushing himself up with help from an unwilling body. His skin is red from blood and scarred with glass.

Dahlia tries to push herself up. She is lucky. The glass has only scratched her, and she rises with more ease than her father. Nothing has bitten into her. Yet.

Her group lies unconscious on the floor beside her, and she doesn't know whether to save them or follow her father.

You can't afford too many charities at times like these.

She has a moment of existential dread as she agrees with her father. With his saying. With what he told her when she was a child. But he's right, and now he's getting away, limping with one hand on his leg.

She can't afford — no. Dahlia rushes toward Seraphina and The Chief, who are grunting but not yet up. She lends them a hand, bringing Seraphina squarely back on her feet. They do not seem injured. They never came far into the room, where those most affected seem to be. The others, the ones she brought with her... she can afford *some* charities, but...

"Let's go!" Dahlia yells as loud as her vocal cords allow, hoping to outshout the tinnitus.

The Chief is already up and helping Seraphina, but she is too distracted. She is completely paralyzed, her eyes filled with tears and dread. She refuses to be moved, standing firm with all the power she can muster while watching the scene, the oversized bite marks, the growing pools of blood. What is that from? The shadows stretch themselves long and leap at her.

The Chief uses his size against her, lifts her up, and carries her away in his arms.

They make their way out the door. The father is already limping down the dark hallway, lit only by the occasional flickering light. Here, every little grunt and breath and beating heart drums off the naked walls.

They follow. The banging continues. They flinch with every distant explosion.

Explosion — that's what has happened here. That was what made the mammoth sound that tore the compound apart. The bomb. It went off. The father is here, in front of them, standing by the chasm, staring at his ravaged compound, sweat visibly dripping off him. A torso and a leg lay scattered, the two men torn apart. There is a huge hole exposing the completely dark outside. It looks like a black hole into nothing. The floor is gone, but only one floor down. The father must be considering whether there is a better way down than jumping.

The walls stop banging. They realize now, more than ever, how loud it had been. In its absence, the compound seems too quiet. Then, there is another sound. A deep, throaty growl, like a bear or a wolf. It sounds large and predatory. When the lights flicker off again, the growl gets closer, much closer, and multiplies. Feet or paws patter on the floor. The lights flicker back on and the sound disappears.

The father turns to a utility locker mounted against on a wall nearby. He reaches in and finds a flashlight.

The light goes off again. The sounds get closer. It is definitely the sound of predators—panting, growling, pattering. The father shines the light behind them, down the hallway, and they catch a glimpse of something: huge monsters, black but not just black. Deep black, like the black at the end of a well, drawing you in. There are eyes peering from the void. The monsters whimper in the light and retreat into the darkness.

The lights flicker back on.

Dahlia checks the locker for more flashlights, but there was only the one. She feels the sudden pull of a firm hand on her back. She falls back, swept off her feet by a force so powerful as to defy nature. Everything goes dark again as she disappears, her scream choked, her body suddenly light and her mind empty.

Oh, no.

That wasn't me. I didn't take her. I took something of His and now He has taken something of mine.

CHAPTER
32

THE PRIEST WAKES TO COMPLETE chaos. He tries to move but his body is not obeying. It is as if he is already dead. All he can do is look around at the many dead or soon to be dead bodies. It is a surreal scene.

What can he do now?

Why did he come here?

He feels ashamed. He feels as if this is his punishment for defying his Dear Creator. After a lifetime of servitude, things can so soon, with such ease, turn. They said they wanted to fight their Creator, *his* Creator, and he went with them of his own free will.

The shame consumes him.

The walls are still banging.

He prays. What else is there to do?

"Dear Creator," he whispers. As he talks, he suddenly feels a sharp pain in his back and something warm and gooey spreads all over. There is so much blood.

"I am scared and I am weak-minded. I am ashamed of

myself, that I might doubt your goodness." He continues, groaning. "I am afraid that I have not passed your test, and although I apologize—deeply, from the depths of my heart—I hope you might see that I am only human. When you birthed us, we needed your wife's guidance, but we are still young and foolish. I fear we may need her again." He takes a deep breath, determined to complete what he is sure will be his final prayer. "I will not insult you by asking you not to hurt me, or not to hurt my friends. What happens is going to happen because you will it, but please see us, and please hear me. By your will, let me not succumb to this fire."

The banging stops. He thinks that's a good sign, that maybe his Creator has heard him. He continues, fueled by hope.

"Please understand that it is hard to love that which you fear, and it is hard not to fear that which hurts you. Please grant me the strength to not be afraid so I may love you the way you intend me to."

A low growl rises from the silence, then grows louder and angrier. He opens his eyes to find himself surrounded by a sea of red gems hovering in the darkness, watching him.

"Oh, Dear Creator!" the priest yells. In a last, desperate attempt, he screams, "Please, not me!"

The shadows with red eyes and needle-sharp teeth engulf him in seconds, attacking his throat, spine, feet, and hands all at the same time. They are like piranhas, tearing him apart, leaving no trace that he was ever alive. Only his clothes remain and a pile of bones. Nothing identifiable.

Of the teenager, something else remains: a picture of her late mother stuck to the back of her clear phone case. On the back of this picture and hidden from the world is her mother's last words before she met a death almost as painful as her daughter's.

Pray you never meet an angry god.

CHAPTER
33

THE CHIEF WATCHES THE FATHER shine his flashlight down the chasm. *Is he going to jump?* he wonders. *Should they follow?*

Seraphina has calmed down in his grasp. He sets her down. Still a little wobbly on her feet, she dries her red eyes and looks from the father to The Chief and then toward —

Dahlia is gone.

They realize it at the same time.

"Dahlia?" The Chief cries out, but there is no response beyond that of the predators lurking. The father turns around as well, lighting up the hallway behind them with his flashlight. He looks, for a moment, concerned. The Chief is filled with rage as the father shakes his head, turns back toward the chasms, and sits down in front of it.

"Dahlia!" Seraphina cries out, her voice breaking.

She's gone. She's hundreds of miles away by now.

There's no response. Seraphina steps further into the darkness, closer to the growling, lurking shadows. The Chief grabs her arm to stop her. They can't see Dahlia anywhere. To them, it looks as if she's disappeared into thin air.

"Dahlia!" they both yell as loud as they can.

Oh, how quiet this moment is. How safe and nice and temporary and in no way sustainable. They are runners before the race, before the gun shoots and sends them off. Dear, how fast they will have to run. I can barely watch.

The father leaps. The hallway is plunged into darkness, and danger covers them like a blanket. The Chief pulls at Seraphina's arm and they also jump.

Try to outrun a bear, lion, or wolf — or any predator at all — and I believe you'll find humans are not meant to win such chases, and surely not down an absurdly long, perfectly straight hallway. That's the price your kind pays for opposable thumbs and higher consciousnesses. The Chief and Seraphina would easily perish were they not blessed with backup generators for the backup generators, which attempt with a stubborn heroism to keep the flickering lights alive and the monsters at bay.

I have calculated exactly how long the last set of backup generators will last: one minute and twenty-seven seconds. It is not possible for Seraphina and The Chief to outrun the monsters. Humans and banshees alike aren't built for it. They're outrunning time — or attempting to, anyway. I calculate it will take them at least two minutes to reach the end of the hallway and get through the door to the basement, and not even then will they be safe.

Let's see how they do.

The landing sends shooting pain through their feet, radiating up their legs to their spines. It takes them only a second to recover, then a survival instinct takes over. Something brushes their ankles with sharp, grazing fangs, and their legs start moving all by themselves, pain or no pain.

The father has stopped limping. He yields his flashlight like a sword, but only in front of him. The Chief and Seraphina will be eaten before anything grabs him from behind. He does not care what happens to them. In fact, he would prefer them out of the picture sooner rather than later.

One minute, fifteen seconds.

Seraphina reaches for The Chief's hand as they run, but he holds his hands close to his body. The situation is too familiar. It makes his stomach uneasy. He doesn't trust himself.

One minute.

The lights flicker. The monsters are playing musical statues, moving only in the millisecond where the lights are out, hiding in the shadows in the creases of the walls whenever they are back on. The Chief's wheezing is almost louder than their feet slapping the floor. Adrenaline or no adrenaline, he is not fit for running, no less sprinting. Seraphina looks back at him, worried.

Forty seconds.

He considers stopping, staying back to give her a better chance, but only for a moment because that is not who he is. That's who he'd like to be, but never who he is. This whole situation is too familiar. If one of them has to sacrifice themselves, would he be a willing volunteer?

Twenty-five seconds.

They don't even know where they are going. They are just running. Running after the man in front of them, the man whose name they don't even know. The father is simply the father.

Fifteen seconds.

Oh, dear. They're still far from the door. The father hasn't even reached it, and they haven't caught up to him. They won't make it. I'm not trying to be suspenseful, I promise. They won't make it with those short, useless legs.

Ten seconds.

The father's flashlight shines on the door. Maybe there's some hope.

Five seconds.

The backup generator caves in and the lights flicker off. The monsters close in, ripping at their flesh and pulling at their hair. The darkness takes a bite out of them. The father runs through the door to the basement and shuts it behind him. Seraphina slams into it, fumbling with the handle.

The Chief screams out in pain. He raises a hand, searching for Seraphina's, and falls against the wall. His legs are unable to carry him, if they're even still there. He is not sure. The pain is so intense his mind is reeling. He can't focus, can't comprehend that he is being eaten alive.

Seraphina yanks open the door so hard the father nearly falls backward, down the staircase. He swears and turns, running down with the flashlight's beam bouncing ahead of him.

She looks over her shoulder. The darkness has engulfed The Chief. All she hears are low whimpers, then something large bowls her over and she falls rolling down the stairs. She reaches the bottom in a tangled mess of twisted limbs and realizes it was The Chief that knocked her over. Adrenaline pumps through their bodies and even a second of inactiveness makes them feel as if they are about to burst open, pure energy tearing their flesh-cages apart as they untangle themselves.

Seraphina looks down and realizes his left leg is barely held together. Thin slices of meat and skin dangle from deep gashes, the bones exposed. A trail of blood flows down the staircase like a mountain creek cascading into the basement.

She stands up, not sure how to help him. She tries to orient herself. The basement is wild and messy. Beast-like monsters are creeping in the corners — strange shapes and swirling shadows with outlines of fur. In the middle of the room is a huge monstrosity of a thing hidden beneath several layers of white sheets.

The father is shining the flashlight every which way as he approaches the hidden monstrosity and pulls the sheet away to reveal a tank. An enormous military tank with the barrel of the huge cannon pointed straight at her.

There is no time to waste being amazed or surprised. The Chief crawls, dragging a bloody trail behind him. Seraphina runs. The light in the ceiling flickers as she scales the tank. The father has already climbed on top and is fumbling with the lever of the hatch, which seems stuck.

"I help," she offers and holds out her hand for the flashlight. The father looks back at her, frowning. "Trust," she tries.

He snarls at her in response. "You're a banshee." He turns his attention back to the hatch.

"I help."

Stubbornly, he tries to hold the flashlight with his mouth as he grasps the stubborn lever in both hands, but he fumbles and drops the light. Seraphina picks it up before he does. Their eyes meet in a stare as he almost fights her for it.

Where is The Chief?

She hears his scared, pained whimpers and finds him with the flashlight. He's halfway up the tank and a monster has its sharp fangs buried in his remaining leg. As she shines the light on it, it retreats, but keeps its grip around his leg, pulling him down the tank.

"Here!" the father yells in desperation. "I can't see!"

The hungry snarls grow louder. She tries to divide the flashlight's attention between the father and The Chief. Every time the light leaves The Chief, he screams and is dragged further down the tank, the monsters eating into him.

Something yanks her foot, throwing her back. She slams her chin against the cold iron surface and bites through her tongue. Her mouth fills with blood. The monster pulls again. She drops the flashlight and feels its teeth sinking into her ankle. The flashlight rolls and falls down the side of the tank.

She hears a metallic thump from the hatch finally being opened. A ray of light emerges from the hole, which the father dives into.

She turns around and throws a fist at whatever is behind her, but her strike passes through thin air. She screams and looks back to see the father reaching out his arm, fumbling for the handle to close the hatch. The monster pulls at her again, and she reaches out for a handhold on the hull to hold on to.

A bright light blinds her. She covers her eyes with one hand until the light passes. She looks over to see The Chief on top of the tank, flashlight in hand. He aims it at the monster behind her, which lets go of her ankle and cowers away. He must have caught the flashlight when it rolled away.

The father has found the handle. Through pure will, it seems, The Chief forces his maimed body around, placing his mangled leg in front of the hatch just as the father tries to close it. There's a loud smack as the metal slams against The Chief's leg and he screams out in pain.

With Seraphina's last effort, she pushes herself against the hull and leaps for the opening, throwing herself down. The Chief follows right after.

CHAPTER
34

THE INSIDE OF THE TANK is narrow, barely fitting the three of them. The Chief is bleeding out on a seat under the hatch, while Seraphina stands in between him and the father, who is in a seat opposite. Pipes and metal surrounds them, threatens to narrow in and squish them, she feels. Her arms are stretched to either side, both to keep balance and to hold back the walls.

The monsters smash against the sides, trying to force their way in. It sounds like crashing thunder. Their claws screech against the metal.

Seraphina searches for a first aid kit. The father is also searching for something, though doubtfully the same. In a rare moment of luck, Seraphina is the first to succeed, retrieving a kit from a corner. She opens it and quickly glances over the insides to assemble parts for an improvised tourniquet.

The Chief's face is paling, and he has stopped screaming. Instead, he mumbles incoherently. The mutilated leftovers of his leg paint the floor and chair red, sprays on buttons and screens. It seems to Seraphina that he should surely have passed out, if not died, by now. Still, she continues her quest to assemble a tourniquet, finally settling on a roll of bandages and a thermometer to use as a stick. She fumbles. It is not in her nature to save people. She feels like a barking cat. She places the cut bandages above where his leg has been mangled and wraps the end around the thermometer, spinning it to tighten it. The Chief gasps in pain but she continues until she can't get it any tighter, then ties it down. She isn't fully satisfied when The Chief's eyes widen and he exerts himself to produce some gesture, as if pointing at something.

She glances behind her to find the father holding a gun, and she is staring down the barrel. She is paralyzed, her hairs strutting on end.

"Oh, you are scared now?" The father mocks, his voice low and sinister. His eyes are nothing but darkness and she finds not an inch of kindness within them. "Why, how the tables have turned. Isn't it ironic?"

She does not understand and worries that she has met the limit of her language abilities.

"Huh?" he prompts, giving the pointed gun a slight shake.

"What?" she squeaks. Her heart is beating so hard it feels as if it is about to leap from her throat.

He scoffs. "It's usually the other way around, isn't it? Your kind is usually the one behind the barrel, not in front of it. You are the ones who bring death, not the other way around."

She looks no less confused. "We warn," she says, her voice as light and soft as feathers. "Not kill. Warn. So say goodbye."

His jaw clenches in an attempt to stay calm. A vein pulsates across his forehead. "Imagine foreseeing every disaster and doing nothing to stop them. Imagine being so void of emotions that you don't care about anyone else's misery. Oh, don't tell me you cared. Don't tell me you ever shed a single tear. You can't because you didn't."

He is right; she never felt like crying then. But now the tears are welling up inside of her, threatening to burst forth. There are so few names still tugging at her throat, and that's somehow worse. There's barely anyone left to kill.

"And your god?" he continues through gritted teeth. "The one you've so obediently supported for millions of years. How about that? Do you still support Him?"

Does she?

"You know what?" he asks, smirking. "Tell me you don't love Gluskab. Right here, right now, and I might let you go."

How can she? Love is such an abstract shape. She was made to love Gluskab. She is not sure she could ever stop loving Him, no matter what He did. No matter how many worlds, He tortured. She is not sure she supports Him anymore, but she could never not love Him.

The father disables the safety with a click and wets his lips.

Lie! Just lie, you silly, moral creature.

"You old," she says instead.

The father raises his eyebrow. "An odd choice of last words."

"No," she says, shaking her head. She tries again. "You old," she repeats, searching for words. "So... before. You remember. You felt. What? The Dear Creator."

"You should learn to speak properly. Your kind isn't very smart, are you? You can't even speak."

She takes a deep breath, shaking. "You remember. The Dear Creator before. Before. You hated Him?"

"Yes," the father says without hesitation.

"Why?"

"I don't want anyone deciding my fate. He has no right to decide for me, to decide what I can and cannot do. It's like we're His dolls in His dollhouse and He doesn't understand that we are as real as Him—that we are worth as much as Him. What if a single human got to decide for every other human? That wouldn't be right. We wouldn't allow that. But He's stronger than all of us, so we can't do anything about it and just accept it. There's no choice here. We *have* to obey. It's a divine dictatorship, is what it is."

"He not human. Perfect."

"He's perfect? Does this look perfect to you?" The father waves the gun with a scoff. "Does this look like the result of a perfect being making a perfect decision? Maybe for Himself. That's all He cares about. Himself. His wife? No, He created her because He was lonely, and everything else was created as an extension of that original loneliness. That's all we do, that's all living is—loneliness and creation. It's not right. And why would you care about anyone else when you're at the top of the food chain, anyway? I tell you, you dirty Knower-nothing, you shouldn't trust anyone who claims to be perfect."

"You upset He left."

He scoffs louder. "Leaving is the best thing He ever did. We got to do what we wanted to do. It's like a child finally being allowed to move out. We weren't His dolls anymore. It's the coming back I mind. He should never have come back. He should always have been gone. He should never have been here, only that way would we have been allowed to be. To just *be*. But He could never give us that; His ego is too big. But now, I'm going to remove Him from this world forever. The creation should always outlive the creator."

"But. No Gluskab—"

"Without Him, I wouldn't be alive, you're right. I would have never existed. But neither would my pain. On the whole, in my life, pain outweighs happiness. I wish I would have never been. But let me ask you this: without me, my children would have never existed, either. Does that give me any right to kill them?"

She does not reply.

"So why does that logic apply to Him, but not to me?" he prompts again.

She looks away. Then back.

"How?" she says. "Kill him. Bomb. How?"

"The bomb's gone, yeah, but I've got something else up my sleeve. But you won't be around to see what it is. I've prepared for this for a very long time. I always knew He'd come back. He could never leave us alone. He could never give us that. But I've got my tricks." He laughs. "You don't even know. You really don't know. But I do. I know how to kill Him. Try to see if you can figure it out, and I'll leave you alone."

She cannot.

I think I know what he means. I recognize that gun. I *made* that gun.

"Your kind really isn't very smart," he concludes with a self-righteous smile. "If that's all you've got—"

He aims the gun, ready to shoot, but right as he does, The Chief leaps across Seraphina. He grabs hold of the barrel, pointing it away from her and towards him. In surprise, the father shoots anyway. The thunderous explosion fills the tank as the bullet swishes past The Chief. It hits the interior and ricochets. Quiet falls on the vehicle. No one breathes. Seconds feel like they drag into minutes.

Seraphina sits up, having thrown herself to the deck. She inspects her body and finds no holes. She looks back at The Chief. He is still there, in his pool of blood, but with no fresh wounds. She turns back to the father to find another pool of blood spreading from a massive cavity drilled through his forehead where the bullet has gone straight through, killing him instantly.

The Chief is not breathing anymore. He has no pulse. Seraphina hunches over him, holding him in her arms. She imagines his veins will start throbbing again, his heart suddenly beating, his leg growing out, and blood returning to his body. She hopes that her imagining it will somehow make it real, a glitch in the world, a secret for her to uncover in the most dire time.

But The Chief remains dead. The father remains dead. The world remains dead.

DAY 4

At some point, even gods waste away.

CHAPTER 35

WHAT DO YOU THINK? THAT because I am a demigod and because my father is the Dear Creator that I would be exempt from this night's bout of terror? Maybe you think the monsters would come knocking at my door and say, "Excuse me, sir, we've come to maul and tear and slaughter, do you have a minute?" Should I reply, "Actually, I'm a demigod, so I shouldn't like any mauling and tearing and slaughtering, thank you very much."

Did *your* god exempt *his* son from suffering?

Last night, I lost and regrew so many limbs that I feel born anew. Except for a limp stemming from one leg having grown back longer than the other, I've no complaints about this new body. The pain is another matter entirely, but let us not dwell on that.

Vallesia is in one piece. I'm very proud of that, but then, she will have to be in one piece. She will have to not be broken. She is so beautiful, lying there, sleeping next to me.

She's waking now. Dear, her eyes. They just draw you in,

don't they?

"Hello, you," I say. I try to sound pleasant, but find my new voice is that of a young boy. The high pitch is amusing, but the mismatch is far from calming.

She returns my stare with wide eyes and attempts to scoot away with a whimper. This morning, as soon as my body grew back to a somewhat human shape, I cleaned the small hut that we sought refuge in. I took out buckets full of blood and bags full of bones and dumped it all in the forest out back. It was odd, getting rid of your own previous bodies like that, my old snakeskins, but imagine if she woke up in that mess. Even now, she is shaking, her eyes darting around, from me to the room, searching for weapons, anything to defend herself with.

"Don't worry," I say. "It's just me." But she doesn't remember who 'just me' is, and then I realize that I have gone through many bodies since last she's seen me. I'm not even that tall anymore. And less lanky. Even if she remembers me, how would she recognize me?

Where is that mask? She watches as I move to the corner where the mask is propped up on a chair. I put it on, struggling to fit it properly over my new head, which is bigger and squarer than before. I am happy with it, though, because it has grown out in one piece. It is a full head with eyes, ears, a nose, and a mouth, which all makes sense together. With my last face, I had so gradually lost an eye, a nose, a cheek, and so on, that when the parts grew out one by one, they grew out mismatched and created a monster. That was the original idea behind the mask, to hide the monster, though now it is the only way I recognize myself.

When I turn around, masked, I see a glimmer of recognition, then disbelief.

"You're not real," she whispers.

"I'm as real as you are."

She blinks and furrows her brow. "You were my childhood imaginary friend."

"I thought you'd think that. Maybe I shouldn't have stopped

visiting you, but you were growing older and I was afraid. If you kept talking about me, they would think you were crazy. And if you didn't... I never wanted you to *feel* crazy, either."

She looks as if she believes I might be crazy, though that doesn't make any more sense of it.

"I'm sorry," I continue. "I should have visited. Or not. I'm not sure. I'm doing the best I can. But I've been there with you always. I really have. Very, very small and—oh, it doesn't matter."

I try to smile, but the mask covers my mouth. I see her looking around the room for an escape route.

"Please don't leave," I say. "These have been some hard and confusing days for you, I know. I'm sorry about that. I wanted to protect you better. I just don't have many powers left. I needed to time everything perfectly. I could never, I'm sure you know, have rivaled the Creator. My powers are nowhere near..."

I stop myself. She isn't listening, and she doesn't understand what she hears.

"I'm sorry," I say, taking a deep breath. "This is not helping. Let me try again. I'll start from the top: I'm your childhood friend, yes. But I am also real. And I am also the son of Jarda and the Creator and I have watched you since you were a child, preparing you for this. One day, you'll forgive me for everything I've forced you to sacrifice—everything I *will* force you to sacrifice. Or maybe you won't. Now, there are important things I need to tell you. First, how we stop all of this. Then, how we save your family."

She looks right at me, her eyes wide. She is finally listening.

CHAPTER
36

THE SUN SETS RELUCTANTLY. IT crawls across the landscape, one hand on a mountain, and peers over it with teeth barred and a low, nervous hum. It spends a long time considering whether it dares moving to the top and, once it has, decides it will not leave again. Every time it leaves, it has noticed, the world goes awry. Today, it will stand its ground and protect what little there is left. Is there anything left? It can see no one.

The world is empty except for the chirping of birds and croaking of frogs.

Where are all the people?

It is by far the cleanest of the apocalypse days. The shadow demons leave little from their dinners: bones, teeth, clothing, shoes, and blood — mainly blood. They even clean up the corpses from previous trials and help rid the world of the rancid stench of decomposing bodies. If it wasn't for their entirely murderous nature, one might even briefly, very briefly, consider appreciating their fastidiousness.

There! There is one. A person, though not a human. The sun breathes out in relief.

Seraphina is inside a tank forcing its way through Capital City's densest traffic jam. Last night, after the monsters stopped banging the sides and the bodies started going stiff in each seat, she crawled into the front with the controls. Seraphina has never even driven a car, much less a tank, but when she pressed the screen, it seemed to come alive all by itself. The garage door rolled up with a loud roar, and the wheels started rolling.

She has been staring straight ahead all night, her muscles tense, her teeth well in the process of grinding themselves down. She is shaking, sure that she has never felt anything this intense before, sure that she isn't meant to. Fear? Anger? Whatever it is, there is a fault in her program, and she feels ready for a dysfunction, her whole body coming apart like cogs in a wheel. This is what one gets when they pursue things not within their nature. This is her own fault.

The city is a ghost city now, completely empty and eerie, the dust still settling. Even the animals are hiding. Store windows are shattered. Bones crunch under the weight of the tank and she leaves a trail of blood behind her as she drives.

The tank climbs cars and crushes them under its weight. Every obstacle is pushed aside, torn apart, climbed over, crushed, or massacred, crunching and shattering. The tank clears chasms in the pavement where the earthquakes opened the land and pushes through the debris of fallen buildings. The tank seems to press on through sheer will, crushing even whole busses in its way.

She makes it to the middle of Capital City where the tank stops for a moment. She watches the screen displaying the outside world. In front of her towers her old home, the Forest of Magnificent Trees. The trees reach far to the sky, guarding the once so familiar grass, flowers, animals, and huts. Are the huts still there? Is the brook? The swing? The cherry bushes? She can almost taste the cherries.

It is a trap. She soon recollects her childhood, the banshees and their maker, the Creator and his wife. Playing games like hide and seek and hopscotch, having fun. It is thousands of years ago, surely, but having fun? That was before the humans were created. It was before the banshees were stripped of their individuality and molded to fit their one job as sidekicks and support characters. Back then, they were allowed to have *fun*. She cannot even remember now what that feels like. She had friends. Friends among the banshees, playmates she —

Oh. She is remembering me. That's awkward. Yes, I suppose we used to be friends. But then, I was a little boy and would play with anyone who would play with me. The forest was filled with banshees just a little older than me, and I would play with them all day. They were my brothers and sisters, all of them. The girls would dress me up and pretend I was their doll. We would play tag, climb trees, and —

No, I'm not being sucked into this series of recollection. She isn't either. Done now.

The tank edges forwards, nearing the edge of the forest, then stops again.

She remembers the day where, without warning and without explanation, a mythical force swept them away. Away from their huts, the brook, and the swing — she had been on the swing. Her wings felt hot. Then, as they neared the exit, they went up in flames. Their backs were like bonfires and the smoke rose to the heavens in a multitude of pillars. They screamed. Masses gathered around them as they fell to the ground and rolled around. Their feathers were gone within minutes, reduced to ashes and carried away by the wind. By the time the people decided fetching water was not an act of blasphemy, their wings were seared off. The remaining stumps had to be operated on. For months, the hospitals were filled with wailing banshees, some even blaspheming, all of them heartbroken, confused, and anxious to get out. To go back — go back where?

Afterward, they swore none of them felt pain. That they were only distressed because they were worried about their Dear Creator. Seraphina told herself that for a long time, so long, in fact, that she stopped doubting if it were true. But it wasn't. She knows that now. It was so painful.

The scars on her back feel as if they are on fire now. Her back is one big scar, damaged tissue covering every inch of it. When Dahlia touched it, just two nights ago, it felt so odd, so strangely removed from her. She'd felt Dahlia retreat in disgust, but only at first. Then... then they...

Her back burns, reminding her, warning her. She dares to cross the border again now. Why? Because one of the corpses behind her claimed the tank would be able to? Even then, she will have to leave the safety of the tank at some point. What then? What is the plan, even? She has no plan. What is she going to say to Gluskab if He's in there?

Where is Dahlia? she wonders. *Does He have Dahlia?*

Her fingertips tremble, then the trembling moves up her hands and arms, then down her legs to her feet. The tank begins to drive again, but as it crosses the border, lightning of historical proportions rips through the sky and thunder deafens her for a moment as it envelops the tank. Everything shakes and the tank is lifted off the ground.

Then it is quiet. Everything is quiet. The tank persists, starting to roll again.

But the forest is not done—far from it. The lightning bolts grow larger and more powerful. They hit the tank five at a time, ten at a time, and they stay there for long, ejecting enough electricity to power Capital City for months. The entire sky is illuminated, blinding generations of bunnies and foxes.

But the tank persists. It screams back at the sky with a raised fist and continues on its defiant way unphased. She continues. The lightning can do nothing to the tank. It is just electricity; it is no bother. She has seen worse.

The lightning gives up, but the trees are enraged. Their branches reach down and pull up their roots. They take a massive step forward and fall in a suicidal attempt to crush the tank below their weight. But the tank persists. It continues on its defiant way, unphased, with not a single scratch on its surface. Seraphina isn't steering anymore; the tank has its own mission now, its own life, its own will.

Last is the ground, which grows eyebrows to furrow and shakes its mighty back so everything goes flying: the rocks, the trees, the rubbles, the animals, and the tank. But the tank persists. It bounces as if on a trampoline and flies forward, Seraphina holding on tight, gravity a mess, bruises all over and the creaking—she thinks the tank might be coming apart, but then it lands.

Everything is quiet. The sky is quiet, the trees are quiet, and the ground is quiet. Here, in front of the palace, where the tank landed, nothing dares to touch them or even get too close. Not even the wind, the bravest of everyone, which goes everywhere, dares to go here. The flowers have migrated from the porch.

She remembers this place from long ago, yet almost doesn't recognize it. It towers tall, like Dahlia's father's compound, enveloped by the magnificent trees. The wood front is rotting, falling apart, with big, gray boils of mold spreading all over. It is hairy and disgusting. It looks as if it smells of rancid death and decay. There is something ominous about it, as if there is a filter in front of it. She half expects the sound of crows, but crows do not dare to go here. The silence is like nothing before, as if the whole place is in a bubble.

She is terrified, but more than this, she is angry. The tank and her are the same now. With bared teeth and a war cry, they charge forward. The tank climbs the staircase, which easily caves in. It runs across the porch, smashing through the front door, and into the living room.

———

There is a gaping hole in the wall of the Creator's palace. There is a tank in His living room. You would think the god at least somewhat responsive; you would imagine Him jumping right out of His plush, floral couch and storming to the tank to demand an explanation. At the very least, you might imagine

Him turning His head in the direction of the enormous crash. Maybe He would make a faint 'oh' sound. But He does nothing of that sort.

Seraphina climbs out the top of the tank, still vibrating. She jumps down, landing on gray and brown carpeted floors in a whirl of dust, disturbing her mutinous swagger with a coughing fit. She persists, regardless, making her way across the enlarged, empty seating area and nearing the single couch situated in front of an ashen fireplace covered in cobwebs. The mold is inside too. The walls are a gray-green and hairy. It is like being inside a dying monster. Something slimy sticks to her shoes.

The god does not stir. She stands in front of the couch, behind which an enormous painting of Jarda hangs above the fireplace, regal, dusty, and looking down at her husband, her widower, with a smirk. The picture and Seraphina both watch Him. His beard and hair have grown long, tousled, and so greasy it looks wet. Fluffy cushions envelop his thin body, almost swallowing Him. His arms lay limp on either side, palms up, fingers unresponsive. He gazes straight ahead, as if seeing through her. He looks dead.

She steps closer, listening for His breathing. It is so faint she cannot be sure she is not imagining it. She places her finger on His neck, searching for a pulse. Again, it is so weak she cannot be certain.

She has seen Gluskab before and she *knows* that what is before her is the Creator, but it is hard to believe. It is not so much that He does not look like *the* Creator, it is more that He does not look like *a* Creator. He looks human. He looks so feeble, weak, and pathetic; and He stinks. He stinks of piss, sweat, and mold. He smells as if He is rotting. An image of Dahlia flashes through her mind as she extends her hand and slaps Him. The smack echoes from the high ceilings and bounces off the fuzzy marble walls.

This receives a reaction. The god emits a low wheeze and slowly turns His head toward her. She leaps back in surprise, bumping into a coffee table behind her as He moves His hand to His flushed cheek. He touches the sore spot in slow motion.

"Ouch," He says in a tone so feeble and pathetic that she feels embarrassed to have hurt someone so innocent and defenseless. But His transgressions are many, and she doesn't feel guilty for long.

"Why did you do that?" He asks.

She is at a loss for words, more than normally. She stutters before managing to say, "Thought dead."

"So you hit me? What would that have accomplished?" His response is slow and lethargic. He doesn't sound angry or accusing.

She cannot produce an answer.

"Ah," He says. "I thought for a while there you had learned how to speak, but banshees don't speak, so that can't be. I suppose I might be losing it. You might not be real, either, although the slap felt real."

He looks to His hands as if considering whether He might have slapped himself.

"Am real," she promptly replies, summoning enough defiance to puff up her chest.

"You do talk. Why have you taught yourself to speak? You aren't supposed to."

She wishes she had taught herself to speak better. This conversation is not what she had expected, nor what she prepared for all night. She reaches behind her, stroking the gun in her belt with her index finger. Dahlia's father's gun.

Gluskab sighs. "Whatever. I suppose it doesn't matter."

He turns His head toward the tank and the gaping hole. He appears deep in thought, though still not upset.

"Does matter," she ventures.

"Does it? I suppose. If you think so."

It occurs to her that the god, or man, or whatever in front of her, cannot have much to do with what is going on outside. He doesn't look capable.

"You do this?" she asks, stressing the question as best she can. Intonations are not her strong suit, but He seems to understand. He looks around.

"Which?" He asks.

"All."

"All? What are you asking me—you want to know if I'm the Creator? I suppose I am, although at present that is not a simple question for me to answer. Or perhaps, do you want to know if I've done…" He looks out the gaping hole again, pressing each bit of air out of Him in a deep sigh. He must breathe in again before He can finish His sentence. "I suppose that would also be a hesitant yes. Pardon my riddles. I'm not doing it on purpose. Dear, talking tires me. I might just take a nap if that's okay…"

She reaches out to shake Him awake. His arm is nothing but bones wrapped in parchment-thin skin. She looks panicked.

He opens his eyes again. "Ah, you. Still. Could you leave me alone, please? I just want to lay here. At some point, even gods waste away."

"No. Not sleep."

"Why? What do you want with me? I can't fix any of this, if that's what you're wondering. I did this, but I didn't do it. You'll see, I'm on my way here. I know you're here, just so you know. Ah, I'm speaking in riddles again now, am I? I must seem like a crazy old man to you."

He does. But He isn't; I know what He means. The other one. The angry one. He's coming.

Gluskab turns His head in my direction. I think He is noticing the vase with the pretty flowers I brought for Him and placed on a small table by the door, then I realize He is not looking at the flowers. He's looking at me. I feel naked and exposed. I make myself smaller, trying harder to hide myself in the corner, but he keeps looking at me. Seraphina cannot see me and looks with confusion in the same direction, wondering what has caught His attention. He doesn't address me.

"Need answers," she says, trying to frown, but it looks more as if she is pretending to frown. Copying something she's seen in a movie.

"Right. Just be quick so I can get back to sleep. And then

promise not to disturb me anymore."

"Why," she says. "Why this?"

"It's not that I don't want to answer you. It's just a little difficult to answer you because, as I've stated, I haven't technically done this. Or am doing this. I suppose I'm not done yet. Far from it. Here's an answer you might use, though: I am very sad *and* I am very angry. Just like you weren't made for these emotions—and for the life of me, I cannot comprehend why you have gone out of your way to learn them—I wasn't either. It's too much for me. It has *literally* torn me apart. But you... It is just like the speaking. Why have you learned to speak? Why have you learned to feel? Life was so much easier for you before, wouldn't you agree?"

"Because friends dead."

"You think you're sad because your friends are dead? Ah. Though you didn't have friends to worry about back then, did you? You would have perished easily and quickly and by your dying thought, you would have repented to me. You wouldn't have made such a hassle. Now, you know, you're only torturing yourself by resisting. I'm mostly taking your side in this, but this one's on you, I'd say."

He looks at me again. "Wouldn't you agree, son?"

I don't reply. I pretend to be a vase. I don't want to be part of this story. I'm only watching.

He yawns. "Neither one of you are being very talkative. If that's all, I'd like to go back to sleep. Please let me. I really enjoy sleeping. And He, I, the other one, is coming now. I don't think He'll like the mess, by the way."

He lifts His legs with an exaggerated grunt and folds them beneath Him. Then He leans over to the side, cocooning himself on the much too small two-man couch. Seraphina tries to wake Him again, but He is fast asleep this time or pretends to be.

I can hear Him now, the other one, nearing the porch. Walking up the remains of the stairs, seething with rage, breathing out in growls. Boots against wood. Is He dragging something behind Him? The old floorboards creak.

CHAPTER 37

GLUSKAB **APPEARS IN THE HOLE,** still dressed in the skin suit of old Mister Crado. He swaggers across the room with a frown, dragging something behind Him. Steam is coming off of Him. When He gets close enough for Seraphina to make out His black, hateful eyes, she finds it both hard to look into and look away from them. They pull her in, but somewhere where she has no desire to be. It makes her feel uneasy all over.

What is He dragging behind Him? He moves slowly, each step shaking the palace, and the thing behind Him—He is holding a wrist. A person.

Dahlia?

He is dragging Dahlia. I shouldn't be surprised, of course, but the worry stabs at me. I wince. Seraphina looks lost, her eyes big, her shoulders lowering, her fingers no longer closing in on the gun. Dahlia? She cannot connect the dots. Who is this, and why does He have Dahlia? He means them both harm, she is certain, because everything about Him is unsettling. Is she breathing? Seraphina wants to run ahead and tend to her, but she doesn't dare.

"What's this?" the god snarls, stopping in front of the tank. He looks from it to Seraphina. A low growl rises from His throat. "Tell me."

She tries to step backward but bumps into the coffee table again. Her face is the color of the walls — white and gray and greenish.

"I—I," she stutters.

His nostrils flare as He fills His lungs, the old man's chest expanding rapidly. Now He is big, big and threatening, and when He releases the air again, He seems no less large. He is growing in height and width. The old body seems less old, wrinkles disappearing and muscles growing, bulging underneath the ragged uniform. He walks toward Seraphina. Dahlia's unconscious body drags against the soft, hairy carpets.

"You did this," He says, His free finger pointing to her in indignation as His face flushes to a deep maroon. "You did this to my beautiful palace. How dare you! Disrespectful, that's what I say. I'll have you whipped, I will."

She wishes she could make herself smaller. She wishes she'd never come. She wishes her courage had not dispersed so fast. What was she expecting?

He lets go of Dahlia's wrist when He reaches her, couch between them, teeth barred like a wild animal. She should run away, bolt for the door, and perhaps scoop Dahlia up with her. But her feet are planted on the floor and not the strongest wind could move her. What now? What will He do to her? She feels so uncomfortable in her body, the angst of each tensed muscle and wavering hair tangible.

"And you!" He turns, finger now raised in indignation at me instead. "You disloyal son. Locking me in. Trying to unravel this whole thing. Scheming. Whispering. Do you hate me so much? I hear you. Disrespectful, the bunch of you. Don't you have somewhere to be? Go fetch my wife."

I crouch on the floor and pull the small table over, trying

to hide myself behind it. Vallesia is still sleeping. She got overwhelmed and I had to put her to sleep. I'll get her in a minute.

Dahlia grunts in the pocket of silence and Seraphina turns to her, her heart leaping with joy that she is alive. She watches as her soft lips quiver, her fingertips flinch with effort, and listens for another grunt of displeasure. She almost forgets their impending doom. At least Dahlia is alive. She needs to wake her up. Seraphina is certain that she will know what to do. She will fix this whole thing.

"You know her," the god observes, a creepy softness in His voice and a crooked smile. "It really is a small world, after all. And narrowing in. Ah, I can see right through you. No, she won't be waking up anytime soon. At least, you should wish that she doesn't." He moves in closer and lowers His voice, as if telling a secret. "Or I'll just have to put her down again."

"Why?"

"It speaks! My. Wow. How incredibly useless," He marvels at her stupidity before continuing, entertained. "Why? I'm waiting for her sister. My pathetic son took her sister, and I want her back. She can't run away from me now. Do you hear that, son? Wherever you're hiding her—she won't leave her sister behind. Ha!"

Does he think it beneath me to not tell Vallesia about her sister? This is the plan of a madman.

Seraphina does not understand what He means; she has barely understood anything since she entered the room. If only Dahlia could—

"Seraphina..." Dahlia whispers, her lips barely moving as she speaks, but her head turning in an expression of pain.

Seraphina's heart flutters with joy again before the god turns around with a huff and stomps down on Dahlia's face. A small squeak is lost in the cracking of broken bones. Her face erupts in a gushing of blood, then a pop, then a gasp and choked scream from Seraphina, and then silence.

"Told ya'," He says.

When he looks back to Seraphina, it is His turn to be

surprised. She is pointing the gun at Him. Her lips are pale and she is trembling with terror. She is shaking too much to aim properly. If she shoots Him, it will only be by luck.

Gluskab remains unfazed and merely laughs at her.

His being unfazed clearly fazes her as she repositions her feet.

"Talk," she manages. "Or I shoot."

"That's a toy gun, or it might as well be. Do you not know who I am?"

She does not.

He laughs again and points to the other version of Him, snoozing on the couch. "He is me. I am Him. We split, so to speak. Why wouldn't we? There are no rules when you are a god. I can do whatever I want to. So, I tore away the weak parts of myself. Look at Him! How pathetic He looks! I'll enjoy getting rid of Him later. If you want, you can call *Him* the Creator, and me — I can be the *Destroyer*."

She tries and fails to look unsurprised. The gun, then, really is useless, but she keeps it raised, if only for the feeling of her being in any kind of control.

"You did this." she says.

"Yes."

"Why?"

"Why?" He beams. His hair hovers as He speaks, floating above Him in pure anger. The air vibrates with danger. The snoozing god finds it difficult to breathe in the fog and wakes up, one eye propped open. "Why? Why did I do this? Who are you to ask me that? A weak, puny banshee. Pathetic."

He punches the side of the couch and she leaps back with a small squeak. She is still trying to aim with the gun. How did Dahlia's father shoot it? Is it even loaded? Is the safety on — how does she turn the safety off? How does she aim?

"I shoot," she says, voice trembling, eyes watering. She is crouched, shoulders so far up they reach her ears.

"My wife," He sneers.

"Jarda?"

He nods, His lips a thin line. "That's right," He says. "She's dead, and it's because of you. You whole lot are all spoiled rotten. It's the whole species. It's broken, and should have never been. I never wanted you here; that was all Jarda. I made you for her, but I never should have. Everything was better before I made you. Do you know how often I've worried about you? How difficult you've made my life? But not anymore. Jarda's dead, and that was *your* fault."

"Me?"

"You. The banshees. The whole human race. She was happy before all of you."

No, she wasn't.

"I was happy before all of you," He adds.

He wasn't.

"You shut up!" He yells toward the corner where I'm cowering. "I told you to leave and take your snide comments with you! You think you could have done this better, huh? Locking me up all these years as if I were a lowly dog. I'll tell you something. I was happier before I made *you*."

He laughs again. It is a villainous laughter, cartoonish, even.

"And here's something else for *you*," He adds, returning to Seraphina. "You think I'm just going to kill all of you, and that's it? And then you'll be reborn as a flower or a tree? Maybe a cute little puppy? You'd like that, wouldn't you? Ha! No. That's too good for you. I am going to finish you off, you and your little lovebug behind you, and then I am going to rid the world of every sentient being and every non-sentient being, and then your souls will have nowhere to go. Did you consider that? What happens to your souls when they have nowhere to go?"

She has no idea. I have some.

"They linger. Why do you think they fly into the next empty vessel they see? Why not stick around, wait for a nice vessel, a pampered puppy, a spoiled child? Because non-existence is *pain*. Every second hurts more than anything you could ever imagine. That's what I've got in store for you, for all of you! As soon as I've found her — that wretched, spoiled wife of mine has crossed me one too many times — I'll leave this world behind and start over somewhere where the people will appreciate me. Or maybe I'll be all alone, and that will be just fine. There will be no one to disappoint me, then."

Dahlia regains conscience, groaning in pain, trying to push herself up with her palms. The cracking replays for Seraphina. Dahlia's face is still covered in blood. He won't stomp on her again. She can't let Him do that. But what is she going to do? What can she do if that's the will of the Creator? Nothing. She can do nothing.

She looks to the other god for help, pleading with big, watery doe eyes, but He just sighs. The gun feels heavy in Seraphina's hands.

"He won't help you. He wants this too. He wants to die and only I can give Him that. Besides, He is too weak. He couldn't do anything, even if He wanted."

"Please," she begs the Creator, fluids escaping from her eyes and nose in a sudden rush, but He turns and hides between the couch cushions.

"I'm afraid," the *Destroyer* says, puffing His old man's veiny chest as His villainous laughter bellows confidence and power, "your time is up."

But Dahlia is standing up. Slowly, her knees wobbling as she does, her bloodied face dropped towards the floor, her body slumped over. She groans and wheezes, then forms a fist and wields it with her last bout of energy, just barely reaching His chin from below. He stumbles backwards in response, His chin forced upwards, then He looks down and meets her eyes. His are completely black and filled with seething rage. They make her shiver, but she doesn't look away; instead, she holds the gaze with intense determination, while He, too, forms a fist.

Seraphina pulls the trigger and drops the gun. The bullet is ejected in a small explosion, the last hope for sentience. The explosion deafens her, bounces off the walls and high ceilings and moves outside and the sound, the heroic sound of one last act of resistance, momentarily fills the entire world. Even the stars gasp in amazement and then — against all logic — the bullet penetrates Him.

It reaches His chest, right where His heart has shriveled to the size of a nut. It splinters His ribcage and punches through a main aorta and explodes. It takes only a second, then the blood comes rushing out. His confidence, once so bulletproof, tears as His face whitens. His smile fades. Regret floods His flickering eyes.

What is this? He must be thinking. *What did she do to me?* He is freezing, frostbite spreading down his arms, clashing with His boiling blood. He is numb, then He falls, first to his knees, then all the way. He looks up at the puny thing in disbelief; the bird-like angel, the one who talks in a whisper, the one who looks just as horrified as Him.

Did you think, Father, that I would leave humanity without one last chance?

CHAPTER
38

I **SHOULD TELL YOU ABOUT** that day, with the dark gray sky and the mourning and the crying. The day my mother, Jarda, died. I have been putting it off, but now you need to know. How else would you understand?

That day, there was a beautiful sunrise and every single color greeted the sky. There was something not terrible in the air, a sort of electricity that hummed a hymn from my childhood. Perhaps you think I should say that I woke up with a feeling of ominous dread, that I *knew* from the way the trees moved or the clucking of the stream. Or that the clouds, perhaps, spelled out danger. However, it was a beautiful morning. I wanted to bottle the air and breathe it in on a rainy day. It was sweet and charming. It tasted like honey.

Maybe she wanted to end it on a good note, or maybe she saw but didn't feel the world around her, the way you read an old poem and know that it contains every truth, but the words are jangled and for you, and for you alone, indecipherable. I've thought a lot about this.

My mother went for a walk after the morning procession. It was the perfect day to go for a walk, and she often told me that the sun powered her when it showered her, like a flower. To me, she was always small and fragile and lovely. She used to say I knew her better than anyone and that I could see right through her. Maybe I wasn't looking. Those words are the ones which stick with me, even now.

Jarda wasn't as impressed by the weather as I was. Now that I've explained it to you, I think my poem analogy was actually just right. She asked me, instead, to take her to another world. When she described your world, I was surprised. Jarda always liked your world, but I never understood why. I've always seen your world as a pale comparison to mine, a world filled with so many atrocities, so much hurt, and so much pain.

She wouldn't talk to me. I remember that. She was in a bad mood.

Her responses became less and less syllabic until they stopped altogether and my questions and attempts at small talk faltered as well. I was growing annoyed with her. The sky in your world was covered in clouds and fine rain fell on us like dust. My shoes and socks were soaked. I worried about getting a cold. Meanwhile, she charged on, her stride determined and her eyes not even glancing over the bland setting. She could be like that sometimes, lost—not in the world or any worlds—but somewhere else.

We reached the top of a cliff which was completely barren, a solid piece of rock with few weeds persisting through the cracks. She sat down on the edge despite the moist surface, her beautiful dress already dirty from the walk. I waited some time for her to invite me to sit next to her, but she didn't. Annoyed, I sat down anyway.

I can't forgive myself for being annoyed with her.

From the cliff, we could see a wide ocean spanning far enough that the curvature hid the land behind. It looked as if the blue went on for an eternity. The nuances of the water and the heavens merged and became one. Behind us, the approaching clouds were almost black.

"What do you like about this place, anyway?" I asked, not expecting an answer.

Her gaze was straight ahead. She kicked her boots against the steep drop of the cliff, which loosened some rocks. They clattered all the way down to the shore, where the tide rushed in with loud roars that echoed up to us.

"Self-determination," she replied, just as I had given up.

"Yeah?"

Silence.

"How so?" I asked.

"There is a god here. There must be. He's built this whole thing, this beautiful and terrible place where no one is wholly happy or wholly sad, and then he went away, or maybe he didn't. He sits somewhere, I think, and stares. But the people can't stare back because they don't know where he is."

"What's good about that?"

"The people here have a choice. Whether to believe in him and whether to love him. Who he is, what he likes and what he doesn't like. Their only books, the only words he's ever spoken to them, are so contextualized that no one can agree which parts are true and which aren't. And it contradicts itself. It's vague. That way, it fits everyone and no one."

"It sounds difficult."

"It sounds amazing. Imagine having that choice. That's living. That's being a person. Self-determination. I feel like a doll."

"You're not a doll."

I should have said something deeper or more comforting, or true.

"No," she said. Then, just like that, with no goodbye of any meaningful kind, she pressed her palms against the rock and pushed herself off the cliff.

She tumbled down. I leaned over to catch her, but she was already gone. I couldn't have caught her. I couldn't have. She fell and fell, her head hitting every rock with a loud crack as her skull split wide open. By the time she reached the shore, she was a bloodied mess, the dress torn and the crystals scattered, and her body… the way her body twisted was not natural.

My mother's soul was lost to a foreign world, anonymous in the wind, or wherever souls go where we were. If your god is real, I wonder if he'd let her into Heaven. He would have, wouldn't he? I like to imagine her there.

There is one thing I can't forgive my mother for. I've told you about how my world works; I've given you an insight into the history and culture, and most notably, I've explained regeneration to you. It's important to us. It's the only way we deal with the enormous sorrow that is death.

How could I have told my father that my mother, the only one He ever really cared about, wouldn't regenerate because her soul was lost to another world? A world without regeneration?

I couldn't. Instead, I told Him that Jarda had fallen from a cliff. I told Him she died instantly. All of that was true. But the cliff I told Him she fell from was a cliff in my world, not yours. And when I showed Him the body, the body of my poor, bloody mother with her cracked skull, that I carried in my own hands all the way across dimensions, I also gave Him the name of a child who had been ensouled at a nearby picnic spot at just that time.

I gave Him Vallesia's name.

It is not Vallesia's fault that she was ensouled at that picnic spot at just that time. Now, she has been caught up in this web of lies, this scheming to save the world. It is my mother's fault, or maybe it's mine, or maybe it's no one's.

Vallesia looks at me now with big eyes, her chin on her knees and her arms around her legs. I tell her she's Jarda. I tell her just like that, I say, "You're Jarda. You're Jarda's regeneration. You always were". If she knew she wasn't, He would know, too. This only works if she believes.

She opens her mouth many times, attempting to speak before hesitating and closing it again. I understand. It's a lot to take in. I try to give her space to process.

"How do you know?" she finally asks, her voice grainy.

"I was there when she fell. When I carried her body back, I saw your parents. Your mother, her water broken. You were ensouled right then, right there," I lie. "And your eyes are just like hers. And you are so strong and determined and—don't you know? You are just like her."

Sometimes when I look at her, I really do think that she is my mother. I've nearly convinced myself of it, but she's only like this because I've been hunched over her bed every night for years, whispering lies. Preparing her. Giving her pictures of my mother.

"I can't be Jarda."

"Why not? Who else?"

She doesn't answer. She looks at the floor and twirls a tiny rock around her finger. What is it, my love? Do you believe me? Please believe me. Even if I'm not telling the truth. Her lips are thin and quivering.

"Mario," she finally says.

"Mario." I sigh. "Mario… He isn't… He didn't…"

I think she's stopped breathing. Her shoulders quiver and she doesn't look up. She presses the sharp edges of the rock between her fingers until their tips turn pale and she bites her cheek.

"How?" she asks.

"He was shot. Suddenly. It was an accident. It went through his heart and he died before he even knew he was dying. It was quick and not painful at all. It was a good way to die."

She breathes in deeply and bites her cheek. I can tell she wants to cry. Who wouldn't? I don't know how she's holding it together.

I should have told her this before. Before she got married, certainly. Maybe before she met Mario, too, or maybe I should have told her already when she was a child. I could have taken her to the shed when she turned eighteen, dressed her in all white and a flower crown, like a bride. Maybe my father would have loved her then. Maybe now is too late. I was so stupid to hope that He would never break out. There are so many excuses I can make for having put this off. My mistakes are so many. I could never count them all.

"We can still save Dahlia," I say. "Please. Let's go save your sister."

CHAPTER 39

GLUSKAB IS A SUPPORT BEAM. Without Him, the world collapses.

Time and space pack up and flee in a suitcase. Reality retreats. Cities rise up to the sky and fold over the plains, which fold over the playgrounds, which fold over the rivers, which fold over the forests, and so on, until the world has warped itself into a dirt sandwich. The sandwich folds until it is the size of a grain, then it blows away and is lost and simply ceases to be. Something not quite but almost like a hungry lawnmower maneuvers around the sky, leaving a trail of darkness, of nothingness, behind. The stars skirt around, but are eventually enveloped by the Great Nothing, and then the Great Nothing is enveloped by absolutely nothing itself.

In the middle of everything, the palace stands. Or rather, in the middle of nothing, the palace single-handedly makes up an entire universe.

Outside, through the hole in the living room, it is quiet. An intense quiet, a loud quiet, a quiet where I feel if I attempted to make a noise, the vacuum would flatten the sound waves. It is a maddening quiet. Inside, Seraphina caresses Dahlia, who has fallen back down again and is groaning. One god melts in a pool of boiling and bubbling blood while the other snores. The house creaks.

Seraphina hums. In one corner, a crack is spreading. "Please..." she whispers, breathing in heavily. "What..." No one can answer her questions. Dahlia is waking up, but too slowly.

Her humming increases. Her brain is working overtime, the cogs spinning rapidly. The ideas jump in from every side, then disappear before she can grapple them, their slimy bodies escaping her tiny hands, and then they stop. There are no ideas and no thoughts except that she doesn't want to not exist, not now, not when she has just begun to truly *live*.

She looks out into the emptiness and thinks that she might slip, might fall backward into it, but there would be nothing for her to fall into. Would something stop her, like striking a wall? What does nothing feel like? Or would she become nothing, as well?

Are all the souls here? Millions, no, billions, no, trillions, no—she cannot estimate how many living souls this world must contain. How many plants are there? Has anyone ever estimated it? Does he know, that god on the couch who was once so great and now is so shriveled and puny? And are they really here, in this house? Are they the thing that creaks? Is it not creaks, but moans?

Is He right? Do they suffer?

She doesn't want to not exist; she cannot imagine not existing. Sometimes, the things we cannot imagine are the scariest.

Dahlia moans with the souls.

The god peeks at her from the couch, a head and a hand above the surface, squinting and yawning. "What happened?" He mutters, still in a sleepy trance.

"I shot..." she says, then trails off. She points to the melting body of His other half. Why would a god melt? If she shot the other one, would He melt, too? Should she? To what point?

"Oh," He offers.

"What..." she asks, trailing off again. Dahlia moves in her lap.

"Ah," He says, half bothered at most.

"Ah."

"That would be the world ending. In a moment, it will tear through this palace, as well. Then, we will cease to be. We will never have existed; that's better than wasting away."

She says nothing.

"Yes. That's very good," He mutters. "I like that. Let's do that. Let's just wait."

"Please," she pleads, to no effect.

He sighs in contentment.

Seraphina moans with the souls.

She could threaten to shoot Him, she thinks, but what would that achieve? He doesn't want to live. She'd be doing Him a favor by ending the waiting.

The palace creaks again, then something crashes upstairs. An entire floor has collapsed. The room feels as if it is spinning, and she is getting dizzy. She falls over like a doll in a soft breeze.

"Please," she sobs.

Another floor gives in. The crash shakes the entire structure. She lies down next to Dahlia, whose eyes are opening slowly, her lashes fluttering.

"Not fair..." she whispers, the tears streaming down her face.

"Seraphina," Dahlia whispers, her voice coarse, her throat like sandpaper.

Seraphina pulls her sleeve down and tries to wipe off the blood, but there is too much. There is too much. She only manages to smear it.

"Dahlia," she whispers.

Another floor is gone. The cacophony sounds like a roaring dragon. Seraphina feels as if she is about to be eaten. My vase falls over, my flowers scattered on the floor. The chandelier falls halfway down, swinging above them as a threatening pendulum. Windows give in and glass splinters everywhere. Dust whirls up and covers them along with the glass like a soft blanket.

Now, she thinks, it looks as if they've been lying here, foreheads pressed together, forever.

"We did it," Dahlia whispers. "We punched the Creator."

Dahlia laughs, and Seraphina joins her. When they've finished, Seraphina sniffs. Dahlia grabs her hand and they twist their fingers around each other as they close their eyes and wait.

Grant us thy peace. According to thy word.

CHAPTER
40

VALLESIA HOVERS IN THE DOOR, biting her parched lip as she watches the scene: the boiling and the sleeping god, the sobbing banshee, holding hands with her sister, whose face is covered in blood. The tank, the hole, the mess. The pathway out into nothing. Her feet are planted on the threshold, her fingers curled around the frame.

She breathes in. A controlled, deep breath, but when the air reaches the bottom of her lungs, it quivers. Maybe she can pretend it's all just a dream. That it isn't real. Is it real?

I nudge her, a gentle push on her back, and she steps forward. First step. Her limbs don't feel like her limbs. She is not herself. She is someone else, and this body, these nerves, do not obey her.

I nudge her again, and she takes another step. She feels paralyzed, yet if she allowed herself, she could run away. Where to?

The god nuzzles on the couch, attempting to make Himself comfortable like a dog or a small gerbil. Dahlia and Seraphina breathe in softly, as if they, too, are falling asleep. The palace rocks, side to side, singing its lullaby of creaks and crashes, moans and weeping.

Vallesia feels invisible. Another step. That's it. She wobbles. The floor might give in at any moment. It might turn into quicksand and gobble her up. She almost wishes it would.

Be brave now, my dear. This is what you were always meant to do – what I've raised you for. Don't you feel that?

Fourth step. Fifth step. She's fully inside. Almost at the center. Dahlia looks up at her through her swollen eyelids, puzzled, not believing what she sees. Vallesia seems like a mirage.

Sixth step. Seventh step.

He hears her. The sound of quiet footsteps, of ragged breathing. Her pulse, out of control, like drums or horses or mountains crashing into each other. She stops, knees weak.

He sits up, eyebrows scrunched together. The palace stops its moaning; the cracks stop to listen and to watch and to smell.

He cocks His head. "Who are you?"

Who is she?

"Jarda," she says, her voice failing to hide her uncertainty. "I'm Jarda."

She fiddles with a string that's come undone from her shirt. He watches her, squinting.

This is Gluskab, she thinks. This is the god who she has grown up defending and worshipping: This is the face of so many statues and paintings. The Creator. She's spent so many nights wondering what she would say if she'd meet Him. She would fawn, no doubt, or so she'd imagined. She'd thank Him and let Him know that she'd never doubted Him. They'd discuss life, ideologies, and politics. She would cling to His every word and remember every expression. She'd count, she once thought, the hairs on His head if He'd let her.

Now, she doesn't even look at Him. There are no questions or comments. He doesn't look like the paintings. He doesn't look like a god. If she'd seen Him on the streets, she would have passed Him by without a second glance. He is – she knows but cannot fathom—her husband now. She imagines explaining this to a younger version of herself, imagines her being disappointed and excited. Both and neither version feels right.

"You're Vallesia Jade," He finally says.

Is she? She is not certain anymore. Who is Vallesia if she is Jarda? Is she both now?

"It's just a name," she says.

"That you go by?"

Language escapes her. She produces sounds, but none of them contain any meaning.

He moves, staring straight ahead at the painting of Jarda sitting on a chair, the dress spread around her, the smirk. Maybe He is comparing them. Fair skin against darker shades; red, fiery, soft hair against untamed black curls; thin frame against burly curves. The nose is bigger, the lips are bigger, the eyes are rounder, the eyebrows are more unruly. Less graceful, less feminine. He doesn't recognize her.

"I know who you are," He says. "He came here the other day. Yesterday? A year ago? Time doesn't mean anything anymore. Anyway. By He, I of course mean…" He stops to gesture at the boiling god, now burned through the carpet and continuing into the marble floor. "Anyway. He told me about you. He'd been to a detective. He came here and raved and ranted."

Vallesia's heart sinks deep into her stomach. A detective? She knows it was Mario, it could only have been Him. She tries to imagine the nameless blob behind her in their apartment, on their couch, drinking tea from their mugs.

"Of course…" He continues, mumbling to Himself. "I… I was never locked in that shed. I have just been sitting here for— how long has it been? Twenty-two years now? And, of course, in my despair, I… *briefly* considered the idea that my darling, beautiful… Well she would have reincarnated, wouldn't she? My son told me she had been."

He moves His neck toward her. "I saw you when you came to my forest. I saw you and thought you'd be the right age. Exactly the right age. That's why I opened the gates for you, but—" He looks back at the painting, sighing. "It can't be. What are the chances? No. Just a birthdate won't do. It's not certain. You might just be a stranger."

The palace creaks, then a crack runs from one end of the ceiling to the other. Dust rains on them.

"I'm not just a stranger."

"So you say."

"And so I mean."

"How can you be so sure?"

She can't be. She isn't.

"I'm just like her," she tries.

"You didn't know her. Do you think anyone is ever the sum of their stories? You could have copied her, for all I know. Your father is a very bitter man. He sent you to military boarding school to train as a spy, didn't he? Are you still a spy? Did he make you into a copy of my wife, as well? It could be a ruse, couldn't it?"

"It isn't."

"It isn't?"

"A ruse."

"You wouldn't know if it was a ruse, would you?"

She bites her lip, furrows her brows, shuffles her feet.

"I'm just me," she says.

"Yes. Just *you*. Not *her*."

"Why can't I be?"

"You *can* be. But how would I know if—"

"I was ensouled right when—"

"Who cares?"

"And I am just like—"

"Just like her, right, aren't you? I don't care. How did she die, then? Do you remember how she died?"

"I do."

"Let me hear, then."

"I fell off a cliff. There was a beach. I cracked my skull."

He quiets, His bottom lip quivering, His hands trembling. Then, His eyes glaze over and His face contorts in gloomy wrinkles.

"Who told you that?" He asks.

"No one."

"Who was it? No one knows about that. How did you even know she died? No one knows. I haven't told anyone."

"I had dreams. During my exam, and that night, I dreamed that—"

"*He* knew! Where is he?"

My father looks around the room, trying to locate me, but I am behind the door, hiding. Vallesia looks with Him, perhaps hoping that I will be revealed so I can help. But He can't know that I have anything to do with this.

"Come to think of it, he's the *only one* who knows," my father continues. "He was the one who found her and carried her to me. He told me what had happened and where it had happened. Her injuries were consistent with his story, but... he would know everything, wouldn't he?"

"I don't know who you're talking about."

With a strained grunt, my father stands up from the couch, every limb cracking as He does. He wobbles, having not stood up for over twenty-two years, and stretches. More cracking echoes through the hall before He turns to look Vallesia in the eyes, His own sad and huge on His emaciated face, His cheekbones sticking out like knives.

"I'm not angry. Really. I just want to understand. My son, he did all this, didn't he? He found someone just the right age and raised her to be just like my precious, beautiful wife. Then he told her how she'd died and brought her here in hopes I wouldn't... wouldn't realize..."

My heart skips beat.

"That's not true," Vallesia tries.

"Who brought you here?"

"He did, but—"

No, no, no.

"I'm so sorry, my dear, but..."

No! No! No!

"I'm afraid that my wife, she is…"

This can't happen!

"And even if you were her, well…" He throws His arms up in the air. "Oh, I just don't know! How can you ever know? I don't know who you are, no. I'm sorry."

Dust rains on us again and the palace screams a high-pitched, metallic screech. The basement collapses, the floor above us collapses, the hallway collapses, and I leap in through the door as there is now only this room. The walls are covered in cracks. We are thrown around as the floor shakes and what is left of the world enters its final throes of death. We will all cease to exist soon. I have failed and it will all end and—

Vallesia bites her left cheek with soft nibbles in a circular motion, just like my mother used to do. Just like I taught her to do.

The destruction halts. The creaking fizzles out. Quiet fills the world. My father stands in the middle of the large room, watching Vallesia with his head tilted and eyes filled to the brim with tears. He looks so small, so fragile. His skinny arms, The oversized, threadbare sweater. He just watches her. I realize He saw her biting her cheek. The last of the regenerative proofs.

"Jarda?" He whispers, His voice is faint, like a squeak.

She nods. Tears fill her eyes and she starts to cry. Her whole body shakes and loud sobs pour from her, then become wails. Her breathing is strained as she covers her wet face with her hands. My father approaches her with hesitant, slow steps. I can't read Him. When He is right by her, He spreads His arms and embraces her, holding her tight.

The carpet underneath them changes color from gray and brown to a vibrant red with gold details swirled in intricate patterns. The dust sparkles pink and purple, and the color spreads in a circle around them, washing clean the marble floors and marble walls, polishing brass work, restoring paint-ings, and resurrecting old flowers. The chandelier above us hangs proud and secure, the couch is refreshed to look brand new, and the fireplace lights up. The shattered glass is gone as the windows are made whole again, and the cracks are gone from the walls and ceiling. The room glistens. There are no more creaks.

I haven't seen my house like this in twenty-two years.

I look to the painting hanging above the fireplace, at my mother, sitting on a chair with her big, puffy, regal dress, with flowers in her hair. She smirks as if this was her plan all along.

"It's really you, Jarda," my father whisper to Vallesia. "I missed you so much, my love. Why did you leave me? Don't ever leave me again. I missed you."

Vallesia says nothing in return. She can only cry. Dahlia and Seraphina have pushed themselves up to stare in awed wonder. Blood still drips down Dahlia's chin, but when it hits the carpet, it disappears, evaporates. I could swear they are looking right at me.

"I'll take care of you now, my love," my father whispers. "You don't ever have to worry again. I'll take care of you. I won't ever let you leave my sight."

I look outside, through the hole leading out into the abyss, and see the darkness disappearing. Green and blue stretch out instead, growing, and the world reforms itself into an infinite field of flowers, a sea of forget-me-nots, under a clear blue sky. The wind breezes through the flowers and I hear them hum in unison, like a sigh of relief.

Epilogue

I'M TRYING TO FIND THE right words. I wanted to tell you this record of my people because there is some truth in it, and because it bothers me. I can't quite put my finger on what it is that bothers me.

Seraphina and Dahlia couldn't live in their world after everything that happened, so they live in yours now. Just down the street, in fact, in that red house with all the bird feeders. You pass by it every day to work. Their garden is full of daffodils. They don't have any forget-me-nots. I think they felt that there was a certain knowledge that you can't back away from once you have it, and I think, if they had stayed, they would have ended up feeling like Jarda—like they were dolls incapable of making their own decisions. In your world, they feel much more at ease. Much more autonomous.

Vallesia and Gluskab got married a few months ago. I officiated them, and the entire world were invited as guests. That is, the world now full of flowers, a sea of forget-me-nots in all possible shades reaching out from their palace. I like to believe they are happy. I rarely visit, and when I do, I stay in the distance and watch them. They sit in the garden all day and drink tea and stare at all the flowers. I overheard Vallesia suggest the other day that they should add bees.

None of these are the right words.

I wonder if my father will ever understand Vallesia. He definitely does not, just like He never understood Jarda. He understood none of the people in His world, or me. I don't think any of us understood Him, either. He is another shape. I feel torn in both directions, the empirical and the eternal essence tearing at me from both sides. I think it's important to understand that you don't understand everything. There are things you can't understand.

Maybe your god isn't a fixed thing. Maybe he doesn't have a beard or a couch. Maybe he's more of an abstract thing that you can mold into whatever you need to? I'm not sure. I haven't finished your Bible yet. I'm still stuck on the Book of Job.

I have been thinking of something lately. I have been thinking that maybe my world is as good now as it was before. There were certainly immeasurable amounts of pain over those few days, but it's evened out now, hasn't it? The souls are happy being flowers, and one day they may become bees, and maybe something with more existential questions after that. So perhaps, in the grand scheme of things, no harm was really done? Dying is so infinitely worse than being dead when being dead is so brief a thing. I don't think being dead in your world can be so bad. I can't wrap my head around it. It doesn't sound like something a loving father would do.

Maybe I know what it is that's bothering me.

There are two kinds of belief in a god. There's the belief that he exists; that he, in some sort of abstract form, is real. That's plain for me. I know who my father is. But there is also the belief that he is good and that he has the best intentions for you in mind, that he created you wanting the best for you, and that he sees you and knows you and that he would never, ever hurt you.

What do you think about that?

I am struggling to believe in my father nowadays. I don't know what to do with that, because if He exists, and He doesn't want what's best for me, then what do I do with that?

It bothers me how helpless we are.

ACKNOWLEDGEMENTS

Firstly, thank you to my publisher, D.W. Hitz, as well as my editors, Renée Gendron and B.K. Bass, for their time, patience, and eagle-eyed observations. Your contributions not only greatly improved this novel, but it also made me improve as a writer (or so I hope!). In addition, thank you to D.W. Hitz for taking a chance on my story, and on me.

Thank you to my husband, Benjamin, who is my biggest and loudest fan. This book wouldn't have happened without your endless confidence in me and my story. I'm sure at least half of my readers will be from your incessant bragging; I only wish you'd stop trying to sell my gory apocalypse book to old people at church.

Thank you to my parents, who have always made me feel incredibly loved. Thank you for driving me to writer's camps and always encouraging my ridiculous dream of writing books (absurd!). Thank you to my dad for buying me gummy bears to eat for every 100 words during NaNoWriMo.

Thank you to Seth, the first person to read a draft of this book. From proofreading to website tweaking, advise and problem-solving — you're the most helpful person I've met, and I know I can always count on you.

Thank you to my writers group: to Ana, Esmee, Isabella, Reagan, Sophie, and Vin, who are always there to share in my excitement and give me honest feedback. Also thank you to Amalie and Caed for enduring my many rambles.

Finally, when I was a child, I often asked for a favor or an extra slice of cake in exchange for an acknowledgement in my first novel. I wish I'd written down your names. Please accept this blanket thank you as a late payment.

About the Author

Asta Geil started writing the moment she learned how to and has been obsessed with everything words ever since. Originally from Denmark, she fell in love with English during an exchange year in New Jersey, USA. She has since worked in London and now lives in Edinburgh with her husband while completing an MA (Hons) in Linguistics and English Language at the University of Edinburgh.

Dear Creator is her debut novel and a testament to her love of the bizarre and horrific.

Find out more about Asta on Twitter or Instagram.

WHAT'S NEXT?

Find more great speculative fiction from Fedowar Press at www.FedowarPress.com. Sign up for our newsletter to be sure you don't miss a thing.

www.FedowarPress.com

Lightning Source UK Ltd.
Milton Keynes UK
UKHW041902111122
412065UK00002B/30